SANDSTORM

Fiction

The Eye of Ra
Firebird
Rare Earth

Non-Fiction

In Search of the Forty Days Road
A Desert Dies
Impossible Journey – Two Against the Sahara
Shoot To Kill – A Soldier's Journey Through Violence
Thesiger – A Biography
Last of the Bedu – In Search of the Myth
Lawrence – the Uncrowned King of Arabia
The Real Bravo Two Zero
Sahara (with Kazoyoshi Nomachi)
Phoenix Rising – The UAE, Past, Present & Future (with Werner Forman)

SANDSTORM

MICHAEL ASHER

HarperCollins*Publishers*

HarperCollins*Publishers*
77–85 Fulham Palace Road,
Hammersmith, London W6 8JB

www.harpercollins.co.uk

Published by HarperCollins*Publishers* 2003
1 3 5 7 9 8 6 4 2

This novel is entirely a work of fiction. The names,
characters and incidents portrayed in it are the work of the
author's imagination. Any resemblance to actual persons,
living or dead, events or localities is entirely coincidental.

A catalogue record for this book
is available from the British Library

ISBN 0 00 714155 6

Typeset in Times New Roman by Palimpsest Book Production Limited,
Polmont, Stirlingshire

Printed and bound in Great Britain by
Clays Ltd, St Ives plc

ACKNOWLEDGEMENTS

I would like to thank my agent Anthony Goff for his continuous encouragement and support, and his assistant, Georgia Glover.

As ever, I owe a great deal to Susan Watt and Katie Espiner of HarperCollins. A very special thanks to John Mercer, whose excellent work, *Spanish Sahara*, became my bible during research for this book. Any mistakes or inaccuracies are mine, not his. Last but not least, to Burton, and to Mariantonietta and Jade, my princesses big and small.

Michael Asher
Written in Rabat, Morocco,
Frazione Agnata, Sardinia,
& Nairobi, Kenya
January–November, 2002

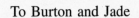

To Burton and Jade

Quid non mortalia pectora cogis,
Auri sacra fames!

Virgil, *The Aeneid, III.56*

'A spot of piracy on the high desert . . .'

RALPH BAGNOLD,
founder of the Long Range Desert Group

Storm and adventure, heat and cold,
. . . And Buccaneers and buried Gold,
And all the old romance, retold,
Exactly in the ancient way . . .

ROBERT LOUIS STEVENSON, *Treasure Island*

1

IN THE WHOLE VAST IMMENSITY OF the sky, the crows
were the only things moving. There were two of them, and
they circled, rich black dots on translucent blue. The sky had a
heaviness to it, Billy Sterling thought. It was almost as if he was
lying on the bed of the ocean, with the brilliant, heavy blueness
above him and the soft dunes beneath. Its bigness was terrifying
but in a sort of holy way – the way you felt sometimes when
you entered a cathedral. As if you had to tread quietly and speak
in whispers because there were big powers at work here that
were dreadful and unfathomable, and you didn't want to draw
attention to yourself or wake them up.

It was not exactly that the desert was empty – there were
ridges and saw-tooth peaks all around him, layered and polished
to a vermilion lacquer, and even straggled, stunted trees in little
copses that looked almost like family groups of grotesque statu-
ettes. It was more that there was nothing human – no roads, no
tracks, no sign of machinery or habitation. The boy was glad

1

that the crows were here. He understood the attraction they felt to him, the attraction of life to life.

Billy had no idea how long he had lain on the sand. It might have been forever, except that it had been dark when he'd hit the ground and it was now light. Everything seemed tangled up in his head, and he wondered if he had imagined falling out of the sky on a parachute. He reached up and felt the lift webs sprouting from his shoulders like angel wings. His body was firmly strapped in a parachute-harness and, at the end of the webs and cords, about five metres away, a jellyfishlike canopy was fluttering, half inflated. He sat up suddenly, realizing that he had been drifting away down a river of dreams. He looked at his watch – the one that his parents had given him for his thirteenth birthday – but it was gone. Then he remembered: it had been ripped off when he'd lumbered into the bulkhead, just after Corrigan had punched him.

He reached up again and felt his swollen jaw, remembering the shock of the blow. Apart from that, there were only vague, disjointed images – of Corrigan and Craven, with faces screwed up in alarm. The humming aircraft, with the wind roaring beyond the gaping door. The sight of Craven going out on the static line, the slow realization that the plane was going to crash. He remembered how he had screamed and struggled frantically as Corrigan had shoved him through the door – the heady rush of the slipstream; plummeting like a deadweight; the sharp tug as his fall was arrested by the developing canopy; drifting helplessly like a dandelion seed. Then hitting the ground with a crump, and the night silence absorbed by a deeper silence within.

The crows, thwarted by Billy's sudden return to the vertical, flapped away, cawing indignantly. He watched them go with a feeling of desperation. Then, remembering the parachute, he clutched at the release-catch, trying to recall the procedure he'd

2

been taught. He turned to the right and pressed. The catch sprang open. He was free.

The little finger of his left hand began to throb. It ended in a slightly swollen stump at the joint – the result of an accident when he was eight years old. It always became itchy and painful when he was under stress. He had never understood whether the pain was real or imaginary. There was nothing imaginary about this situation, though. He was stranded alone in the middle of the desert.

His heart started drumming like a tom-tom, his breath coming in rasps, his muscles trembling. He was assailed for a moment with wild panic, and felt the urge to run. But he did not know where to go, so he stayed where he was, took a deep breath and glanced around him, letting his senses expand cautiously out into the vastness.

The crows were black commas in the distance now. The huge dimensions of the wasteland played havoc with his perception of scale. The sun was just up, a lopsided beachball bowled along seams of dust, and he could feel the gathering prelude of the day's heat. Billy knew that his best bet was to find the *Rose of Cimarron*. He didn't recall having heard the Dakota pile in, but the way she'd been juddering and yawing before he'd been shoved through the door, he was sure she couldn't have got far.

He scanned into the sun. In the mid-ground, weirdly shaped nodules of rock poked out of the soft down of the dunes – rocks with toadstool heads and slender stems, looking like petrified trees. Billy remembered having studied these things in a geography lesson at Scowcroft with old Jobbins. They were called yardangs – the stems had been eroded near ground level by the abrasion of sand over eons, while the heads had remained intact. What struck Billy as odd about the rocks, though, was not their shapes. It was the fact that, at the base of one of them, stood a vertical splash of orange that seemed curiously vulgar against

3

the desert's subtle colour-scheme. Craven had been wearing a flying-suit of just such a shade of orange.

Catching his breath, not daring to believe it, he shaded his eyes with his hand and peered intensely at the bright-coloured patch. It was human shape, certainly – the upright torso of a human body, and Billy could almost make out Craven's long fingers waving feebly and his overlong hair flopping from side to side as he nodded his head. Billy's heart began to thrust with excitement. For a moment he wondered if he had imagined it, and he peered again. No. There was movement, of that he was certain. He could clearly see Craven's hands oscillating up and down and the head shaking to and fro. But then why wasn't he shouting, trying to attract Billy's attention? The answer was obvious, Billy thought: Craven had been injured in the parachute jump and couldn't move freely or speak.

In his relief at seeing another person, Billy forgot the pilot's cowardly behaviour. Almost sobbing with joy, he rushed towards the yardangs, waving and gesticulating madly. 'Major!' he screamed. 'Keith, I'm coming!'

He was sinking calf-deep into the soft sand of the dunes, but he struggled on until he was gasping for air. The yardangs were further away than they had seemed, and by the time he had come within fifty feet of them, he had run out of steam. As he edged closer, Billy saw that Craven's head was lolling on his chest, as if he were only half conscious; occasionally it raised itself a few inches, as if with tremendous effort. Billy got a glimpse of almost closed eyes and a slack jaw hanging open and slavering froth. The position of Craven's arms, raised at shoulder height in a 'don't shoot' position, seemed unnatural. Billy slowed to a cautious walk and approached the pilot with bated breath. 'Keith?' he said. 'All right, Keith?'

The only answer was a subtle tremor of the hands and the

4

ghost of a nod, and as Billy stepped nearer he suddenly understood Craven's predicament. He was still strapped in his parachute-harness, and the canopy had snagged on the head of one
of the yardangs, suspending him upright, with his feet trailing
on the sand. The lift webs, pulled taut by the weight of his body,
had not been visible from far off. Craven's hands were caught
in the tangle of webs and cord, and the breeze in the snagged
chute was playing his body like a marionette.

On the sand, by Craven's flying-boots, Billy saw the worn leather
map-case the pilot had always carried with him – something so
precious that it was never allowed out of his grasp. Billy gulped,
realizing suddenly that a map might be just the thing he needed
right now. Holding his breath, he lurched forward and grabbed the
map-case, then backed away from the suspended body. 'Keith!' he
recited again, but his voice was a whisper now, lacking conviction.
It occurred to him suddenly that Craven must have slammed into
a yardang, snapping his back like a twig. Craven was dead.

For a second he stood rooted to the spot, not knowing what
to do. A sob issued from somewhere far away and it was only
with a shock that he realized it had pressed itself from his own
throat. Emotions crowded in on him, control and panic battling
for supremacy in his adolescent psyche. Nothing in his life had
prepared him for this. It was the quickness of death that astonished him. Only yesterday this husk had been a living, func-
tioning person. He took a step backwards as a new shockwave
absorbed him. Suddenly his control gave way, and the child in
him panicked. Adrenaline pulsed through his veins and he staggered further away, finally turning his back on Craven's cruci-
fied body and pelting off helter-skelter into the desert, oblivious
to everything but the horror behind him.

In his blind rush to get away, he was almost upon the *Rose of*

Cimarron before he saw her. Panting heavily, he pulled himself up, his mouth falling open. The Dakota lay resplendent in the sunlight, a noble silver artefact from another age and time. She had not piled in, but made a miraculous landing. True, she was nose-deep in sand and her landing gear was gone, but the fuselage and wings had remained remarkably intact. Billy greeted the new apparition with a surge of hope, and for a moment the boy had comic-book visions of piloting the Dakota out of there. Then adult reality intervened. He knew that he would never have been able to fly her, even if her landing gear had been intact.

Still, there had been a wireless on board, and maybe it was still working. Maybe he could talk to somebody on it, get himself rescued. He thrust his head through the open cargo door. The cabin looked undisturbed, the strops of the parachutes' static lines still attached to the overhead brackets where they had been clipped. He crawled into the cabin, gagging in the stink of aviation fuel, but feeling momentarily safe from the immensity of the great void out there. Tools, water-bottles, packets of cigarettes, chewing gum and chocolate bars were strewn across the deck around the long-range fuel tank that extended almost the whole length of the cabin.

Billy pushed through into the cockpit and squirmed into the pilot's chair. A vacuum flask still stood in its bracket under the instrument panel, and a padded flying helmet still hung from the back of the seat where it had been tied. The panel seemed lifeless, and for what seemed an age he tinkered with it, clicking and unclicking switches, desperately trying to recall how the wireless worked. In the end he gave up, and for a long while he sat holding himself tightly, rocking backwards and forwards in the seat, feeling numb, wishing even that the two crows would return to remind him that he was not alone on the planet's face.

Billy shivered and sat up. How long he'd been in the cockpit he didn't know. He did not think he had slept, yet his mind had been filled with images of Craven's dead body. He tried to steer his thoughts away from the horror he had seen, but always it returned. He was brought out of it only by the gnawing rasp of thirst in his throat. It was very hot now. He clambered back into the main cabin and groped under the baggage net for the steel jerry can Craven had left there. The can was only about half full of water and Billy knew that wouldn't last long. He picked up chocolate bars and biscuits from the deck, and collected them in a pile. He poured water from the jerry can into an enamel mug, wolfed down melted chocolate, and gulped water. For the first time he wondered what had happened to Corrigan. Had he met the same fate as Craven, or was he still wandering around out there?

He sat down in the doorway for a moment, and looked at the map-case he had taken from near Craven's inert body. He had always wondered what it contained – the major had seemed so protective of it always. Maybe it was just a keepsake that reminded him of his wartime exploits. Billy's grandfather had told him proudly that Craven had won the DFC and bar flying reconnaissance missions for the army in light aircraft called Wacos. He was one of only a handful of army officers to receive the DFC, and probably the only one with a bar. Grandfather had called Craven, 'the bravest of the brave', but that didn't seem to tally with his abandoning Billy in the Dakota when it was about to crash last night. Impulsively, Billy opened the map-case. He had been expecting to find a detailed air chart – something that would give him an idea, even a vague one, of where he might be. Instead, the case held nothing but a sketch-map; neatly drawn, but a sketch-map nevertheless. Written across the top in bold capitals was the word '*SONNENBLUME*'. The map seemed to be drawn to scale. There were hand-drawn graphics of sand-dunes and rocks, and a pair of crossed swords marked *Sonnenblume* again, this time in

7

smaller letters. A dotted line, starting from the crossed swords, led to an area where a maze of rocky outcrops and contour lines were drawn. There was a series of small crosses marked *Graves*, and nearby a larger cross marked *Gorge*. There was an arrow here, and next to it a tiny box, in which was written:

1) Grave One 570 yards 340° north by northwest. Rum Flask
2) 172 yards NW Wilkinson's Arrow
3) 110 yards Fanny

Billy shook his head. It looked like something from a child's game of pirates – he hadn't a clue what it meant, and it gave no inkling as to where he was. He closed the case and looped it over his neck – it had been important to Craven and it might come in handy later.

Putting the map to the back of his mind, he inched his way round the cabin, collecting anything he thought might be of use to him: spare water canteens with dribbles of liquid in them, an axe, a spanner, a rope, a torch, a cardboard carton containing tinned food. When he had gathered his trophies together, he piled them into the cockpit, where he felt safest. Then, reasoning to himself that a rescue mission was certain to come, he sat down again to wait. He waited, dozing fitfully, but outside the cockpit nothing moved but the shadows and the sun. No help came.

The night fell with frightening suddenness, and with it came an unexpected drop in temperature that had the boy shivering in his cotton shirt. He dozed again, woken every few minutes, it seemed, by the cold. His only comfort was to nibble on the biscuits, but they left him thirsty and he dared not drink too much of the water. A moon came up – a first-quarter moon like a long curved dagger, so close you could almost touch it, and through the aircraft's windscreen he could see familiar patterns of stars he could not name.

The vastness of space only made his sense of impotence more acute.

He slept again, dozing deeply this time. In his dreams a wizened creature – a wolf with a shadowed face – heaved itself up from the sands beneath the plane and clutched his arm with skeletal fingers, twisting it hard until it broke with an audible snap. Billy's eyes flew open.

He sat bolt upright, all his senses alert, wondering if the noise had come from within his dream or without. He strained for sound in the darkness, holding his breath, and listened with his ear cocked to one side. From the outside came the faintest scuffle. He listened again, thinking it might be the wind, but the desert night was as still as the grave, and the faint sound came once more. Billy felt the hairs on the back of his neck prickle, and fought to hold down his breathing. There was something moving outside the aircraft – something that he could sense but could not see. The idea grew upon him that it was a human being out there, and suddenly the irrational notion that it might be Craven vaulted into his mind. Maybe the major wasn't really dead. No, that was crazy. But the events of the previous day and the silence of the night had already blurred the edges of reality. What if he had got it wrong? What if Craven had only been unconscious after all? Billy cursed himself. How could Craven possibly be alive? He had seen him cold and dead as a stone. If there was somebody out there, it had to be Corrigan, not Craven. He considered calling Corrigan's name, but checked himself. He listened again. There was no sound from outside, and again he asked himself if he had dreamed it. The mind could play funny tricks out here.

When at last the night ended and long shadows began to sprout from the trees and under the plane, Billy crawled out, shivering. He watched the sun come into being beyond the vermilion ridges in the distance, a fragile eddy of light at first, flaring in intensity as it strengthened its grip on the day. A gauze of heat shimmered along the jagged skyline, forming and breaking like bubbles of gas.

For a while Billy stood there, sensing the sacred character of the moment, feeling the night's claustrophobia melt into an awe for the hugeness of the world and the smallness of his place in it. It was a shift of absolutes – in the night your world became reduced to the little you could sense around you; in the day you were a mote under the endless sky.

Billy paced around, slapping his arms across his chest as if to beat the cold away. Suddenly he stopped. There, not twenty feet from the *Rose of Cimarron*, the fresh tracks of naked human feet were cut neatly into the sand.

Billy's first instinct was to rush back to the *Rose of Cimarron* in terror, but he was weary of running, knowing that in this great void there could be no hiding-place. Trembling, he began to follow the tracks. It seemed to him that they were more slender and smaller than Craven's would have been, but he could not be sure. The most disquieting thing, though, was that the footprints actually led in the direction of the yardangs, where he had left Craven's body. It was surprisingly far: Billy realized that he must have been completely unconscious of the distance during his mad flight away from the corpse the previous day. As he approached the place his disquiet increased. He had no desire to see Craven's body again, but the sense of unease seemed to come from something else. He could not see the parachute canopy flapping on the rocks. He paused behind the cluster of yardangs, breathing heavily, then made his way around them – and stood petrified.

Craven's body was no longer there. Not a sign or a trace of it. For a fraction of a second Billy wondered if he'd imagined it. For another long moment he thought he must have come to the wrong place. No, he had not imagined it, and this was the right place – the shape of the yardangs here was very distinctive. As he sidled nearer, he saw that the sand was scuffed and broken by the same barefoot tracks. The tracks were there, but Craven had gone, the parachute canopy had gone, everything had gone. Billy staggered backwards; then, for the second time, he turned and fled from the same spot.

Rose of Cimarron glittered in the light of the rising sun. She drew his eye magnetically, seeming two or three times her true size. Billy shambled nearer, knowing that the Dakota could not really protect him, but taking comfort from her presence anyway.

He was about to enter through the open cargo door, when a long shadow fell across his own. Billy put up his arm instinctively to protect himself and saw that the shadow belonged to a dark rider from the deepest reaches of nightmare. He froze, catching his breath, staggered by the sight. It was a man looking like an Old Testament prophet, mounted on a white camel. The man was dressed in a fluttering black head-cloth and blue robes that billowed behind him over the camel's flank. With one hand he held in check the beast's gnashing, snapping, snake-like head, and in the other hand he held a slim stick. An old rifle was slung over his shoulder. He looked as if he'd stepped out of some fantastic dimension, like a wizard from a fairy-tale book. His hands and feet were as thin as a skeleton's, his face etched like desert rock, with only a straggly wisp of beard at the end of a long chin. Smears of dye had rubbed off on his skin, giving the face a patina of raw blueness. The old man's eyes were alive with animal curiosity, wisps of grey hair hanging down from beneath the head-cloth. His teeth were bared under a hawk-like beak of a nose, and Billy could not tell whether he was smiling. He said something, and the words sounded harsh and guttural, as if they had come from deep inside.

Billy was so overwhelmed with the vision that in the moment he might have taken to his heels, he instead stared back at the old man's face, mesmerized. And in that moment the Blue Man slipped out of the saddle with ease, and reached for him.

11

$$\boxed{2}$$

'I GO BACK NOW,' SLIMAN SAID IN tortured English. He applied the Jeep's brakes jerkily and put the gear in neutral. Squinting through the dust-jacketed windscreen, George Bridger Sterling could make out the shape of the kasbah standing on the very edge of the rocky hammada, the desert surface swept clear of sand and dust by the wind. Above it towered orange and yellow dunes. The kasbah looked like a Gothic castle that had melted in the heat. It was at least a mile away.

He glared at the driver harshly. 'We're paying you to take us to the kasbah,' he said. 'We aren't there yet.'

Sliman took a flat packet of cigarettes from the pocket of his djellaba, teased one out with his thumb and forefinger and lit it with a match. He was a thin man with bulging eyes and bulbous lips, a combination that gave him a curiously baleful expression. 'Maybe I get stuck in sand,' he said. 'Or maybe that crazy son-of-a-bitch Sheikh Mafoudh take a shot at me. You get out here.'

Suddenly the driver froze with the cigarette in his mouth. His knuckles went white on the steering wheel. Sterling turned to see that Eric Churchill, in the back seat, was holding the muzzle of his Smith & Wesson .38 flush with the Arab's head. 'I don't think so,' Churchill growled. 'It's not that I'm sorry to find this is the end of the road. Three days of bone shaking across the Atlas is enough. But a deal is a deal. The agreement was that you delivered us to the door.'

Churchill looked intimidating, Sterling had to admit. He was six-foot-three, a powerful, slightly round-shouldered man, who for a moment resembled his namesake, Winston, as he demonstrated the grim-set, turned-down mouth and knitted eyebrows of the 'we will fight on the beaches' speech that Eric knew off by heart. But the resemblance went only so far. At thirty-seven, Eric was a little under half Winnie's age, and the dark eyes and slightly hooked nose held a hint of foreignness that would have been quite out of place on the elder statesman.

Sliman burst into a bout of coughing and dropped the cigarette on his lap, where it burned a hole in the cloth of his djellaba. Sterling retrieved it, and threw it out of the window, while Sliman beat at his burning djellaba and spluttered. 'This Sheikh Mafoudh, he possessed by *yenun*,' he gabbled. 'Crazy, you unnerstan'? He don't like visitors. He even shoot at people. Maybe he shoot you – me too.'

'And if you don't go,' Churchill growled, 'then I shall certainly shoot you.'

Cursing to himself, Sliman nosed the Jeep in the direction of the kasbah.

As they got nearer, it looked less impressive. It was more than half ruined, its outer walls caved in, the roof mostly gone. Behind the rambling building, tamarisk trees grew in the skirts of the dunes, some of them ancient, huge, and grotesquely twisted. Above the tamarisk groves rose the razor-edged creases of the

13

sands, dividing light from dark, climaxing in drifting soft peaks in rose and orange ochre, buff and flame. The highest peak stood at least 500 feet above the hammada.

It was mid-morning, but already the sky was a radiant blue screen. A shimmer of heat rose across the eastern horizon; somewhere over there, Sterling knew, Morocco ended and French Algeria began. The Spanish sector lay almost 400 miles south by west.

Sand drifts had piled up against the kasbah's mud walls, which were the texture of dried beef, and a door stood open, gaping like a missing front tooth. As they drew near, a barefooted Arab in a ragged brown robe and head-cloth stepped into the doorway. He had a face as rough as buckskin, with eyes the colour of slate. He wore a cartridge belt round his waist with a hooked dagger in it, and in his hands he held an old rifle. It was pointed at them.

Sliman began to tremble. He brought the car to a halt and stuck his head out of the window. 'Don't shoot!' he cried in Arabic. 'These are the foreign visitors who arranged to meet Sheikh Mafoudh.'

'*Mirhabban bikum*,' the Arab said. 'Welcome.' His eyes did not lose their slaty coolness, and the rifle stayed pointing at the Jeep. Sterling and Churchill got out and unloaded their canvas kitbags, and Churchill slapped dirhams into the driver's hand. Sliman counted them fastidiously. 'Hey!' he said at last. 'No tip?'

'On your bike,' Churchill said.

The Moroccan narrowed his bug eyes, knowing he'd been put down but trying to grasp what bikes had to do with it. 'You fuck,' he spat.

'As do you,' Churchill said.

The man gave them a last look of hatred, a fearful glance at

14

the Arab with the rifle, and sped off towards the horizon, leaving them alone with the Arab.

Once the Moroccan had gone, the Arab seemed to relax. He shook hands with them both, and led them through the doorway into a yard that was dilapidated and open to the elements. It was carpeted with sand and goat-turds, and a white Hand of Fatima was painted on the wall as protection against the evil eye. Above them there were the remains of a roof of palm-beams, palm-stalks and fibres, much of which had collapsed onto the floor. The walls had mostly fallen in under the pressure of creeping sand; Sterling glimpsed through the spaces the sun glittering on the polished quartz and limestone nodules of the hammada – acres of stone stretching eternally across the void.

Six men were sitting around a hearth in the middle of the shaded bit of the yard. Some were wearing ragged head-cloths, the colour of the desert sands; all wore patched Arab shirts with cartridge-belts and daggers. Their rifles were leaning against the wall nearby. Most had the chiselled features of Arabs, but a couple were distinctly African. To Sterling they looked like wild men – as primitive as the natives of New Guinea he'd seen in *National Geographic* – and yet their manners were gracious. All stood up to welcome the Englishmen, and one, an old man with a white beard and a smoothly shaven head, grinned at Churchill, showing a single yellow tooth, like a claw, that wobbled as he spoke. 'Captain!' he yelled, slapping Churchill's big hand with his own and flinging his emaciated arms round him. 'Captain! Is it really you? They say you are back but I don't believe it. I say, I don't believe till I see the captain hisself! And, God be praised, here you are!' He launched into a stream of Arabic, which Churchill seemed to comprehend, alternately wringing his hand and thumping his broad shoulder.

Churchill introduced him to Sterling and the old man shook

his hand violently. 'Sheikh Mafoudh worked with me as a guide in the war,' Churchill said. 'One of my Baker Street Irregulars. This is his little gang. They're outcasts: ex-slaves, fugitives, Znaga – mostly not true desert people – but they know the desert well enough to get us into the Spanish Sahara.'

Churchill and Sterling shook hands with the whole crew, and were welcomed by the fire. Glasses of hot tea were poured from a decrepit miniature teapot and forced on them.

Sterling stared at the glass – it seemed to have acquired half the substance of the desert in its travels. 'Don't think about it, just drink it,' Churchill whispered. Sterling sipped it gingerly. It tasted like vinegar.

'Tea no good?' Sheikh Mafoudh demanded with mock indignation.

Churchill chuckled. 'You have to slurp it,' he said. 'Or they'll be insulted.'

He demonstrated by slurping his own tea noisily. Mafoudh and his ragged gang nodded with approval.

When the tea-drinking ceremony was finished, Churchill asked Sterling to get out the map. He took it and showed it to Mafoudh, who promptly turned it upside down. '*Afrangi* map,' the old man commented, his single tooth wobbling. 'Arab map is better.' He pointed a callused finger to his smooth pate. 'Arab map up here.'

Churchill handed the map back to Sterling. 'We're looking for an aircraft,' he said. 'An iron bird, like the ones you used to see taking off in Casablanca, Sheikh Mafoudh.'

The old sheikh nodded vigorously.

'It came down in the desert,' Churchill went on. 'In the Seguiet al-Hamra, seven years ago. Did you ever hear tell of such an aircraft?'

The old man tilted his head to one side. 'Many iron birds

16

come down in desert,' he said. 'But the Seguiet al-Hamra . . .
that is Reguibat country – very dangerous. It is far.'

'The man who made the map didn't know the name of the
place,' Churchill said. 'But it is an unusual place. On one side
are high dunes, on another broken hills and empty desert. On
another side there is quicksand. Do you know of a place like
this?'

The sheikh went quiet for a moment, then translated what
Churchill had said to his crew. In a second everyone was talking
at once. After a while, Mafoudh held up his hand for quiet and
looked at Churchill. 'You mean the Ghaydat al-Jahoucha,' he
said grimly. The others nodded and sucked in their breath. 'I
have been there once,' he went on. 'Many, many years ago, when
I was young. It is dangerous. The dunes on the north side are
called the Uruq ash-Shaytan and they stretch across the plain in
an unbroken wall. I never heard of anyone crossing the Uruq
with camels. The quicksand is called Umm al-Khof. It can be
crossed by a single path, but that is known to none but the hunting
people. The third way – across the Zrouft, the Plain of Thirst,
is our only way in, but even that is hard, by God. Seven days
without water for the camels. God only knows, if it is hot, camels
die. Then we all die.'

Churchill was watching him intently now. 'Can you take us
there?' he asked.

Mafoudh looked troubled. He scratched his white beard, and
began to gabble to his men. Once again the yard was filled with
excited voices. One of the men, a squat Arab with a curly mass
of black hair and a twist of beard on his long chin, leapt up,
ripped off his head-cloth and threw it down. One of the black
men – an immensely powerful-looking man with tribal tattoos
on his cheeks – began to bawl at him, gesturing angrily with his
stick. Everyone was shouting.

17

Sterling shot Churchill a look of concern. 'Don't worry,' Churchill smiled. 'You should see them when they're worked up.'

When the noise had quietened down again, the sheikh beamed at Churchill, waggling his one loose tooth with his tongue. 'We can take you,' he said. 'But the way is hard even for us. Very hard for you.' He rubbed his thumb and forefinger together and a crafty look came into his eyes. 'It will cost many, many moneys,' he said.

The tribesmen chattered on exuberantly while Churchill and Sheikh Mafoudh began to reminisce in Arabic about old times. Sterling's Arabic was passable but not perfect, and soon he lost track of the conversation, drifting off into the inner world that had become his familiar resort ever since Margaret had died. Seven years, he thought, since Billy had disappeared in Morocco, and in all that time there hadn't been a hint of what had happened to him. Not a trace of the missing aircraft had been found.

Nothing until the day, only a few weeks back, when Sterling had suddenly received a call at his office in London from a man calling himself 'Mr Black'. 'Mr Black' claimed that he had information about Billy, and had asked Sterling to meet him in a West End pub called the Marquis of Granby that evening. It was an offer Sterling couldn't refuse.

It had been a gloomy, wet night in February. In the pub, clusters of men in shabby raincoats were leaning morosely over a beer-soaked bar, or hobnobbing in alcoves under a haze of tobacco smoke like a camouflage net. Sterling ordered a pint of bitter. When the barman set the glass under the pump, he noticed that there was a clean-sheared stump where the man's hand should have been. He watched the cripple with fascination as he heaved on the handle, holding the glass in place with his stump. The man noticed his gaze and nodded, unembarrassed, at his mutilated limb. 'Dunkirk,' he commented. 'Christ! What a bleeding pig's ear.'

'Isn't it always?' Sterling said, half to himself.

The barman's eyes flickered momentarily on him, taking in the tousled, unkempt hair, the worn greatcoat, the shirt with its flyaway collar. 'What about you?' he growled. 'Come out all right?'

Sterling shrugged, not wanting to get drawn into the subject of what he had done in the war. Some of the worst mutilations, he thought, were on the inside. 'I missed Dunkirk, thank God. I was here and there, you know.'

He paid the sixpence hurriedly, but the barman's eyes followed him as he sat down at a round table in front of a flickering coke fire.

'Mr Sterling?'

The voice was almost a whisper, and the accent was distinctly American. Sterling turned slightly to see a man in a brown over-coat and broad-brimmed hat looming over him. The man was thin and pale looking, with wire-framed glasses that rimmed hollow eyes. He was not old, yet he looked tarnished – as thread-bare as the coat he was wearing. He kept his hands in his pockets as if suffering from the cold, but a copy of the *Daily Mail* was folded under his arm. He glanced nervously around him. 'You alone?' he asked.

Sterling half smiled. 'Yes.'

'Mr Black' continued to gaze around uncertainly, and Sterling saw cold fear behind the spectacles. 'You certain you didn't bring anyone?' he demanded.

'Of course I am. What are you afraid of, anyway?'

The man sat down circumspectly in the chair opposite, and stared at him. 'Werewolves,' he said. He did not smile.

Sterling shivered inwardly. 'I beg your pardon?' he said.

The man seemed to be examining his features minutely. 'Even the walls have ears. Isn't that what they used to say during the war? Careless talk costs lives? Loose lips sink ships?'

'The war's over,' Sterling said.

'Not for some, it's not. For some it's still on.'

'Mr Black' put the newspaper down on the table and tried to warm his hands in the fickle heat of the coke. His fingers were slender and the nails bitten down to the bone. His hands shook slightly as he held them up, Sterling noticed. 'Cold tonight,' he said in the same sandpapery voice. 'At least the rain's stopped.'

He took a packet of Camel cigarettes from his pocket, stuck one in his mouth and lit it shakily with a match. He blew smoke at the fire, then suddenly burst into a paroxysm of coughing. Sterling watched, fascinated, wondering what would come next.

'Still,' the man went on hoarsely, after the coughing had died down, 'the rain's better than one of them pea-soupers, ain't it?' He coughed again briefly. 'You remember that one coupla months back? They reckon it laid upwards of ten thousand in their graves.'

Sterling nodded. 'Yes, but it was an exaggeration by the press. Most of the deaths were actually from asthma or an outbreak of Asian flu.'

He moved his chair back an inch. He found the man's appearance disagreeable. There was an unwashed smell about him, almost as if he had been sleeping rough.

'Mr Black' was staring into the fire, exhaling smoke. 'Hell of a dump, anyway,' he commented. He grinned at Sterling suddenly, and the feeble light of the coke flame glinted on broken teeth. 'Drink'd be nice.'

Sterling swallowed back a rejoinder to this solecism. 'What'll you have?'

'Brandy. Make it a big one.'

'Mr Black' was still staring into the fire, smoking and

coughing alternately, when Sterling returned with the brandy. He took it without thanks and drank half of it greedily in a gulp. 'That's the stuff,' he said. 'Dopes you up good.'

'Mr Black,' Sterling began, but the man held up a lean hand.

'Name's not Black,' he said. 'It's Corrigan. Former Flight Sergeant US Air Force. Currently unemployed.'

The name meant nothing to Sterling. 'What's this about, Mr Corrigan?' he said.

Corrigan sighed and let smoke out through his nose. He coughed.

'OK,' he said. 'I know what happened to your kid and where the *Rose of Cimarron* went down. I can give it to you chapter and verse.'

Sterling's eyes widened. He felt anger simmering inside him; all the old emotions that had been dammed up seemed set to overflow. He swallowed hard to control it and balled his fists under the table. For a moment he glared at Corrigan. 'Are you trying to tell me Billy's alive?' he demanded.

Corrigan raised his eyes. 'Let's get one thing straight,' he rasped. 'I ain't saying the kid's alive. I'm only sayin' I know what happened to him and the kite.'

'You're wasting your time,' Sterling said. 'I might have been taken in by this sort of thing once, but not any longer.'

Corrigan's dark pupils behind the glasses dilated to fiery pinpricks.

'Look,' Sterling went on. 'What you may not know is that I scoured every corner of Morocco looking for the *Rose of Cimarron*. I went over the route time and time again. I even learned to speak Arabic. My father-in-law and I spent a year searching—'

'Oh yeah. That Hobart character. I know all about him. Him and Ravin' was big buddies.'

21

'The point is we went everywhere and talked to everyone, and we didn't hear a damned thing about a downed plane or my son.'

A triumphant, slightly mocking smile played on Corrigan's lips. 'You wouldn't have,' he said. 'See *Rose* never went down in Morocco. She dumped in Spanish Sahara: 'the Spic Zone', we used to call it. The Spic Zone's a damn big place – as big as Britain with only a handful of Ay-rabs trolling about in it. That's why she wasn't found. But she dumped there all right.'

Sterling was tempted to get up and walk out, but something stopped him. It was the shock of realization that Corrigan could be right – they had never even bothered to search beyond Moroccan borders. His grip on the table tightened.

'And how the hell do you know that?' he said.

Corrigan paused for a moment, as if striving for maximum effect.

'I was there,' he said gravely. 'I was on the damn plane.'

Sterling saw red. For a moment the whole room went out of focus, and he felt sick. He wanted to claw Corrigan's head and beat it against the wall. *The impudence of the man. The impertinence. The sheer lying audacity.* He opened his mouth to say something, but Corrigan again held up a wizened hand.

'Lemme finish,' he snapped. 'You wanna hear it or not?'

'All right.'

''kay. It was summer '46. A routine flight over the Atlas – Casa to Zagora. Craven was the pilot – Ravin' Craven, they used to call him. A Dakota normally takes a crew of three – pilot, navigator and radio-op – but on this one there was just me and him. Craven took the kid along as a treat. Some treat. Ravin' was a good pilot, but he didn't know diddly-squat about maintenance. I know Dakotas – crewed them in the war. The whole instrument panel needed overhauling. I told him a million times, but he was a real Clever-Dick Brit. All went smooth till we

22

passed Ouarzazate, then suddenly the navigation gear went down. I wanted to turn back, but Ravin' said Zagora was nearer. Next thing you know we hit a dense fog, and then we was in deep shit. It was too late to turn back, too late to do anything.

'So we go on for an hour and a half, two hours, and by that time the fuel-gauge needle was in the red. Another half-hour and we're losing altitude and we knew we'd have to ditch. Ravin' panicked. It was me that saved Billy. I hooked his chute up myself and kicked him out. I jumped last, did a rivet inspection – head hit the fuselage, which sent me into spins. Canopy developed twisted. By the time I kicked the twists out, I was miles away from *Rose*. To cap it all, I landed heavy and bent my ankle.

'I just lay there till dawn came, then hobbled up a dune. I could see something shiny in the distance and I knew it had to be *Rose*. I decided to walk over there, see if I could find Billy or Craven; maybe the wireless would still be intact. My ankle was swollen so bad I had to take my flying-boots off and walk barefoot. Anyway it took me till the next morning to get to *Rose* and I was too late. I found Craven's body strung up on a jagged rock, still in his parachute-harness, dead as a doornail. He'd piled into the rock and broke his back. I looked for Billy, and found signs he'd been there – his parachute was still billowing not far from Craven's body, and there were tracks leading to the wreck. Trouble was, there were other tracks intersecting with Billy's: camel tracks and human tracks. It didn't take a genius to work out what had happened. Billy got hisself shanghaied by Ay-rabs.'

Corrigan shifted slightly and stared straight into Sterling's eyes. 'Now get this, Sterling,' he said. 'All I'm sayin' is that Billy *was* alive when *Rose* came down, I'd lay my last buck on that. There were signs in the cabin, too: chocolate half eaten, water drunk – even found places near the plane where he'd pissed. I couldn't get the wireless working, and there was no water left in the crate, so I knew I was going to have to bug out. It weren't no joke, I can tell you. I walked for three days, travelling at night, resting up in the day, until I ran into a bunch of Ay-rabs. Cost me every cent I had to get back into Morocco. I asked these guys to put the word out about Billy, but that was all I could do.'

Sterling's eyes were riveted on Corrigan's face, speechless now. He was gripping the edge of the table with both hands, his knuckles bleached. His mouth opened and closed, but no words emerged. 'Why didn't you get in contact before?' he managed to say.

Corrigan shifted awkwardly. 'OK,' he said. 'I had a little trouble with some guys who wanted a word in my ear. After I got out of the blue they were on my trail, and I had to lie low and get a new passport.'

'And that took *seven years*?'

'It took time.'

Sterling looked down at his hands and took deep breaths. 'Pull the other one, Mr Corrigan,' he said. 'You're lying. You made this up.'

Before he had even finished the sentence, he saw that Corrigan was holding up something shiny in his lean hand.

'How'd I guess you'd say that?' he said, gloatingly. 'Here. Look at this.'

Sterling took the object. It was a gold watch with a gilt expanding bracelet that was broken. It was not a very expensive watch, but the Gothic numerals on the face were quite distinctive. Sterling had given it to Billy on his thirteenth birthday. The words, *To Sunshine Boy. Happy Birthday from Mum and Dad*, were engraved on the back in italic script.

'That Billy's watch or not?' Corrigan said.

Sterling's eyes fixed on him murderously. 'Where did you get this?' he said.

'Billy fell into a bulkhead when the aircraft yawed. The watch-strap got caught in the seat-webs and was ripped off. I picked it up after he'd gone out.'

Sterling heard something inside his ears go *snap*. Doubt, distress, confusion, helplessness, despair: all seemed to gush out of him at once in an overpowering torrent, and Corrigan was a twig in the raging waters. Before he knew it, he was on top of the American with the scrawny throat in his hands, trying to squeeze the life out of him. 'You piece of shit!' he spat. 'That's my son you're talking about! You think I don't know what you are? You're a bloody deserter, that's what you are! By Christ, I'll report you to the US Embassy. I'll see you swing, Corrigan!'

He raised his fist for a smashing blow, but it was arrested in mid flight by a steel-like grip. He turned his head, dazed, to see the one-armed barman staring straight into his face. The broad fingers of the cripple's good arm were tight round his wrist.

'Not in here you don't!' the barman growled quietly. 'I knew you was trouble the moment you come in!' Sterling blinked and became aware suddenly that everyone in the pub was watching him. He felt himself shrinking, curling up with shame. It was the first time since his childhood that he had offered anyone violence. 'I'm sorry,' he stammered to the barman. 'I don't know what came over me. It won't happen again.'

'It'd better not,' the man said. 'Because next time you'll be out on your ear.'

Sterling reddened and looked at Corrigan. The American's breathing had become laboured and his complexion pale. He grabbed for his brandy and gulped it down, smoothing down his coat, trying to regain composure. The barman stalked off with a warning scowl, and after a few moments Corrigan leaned across the table. 'You asshole,' he whispered. 'You try that again, you'll never find out if your brat is dead or alive.'

He stared at Sterling in disgust and took another gulp of brandy, his piercing eyes never leaving Sterling's face. 'Gimme a hard time,' he mumbled, 'when I'm here to help you. And don't come that "deserter" shit. Tough guy, eh? I talked to your kid. I know you was a Conchie in the war. They even put you behind bars for it. What's the difference, *pal*?'

Sterling's ears were humming with shock, and Corrigan's words seemed to come from far away. He examined the watch. 'You could have taken this from his dead body,' he said. 'How do I know you didn't?'

Corrigan puffed at his Camel pensively. 'You don't,' he said. 'The only way you're gonna find out if I'm on the level is by going out there. I'm the only one who can tell you where *Rose of Cimarron* went down, so you need me. That's why I'm here.'

Sterling put the watch away in his overcoat pocket. His breathing was steadying now, his thoughts becoming more lucid. He did not want to look at Corrigan, but he forced himself. 'I see,' he said slowly. 'I get it. You want money. If I grease your palm you will tell me where the *Rose of Cimarron* went down, isn't that it?'

Corrigan shook his head. 'Wrong,' he said. 'For all you know I could be lying, like you said.'

Sterling gulped in surprise. 'So what *do* you want?' he demanded. 'You're not doing this for charity.'

Corrigan threw his cigarette stub into the fire. 'Charity begins at home,' he said. 'Least that's what my momma always told me.' He leaned closer to Sterling, elbows on the table. 'No, it ain't charity,' he said. 'But I don't want nothing on the nail. You go out there to look for Billy, you take me with you, that's all I want. You take me with you, all expenses paid. The kid could still be alive. If he ain't, you'll at least be able to bring his remains back. If you find Billy, or find his body, you can make

26

it worth my while. Strictly cash on delivery – but you take me with you is all.'

Sterling shivered. 'And if I refuse?'

'Either I go, or nobody goes: that's the deal.'

Sterling shook his head, trying to make some sense of the confusion spinning in his mind like a carousel.

'I'll give you a coupla hours to decide,' Corrigan said bluntly. He brought a soiled card out of his pocket and pushed it across the table to Sterling. 'This is where you can contact me. No phone number. You'll have to come in person.'

Sterling examined the card, noting the address written on it in pencil. 'I'll be at that address till midnight,' Corrigan said.

'But wait a minute,' Sterling gasped. 'That's impossible . . . I need time.'

'OK,' Corrigan snapped. 'Noon tomorrow at the very latest, but that's the cut-off time. If you ain't there by then, the offer expires. You won't see me again.'

Sterling put the card in his pocket, only half aware he was doing it. 'But wait a minute,' he said. 'This is ludicrous. First of all, even if I agreed, how will you find the *Rose* again? You say the desert is huge. If no one's found her by now, it's not going to be easy. Second, you say Billy was taken by Arabs. Even if you find the aircraft, that doesn't mean you can find my son.'

Corrigan finished off the brandy, belched, set the glass back hard on the table and wiped his lips with the back of his hand. 'I'm a navigator by trade,' he said. 'I made me a chart. As for finding Billy – like I said, I don't guarantee sweet Fanny Adams. But you won't get no help from the authorities – those tribes out there are in conflict with the Spics. You have to go it alone – start with *Rose* and fan out from there.'

He stood up unsteadily, pulled the brim of his trilby over his eyes, and nodded at Sterling. 'Come tonight if you can,' he said, 'but by noon tomorrow latest. I'll be watching out like a hawk. If you bring or send anyone else, the deal's off.'

Corrigan turned on his heel and eased his way through the crowd by the bar like a phantom. Five seconds later, it was as if he had never been there at all.

In the afternoon, when the sun was already descending from its zenith, Sheikh Mafoudh took them outside to see the camels. There were ten of them, and they were couched in the lee of the kasbah's broken walls, mewling, grumbling and gnashing their teeth as the Arabs loaded them with huge basketwork panniers and water-skins like bloated sea cucumbers. Sterling thought the animals looked decidedly underfed.

Mafoudh pointed out the provisions he had brought along for the journey: dates, rice, couscous, flour, tea, coffee, solid cones of sugar weighing four or five pounds each, skins of liquid butter, flakes of sun-dried meat, called *tishtar*, in dirty goatskin pouches. The camel-men squabbled as they worked, bawling at each other and at the camels, packing and repacking loads, stringing and restringing ropes. The camels roared and lurched to their feet, only to be jerked down again amid streams of what sounded like curses. To Sterling it looked like pandemonium had broken loose – yet, despite everything, the loads seemed to go on quickly and efficiently.

While Mafoudh took charge of the loading, shouting redundant orders at the men, Sterling took Churchill aside. 'Are you sure we can trust these boys?' he asked. 'I mean, they look like savages. What did you mean they are ex-slaves, Znaga and outcasts?'

Churchill gave a Cheshire-cat grin. 'Slavery's illegal in Morocco,' he said, 'but down in the Sahara it still goes on. You

28

see the two black men – Hamdu and Faris? They got fed up with being slaves and left their masters to make their own way. In Sahara society slaves are a caste, so are Znaga – they're Arabs, but from so-called 'weak' tribes, who aren't allowed to carry arms or own camels. They work as herdsmen, looking after the camels of the powerful warrior tribes, like the Reguibat and the Delim. The warrior tribes are supposed to protect them. The chap with the long black hair who threw down his head-cloth – his name is Jafar. He's a runaway Znaga who thought he could do better in life than look after someone else's property. As for outcasts – they're Berber villagers from the fringes of the desert, Ait Atta and Ait Kabbash, who committed an unforgivable sin and have been expelled from their own tribes. Usually involves some sort of treachery, like violating the hospitality laws or killing a travelling companion.'

Sterling stared at him aghast. 'And yet you're willing to put your life in their hands?'

Churchill shrugged his rounded shoulders. 'They're the best I could get,' he said. 'Sheikh Mafoudh worked for me when I was with Field Security in Casablanca – that's where he learned his English. I sometimes needed to follow up leads in the desert and he was my guide. He never let me down.'

There was a salvo of snorts and growls as the camels rose to their feet, finally loaded. Mafoudh called the Englishmen over and inspected them. 'You travel in clothes like that?' he inquired, in Arabic.

Churchill and Sterling were dressed in broad-brimmed hats and army-surplus desert fatigues – khaki trousers, drill shirts, and *chaplis*, the Indian-style sandals that had been favoured in the war by the desert commandos. Both had greased pullovers and special-forces smocks stuffed in their kitbags for the cold desert nights. Both had equipped themselves with prismatic compasses, and Sterling had brought a standard French survey map. Both had army water-bottles – steel with felt covers and cork caps.

'Why?' Churchill said. 'What's wrong with this? I am an Englishman and proud of it.'

The sheikh smirked. 'You look like crazy men,' he said. 'But no matter.' He turned and grabbed the head-rope of the first camel, which snapped at him. He tapped it smartly on the nose. 'This is how we do it,' he announced. 'First we walk, maybe two hours, maybe two and a half. Then we ride till sunset. Then we make camp. In the morning the same – walk, ride, camp when the sun is high; the same every day. You have water. You drink when you like, but you don't fill the bottles till I say. We all fill our bottles at the same time, all right?'

Churchill nodded and looked at Sterling to see if he'd picked up the Arabic. Sterling nodded back.

'In the name of God, the Compassionate, the Merciful,' Mafoudh chanted. 'Let God be our agent.'

'Amen!' the camel-men chimed in.

The caravan moved off into the hammada and the voices grew less strident and more reverent as the Sahara closed in around them by degrees, humbling them with the immensity of its silence.

As he tramped on behind the camels, Sterling remembered how he had stood in the rain outside the Marquis of Granby after meeting Corrigan. He'd felt confused and angry, just as he'd done when he had first heard the news of Billy's disappearance. The wound had suddenly been opened up, just when he'd thought it had healed. Worse than the anger was the helplessness, the feeling of terrible uncertainty. Sterling knew he needed help. He needed to talk to someone, and the only person he could confide in about this was his father-in-law, Arnold Hobart. Billy had been staying with Hobart when he had gone for a trip in the aircraft with Craven, and the old man had never forgiven himself. He had spent a large amount of money that he could not afford on trying to find out what had happened to the *Rose of Cimarron*, but to no avail. Since Corrigan claimed to have been Craven's co-pilot, Hobart might even have known him in Casablanca, and could testify at least that Corrigan was who he claimed to be. Sterling felt for change and hailed a passing taxi.

The rain had stopped by the time he reached Hobart's building in White Street. Sterling climbed the three floors up the polished stairs and knocked on his father-in-law's door. 'Come in!' a voice said. Sterling entered and walked into the living room. Arnold Hobart sat contentedly in his favourite armchair by a blazing fire, puffing a Turkish meerschaum pipe, whose bowl was carved in the effigy of a bearded janissary. As he entered, the old man lifted his head amiably. 'Oh, hallo, George,' he said.

Hobart's face was roseate from the fire, or perhaps it was from the tumbler of Cognac he held in one hand. His stiff leg – the left, hit in a shootout with Nazi Fifth Columnists in Morocco in '45 – was stretched out in front of him. The wound had almost cost him the leg, but before that Hobart had been both captain of the army heavyweight boxing team and a national standard swimmer, and he still had the trimness and the massive, top-heavy shoulders to show for it. Hobart wasn't tall, but everything else about him was larger than life – giant hands and feet and an enormous head that would hardly have disgraced a Siberian tiger. He was wearing what Sterling had come to think of as his 'uniform': shapeless tweed jacket with leather elbow-patches, cavalry twill trousers, hand-stitched shoes – all of which had seen better days, a shirt with frayed collar, and a Long Range Desert Group tie with its famous scorpion badge. A leather-bound book was balanced precariously on his knees, and he steadied it with his pipe-hand as he turned to Sterling, his face as lined as a piece of old parchment, his silver Kitchener moustache carefully trained at the ends.

He beamed at his son-in-law. 'Glad to see you, George,' he said. He examined the golden liquor in his glass, warming it against the flames, then downed his brandy in a gulp and winked at Sterling, holding the glass out. 'You look like a man who could do with a drink,' he said. 'Be a sport. Pour us a couple of tots of Cognac, would you?'

Sterling took the tumbler obediently, and carried it over to the well-worn sideboard nearby, where tumblers shared space with a clutter of photographs – of Margaret and Billy, of a bearded Hobart in Arab head-dress sitting in a Chevrolet truck bristling with machine guns against the background of the desert. There were other photos of Hobart in uniform with the almost legendary founder of the Long Range Desert Group, Ralph Bagnold, and another with an officer completely kitted out in Arab dress, who Sterling knew was Jock Hasleden, the equally legendary British intelligence agent.

He picked up another tumbler, examined it for specks of dust, then poured a generous measure of Napoleon for each of them. He arranged the remaining glasses in line abreast, then brought the full tumblers back to the fire. Hobart laid his pipe in the ashtray on the occasional table, and took the brandy glass in his left palm. He swilled the liquor around and tasted it with a look of deep enjoyment, then made a gesture to the chair opposite. Sterling sat down.

'Isn't it a bit dangerous to leave the front door open like that?' Sterling said. 'I mean, anyone could just walk in.'

Hobart shrugged. 'Let them,' he said. 'They're welcome to anything I've got, except the wife. Come to think of it, they're welcome to the wife, too.'

32

Sterling grinned weakly, glancing around the flat, at the thread-bare Persian rugs, the dilapidated leather suite, the notched dining table, the overstuffed bookshelves, and was inclined to agree. 'Where *is* Molly?' he inquired.

'Ladies bridge night.' Hobart winked. 'Gives her a break from the old bore, anyway.'

Sterling smiled, thinking that his father-in-law had turned out to be a very different kettle of fish from what he'd imagined when he'd first met Margaret Hobart at Cambridge back in 1930. Even then, Sterling had been a committed pacifist and, after they'd decided to get married, he'd dreaded the inevitable confrontation with Arnold, who had loomed in his mind as formidably as the famous Kitchener recruiting poster: '*Your country needs YOU.*'

He'd known then that Hobart had led a bayonet charge at Gallipoli in the First World War, and imagined him a dyed-in-the-wool imperialist. This was true, but Hobart had merely pointed mild fun at Sterling's idealism, and had largely accepted it. Even when his son-in-law had been jailed for refusing to serve, Hobart had kept quiet. On that first dinner invitation, a decade earlier, he had astonished Sterling by taking him aside when the ladies had withdrawn after the meal and confiding, 'Margaret's dippy, you know, but that won't mean anything to you, will it? Fact is, she's beautiful, and that's all you can see. I know. Been through it all myself. Nobody ever learns. I didn't.'

Hobart belonged to old landed gentry, but his grandfather had squandered all the family money. He had had to accept his daughter's marriage to a conscientious objector, had lost his only son, Justin, on Crete in 1941, his first wife in the blitz, his daughter to suicide, and his only grandson in an air-crash in Morocco while in his charge. And yet, incredibly almost, Hobart had remained balanced and reasonable – one of those old war-dogs of the British Empire who always knew the best thing to do.

Now, he eyed Sterling appraisingly. 'You look a bit piqued, old boy,' he said. 'Cheer up. The war's over.'

'Not for some, it's not,' Sterling said. 'At least that's what a man I met tonight told me – an American called Corrigan. He claimed to have been on the *Rose of Cimarron* when she went down.'

Hobart stiffened visibly. His eyes widened and went ice-cold. He put his drink down. 'After seven years?' he said. 'This has to be a hoax, George.'

'That's what I thought at first, but I tell you, Arnold, the man was bloody convincing. Said he had a map of the crash site.'

Hobart was staring at him with deep interest now; his deeply lined face had gone buff, with only raw red patches showing on the cheeks. 'I don't believe it,' he said. 'We searched every inch of that route.'

'Corrigan reckoned the aircraft crash-landed in Spanish Sahara, miles off course.'

Hobart gripped the arm of his chair, his eyes searching Sterling's face. 'That's impossible,' he snorted. 'A Dakota wouldn't have the range. Not unless it had an extra fuel tank fitted. A Dakota C47 has a range of about 1200 kilometres on normal tanks – enough to get to Zagora with a full payload. So why would *Rose of Cimarron* have an extra fuel tank fitted for a standard run? That would have meant cutting down on her payload. It would have cost the company money.'

Sterling recounted the story Corrigan had told him, while Hobart listened in silence. He finished by pulling out Billy's watch. 'Margaret and I gave Billy this for his thirteenth birthday,' he said.

Hobart turned a shade paler. He took the watch and examined

34

it. 'I remember,' he said. 'But Corrigan could have got this anywhere . . .' He paused for a moment, and with great effort picked up his pipe. 'Go to the police, George,' he said. 'This chap should be publicly horsewhipped. As if it isn't enough that we've all suffered so much, these vermin have to crawl out of the woodwork just when everything's starting to run smoothly again and rub salt in the old wounds. Man's a deserter, you say? I can't imagine a chap like Keith Craven taking him on. I mean, I knew a lot of the expatriates in Casablanca in '46 and I don't recall any Corrigan. Admittedly, the shower that Craven worked for employed all sorts of riff-raff, but I don't remember Keith ever mentioning a Corrigan. My advice is to ring the police straight away. You say you have the chap's address?'

Sterling remembered the dog-eared card Corrigan had given him and fished it out. He handed it to his father-in-law and Hobart turned it over in his big boxer's hand.

'Rotherhithe,' he commented. 'Near the docks.'

He handed it back to Sterling, who put it away.

'Let the police go round there,' Hobart said. 'They'll sort him out. He's playing on your emotions. My God, good job Margaret's not with us . . .'

He broke off, clenching the big fists. Sterling remembered with a shudder how he had come home one day to find his wife Margaret, Hobart's daughter, lying naked in a bathtub full of water and blood, her wrists slashed. He shook his head slightly to chase the horrific image away.

'But say Corrigan's telling the truth,' he went on in a quiet voice. 'The police would wreck everything – he was right about that. If he really has the map, I'd never get it. Look, I know it's probably a hoax, Arnold, but to be sure I have to see that map.'

Hobart scratched his moustache with the stem of his pipe. 'If it exists,' he said. 'It just doesn't ring true. It's taken him seven

35

years to come forward? The idea of "going out there with you", and everything. I reckon it was just a ploy to gain your confidence. Clever – but that's how these chaps work.' He watched Sterling with curiosity. 'Go through the proper channels, George,' he said.

'I'm sure you're right, but promise me you won't breathe a word until I've decided.'

'George,' Hobart said. 'You know Billy's . . . disappearance . . . was one of the worst things that ever happened to me. Worse than Justin on Crete in forty-one, and that was bad enough. I mean, at least Justin was a soldier and we all knew what the chances were. But Billy was only a boy, and he was in my charge. I should never, never have let him go with Keith, but then Keith was the best flier I ever met. DFC and *bar,* George – and he was army, not RAF. I couldn't believe that the kite had gone down. But she did go down – in the Atlas, in the desert – what's the difference? It's seven years, George, and Billy's not going to come back. I hate myself for saying it, but why open old wounds? Let the dead rest in peace. Accept it. Accept.'

To Sterling's embarrassment, two tears streaked down the old man's leathery face. Hobart sniffed and brushed them off. 'I promise I won't report it to the police,' he said, 'but don't do anything in a rush, George. Don't go round there tonight.'

Sterling sighed. 'All right,' he said. 'It's too late to be tramping round the docks, anyway.' He paused and looked directly at Hobart. 'There is one possibility that occurs to me,' he said, 'but I hesitate to mention it in view of your friendship with Craven.'

'What's that?'

'Well, if Corrigan was telling the truth about . . . you know, about wanting to join me on a search mission . . . Well, maybe there's something on the *Rose of Cimarron* that he wants. I mean something quite unrelated to Billy.'

36

'What on earth are you getting at?'

'All right, it's a shot in the dark – but, say the kite was carrying something valuable. I mean, it's curious that Corrigan never referred to the cargo. What if something went down with *Rose* that he wants to get back?'

Hobart snorted. 'You mean like contraband? But, George, we went into the cargo issue when we investigated it all in '46. We even saw the manifest. The *Rose* was carrying supplies for the French Foreign Legion in Zagora – bully beef, oatmeal and sardines. Nothing more exotic than that. The French military confirmed it. Anyway, Keith was as honourable a man as you'd find anywhere. He'd never have got mixed up with any sort of smuggling operation.'

Sterling considered it for a moment. His memory differed slightly from that of his father-in-law – he recalled that they had not seen the flight manifest, only conferred with a slightly flaky French army clerk who'd told them so verbally. But Hobart was showing signs of irritation now, and Sterling decided he shouldn't push it. His father-in-law had always made it clear that he held himself totally responsible for what had happened to Billy, and Sterling knew this would be adding insult to injury. 'You're right,' he said submissively. 'It was just a thought. Ninety-nine point nine per cent the man's crooked, as you say.'

There was a movement from the hall outside and Sterling jumped. 'It's me!' a female voice cried. 'I'm home!'

A moment later Molly Hobart came striding through the doorway, a statuesque figure, five foot ten, with a bushy mop of hair going grey at the roots, and a rather severe face, heavily made up. Her ankle-length blue dress was not expensive, but it fitted her like a glove. She was a handsome looking woman, George thought, but an ice-maiden if ever there was one. Molly was a war-widow. She'd been a nursing sister in Queen Anne's during the war, and Arnold had met her while recovering from a gunshot wound in a hospital in Algiers – the one he'd received in a shootout with Nazi agents in Morocco. She was a good fifteen years younger than his father-in-law, and Sterling often thought that Hobart had chosen her to look after him in his old age. He wondered if he had chosen well. She was efficient at making him comfortable, all right, but to Sterling it was the cold efficiency of a drill sergeant. 'George,' she said, smiling thinly, 'how nice to see you.'

Hobart and Sterling both rose politely, but when Hobart sat down, Sterling remained standing. 'I'm just off,' he said.

'Oh, do you have to?' Molly said, pouting, but not making much effort to sound as if she meant it. He and Molly had never got on. Her husband had been killed at Tobruk in 1942, and somehow she seemed to feel that Sterling was responsible. Although Sterling hadn't heard it himself, she'd reportedly once expressed the opinion that all conscientious objectors ought to have been lined up and shot.

'Yes, it's late,' Sterling said.

'How did it go?' Hobart asked.

Molly pouted again. 'Rotten show,' she said. 'I got partnered with Jean Leithstone, who hasn't got a clue. We lost an arm and a leg.'

'You don't mean you're playing for money now?' Hobart growled.

'But, darling, did you think we played for matchsticks? It wouldn't be much fun otherwise, would it?'

'God,' Hobart said. 'Another fortune down the drain.'

'Well, I'll be off,' Sterling said. 'Don't get up, Arnold.'

'All right,' Hobart said. 'I'll leave it to you, but just keep me informed, won't you, old boy.'

* * *

At camp that night, Sterling's back and legs were sore from the constant jogging of his camel, though he had ridden for only the last couple of hours. 'Don't worry,' Churchill said, 'you get used to it after a year or two.'

Sterling snorted. 'Or maybe fifty years. Or maybe never.'

They were sitting amid their saddlery, at a distance from the camel-men who seemed furiously busy, hanging water-skins, stitching saddles, greasing the flanks of their camels with animal fat. The night was clear and cold, the stars out in myriads above them. Churchill seemed at home, but Sterling felt awkward, conspicuous and out of place.

Churchill groped in his kitbag and brought out a bottle of whisky. He unscrewed it and passed it to Sterling. 'Only don't let them see it,' he said.

Sterling took the bottle gratefully. 'Why?' he enquired. 'They'll be insulted?'

'You're joking. No, they'll want their share, and there isn't enough.'

Sterling smiled and swigged whisky, feeling it burning down his gullet, warming the blood. He handed the bottle back to Churchill, who had a good swig and screwed the cap on again. 'Well,' he said. 'We're off, at any rate. We haven't done too badly, after all.'

Sterling nodded. Churchill had certainly pulled out all the stops on this one. In Casablanca he had used his contacts among former French cronies, who had managed to get in touch by telephone with Sheikh Mafoudh, now residing near Rissani, an oasis in the pre-Sahara. The old man had agreed to meet them at the ruined kasbah of Tamerdanit, near the dunes of the Erg Chebbi. It had all gone smoothly – almost too smoothly – and no one had asked questions. Cash had eased away any difficulties that might have arisen. Sterling had to admit that Churchill had been a tower of strength and efficiency; his polyglot grasp of languages – Arabic, French, German, Spanish and God-knew-what-else – especially surprised him. If Churchill's continuous rendering of his namesake's speeches was starting to irritate Sterling, he had also revealed himself as a man of hidden depths.

'*Let us therefore brace ourselves to our duty,*' the big man was reciting now. '*And so bear ourselves that, if the British Empire and its Commonwealth last for a thousand years, men will still say, "This was their finest hour".*'

Sterling grimaced. 'Old Winnie was being a bit optimistic there,' he commented. 'The Empire's already had it. In fact, it'd had it long before the war even started. The economists reckon now that in September 1939 we only had enough resources to last four months. Thank providence for the US of A.'

'Maybe,' Churchill agreed morosely. 'But it was great while it lasted.'

Sterling watched him in the light of the half-moon. 'You strike me as a genuine patriot, Eric,' he said. 'Something I could never be, not if it meant killing supposed enemies of the state.'

'It takes all sorts,' Churchill said, primly. 'Who was it who said *patriotism is the last resort of the scoundrel*?'

'God knows – but I'd lay odds it wasn't Winston Churchill. Tell me, you aren't really related to him, are you?'

Churchill knitted his eyebrows as if he were about to deliver another speech, then thought better of it. 'A minor branch of the family,' he said.

Sterling watched him inquisitively, waiting for more, but Churchill only gave him a bulldog grimace, knowing that it made him look more like Winston than ever. Actually, the idea that he was related to the British wartime Prime-Minister – the man who'd provided 'the British Empire's roar' – had worked a blinder for him. His private-investigation business had flourished in the years immediately after the war, when thousands were clamouring to find out what had happened to sons, brothers and fathers lost in the conflict. Churchill specialized in tracking down Forces personnel who'd gone missing in Europe or North Africa during the war years – particularly American aircrew. His US clients were tickled to tell their friends back home that they'd been helped 'by one of the Churchills', and Eric had cashed in on his image by cultivating a suitably Churchillian appearance, complete with glowering brow-ridges, big cigars when he could afford them, and almost word-perfect renditions of the wartime speeches in a voice that seemed suitably pickled in whisky and cigar-smoke, and sometimes was.

He'd been spectacularly successful for a while – he'd even managed to locate USAF airmen who were happily but bigamously married to French wives and didn't want to come home, and had paid him to keep quiet. But inevitably the bottom had fallen out of the market. It was now seven years since the Armistice, and the world had begun to move into a new era. Most of the boys who were going to come home were home, and those who weren't could be left in peace.

Churchill's relationship with Sterling had begun at precisely 4.35 p.m. on 15 February when the telephone had rung just as Churchill was locking up his office in Borough High Street. Normally Churchill didn't shut up shop until five, but there had been nothing doing all that day – nothing for the past two weeks, actually – and finally there'd seemed no point in keeping up appearances.

He'd sent his secretary, Madge, home at three, and since she hadn't been paid for a month, Churchill wouldn't have blamed her if she'd never come back. For a time they had had a cosy *affaire* going and plenty of time to indulge in it on the office couch. Churchill was married to Sonja, a dark-haired, attractive, pint-sized woman, but didn't believe men were made to be monogamous – at least, not himself. Actually he blamed his mother for his own promiscuity. She'd been an extraordinarily beautiful woman, and a wonderful *artiste*, who had treated him as if he were the most special person on earth. Somehow, no one quite managed to live up to his mother's standards.

His wife, Sonja, had finally walked out on him ten days before, saying she was going back to her mother's. She'd grown tired of Churchill's promises that something better was just round the corner. As she had packed her case, her mouth set with grim determination, Churchill had held her arm gently in his big hand. 'What about for better or for worse?' he'd asked.

Sonja laughed bitterly, her dark eyes flashing. 'Promises don't pay the rent,' she said.

'Just hang on a bit longer,' Churchill had begged her. 'There's a big job coming up any day now.'

'Yes,' she said. 'And pigs might fly.'

Since Sonja had walked out, the *affaire* with Madge had somehow diminished in intensity. It had begun to dawn on him that the forbidden fruit lost its flavour once it was un-forbidden.

For a moment Churchill had been tempted to leave the ringing phone, then he turned and unlocked the door again. He realized that he hoped the caller was Sonja, ringing to tell him that everything was all right and they could start again.

He lifted the receiver. A rather nasal, slightly high-pitched male voice asked, 'Mr Churchill?'

'Yes,' Churchill assented. 'Who is this?'

'My name is George Bridger Sterling.'

Churchill sniffed. 'How can I help you, Mr Sterling?'

'Your name was given to me by a friend.'

There was a pause, and Churchill realized that the man on the other end of the line was finding it difficult to go on. 'Do you need help finding a lost relative?' he asked coaxingly.

'Yes. My son disappeared.'

'He was lost in the war?'

'No. He's – or he *was* – only a boy. Fourteen years old.'

'When did it happen?'

There was another pause. 'In nineteen forty-six,' Sterling said. There was an intake of breath as if he intended to add something. Then he paused again.

Churchill scratched his head. 'That's still a heck of a long time ago, Mr Sterling,' he said. 'I'm sorry to say this, but the likelihood is that your son is—'

'Dead, I know. I faced that a long while ago. But some new evidence has come up, and I have to know for certain.'

'Have you tried the police?'

There was a longer pause from the other end. 'The police can't help with this. My son disappeared in Morocco.'

Churchill sighed. There was really no question about whether he would take the job – it was the one he'd been waiting for, the one he'd told Sonja was just around the corner, and there was no way he could turn it down. He was an old enough hand not to seem too eager, though. 'I usually do lost Forces personnel,' he said.

'I realize that, but I understand you know Morocco well.'

'I'd hardly say "know". I was stationed there for a time at the end of the war, yes, but I can't say I'm the world's expert. Who gave you my name?'

'Vernon Dakin, my business partner.'

'Ah yes, Mr Dakin – *Major* Dakin, wasn't it? We've met at various functions – he's a friend of a couple of my clients. I remember now, Dakin runs a string of chemists' shops called *Dakin & Sterling* I take it you're the Sterling?'

43

Sterling ignored the question. 'Can I rely on your discretion, Mr Churchill?' he asked.

'The relationship between a private investigator and his client is sacrosanct. Think of yourself as a confessor with his priest.'

'I'm not a Catholic. Not even a practising Christian. I've never been to confession and am never likely to.'

'Maybe it was a bad analogy. Think of a lawyer and his client or a doctor and his patient.'

'So I can take it you accept the job?'

Churchill chuckled mirthlessly. 'Whoa, hold your horses, old boy,' he said. 'I need to know a bit more about it.'

'Then we should meet. I'm at Kew. Can you come here?'

'When?'

'Now?'

Churchill grunted. 'Well, it's a bit short notice . . .' he began.

'Get a taxi,' Sterling said.

'I'm in Borough. A taxi is going to cost.'

'Don't worry about the money. Got a pen?'

'Yes.' Churchill groped on his desk for a pencil and scribbled down the address that Sterling gave him on the margin of the *Daily Express*.

'Thirty minutes,' Sterling said, and hung up.

Churchill put the phone down and made a 'V for Victory' sign, and glanced triumphantly in the mirror. '*Now this is not the end*,' he growled at his reflection. '*It is not even the beginning of the end. But it is perhaps the end of the beginning.*'

He was about to go out again, when he hesitated, turned around and unlocked the drawer of his desk. He took out the loaded .38 Smith & Wesson revolver concealed there, and stuffed it in his pocket.

* * *

44

Every day followed the same routine. The Arabs would be up before dawn, rousing the camels, feeding them grain in nosebags, growling at each other in guttural voices. Churchill and Sterling would roll out of their sleeping bags, splash a little water over their faces and hands, and join the others by the fire for tea. As the sun rose, turning the campsite into a mandala of grotesque shadows, the caravan would form, and Sheikh Mafoudh would lead them off, shambling towards yet another horizon. For the first hours they tramped alongside the camels, then, as the day grew hotter, they would couch their animals and ride for the rest of the morning, halting at noon for a rest and a meal.

For the first few days they passed black tents in the distance, and occasionally tiny mud-built cabins amid clumps of tamarisk trees. After that, there was nothing but the endless plain of stone, sand and gravel, sandy arroyos, seams of dunes like the scales of goldfish, jagged spurs of rock that rose out of the hammada like vast monuments. Day blended imperceptibly into day, each one almost interchangeable, and Sterling grew increasingly footsore, weary, thirsty and ragged as the monotony gnawed away at his soul. The filth irritated him, the flies, the constant shouting of the Arabs, the smell of the camels, the total lack of privacy. In the desert there was no hiding place. Everything he did was watched and, he suspected, commented on and judged. One evening at dinner, Sheikh Mafoudh had asked why he carried no weapon. Churchill, he pointed out, wore his Smith & Wesson openly in a holster on his belt, why not Sterling? There was an awkward silence, which even the loquacious Churchill couldn't cover up.

'I'm not a fighter, that's all,' Sterling said.

'But how can that be?' Mafoudh demanded in Arabic. 'You are an Englishman and the English are warriors.'

'Not at all. I'm not a warrior.'

Mafoudh made a scoffing noise. 'What are you then?' he demanded. 'Znaga?'

'He is a wise man,' Churchill cut in. 'A marabout.'

Mafoudh seemed to accept this, but afterwards Sterling noticed a definite coolness towards him on the part of the camel-men. Mafoudh adopted a sneering tone when addressing him, dropping hints about 'yellow-bellies' and 'weak peoples'.

It was ironic, Sterling thought, that most of these men had broken away from old lives in which they'd had inferior status in order to become warriors. He'd been born a 'warrior' – at least in their eyes – and had rejected it.

On the fifth morning they awoke to find the horizons occluded by a pall of dust, and a sharp wind raking fragments of dust across their faces. Mafoudh sniffed the air. 'Smell!' he said. 'See! There is a storm coming – an *irifi*. It will reach us before noon.'

They loaded the camels and moved out as usual, tramping into the tentacles of dust that were already thrashing across the landscape. By mid-morning they could see a wall of thick dust moving across the horizon like a fast-encroaching fire. The sky had gone dark, and was filled with a single giant black cloud, like a vast hand poised to pluck them from the face of the earth. Only minutes after they mounted their camels, the storm hit them, smashing into the caravan like a shock wave, almost bowling the camels over. The screech and rasp of the wind was deafening, the wind so violent that it seemed to Sterling that the planet itself was in upheaval, a live organism trying with all its power to buck them off. They leaned into their saddles, turning their heads out of the wind, forcing the camels onwards. Soon, though, Sheikh Mafoudh reined in, his mount turning immediately out of the storm.

He beckoned to Churchill, who nudged his camel closer. Sterling followed, and all three leaned close across their saddles, forming a tiny bubble against the storm.

46

'We have to stop,' the sheikh hissed. 'I can't find the way in the *irifi*. We will get lost.'

'But what about water?' Churchill yelled. 'We only have enough for a day. If the storm goes on longer, we'll die.'

'God is generous!' Mafoudh shouted. 'We all die when the time comes.'

'No!' Sterling bawled. He pulled the prismatic compass from the pocket of his coat. 'We can go on with this.'

Mafoudh swept sand out of his eyes and stared at it, then at Churchill. 'He is a crazy man,' he said.

'You sure you can use that thing?' Churchill demanded.

'Yes,' Sterling yelled. 'I've been keeping tabs on our direction just in case.'

'All right,' Churchill said. 'Lead on MacDuff!'

Sterling took the lead position, balancing the compass in his hand. The next two hours were among the most difficult he had ever experienced. The sound of the wind alone was terrifying, the airborne sand lashed at their faces, the power of the storm threatening constantly to hurl them out of the saddle. There was no respite, even for a moment, and the camels fought their riders, trying to turn aside, so that Sterling always had to jerk his mount's head in the right direction. It was exhausting work. The sand built up on their faces, working its way into their eyes, mouth, nostrils and ears, penetrating every layer of clothing with the persistence of water.

Suddenly there was a shout from the rear. Sterling didn't hear it at first, until Churchill spurred his mount beside him and grabbed his arm. 'Hamdu is missing!' he bawled. 'His camel is here, but he's gone!' Sterling halted his mount, which turned its back to the storm gratefully.

'How?' he asked. 'When was he last seen?'

The camel-men had already formed a huddle, their camels

47

pressing shoulder to shoulder, backs to the wind. They looked persecuted and fearful, Sterling thought.

'Last time I saw him was when you took over as guide,' Mafoudh shouted in Arabic.

'Jesus Christ!' Sterling spat. 'That's hours ago.'

'Leave him,' Mafoudh bawled. 'We go on.'

For a moment Sterling listened to the howl of the storm and shivered.

'Alone in this he'll die,' he yelled.

'It is the Will of God!' Mafoudh protested. 'If we go back we all die. He's only a slave, after all. What does a slave matter? We all die when it is time – the Almighty has decreed it. What does one life matter more or less?'

Sterling's camel jerked its head suddenly, and he drew back the head-rope to restrain it. 'It matters,' he hissed angrily. 'If it doesn't matter, what are we doing here?'

He brought his camel-stick down smartly on the camel's rump and it shot forward.

Mafoudh put out a bony hand and grabbed his head-rope. 'Where are you going, crazy man?' he demanded.

'I'm going to get Hamdu,' Sterling shouted. 'Let go of my camel!'

'You crazy!' Mafoudh yelled in broken English. 'You die. Mebbe we all die. Tell him, Captain!'

He shot a glance at Churchill, who was looking on, perturbed. 'He's right, George,' Churchill shouted. 'You'll never find him in this.'

'Then I'll die,' Sterling growled. He ripped his head-rope smartly from the sheikh's hand. 'Get out of my way!' he hissed.

Mafoudh looked as if he would protest, but something in Sterling's demeanour stopped him. 'Crazy fool!' he said. 'The English Znaga will bring back the worthless slave. Ha! Ha! If

48

we'd stopped like I said back there, Hamdu would not have got lost. By God, this is your fault Englishman!'

'Yes,' Sterling spat. 'Then it's only right I go back for him.' He brushed dust out of his eyes and stared at Churchill. 'Wait here,' he ordered. 'If I'm not back in an hour, you continue to the next well, all right? You've got a compass, Eric. You can lead, can't you?'

'Yes, but . . .'

Sterling lifted his compass. 'You're going two hundred and thirty degrees,' he yelled. 'Southwest by south.' He shifted the scale on his own compass, setting it on a back bearing. Then he belted his camel's flank again and shot off into the storm. Seconds later he was out of sight.

The storm closed in around him, enveloping him in its folds, but it was behind him now and he could feel it at his back, pushing him on. The camel seemed to feel it too, and began to step out, thinking it was going home. Sterling was glad of this – he was still a novice at camel-handling, but the beast's homing instinct seemed to keep it on his bearing almost exactly. The wind screeched beside him, coming in gusts, now allowing a momentary glimpse of the larger landscape, now shutting him in once again. Sterling did not know exactly what had made him turn back – he was a complete stranger to the desert and he'd hated almost every minute of it so far. It was the thought of a man dying alone in the desolation that had decided him, he realized. It reminded him of what might have been Billy's fate.

He held his watch up to his eyes and saw that he'd been gone almost half an hour. Riding back into the wind would be slower, so unless he turned back now the caravan would go on without him, at least to the next well. Sterling knew that finding a well he'd never seen before in this storm was going to be far more difficult than travelling on a bearing. If he didn't turn now he might never see them again. But he could not leave Hamdu to die, he thought, and in the end Mafoudh was right. If he hadn't insisted on travelling by compass, the fellow wouldn't have been lost at all. After a while he held up his watch again. Now he had been gone forty minutes – too late to catch up with the others unless he turned right now and raced back. He stopped his camel, hesitating. The storm howled in his ears, wailing like a cacophony of banshees. What he did now, he thought, might condemn a man to death. He was about to jerk the camel's head back into the storm, when he glanced up to see something dark looming out of the sand-mist. At once Sterling shifted his camel to face the dark thing. 'Hamdu?' he roared. 'Hamdu, is that you?'

Sterling urged the camel forwards a few paces and saw that the dark figure was indeed Hamdu, his eyes almost blinded by the sand, his head-cloth lost, his face contorted with terror, pain and thirst. When he saw Sterling he froze, rooted to the spot as if he'd seen a ghost. '*Alhamdulillah*! Thanks be to God!' he mumbled.

Sterling made his camel kneel and helped the ex-slave onto its rump, behind the saddle. 'Hang on!' was all he could think to say. As soon as the camel rose, he tapped its rear leg with his stick and headed it in the direction from which he had come.

The camel-men sat close together, in the lee of the couched camels, heads drooping, cloaks and scarves covering their heads. 'How long has he been gone?' Sheikh Mafoudh asked.

Churchill peered at his watch. 'It's almost an hour,' he said.

'Your friend is a crazy man,' Mafoudh said. 'Why did you bring him here, Captain? He'll get us all killed. He'll never find Hamdu, not in this. I say let Hamdu go. These slaves are no good in the desert. Maybe he fell asleep, fell off his camel and

50

hit his head. Your friend – he'll never come back now. Better we go on.'

Churchill shifted uneasily, wishing he'd prevented Sterling from going back. He could have used force; in fact he couldn't think why he hadn't. It was just that, for a moment, Sterling had seemed full of confidence and authority, fully in charge of his own fate. Churchill looked at his watch. Sterling had been away an hour now, and Mafoudh was right – there was little chance of him getting back.

That bloody fool, he thought suddenly. *He's gone and ruined everything now. There's a hell of a lot riding on this.*

'Give him another few minutes,' he told the sheikh. 'You never know.'

'God is generous,' Mafoudh said, scratching a crust of sand out of his eyes.

There was silence but for the roaring of the storm. The minutes ticked past. Finally, Sheikh Mafoudh poked Churchill's leg with his camel-stick, and the big man looked at his watch. It was an hour and fifteen minutes since Sterling had disappeared. 'Come on,' the sheikh said. 'He's not coming back now.'

The men got to their feet awkwardly, muffling their heads, cursing the storm, and trying to rouse the camels and turn them once more into the wind.

Churchill groped for his compass.

'You can find the way?' Mafoudh yelled to him.

'I suppose I could,' Churchill said.

'Come on then. Let's go.'

'No, wait!' came a voice from the back of the caravan. It was the ex-Znaga, Jafar, and he was standing stock-still, staring into the tails of the storm. 'I saw something!' he bawled.

'Nonsense!' Mafoudh screamed back. 'Just the wind.'

'No!' Jafar shouted back. 'Something – there!'

At that moment, Sterling's camel emerged from the sand-mist like an apparition, with Hamdu still clinging on at the rear.

Churchill's eyes opened wide in amazement, and Mafoudh's mouth fell. 'God preserve us,' he gasped. 'I don't believe it.'

The storm had blown itself out by sunset, when they reached the Hassi Messoud. The well was deep and the camel-men drew the buckets up in teams, watering the camels in a stone trough that looked as if it had been there since the beginning of time. Meanwhile, Mafoudh and the Englishmen made camp in the shelter of some tamarisk trees nearby. By nightfall, the camels had all drunk their fill, and the Arabs drove them back into the trees in a tight squad. The sheikh called to the men to come and sit by the fire. He made tea with the usual ceremony, offering Sterling the first glass – a singular honour. 'I was wrong,' the sheikh said graciously in Arabic. 'You are neither a Znaga nor a slave. You may not carry a weapon, but you are a man of courage.' He turned and glared scornfully at Hamdu, who sat in silence with his head on his chest. 'And you risked your life for this worthless piece of camel's turd,' he said, poking at the black man with his stick. 'For this slave, who fell asleep in a storm and put us all at risk.'

Sterling was about to argue, but didn't. Altogether, he thought, there had been too much dying in the world over the past fifteen years – 30 million dead in the war they now reckoned. He could never get his head around such a figure. He thought of Corrigan again, remembering how he had struggled with his alternatives: going to the police, as Arnold had insisted, or taking the American up on his offer. He had lain awake thinking about it all night, stroking Billy's watch. In the morning he'd taken a bus to Rotherhithe.

* * *

Corrigan's address turned out to be a Victorian tenement, standing precariously on walls whose foundations had been shaken by Luftwaffe bombs intended for the nearby docks. The tiny Presbyterian Seamen's Church that stood next door had remained untouched, as if protected by an invisible aura of sanctity, but the block was like a mangled, rotten cake with bites taken out of it – each bite a ruined apartment, a burned-out home. The place should have been demolished long ago. By the entrance, in a small shelter of brickbats and debris, two men made obese by layers of sacks and newspapers huddled up to a fire lit in a rusty oilcan. They did not greet Sterling as he passed.

He went through the big arched doorway, up a dark spiral of stairs whose ornate banister had been rubbed a slick grey from the grease of countless hands. He passed two landings before he found the number on the card, and halted outside a four-panelled wooden door, intact but colourless under generations of peeling paint.

Sterling knocked. There was no answer, but the door gave slightly and he realized it wasn't locked. He called Corrigan's name, knocked again. Still no answer. He waited a moment, then pushed the door open with his fist. Inside, a short hallway stretched to the half-open door of a parlour. There was a smell of damp carpets and the reek of burned cooking. He closed the door gently and advanced into the hall. 'Corrigan?' he shouted. 'You there?'

He shoved open the second door. Corrigan was in front of him, naked from the waist up, sitting in a battered upright chair, his head lolling backwards at a curious angle, his bulging eyes staring at the ceiling. His arms were strapped to the chair with piano-wire, and a piece of the same wire was wrapped around his neck.

For a second Sterling stood rooted, as the image gouged itself

53

upon his retina – the ivory-coloured hands, the face that was almost the colour and texture of Wedgwood porcelain, the eyes wide open, the lips drawn back over the broken teeth in an agonizing rictus. The piano-wire had cut almost a quarter of an inch into the flesh of the neck, but the blood that had streamed down Corrigan's naked torso had long since congealed. His wire-framed spectacles lay beside him on the floorboards.

Sterling was shocked, but not panic-stricken. This was not his first experience of violent death. He squatted down, saw Corrigan's mouth was blocked by a bloated tongue. The tongue was bloody where Corrigan's teeth had clamped down on it. He cleared the obstruction expertly, straining for a whisper of breath. Nothing. The tongue felt as dry and rough as emery cloth. He probed the chest and finally the left wrist. There was no movement, no pulse; the body was cold and inert, the muscles already set hard in rigor mortis. As he stood up he noticed that Corrigan's bare left arm was covered in what looked like cigarette-burns, and for the first time he shuddered. Someone had made the American suffer before he died.

A fly settled on Corrigan's tongue and Sterling brushed it off. He felt a pang of pity, but then he thought of Billy. Corrigan's death might have robbed him of his last chance of finding the boy, just when he had finally set his mind to it. He had come here to find the map – the map that Corrigan had said could lead him back to Billy – and it occurred to him suddenly that whoever had tortured and murdered Corrigan might have been after the same thing.

He stood up and made a quick inventory of the flat. It was a cramped and bleak place – no pictures, no ornaments, nothing of a personal nature. It carried the carrion smell of wet rugs and stale cigarettes. It was as cold as an icebox and the only light came from a great sash window, which was half open.

54

Sterling knew he ought to call the police at once, but there was no phone and it would mean going out to find a Bobby on the beat, which might take some time. If he did that, he wouldn't get the chance to look for the map that he so desperately needed. For a moment he struggled with himself. Corrigan was dead, and wouldn't get any deader with half an hour's delay. But it would take more than that to search the flat properly, and perhaps the map didn't exist anyway.

His internal debate was cut short abruptly by the sound of voices from outside. There was a rap on the front door, brusque, businesslike and brutal. Sterling's first instinct was to open the door, but he held back. Finding a policeman in the street was one thing, but it now occurred to him that his situation might look very bad, standing over a murdered man in a flat he'd had no right to enter. He looked down and saw that there was blood on his hands where he had felt Corrigan's chest. That would be hard to explain. A score of witnesses in the Marquis of Granby had seen him assault Corrigan the previous night and, after all, he was a jailbird with a record – who would take his word for anything?

Sterling wavered. Then he heard the sound of the door being flung open and the growling of voices in the corridor, and he went instinctively for the sash window. It was open just wide enough for him to squirm through. The window ledge outside was slippery but wide, and he raised himself to his feet and inched into the cover of the torn, grimy curtain just as a group of men moved into the sitting room. He could see them clearly through the gap in the curtain. There were four of them. They were dressed in dark overcoats, and they had the unhurried, coolly professional air of policemen. They bent out of sight and he guessed they were searching Corrigan's body. A moment later there was the sound of crashing and hammering as they began to take the flat apart.

Sterling edged as far along the ledge as he could, not daring to look down. His hand came into contact with a piece of piping, so rusted that it had snapped in two, and for a perilous second he wobbled. He grabbed at the brickwork behind him to steady himself, and as he did so saw that something had been pushed into the jagged end of the broken pipe. It looked like an oilskin packet – the kind of thing commandos used to wrap their pistols in during the war. Bracing his legs for balance, he reached out and pulled the packet out of the pipe, holding it for a moment between his thumb and forefinger. It was light – but it certainly might contain a map. He shoved it hastily into the pocket of his coat, then peered back through the slit between the curtain and the wall. One of the men – a gorilla with a pugilist's broken nose – turned suddenly in his direction and pointed at the window. 'Hey, Inspector!' he grunted in a Cockney accent. 'What about out there?'

Inspector. So they were police. The thought turned Sterling's blood cold. He should have stayed there and confronted them. Running away and hiding would only confirm his guilt, but it was too late to change his mind now. He could not see the other man from where he stood, but he heard a crisp order and suddenly the inspector came into view – an unusually tall man, ramrod straight, with a clean-shaven face, pale blue eyes and close-cropped blond hair. There was a V-shaped scar in the very centre of his right cheek, which might have been an old knife-wound. He was holding a revolver – the kind issued to officers in the war: a Webley .38.

Sterling was already shaking. His foothold on the ledge was precarious and he was aware that he was unlikely to survive a fall, at least not in one piece. He could creep no further along the ledge. The pipe wouldn't bear his weight, that was certain. Further to his right there was a rusted fire ladder, but it was five or six feet away, far beyond his reach. In any case, the ladder looked as if it hadn't been used or serviced in years. The brackets that fixed it to the wall were set in mortar that had softened and crumbled. Any weight on it and it might go down like a ton of bricks.

The blond man approached the window. In a moment he would thrust his head out and see Sterling on the ledge. It was flight or fight time. He turned himself towards the teetering fire escape and measured the distance frantically. A good leap would do it, but the chances of it holding were no more than fifty-fifty. There were no certainties whichever way you looked at it.

He braced his calf muscles and flung himself off the ledge. One hand came into contact with a rusted rung and the second quickly followed, but as Sterling struggled to get a foothold there was an eerie scraping and he felt the ladder give as his weight wrenched it out of the wall. The breath rushed from his body. For a moment he hung in the balance, frigid inside. The iron bracket above him slid out six inches, then stopped abruptly. Sterling's feet hit the rungs and he knew he was back from the jaws of death. He slithered, shimmied, scampered down, hardly touching the rungs at all, feeling the iron shivering under his weight. He heard someone bellow after him, and the sound of a sash window being wrenched up, but he did not pause to look. In only seconds he had dropped down among the garbage of an alley, and then he was on his feet and running for his life.

Sterling kept running until he came to a phone-box, standing outside a newsagent's shop on the corner of a major intersection. He stopped and looked behind him, seeing only down-at-heel Londoners pacing the street. Sterling eased into the box, panting, and steadied himself against its solid iron frame. It suddenly began to dawn on him that he was in the worst mess

57

of his life. It was worse than his conviction for refusing to serve in 1940. Much worse. He'd been spotted hiding from the police outside the room of a man who'd been tortured and brutally murdered, a man a couple of dozen eyewitnesses could testify he'd actually assaulted and threatened only the previous night. It was clear he needed help, and needed it fast.

On impulse he drew the oilskin packet from his pocket. It was fastened with buckles and press-studs that he opened with frantic haste. An old lady in a woolly coat and a hat like a hayrick shuffled out of the newsagent's, carrying a heavy basket. She plumped it down next to the box and glared at him through the glass.

Sterling opened the packet. Inside was a neatly folded piece of thick yellow card, on which was drawn a map. The legend 'ROC' was spelt out almost in the exact centre, next to a tiny precision drawing of a Dakota aircraft. Relief, sand dunes and landmarks were all filled in with professional skill. A grid of latitude and longitude had been carefully drawn over the chart, and in the bottom right corner was a key, with a stylized compass and the words 'Spanish Sahara' at its head. There was even a scale marked along the base with distances in miles and kilometres. Sterling was amazed at its neatness.

A rap on the glass made him jump. The old lady outside was peering at him with raised eyebrows. 'You goin' to be there all day?' she mouthed.

Sterling closed the packet and shoved the map back into his coat, shooting her a hot murderous glance until she turned and walked away. He lifted the receiver, fed his penny into slot 'A' and dialled Hobart's number. As soon as the receiver was lifted at the other end, he pressed button 'B' and heard the coin drop.

It was Hobart himself who answered. 'George?' he said. 'Did you see him?'

Sterling closed his eyes momentarily. Hobart's confident no-nonsense voice, with centuries of his ancestors' reasonableness behind it, was the lifeline he needed.

'Corrigan's dead, Arnold,' Sterling said. 'Someone got there first and . . . garrotted him.'

'Good Lord!' he heard Hobart gasp. 'Now you have to go to the police, George. Ring them straight away.'

'I can't. They're after me.'

'What?'

'I don't know if they were watching Corrigan's place or if someone alerted them, but they arrived while I was in there with Corrigan's dead body, and I had blood on my hands. . . . I ran for it.'

'That was pretty silly, George.'

'I know, but it looked bad. Anyway, I found the map.'

There was silence again, and Sterling could hear his father-in-law taking a deep breath. 'All right, George,' he said at last. 'You'd better come round here. I expect we can sort it out.'

Suddenly, Sterling went rigid. From one side of the kiosk he had a view back down the street he'd just run up. Four men in dark coats were advancing up it now, two on each side of the road, spread out ten yards apart in military-style formation. They moved easily and purposefully, without attracting attention from the other passers-by. As they came nearer, Sterling recognized the pug-nosed gorilla and the blond-haired inspector among them.

'George?' Hobart's voice said, sounding distant now. 'George, are you there?'

Sterling replaced the receiver carefully, wondering what to do. His immediate impulse was to give himself up, but something still held him back – perhaps the memory of those bitter eighteen months in Wormwood Scrubs, perhaps Hobart's confidence that it could be sorted out, perhaps a lifetime of non-conformity. For a few seconds he stood there, drawing breath. The men were coming closer now, unmistakably menacing. Sterling glanced towards the street at right angles to the street along which the men were walking. He could see – as the advancing men could not – that a double-decker bus was heading in his direction. He checked the impulse to move. He measured the distance and speed of the bus against that of the approaching men. The bus was fifty yards away, then thirty. He could make out the face of the driver and the word 'Waterloo' on the signboard. The bus was twenty yards away; Sterling realized that the men were going to reach him first.

They were almost on him. Sterling could see the distorted features of the gorilla clearly now, within only a couple of feet of the box. He turned to face the man through the glass, and saw sudden recognition on his features. The gorilla's mouth formed fishlike into a call for help, but in that instant Sterling slammed the heavy door open, pressing all his weight against it. There was an audible crack as the steel door crashed against the gorilla's head, then Sterling was out and running. The bus was just passing the end of the street, going no more than twenty m.p.h., and Sterling ran for it, ignoring the shouts behind him. In five seconds he was racing alongside the bus's open rear entrance. He made a grab for the chrome bar and caught it, and at that moment a dark uniformed arm shot out from inside, caught hold of his belt and hauled him aboard. The bus accelerated. Sterling looked up to see a conductor in a tattered London Transport uniform, with a ticket-machine hung round his neck - a thickset man with a stubble of hair and an eye half closed by a purple bruise. 'You don't wanna try that too often, squire,' the conductor said. For a second Sterling wondered if the man had seen the plain-clothes policemen chasing him.

'Break your bloody neck,' the conductor said, and winked at Sterling with his good eye. 'Where to, squire?' he enquired.

This time, Hobart's door was locked, and when his father-in-law opened it, he gave Sterling a momentarily harassed look. A second later, though, the look was gone and replaced by one of concern. When Sterling was seated by the fire in the sitting room with a brandy in his shaky hand, Hobart sat down opposite. 'Are you sure they were policemen?' he asked.

Sterling wiped his brow with his fingers, feeling its stickiness. 'I'm not sure of anything,' he said. 'They looked like plainclothes cops – CID or whatever. But one of them had a gun – CID don't normally carry guns, do they?'

'Special Branch do,' Hobart said. 'On occasions.'

'I heard one of them call another "Inspector". He had a Cockney accent. But they never shouted "Police", or anything. Corrigan was tied to a chair with piano-wire, half naked, covered in blood, and had cigarette-burns on his arms. He had wire wrapped round his neck . . . Jesus Christ, what the hell is this about, Arnold?'

Hobart picked up his meerschaum pipe from the ashtray but didn't light it. 'I don't know,' he said gravely, 'but I still think you ought to turn yourself in. Nothing good can come of this.' He played with the pipe, and Sterling's gaze fell on the carved white face of the janissary. He felt very tired suddenly, and realized his mind was losing focus. He knew Hobart was right about turning himself in. 'What I want to know,' he said, 'is who did that to Corrigan. When I met him last night, he was scared stiff of something. He even mumbled about werewolves.'

'The chap was off his rocker.'

'Maybe, Arnold. But somebody had a bone to pick with him, that's for certain. It can only have been the map they were after.'

Hobart frowned, put the unlit pipe in his mouth and took it out again. 'Don't jump the gun,' he said. 'After you went last night, I made some phone-calls . . . no, don't worry, not to the police. Just to certain old colleagues from the "I" Corps boys. They were stationed in Morocco at the end of the war. Some discreet enquiries about Corrigan.'

'Discreet?' Sterling exploded. 'Christ, Arnold! You've bloody well compromised yourself. His death is going to be all over the papers tomorrow, and I don't care how discreet your old chums are, somebody will be wondering why you were checking up on him the night before!'

Hobart shrugged magnificently, and Sterling had to admire his ability to stay unruffled. 'How was I to know the chap was going to get bumped off?' he said calmly. 'Anyway, no good crying over spilt milk. The point is that I got a whisper from Frank Quayle, who was liaison to the French *Deuxième Bureau* that there *was* a Corrigan in Casablanca in 1946. The word is that he belonged to one of those mafia gangs that hung out there after the war – deserters, war criminals; all the scum of the earth. They were into everything shady – a bit of dope, a bit of white slavery, the odd smuggling deal. Frank wasn't sure, but he thinks he remembers seeing a French file about a Corrigan, a USAF deserter, who did the dirty on his gang. Stole fifty thousand dollars of their money and disappeared. These people have memories like elephants, George. If it's true, it could explain what happened to him.'

Sterling looked at him aghast. 'It fits,' he said slowly. 'But why would Craven fly with a fellow like that?'

Hobart shook the leonine head. 'I can't answer that,' he said. 'And anyway, it assumes Corrigan was telling the truth. Maybe he just heard what happened to *Rose of Cimarron* and decided to cash in on it once his funds ran out.'

'The map looks genuine enough to me.'

Hobart leaned forward with a new spark of interest in his eyes. 'Where is the map?' he asked gently. 'Can I see it?'

Sterling took out the oilskin packet, slipped the map out of it and handed it to Hobart. The old man took it and held it up to the light. Moments passed in silence as the fire crackled and the grandfather clock beat time. Hobart seemed totally absorbed in it. Finally, he said, 'It certainly looks genuine, but how can you be sure?'

Sterling took it back and replaced it in its packet. 'As I said, I'm not sure of anything. I've spent too much time pretending that there's such a thing as certainty, Arnold. I don't know why the hell I just accepted Billy's death as cut and dried. It's as if I've done a Rip Van Winkle act – been asleep for seven years, and now I've woken up. I'm going back there, and I'm going to face the uncertainty.'

Hobart took a deep breath. 'All right,' he said. 'What can I say? It was my fault Billy went off with Craven and, believe me, there hasn't been a day since that I didn't wish I'd said no. I'm responsible, and I'll support you, George, in any way I can, even if things get hot here.'

'I'm sorry—' Sterling began, but his father-in-law cut him short.

'I owe it to you,' he said. 'I owe it to Billy and to Margaret.' He put out his boxer's mitt and Sterling shook it. 'That's all I can do,' Hobart said. 'If I were a bit younger I'd come with you, but you know . . . and there's Molly.'

Sterling felt a lump in his throat. 'Thanks, Arnold,' he said.

Hobart looked at him through narrowed eyes, and it reminded Sterling of the day they'd first met, all those years ago when he'd been an aspiring chemistry undergrad at Cambridge and the world had seemed his oyster. Before the damn war came along and changed it all.

'You take care of yourself,' Hobart said.

* * *

Four days after leaving Hassi Messoud, the caravan reached 'Ushub al-Maraya. It was a region of succulent grasses and tamarisk, their last chance to graze the camels before the terrible plains of the Zrouft, which stretched endlessly beyond to the south. Groups of nomads were pasturing their animals here: for the first time in days, Sterling and Churchill saw faces other than those of their travelling companions. They realized that here they were in the presence of true desert people. These tribesmen dressed in blue robes and black head-cloths and spoke in a dialect less harsh and more melodious than that of Mafoudh's men. They looked askance at the sheikh and his outcasts, yet they were eminently hospitable – it was impossible to pass a camp without being called to drink camels' milk and eat dates. These tribesmen were as happy as they ever could be in their harsh lives, Sheikh Mafoudh pointed out – there was grazing here, their camels were fat and in milk, and they wanted for nothing.

Two days passed, and Mafoudh himself showed no sign of leaving. When Churchill pushed him over it, he protested that the camels were weak and needed feeding up. On the third day, though, Churchill and Sterling decided that enough was enough. That evening, after dinner, Churchill announced that they would be leaving in the morning. Mafoudh looked at him uneasily, then said, 'Captain, that is as far as we go.'

For a moment Sterling thought he hadn't heard right. 'What?' he said. 'But you agreed to take us into the Spanish Zone.'

The old sheikh wobbled his tooth. 'The camels are weak,' he said. 'And it is far. There is no water at all in the Zrouft. If we go on we will die.'

Churchill looked at him aghast. His features assumed their most Winstonian ferocity and he thumped the nearest saddle with his massive fist. 'We all die when it's time for us to die!' he thundered. 'What happened to all that bullshit, then? What happened to the honour of the tribe?'

The old man hung his head, and Sterling suddenly understood that he was desperately afraid. Churchill had said these people weren't true desert nomads; now he'd met the real thing here, he glimpsed what his friend had meant. Mafoudh looked old, washed out and defeated. He was far from his own country, and the Zrouft terrified him. Argue as they might, the old man would not change his mind. Sterling cast round at the starlit faces, seeing that most of them were set with the same determination that the old sheikh was showing. Only Hamdu, who had been unusually quiet since the storm, showed signs of unrest. 'What about you, Hamdu?' Sterling asked in Arabic.

The Negro raised his head and stared back at Sterling. 'You saved me,' he said, slowly. 'If you wish it, I will go with you.'

Faris, the other ex-slave, who was sitting next to Hamdu, chimed in. 'If Hamdu goes, then I too will go.'

'By God!' the ex-Znaga Jafar cut in, standing up and gripping the Martini-Henri rifle that was always by his side. 'Am I to be outdone by a couple of slaves? By the heavens, I will go, too!'

That evening Sterling paid Mafoudh and the others and they divided up the food and the water-skins. After it was done, Churchill and Sterling sat together on their saddles, sharing the last of the whisky. 'It's a shame about Mafoudh,' Churchill said, passing the open bottle to Sterling. 'He's let the fear get to him. I've seen it happen before.'

Sterling shivered involuntarily and took a gulp of whisky to cover it. 'You can't blame him,' he said. 'The Zrouft sounds like it's a little bit south of hell.'

'That doesn't seem to have put *you* off.'

'I have an incentive.'

Churchill smiled and took the bottle. 'I must admit,' he said, 'when you told me you were a Conchie in the war, I had you down as a sissy. But when you brought Hamdu back . . . well, I've never seen anything so brave. It paid off too. You were having me on about being a Conchie, weren't you? Come on, what did you *really* do in the war?'

Sterling felt the whisky loosening his tongue. It had been one of the harder, scarier periods of his life, and he needed relief. He took the bottle from Churchill again and treated himself to another long swig.

'All right,' he said. 'I'll tell you. I *was* a Conchie in the war. I refused to be called up. You can call it idealism, or just plain cowardice, but to me it was a kind of protest. My father was killed in the first hour on the Somme in nineteen sixteen, the most devastating hour in the history of war. Someone had to stand up against that, make sure it never happened again. Anyway, they put me inside – Wormwood Scrubs. When they let me out in 1942, I had a choice. I'd made my name as an experimental research chemist at Cambridge before the war, and I had a good knowledge of the new physics – relativity and quantum mechanics, that is. They wanted me to take part in the heavy-water project they were planning. Nothing was said about hydrogen bombs in those days, of course, but I knew enough to guess which way the wind was blowing, and I refused to be part of it.'

'And the other choice?' Churchill asked, taking the bottle back.

'Was to be an ambulance driver on *Overlord*,' Sterling said. 'Auxiliary Ambulance Corps. You didn't have to carry a gun, but they threw you right in at the deep end. Anyway, to cut a long story short, I settled for that.

Churchill grinned. 'So you were there on D-Day.'

66

'D-Day and every other damn day. Of course, I never fired a shot, never even held a weapon. But Eric, the carnage I saw, you wouldn't believe. Chaps with their eyes hanging out on strings, with both their legs blown off, still alive with half their heads missing. The horror of wounds like that is almost . . . mystical. Then, one day, near the end, we were in action with Seventh Armoured Brigade. There was some kind of obstruction on the road ahead, and a Daimler scout car was pinned down by anti-tank fire. There was a driver and an officer in the vehicle, both severely wounded. The car was blocking the road and halting the advance, and they sent an armoured bulldozer up to shift it out of the way. I don't know what happened – something just snapped inside at the sheer inhumanity of it. I got out of the ambulance, ran to the scout car and pulled the two men clear before the bulldozer got there. I didn't even notice that the Germans were shooting at me. Once I'd got them out, some other medics came up to help and we stretchered them to the ambulance. To me, it was just an act of humanity, but the CO of the brigade saw it happen, and made a big hoo-ha, so they gave me a George Medal for bravery. First time in the history of war that a coward gets a bravery award! But actually it was nothing – some of the acts of courage I saw among my "Conchie" comrades in the Ambulance Corps were unbelievable.'

Churchill handed him the bottle. 'Here,' he said, 'you deserve this. I don't know what to say.'

Sterling grinned at him. He swilled around the little whisky remaining in the bottle, holding it up in the moonlight. 'Since we're doing last confessions,' he said. 'Why don't you tell me about yourself? After all, there are no minor branches of the Churchill family, are there?'

The big man chuckled and looked at the stars. 'Hard keeping secrets in the desert,' he said. He took a deep breath. 'All right,

I suppose you've bared all, so let me follow suit. Churchill isn't my name – I'm not even British, actually.'

For a moment Sterling was taken by surprise, and his mouth fell open.

'I mean, I am legally a British citizen,' Churchill assured him, 'and the name Churchill is on my birth certificate, but my father's name was Joe Gusenkian. He was an Armenian who fled from the massacres in western Turkey in nineteen fifteen. My mother was French. I was born in London, but we spoke Armenian and French at home, and I grew up in a sort of extended family where a lot of languages were spoken – German, Italian, even Russian. I only really learned English at school – the little I got of it. My father hated the Turks, and he was a great admirer of Winston Churchill, who'd pushed the British into the Dardanelles Campaign. It didn't matter that they got their backsides kicked; anyone who bashed the Turks was a friend of dad's. That was why he decided to change his name by deed poll to Joe Churchill.'

'So you became more British than the British to fit in,' Sterling said.

Churchill shrugged. 'Refugee syndrome,' he said. 'Don't stand out. Blend in. But the odd thing is, I never really felt British, not even in the war. I already spoke five languages by the time I was twenty, and when the war came they tried to draft me into the Special Operations Executive. I was all for the Empire and everything, but SOE agents in France were going down like flies – there was only about an even chance of survival. That was no way to fight a war, so I refused. Instead, or maybe as a punishment I often thought, they put me in Field Security – the spy-catchers' department – where languages were also crucial, but you got to wear a uniform . . . sometimes, anyway. I started to pick up Arabic when I was with Defence Security in Egypt on the desert border.'

'What was that like?'

'Bloody dicey, I'll tell you. The day after I was posted there they sent me – in uniform – with an Arab, to meet a Libyan agent who was supposed to be supplying info on the Eyeties. When I saw the chap I smelt a rat, and he must have read my face, because he drew his Beretta and said, "Hands up!" Mustafa went for him like a terrier, and he fired. The shot went wide, and Mustafa got hold of his weapon. I tell you, he'd very nearly got the muzzle stuck in Mustafa's ribs when I ran up and gave him a round through the head. Point-blank. Mustafa was livid. He said we could have got a lot out of him if we'd just over-powered him. That was the first time I ever killed a man, and I lost my breakfast all over the shop. I've shot four people since then, but I still can't stomach the sight of blood. Anyway, there I was, spilling my guts, when Mustafa yelled that there was an Italian patrol advancing to contact. My nose'd been right. We only got out by the skin of our teeth.'

There was a moment's silence as both reflected.

'Sorry,' Churchill said suddenly. 'Maybe I shouldn't have told that story. You being a Conch . . . a pacifist and everything.'

'That's all right,' Sterling said. He paused again, then asked, 'So what did you do before the war?'

Churchill sighed. 'You won't believe me if I tell you.'

'Try me.'

'I tell you, you'll think I'm kidding.'

'No I won't. Go on.'

'All right. I was a circus performer.'

'What? You're kidding?'

'Indeed I am not, sir. My father ran "Gusenkian's Travelling Circus". We had ten Siberian tigers, six white Arab horses, two camels, a hippo, performing poodles, an ostrich, assorted giant snakes, and an Indian elephant called Rajah. My father did a bit

69

of everything – acrobatics, clowning, animal-taming. He even played the trumpet.'

'He didn't bring all that menagerie to London with him?'

'Good God, no! He had to ditch his old circus in Turkey, and he started it up in Britain around a cadre of acts he'd brought out with him. Did very well, actually. When I wasn't at school I was trained as an acrobat with my mother, brothers and cousins. My mother was small and slender – a beautiful mover. But at fifteen I was already six foot tall and fifteen stone. My father tried me out in animal-taming, but I just didn't have the nerve for it. I was petrified of those damn tigers. So he talked me into doing strong-man stunts, like lifting Rajah the elephant or being sat on by a hippo. For a while I was anchor for a human pyramid, but that fell through – literally. I dropped eight people, and the top man broke a collarbone. All I ever really wanted was to be accepted as a conventional Englishman, but with my background there was fat chance. Then the war came along and changed all that. I mean, they'd never have looked at me except that I spoke six languages, and suddenly there was a premium on that and I walked into a commission. The day I got that first pip was the best day of my life. I'd made it. I was in the officers' mess.'

'So what were you actually doing in Casablanca at the end of the war?'

Churchill flapped his large hand noncommittally. 'You ever see the film *Casablanca*?' he enquired, 'with Humphrey Bogart? You know – "Play it again, Sam?" Yes, well, Casa really was like that in the nineteen forties. Full of Nazis and mafia and criminals of every nationality. Part of my job was to investigate links between organized crime and the military. I never got very far.' He sighed. 'The Germans collapsed and Hitler topped himself, and my bubble burst. They didn't need me any more.

70

I'd have happily stayed on. The war raised my expectations, but I never really achieved my goal in the end . . .'

They looked up as old Mafoudh shuffled shamefacedly over and invited them to the fire to drink tea. Later, Hamdu cooked rice with dried meat pounded to a green powder with stones. To Sterling it had the flavour of old socks.

In the morning they parted formally. Sheikh Mafoudh avoided meeting Churchill's eye but, after they had shaken hands, he raised both his arms and pointed southwest. 'There is no water in the Zrouft,' he said in Arabic, 'but after seven days you will come to a wall of dunes. The dunes are not wide – they are not the Uruq ash-Shaytan, which is on the other side of the Ghayda, and there is a way through them. Set in the dunes is an over-hanging cliff, and at its base is a spring, Ain Effet, which can be reached by climbing down a crevasse between the cliff and the sand. If you wish to live, you must water there.'

Churchill bowed theatrically and declared, *'We shall not flag or fail. We shall go on to the end . . . whatever the cost may be. We shall fight on the beaches, we shall fight on the landing grounds, we shall fight in the fields and in the streets, we shall fight in the hills; we shall never surrender.'*

Then, leaving the bemused Sheikh behind them, the two Englishmen and their three companions took their head-ropes and led their caravan off into the Zrouft.

3

I T WAS THE SILENCE OF THE camels that woke him. There
were twenty of them hobbled around the remains of the camp
fire, mostly females and young, and all night their rhythmic
chewing had formed the backdrop of his sleep. Suddenly they
had stopped, and their silence felt as shrill as a scream. When
Taha opened his eyes and saw that they were craning their necks
and gawking fearfully towards the saltwort thickets fifty paces
behind him, he knew there had to be a big predator lurking there.

It was a sharp night and the full moon was out, bathing the
desert in velveteen blue. There was no wind. Taha pushed his
furled black head-cloth out of his eyes and adjusted his robes,
then grasped for the old rifle his father had given him. The octag-
onal barrel was cold to his touch.

He eased himself up silently, letting the weapon nuzzle loosely
against his shoulder, straining the cold air in through his nostrils
to try and scent the beast. He smelt only the musk of the camels,
the potash odours of the dead fire, the chalk scent of the desert.

He wondered what kind of animal it could be. Not a hyena: they hunted in pairs and would have given themselves away with their deep-throated hunting-call. A lion? It was unlikely. There were a few lions in Jebel Zemmour, but none had been seen this far up the Seguiet al-Hamra in years. Suddenly there was a dry cough from the saltwort thickets. Taha froze.

Only a leopard coughed like that, and a she-leopard had been harassing the flocks of the Ulad al-Mizna for the past year. His brother, Fahal, had once winged her in the back leg, but she had escaped and eluded even the tribe's best trackers. For some months the attacks had ceased, but then she had returned with a vengeance, more savage and cunning than ever. Those who had glimpsed her had noticed that her rear right leg had been slightly twisted by Fahal's shot. Ever since, they had called her the Twisted One.

Taha shivered. A leopard was the most fearsome of all beasts. Shy, retiring, she was a mistress of stealth and concealment, but once she had decided to attack she was as fleet as the wind, capable of outrunning even a gazelle. The hyena and the lion were lumbering and slow by comparison. Leopards were also incredibly strong. His father, Belhaan, had once tracked a missing camel-calf for three days and found its remains high in the branches of a tamarisk tree where a leopard had dragged it.

Taha took a step forward, bracing the old rifle hard against his body. It was a weapon made long ago by the *mu'allimin*, the travelling smiths who occasionally visited his tribe here in the remote desert. The rifle was already loaded with a blunt round he had moulded himself, no more than a flat-nosed slug of lead wedged into an old brass cartridge case. Taha knew that whatever happened he would get only one shot. Once fired, the cartridge-case had to be prised out with a knife and another inserted, and no leopard he had ever heard of was going to wait patiently while he did that.

He narrowed his eyes trying to observe movement in the thickets, which rose out of the desert like a white mist. He thought of calling out for his brother, Fahal, who was sleeping with his own camels down the wadi, but he hesitated. A shout might startle the leopard and goad her into attack, and in any case he judged that his brother was too far away to hear him. The idea was put out of his mind when the leopard suddenly emerged from cover.

She was big, bigger than Taha could ever have imagined, her head massive, her jaw hanging open so that her fangs gleamed dully. Her body was long and lean, the hide not speckled as Taha had expected, but a dull ochre colour in the moonlight. The creature paused, and Taha saw the flecks of vapour that rose from her nostrils, heard the snarl that seemed to come from deep in her belly. He saw clearly that her back right foot was slightly askew, and knew that this was indeed the terrible Twisted One that had been plaguing his family's flocks all winter.

He closed one eye and peered at the beast across the rifle's crude sights. For a moment the leopard's eyes were locked on his own, and then the beast sprang forward, her feet leaving puffs of dust as they pawed the earth. Taha felt the urge to scream out and run away in terror, but instead he held his ground and squeezed the trigger.

There was a fearsome recoil, a clap like thunder, and a tongue of flame and smoke that belched from the weapon's muzzle. The leopard kept on coming. Taha shut his eyes and dropped the rifle. He had half turned to run when the beast smashed into him, knocking him down. He felt the creature's weight on him, smelt her rank breath, felt the searing pain in his left hand as the leopard's claws mauled him. In that moment, though, he ceased to be afraid. It was almost as if he suddenly stood apart from himself, looking on with no more than curiosity to see what

74

transpired. He heard the camels mewling, and as he rolled he noticed the glorious brightness of the stars above him. Then the stars went out.

When he came to, his brother was bending over him, deep concern etched on his broad face. Taha's first thought was for the camels, and he sat up suddenly to check them; but where they had been there was now only a mush of churned-up ground and fresh droppings. 'Where are they?' he demanded, clutching Fahal's arm. 'Did the Twisted One get them?'

Fahal chuckled. 'I let them off the hobbles,' he said. 'The Twisted One is dead.'

'But I missed her.'

'No. The blessing of God was with you. Look.'

Taha looked to where his brother pointed and saw the cadaver of the leopard sprawled sideways in the sand. Her mouth was open slightly showing yellowed fangs, and blood trickled from one nostril. Somehow, she looked smaller and less fearsome than she had done just before she attacked.

Taha stood up to examine her more closely and felt a biting pain in his left hand. He looked down in surprise to see that the skin had been torn away where the Twisted One's claws had raked it. Fahal lifted his brother's hand to inspect it, and saw that the wound wasn't deep and that the bleeding had stopped. 'It is not so bad as it looks,' he said. 'Praise God it wasn't the right.'

Fahal took some strips of bark and a small leather flask out of the skin bag he wore slung across his blue *dara'a*. He tipped oil from the flask, smeared it on the strips and bound them around Taha's hand. For such a big, strong man, his touch was surprisingly gentle, Taha thought. He did not flinch as Fahal worked on him, but he wrinkled up his nose at the oil, which smelt of rotten fish.

75

When Fahal had finished dressing the wound, he knelt down next to the leopard, and slid out the curved knife he wore at his waist. It was razor-sharp from constant honing. Then, with a sawing movement, he sliced off the leopard's left front paw. 'This is your prize,' he said, handing it to Taha. 'When the clan know you have killed the Twisted One, there will be rejoicing indeed.'

It was a day's journey back to their camp under the cliffs of al-Lehauf. The brothers left at first light, saddling their riding camels and slinging the leopard's cadaver on the back of one of them. Taha knew they must skin it soon or the pelt would be spoiled.

For the first hours after sunrise the brothers walked, leading their mounts, driving the rest of the herd before them. Taha's hand did not trouble him – the fish-oil and bark poultice had dulled the pain to a throb. The desert stretched to every horizon, ochre-coloured dunes in fish-scale patterns, rocky outcrops, plains where cores of quartz sparkled from the wind-graded, gravel-covered desert, the serir.

Before noon they arrived at the lone black tent of a *mu'allim* – one of the gypsy metal-smiths who wandered from tribe to tribe – and they halted to get the news. They stopped the camels twenty-five paces from the tent, as politeness demanded, and waited until their host came to greet them. He was a sullen man named Khamis, powerful and dark-skinned, as many smiths were. His rough shirt was a ragged mess of dirt, grease and tatters. His eyes, narrow and suspicious, missed nothing, lingering on Taha's bound hand and the leopard slung across the saddle of his mount.

They greeted him in turn, shaking hands over and over. 'Come to my tent,' he growled.

The brothers accepted the offer mutely. Hospitality was the code of the desert, and anyone who refused it would be branded a miser for life. To be known as a miser was as bad as being known as a coward, for the nomads considered courage and generosity to be the same thing. Wealth and possessions mattered little to Taha's people. A man's status was not assessed by what he owned but by his reputation, and reputation could only be gained by the display of generosity, hospitality, courage, endurance and loyalty. These five qualities constituted what the nomads called *miruwa* or 'humanness'. To be known for one's humanness was the ambition of every man, and though the smiths were not considered tribesmen, even they were not immune from the code.

There were four almost-naked brown children in the tent, and a Negroid woman who greeted them but did not shake hands. Beside the tent there was an ill-made shack of wood and straw where the mud oven was housed; a few thin goats grazed in the thorn-brush round about. An elderly bull-camel with almost no hump was tethered to a peg a little distance away. It bore the curious diamond-shaped brand of the smiths on its neck, Taha saw.

Khamis wordlessly spread an esparto mat for them in a square of shade outside. His manner was surly, but Taha did not expect anything else from a smith. They were a people apart, a fraternity who married only within each other's families. They were not trusted by the tribesmen, who thought of them as sorcerers and feared their ability to work with fire, to change metal from one shape to another. Some said they were skin-changers themselves, able to turn into werewolves or were-hyenas at the time of the full moon. 'Better trust a slave than a smith,' the saying went. Yet the nomads could not survive without them, since no one else had the skill to work metal that the smiths had passed down from generation to generation.

77

After Khamis had brought them goats' milk in a grease-smeared esparto bowl, and they had drunk deeply, Taha showed the smith his old rifle. The cartridge case had jammed in the breech after his single shot at the leopard. 'Can you get it out?' he enquired.

Khamis sniffed and examined the weapon disdainfully. 'This is a poor firearm,' he commented finally. 'It was not made by me, nor my brothers nor my father. Not even by my grand-father.'

Taha did not register his irritation. 'Perhaps,' he said. 'But it killed the Twisted One.'

The smith's jaundiced eyes fell on the severed leopard paw that Taha had strung around his neck. It was caked with blood and already stank. 'The Twisted One?' he repeated, and there was new respect in his voice. 'You killed that beast?'

'Can you get the cartridge out?' Taha repeated.

Khamis shrugged noncommittally. 'Inshallah,' he said, 'but what will you pay me?' He nodded towards Taha's riding camel, now hobbled and grazing with the others some distance away. 'What about the leopard skin?'

Taha smiled. 'The leopard skin is not for barter,' he said. 'I offer you half a cone of sugar. For you, it's only a small job.'

The smith grinned for the first time, showing teeth like yellow fangs. 'All right,' he said.

A while later, after they had exchanged news about the pasture and the wells, Khamis brought his tea set and his tools. He wavered for a moment, wondering whom to give the tea set to, but in deference to Taha's injured hand he laid it before Fahal – a charcoal brazier, a tiny kettle, an ostrich-skin sleeve containing glasses, an iron box that held a plug of sugar and a hammer, a pouch of green tea and a saucer-sized brass tray. 'You make the tea,' he told Fahal, 'and I will fix the weapon.'

78

As Fahal kindled a fire, striking a flint against his blade, Taha watched the smith unwrap his miniature anvil from its skin cover. The anvil was no more than half a forearm's length. It stood on a long spike, which Khamis drove into the sand. Taha looked on with fascination as the dark man unrolled his toolkit. Everything else about Khamis was dirty and unkempt, but the tools were immaculately clean; Khamis handled them with loving care. The smith took out a pair of pincers, and broke open the rifle on its pin, gripping the barrel with the pincers. He slipped a slim, pointed file from the toolkit and began to work delicately on the rim of the cartridge case.

Suddenly he stopped and looked up from his work. His eyes fixed on Taha's, and the young man saw recognition in them. 'I know you,' he growled slowly. 'I know who you are. You were not born among the tribes. You are the *afrangi* that Belhaan bin Hamed took as a son. The one they call Taha Minan Nijum: Fell-From-The-Stars.'

The word *afrangi* – 'Frank' – evoked a flood of memories for Taha. It was what the Blue Men had called him when he had first been brought to the camp of his adoptive father, Belhaan. He had long since ceased thinking of himself as a 'Frank'. Indeed, he no longer thought – at least, not in waking moments – about anything that had happened to him before Belhaan had found him in the desert. That old life, when his name had been 'Billy', was a dream to him now. He was Taha, son of Belhaan, of the great nomad tribe of Reguibat, the Ulad al-Mizna, the People of the Clouds.

It was as if he had locked those earlier memories in a box somewhere and thrown away the key. They were of no use to him here in the desert. It was a harsh landscape where only the strong survived, and to be strong you had to keep your mind on those things that were of use – how to track and shoot and ride; how to find food, water and shelter; how to tend your camels; how to defend your wife and children. At first he had not believed that the landscape was inhabited by spirits, malevolent and benign, but now he accepted it fully. Once he had believed that the earth was round, but now, like his adopted people, he knew that it was flat.

At first he had been defensive and afraid, had fought Belhaan and the other men of the clan. Twice he had run away in the night, and twice Belhaan had tracked him down and brought him back. The third time he'd escaped, though, Belhaan had not come after him. Taha remembered that day – how he had lain cowering in the thorn scrub, seeing the trackless desert stretching to every horizon, knowing he could not survive alone.

His real father was a coward who had refused to fight, who had made him leave home and live among other boys he had hated, boys who'd made fun of him and called his dad a 'yellow-belly'. He had never forgotten the shame of that, even now. His mother was a useless woman who did everything on whims, and his grandfather had entrusted him to the safekeeping of a *bowqaa* – a traitor. None of them had come for him, but now he did not care. It was only in his dreams, at night, sometimes, that he had visions of happier times – playing football with his 'dad', going to the cinema, flying kites on the beach – and felt a stirring of something he could not or did not want to name. But these visions had no place in the waking world, and when he awoke he deliberately banished them.

The people he had found himself amongst – he called them the 'Blue Men' because, apart from their black head-cloths, blue was the only colour they wore – had been alien to him. They were primitive savages, he had thought, who never washed, who lived in flyblown squalor and abject poverty, who had disgusting habits like eating out of a common dish with their right hands, wiping the fat from their fingers on the tent flap, and using the other hand to clean themselves after going to the toilet. The food itself was equally disgusting: they ate lizards, rats, raw camel-liver and uncooked jelly from the camel's hump, with the juice of the animal's gall-bladder squirted over it.

Yet, though he didn't speak their language, he'd felt that they were also good-humoured, honest, generous and warm. Most of all, they knew how to survive here, and they did that by sticking together. Taha had been brought up to see himself as a free individual, but he was astute enough to realize that that brand of freedom meant nothing here. Here you could not live alone. Where was he going to across that great desert, anyway? The world he came from seemed as far away as the moon. Better to stay with these people, learn from them, and escape when the right moment came. When he had returned to the camp that night, parched and exhausted, the old man, Belhaan, had seemed delighted to see him. Taha had known that something important had changed between them that day.

And gradually, as he had learned to speak their tongue and picked up their customs and skills, the idea of escaping had simply melted away. Slowly, he had come to love the primitive harmony of life in the desert. Bit by bit, imperceptibly, he had unlearned his old life and become one of them, had begun to feel that here he had all that he could ever want: a family, a place, an identity, and a sense of belonging he had never known.

Taha ignored the smith and turned away, watching Fahal as he scooped glowing embers of wood into the tea-brazier with a stick, then set the small kettle on top. He and his stepbrother had become so close that he often forgot they were not real brothers. It must have been hard for Fahal, he thought, to find himself suddenly with a strange younger sibling just as he approached full manhood. It said much for Fahal's generosity of spirit that he had never shown any jealousy towards him. Instead he had protected him from the taunts of the others, made it clear that any slight against Taha was a slight against himself, repeating the famous nomad adage:

> Me and my brother against my cousin,
> Me and my cousin against a stranger.

That Fahal did not regard him as a stranger, or even a mere cousin, had always warmed Taha's heart. And since Fahal was the strongest and most enduring of all the clan's youths, his warnings had been heeded. It was not for nothing that his full name – Fahal Raakid – meant Bull-Camel-Running. He could still outwrestle, out-track and outride any of the clan, including Taha himself.

It had been Fahal who had warned him not to cry out during his circumcision ceremony. He still remembered the excruciating pain as the travelling circumciser had sliced off the end of his foreskin with a sharp stone, while he sat on a camel-saddle in full view of the clan. He remembered the blood; how the women had ululated and danced afterwards. Even his father, Belhaan, had praised his fortitude. The same evening Belhaan had shown him the engravings on the rock-shelters of Lehauf for the first time, explained how some of the ancestors of the Ulad al-Mizna had lived here since the Time Before Time, while others had come across the endless desert aeons ago, fleeing from the great tribe of Rumm who had driven them from their homeland, the legendary Garama. That night, his father had given him his first taste of afyun, a mixture of hashish and the dried leaves of the efelehleh plant, inhaled from a ceremonial pipe. The narcotic had bowled him over, sent him into a trance in which he had suddenly perceived that the world was not the random juxtaposition of qualities that he had always supposed it to be, but a matrix of living dreams.

In trance his astral spirit had roamed a broad, sunlit plain in disembodied form, seen a white antelope running across it – a magnificent, powerful animal that seemed to carry the sun on its head. In the trance he had seen himself tracking and shooting the antelope, taking from its stomach the small black bezoar stones that were to be found there, and which the Ulad al-Mizna considered sacred. He had come out of the trance knowing that an initiation task had been granted him.

When the circumcision wound had healed, he had set off alone into the desert to track down the white antelope, the most elusive of desert creatures. It had taken him twelve days, and in that time he had learned more about the desert and how to survive there than in the whole of the previous year. Finally he had identified the tracks of a white antelope bull of advanced age, a creature that had lived long and produced many offspring, and would soon fall to a leopard or a hyena pack. He had followed the antelope's spoor for two days without food and water, right to the foot of Jebel Sarhro, where he had trapped it in a gorge and killed it with a single shot. It was only after he had butchered it and retrieved the bezoar stones from its belly that he realized he was in Morocco, and could easily have found his way back to civilization. The chance he had been waiting for had presented itself at last, and there was no one and nothing to prevent him leaving. That he no longer wanted to return came as a revelation to him; so did the sudden insight that it was this, not the tracking of the white antelope, that had been the real test.

*   *   *

Taha felt the black stones now. They hung around his neck on a thong of gazelle sinew, next to the leopard paw, to remind him of that momentous insight, the realization that he himself had become one of the 'Blue Men'.

He was drawn out of his recollections by an imprecation to God from the smith, who was smiling through his yellow teeth and proudly holding up the empty brass cartridge casing in his pincers. Taha took the casing and examined it. 'God reward you for your skill,' he said.

The tea was ready, and Fahal offered them the first round in tiny glasses on the brass tray. Khamis took the glass and drank the strong tea in a single gulp. Taha sipped the liquid with polite slurping sounds of appreciation. Both returned the glasses to the tray, and Fahal refilled them. It was the custom among the nomads to drink three rounds of tea – no more and no less. Each successive glass was strikingly different from the one before. The first was bitter, the second slightly sweet, and the third cloyingly sweet. The server would not drink until the others had finished their three glasses; the tea ceremony could not be rushed.

The smith smacked his lips as he finished his third glass and returned it to the tray. As Fahal poured himself a glass, Khamis looked around him and scratched under his ragged head-cloth. 'Strange thing,' he said. 'A week back I came across a lot of camel-tracks heading north across the Seguiet al-Hamra. Fresh ones. I have smithied for most of the Reguibat clans at one time or another, and I know the tracks of their camels, but I didn't recognize any Reguibat camels amongst these. No, by God, it was a Delim raiding party, and a big one, too.'

Both Fahal and Taha were suddenly watching him with rapt attention. The smith grinned triumphantly, and Taha realized he'd been holding back this important morsel of news deliberately, for effect.

'No Delim raiders have come into this territory for years,'
Fahal said. 'Not since their *yama'a* agreed to the treaty.'

'Where were they going?' Taha asked.

Khamis gulped compulsively. 'That was the curious thing,'
he said. 'They went in the direction of the Ghaydat al-Jahoucha.'

Taha stared in surprise. 'The only ways in are through the
dunes of Uruq ash-Shaytan or the quicksand. I doubt if any of
the Delim know the path through the quicksand, and the dunes
are a hard slog for camels. Unless they were heading north
towards the Zrouft, there is no reason to go there.'

'God only is all-knowing,' Khamis said. 'The only thing of
interest there is the wrecked iron bird.'

He was watching Taha intensely now. 'They must have gone
no further than that,' he said, 'because this morning I found the
same tracks heading back south.'

Taha and Fahal exchanged glances. 'Why would they have
been looking at the wreck?' Taha enquired casually.

'God only knows,' the smith said, making a two-fingered sign
against the evil eye. 'But you mark my words – there's going
to be trouble before the season's out.'

They picked up the raiders' tracks within an hour of leaving the
smith's camp. Fahal slipped out of the saddle and examined them
carefully. 'It is as Khamis said,' he declared. 'Except I reckon
there are nineteen riders, not eighteen. The camels are tired –
they have been ridden hard.'

He picked up a piece of camel-turd, the size and colour of a
large olive, and broke it in his fingers, examining the content.
'The animals are being fed on grain,' he said, 'but they are thirsty.
They are carrying heavy loads, which means they have come a
long way. The raiders are certainly Delim, and they are heading
back into their own country.'

Taha couched his camel and crouched down by his brother, peering at the tracks.

'We should go after them,' he said.

'They passed by after sunrise this morning,' Fahal said. 'That means they have half a day's start. We won't catch them, not with the herd. What can we do against nineteen, anyway?'

'Nothing,' Taha said, 'but I want to know why they came here. Why did they break the treaty? Why were they looking at the iron bird?'

Suddenly the wound in his left hand pained him, and he squeezed it with his right. Fahal shrugged. 'God alone is all-knowing,' he said.

He took a long sniff of the air and suddenly stood upright.

'What is it?' Taha asked.

'Fire,' Fahal said. He shaded his eyes and began to scan the horizon methodically. 'There!' he gasped suddenly. 'South!'

Taha followed his gaze until, on the southern horizon, far across the ochre plain, he made out a pall of black smoke curling up into the cloudless screen of the sky.

'That's no cooking fire,' Fahal said. 'Come on, mount up.'

It took them many minutes to reach the source of the fire, but even from far off they could tell it was a camp that had gone up in flames. 'By God, this is Delim work!' Fahal declared.

Closer up, the devastation became only too clear. The camp had stood on a low, pebbly promontory over a dry stream bed, in a copse of thorn trees, but now there was nothing left of it but a smouldering ruin. Three black tents had been burned to cinders, and their contents – old saddles, saddlebags, sacks, milking-vessels, bowls, tin boxes and tea things had been smashed and scattered about over a large area. Taha counted five goats and three camels lying hacked and mutilated in pools of congealing blood. There was a smell of singed flesh on the air that made their stomachs turn, and suddenly their camels began to shy, backing away and quivering. The brothers leapt out of the saddle and hobbled them tightly, tying the riding animals to thorn bushes by their head-ropes.

Taha gagged, but forced himself to examine one of the dead camels. Its neck had been severed, its entrails almost ripped out. In the shade of a tree nearby stood a rack of water-skins, all of which had been punctured or slashed. The water still dripped out of them into the brown, wet sand beneath.

It was only when the brothers got nearer still that they saw the human victims. Two small children – a girl and a boy – lay by one of the smouldering tents like castaway dolls. Their throats had been slit. A naked woman was splayed out behind a thorn tree, wrists and ankles strapped to stakes driven in the ground. The woman had been shot in the head, but her breasts, arms and thighs had been viciously slashed with knives. One eye stared at them blindly through a mask of thick blood that obscured what was left of her disfigured face and hair. Steeling himself, Fahal knelt down and tried to clean the blood off the woman's face. 'By God!' he said, shocked. 'I know this woman. It is Sara mint Mashili. May they abide in the fires of hell for ever! This is a Znaga camp!'

Taha's mouth fell open, as he too recognized the woman. His senses baulked, his mind groping to grasp the enormity of the crime that had been committed here. Znaga were vassals of either warrior or marabout tribes, and were considered inviolable in raids. They were unarmed and unable to protect themselves, and were not expected to fight. The camels they herded did not even belong to them.

Taha glanced around him. Every desert law had been flouted here, he realized, every decency corrupted. Raids were carried out only for livestock; camps were never touched, let alone burned, children were not harmed, women were not violated, animals the raiders could not take were spared, and water-vessels were never interfered with. The men who had done this could not have been tribesmen, he thought.

'It can't have been the Delim,' he said. 'They wouldn't have done this.'

Fahal pointed out the camel-tracks that had churned up the surface around the camp. 'The same tracks we picked up back there,' he said. 'It's them all right.'

The moan came so unexpectedly that both the brothers were startled. They hunted about quickly, and Fahal found the man lying behind another bush, his hands tied behind his back. His feet and legs were black and blistered where they had been deliberately burned, and he had been stabbed repeatedly. Yet he was still alive. Leaning over him, Taha heard the ragged rattle of breath and saw a flicker of eyelids. 'It is Sara's husband,' he whispered. 'Latif ould Mahjub.'

'Father employs him to look after some of our camels,' Fahal said. 'God have mercy.'

Latif moaned again, and Fahal rushed to his camel and came back with a skin of water. He wetted the Znaga's lips and splashed a little on his face. The man's eyes flickered open momentarily. He stared at Taha, and a flash of recognition came into his eyes. A hand, wet with blood, gripped Taha's wrist. 'Delim raiders,' he gasped, choking. 'They took your father's camels.'

Taha smoothed the man's blood-caked hair. 'Don't try to talk, Latif,' he said. 'We will get you to my father. He will know what to do.'

'Nooo!' Latif cried. 'I don't want to live.'

'God is generous,' Taha said.

'They killed . . . my children. My wife . . . they violated her . . . I had to tell them . . . God help me . . . I had no choice.'

88

'What did you have to tell them?' Taha asked softly. 'What did they want to know?'

Latif clutched his left arm in a vice-like grip. His eyes opened wide as they focused on Taha's bandaged hand and sought out the missing joint of his little finger. 'They . . . wanted to know about . . . Fell-From-The-Stars,' he groaned. 'They . . . wanted . . . to . . . know . . . about . . . *you*.'

The camp of Taha's clan was pitched along the cliff of al-Lehauf. It was made up of nine large black tents and two smaller ones; here there were three dozen men, women and children, as well as camels, goats and sheep. They had camped here every *tifiski* for generations – for as long as time itself. Belhaan was chief of the clan, both counsellor and holy man. People respected him for his wisdom but feared him because he was one of the *inhaden yenun*, those who talked to the spirits.

The morning after his sons returned with the news of the Delim raid, Belhaan left the camp at dawn and walked quietly through the pools of shadow along the base of the cliff. There were rock overhangs here that the old man believed had been the home of the tribe's predecessors, the people they called the Bafour, long ago, when the desert had been greener than it was today. He believed this because the Bafour had left pictures on the rocks: strikingly fresh images of men hunting giraffes with what looked like loops of rope, or spearing elephants or hippopotami. There were words for such animals in Hassaniyya, the dialect of Arabic spoken by the Ulad al-Mizna, though Belhaan had never seen them himself. Every nomad boy had seen ostrich, antelope, gazelle, oryx and addax, jackal, honey-badger, hyena – even leopard and lion, but never the animals in the ancient pictures. Today they lived far to the south of Reguibat territory, in the land around Timbuctou.

89

And the skilful drawings of the Bafour were not the only things on the rocks. There were also writings in Tifinagh, the runic script of the tribe's other ancestors, the Hawwara, who had first brought camels here. The meaning of the old writing had been lost long ago, but an echo of it was still to be found in the camel-brands used by the People of the Clouds.

Belhaan drew comfort from the pictures and the runes because they portrayed the continuity of human life here in the desert. He needed such comfort today, because he was sorely troubled about the Delim incursion reported by Taha and Fahal, and the attack on the Znaga camp.

Until now, he thought, it had been a successful season. The pasture had been abundant and the camels had given plenty of milk. The goats had multiplied, and even one of the women was pregnant. He had guided the clan through the winter, healed the sick, protected the children with his charms and amulets, fought off the evil *yenun* with his potions, propitiated the good spirits of the trees and wells. His standing had risen even higher. True, the Twisted One had taken two of their camel-calves and half a dozen goats, but first his eldest son, Fahal, had wounded her, and then his adopted son, Taha, had finished her off. The Twisted One had already been expertly skinned by his two sons, and her valuable pelt, with the head still attached, now lay pegged out by Taha's tent to cure. It had been a good season until today, when the news of the Twisted One's death had been overshadowed by the Delim's heinous crime. Never had the old man heard of such iniquity.

For the Delim to enter Reguibat territory at all was a serious infringement of the agreement made by the tribal councils of both tribes back in the Year of the Treaty, five summers ago. And in all his years, Belhaan could not recall having heard of Znaga being violated in a raid before – he'd only once known a Delim to transgress the strict code. His own first-born son, Asil, had been a child when he'd been killed in a Delim raid. But that had been before the treaty, and the perpetrator, Agayl ould Selim, had been ostracized even by his own people.

There were many questions to be answered, the old man thought. Why had the Delim broken the treaty? Why had they visited the wrecked iron bird that had brought Taha to him? Why had they killed a family just to get information about his son? He thought he knew the answer, but he didn't yet want to admit it. He shook his head and frowned.

He halted at the edge of the cliff and turned to survey the camp, the tents erected in a perfect line open to the rising sun. The day was windless, and the smoke from early morning cooking fires rose in vertical dark lines from among the tents. Belhaan knew that the men of the clan must decide what was to be done, but before that he wanted to talk to Taha.

Taha had been woken up by his two small sons, Dhaalib and Nofal, who'd thrown themselves on his bed of palm-stalks shrieking and snarling, pretending to be the Twisted One. It was late – already after sunrise – and his wife Rauda was milking the goats behind the tent. Although Taha couldn't see her, he could hear the bleating of the animals and the click of the wooden goat-bells. Taha wrestled with the children until his injured hand stopped him, then took them to see the leopard skin pegged out nearby. It was drying well, he observed; the creature's mouth had set in a satisfyingly ferocious expression.

His twenty camels – sixteen she-camels and calves, and four trained house-camels – were still hobbled by the tent's side. Five of the she-camels were nursing small calves and could not be milked, but the udders of the remaining six were bulging. Taha sent Dhaalib to fetch the milking-bowl, the *aders*, while he and

91

Nofal, the younger of the two boys, let the house-camels off their hobbles and sent them out to graze on the sparse acacia bushes near the camp. When Dhaalib returned with the *aders*, Taha released the first female, encouraging her up with sucking sounds. He unfastened the covers on her udder, and, standing on one leg with the other balanced against his knee, he began to work at the teats, squirting the fresh milk into the bowl. As he worked, wincing occasionally when his hand pained him, he told the story of the Twisted One again for the benefit of the two boys, who listened with wide eyes.

This was the way it had always been, Taha reflected: the women milking the goats behind the tent, the men milking the camels by the side of the tent. It had been like this every day, morning and evening since the ancient Howwara had come across the distant horizons on their camels. It was a pattern prescribed and venerated by time. Nothing could be more satisfying than the simple rhythm of this life. Then a shadow fell across his face as he remembered the Znaga camp.

He had ridden in several raids and counter-raids during his time here, and had killed men in open battle, but he had only once known a tribesman to harm the hair of a child's head – when Belhaan's small son, Asil, had been killed by Agayl ould Selim. The story of Sheikh Sa'adan al-Mutlag, though, was the one most often told around the camp fires. One of the sheikh's warriors had got carried away during a victorious raid against the Tekna, and had tried to ravish a young girl. Sheikh Sa'adan had been so incensed by the dishonour to his name that he'd shot the warrior dead there and then – a member of his own family.

Taha worked on the camels methodically, tying up the udders and letting the boys shoo them out to the grazing after he was done. There was a lot of milk this morning. Every time the bowl was filled, Dhaalib would take it into the tent to top up the great earthenware milk-pot, the *tazua*, balancing the bowl with careful precision. It would have been bad luck to spill a drop.

As Taha drove the last camel off to graze, Rauda came around the tent, struggling with a full skin of goats' milk. Taha did not offer to carry it: to do so would have been an insult to a Reguibat woman, suggesting that she was weak. She was dressed in a blue *mehlafa*, the single-piece wrap-around garment the nomad women wore, with her long braided hair covered, and the customary blue tinge to her skin. As she hurried past their eyes met, locked intensely. There was a small, sensuous smile on her lips, and Taha knew she too was remembering the passionate lovemaking they had enjoyed the previous night, when the boys were asleep. Now, they did not kiss, embrace or even shake hands: physical contact between the sexes was confined to the privacy of the tent. But the eyes said it all. There was a power between them, irresistible and invisible – like magic, Taha thought.

'My uncle is coming,' Rauda said. 'I think he wants to talk to you.'

Rauda was Belhaan's niece and a famous beauty of the Reguibat. Taha could still hardly believe that she was his wife. Belhaan had chosen her for him soon after he'd returned from the north, having completed his successful quest for the bezoar stones. Rauda, whose name meant The-Pool-That-Gathers-After-The-Rain, had been agreeable – she had been intrigued by the fair-skinned boy who'd fallen from the stars. But as she travelled with her family as part of another clan, Taha had been obliged to 'abduct' her in nomad fashion, riding into her family's camp on his best camel, leaping out of the saddle, grabbing her and fighting off her brothers with his stick. They had given him some nasty bruises before he'd ridden off with Rauda bundled across the saddle.

The worst part of the marriage-ritual had been the consummation, when Taha had had to deflower his wife in a small tent of thin cotton specially erected for the purpose, while members of their respective families had stood about outside, making obscene cracks, beating on the tent with their camel-sticks and occasionally even peering inside. Nine months later, Rauda had produced Dhaalib, a miracle that had astonished Taha, and convinced him finally that the Ulad al-Mizna were right: there were powers at work in the universe that could not be comprehended by mortal man.

Taha told Rauda to light a fire for tea and turned to welcome Belhaan, a thin, hunched figure wearing a black cloak thrown over his blue *dara'a*. Taha still remembered vividly the day Belhaan had taken him from near the iron bird. At the time he'd thought the man had been out to kill him. He'd realized only later that Belhaan had been determined to save his life.

He ushered his wife's uncle to the fire in front of the tent, where they sat down together on an esparto mat. While Taha began the tea ceremony, Belhaan filled an ornate brass pipe, as straight and as long as his index finger, with powdery tobacco from an equally ornate pouch. He took a clean spill of wood from his bag and lit it from the fire; to have taken a brand already burning out of the flames would have been to invite the evil eye. He proceeded to light the pipe, taking quick, deep puffs. After five puffs the tobacco was finished and he put the pipe down, feeling a warm glow spreading through his body. They sat there in silence for a while. Taha poured tea into a glass, tasted it, and tipped the remainder back into the kettle. Both knew what the other was thinking, but were aware that such subjects must be approached tentatively.

'You still have it?' the old man asked. 'The *afrangi* paper? The one called *Son-nen* . . . ?'

94

'*Sonnenblume*,' Taha said.

He got up and entered his tent. He returned a minute later with an old tin box and sat down again. He unlocked the box with a key he wore round his neck next to the bezoar stones, and took out the map. It was the one he'd found so long ago near Craven's body – in a different world, a different life.

He handed it to Belhaan, but the old man didn't look at it. He had simply wanted to reassure himself that it was still there. Taha replaced it in the box and locked it. 'You think this is what the Delim came for, Father?' he asked.

Belhaan eyed him inscrutably. 'God is all-knowing,' he said. 'But I fear it. Since the day I found you I have feared that someone would come in search of you and this paper. But time passed and no one came, and I began to hope that you had been forgotten, and to sleep more soundly at night. God alone knows that danger always comes from the direction where it is least expected. The Delim have come into our territory after five years, and they visit the flying machine, they fall on defenceless Znaga, and they torture them to get information about you. This has never happened before, not in my memory, nor that of my father or grandfather, or any of the ancestors whose memories were passed down to me. My inner voice tells me the Delim have sold themselves to the Devil.'

Taha tasted the tea again, nodded to himself, then poured out the first glass for Belhaan. The old man sipped it, then finished it in two more mouthfuls. Taha poured a second glass, but Belhaan did not take it at once. His eyes were focused somewhere far off, and Taha guessed he was thinking of Asil, Fahal's younger brother. Taha had often thought that Belhaan had adopted him to fill the gap created by his son's death. Fahal and he had taken it on themselves to track down Asil's murderer, Agayl ould Selim, who had been driven out of his own tribe and

95

lived alone in the desert. Twice they had come close to catching him, but had learned that he had finally fled to the capital, Layoune, where he would be under the protection of the Spanish police.

Taha hoped only that he had lived up to the old man's expectations.

A moment later Belhaan took the glass, drank the tea noisily and replaced the glass on the tray. Taha handed him his third, sweet glass, and Belhaan drank it with relish. Then he put the glass back with gestures of refusal when Taha offered more. To drink more than three was unheard of, but it was equally impolite not to offer.

Belhaan gritted his teeth. 'Do not discuss the *afrangi* paper with anyone,' he said. 'Hide it. Bury the box in the sand under your tent. I am calling a *yama'a*.'

The council met at Belhaan's tent, all twelve men of the clan, young and old. Belhaan sat cross-legged before a wood fire at the door-gap, listening as Fahal and Taha related the story of the Znaga camp again. The men listened, open mouthed, to the tale. Taha finished by describing how Latif had died in his arms, and how they had buried him on the ridge next to his wife and children.

Then Belhaan spoke quietly, explaining clearly for those who did not know, or had forgotten, the tribal lore in respect of raids. 'No woman or child may be touched,' he said. 'A woman's own property is inviolable – her tent, her jewellery and her camel-saddle. Raiders may take carpets, a spare tent, coffee pots, kettles, and food if it is abundant, but they must leave enough for the family to live on, and at least one camel to fetch water. Water-skins may not be touched.'

He raised his slender hand to emphasize the next point. 'This tradition applies only to warrior-tribes,' he said. 'In the case of

Znaga, who are noncombatants, neither men, nor women, nor children may be harmed, nor any of their possessions taken. Since Latif and his family were under our protection, and they were herding our camels, this attack is a direct insult to us and our honour. We are bound to avenge this attack to restore our honour, and also to retrieve the stolen camels from the Delim. What have you to say?'

Minshaaf 'Al-Fajur, Seen-At-Sunrise, was the youngest adult of the clan. He jumped up and waved his camel-stick, fulminating against the raiders. He pointed out that they could not have got far, even if they were travelling fast, and suggested that the clan should set out on the best racing-camels, cut them off and take their camels back, killing at least one raider for each Znaga who had died.

Fahal agreed with the sentiments but not the plan. He did not mock Minshaaf's suggestion, but he reminded him that they were only a dozen. 'The Delim are nineteen,' he said. 'And besides, we cannot spare everyone. Most of us must stay to tend the herds. The women cannot do it alone.'

'That doesn't matter, by God!' Minshaaf yelled. 'We are Reguibat and each of us is worth two of them!'

'Four of them, by God!'

There were shouts of assent, and the meeting became a battle between those who thought the clan should send a pursuit party at once and those who disagreed.

Saqr Tayaar, Eagle Flying, held up his hand to speak. The voices subsided. He was an old man and known to be cautious, though he had been a renowned warrior in his younger days, and no one would have dared question his courage. 'There is one thing that no one has yet considered,' he said. 'Pursuing the Delim means going into their territory, something which is forbidden by the treaty—'

97

'But they have broken the treaty!' someone objected. 'So we can do the same . . .'

'Maybe,' Saqr said. 'But let us consider this carefully. Once we enter Delim territory, it means war. By tradition, a war between tribes must be declared, either by a letter written by the marabouts, or by a verbal message.'

'But they themselves have flouted that!'

'True, but lack of honour shown by the Ulad Delim does not itself exempt us from honour. If we behave like them, then we are ourselves dishonoured. No, we must follow tribal custom. Send a messenger to the marabouts, have them declare that the treaty has been broken. It is then the duty of the marabouts to call an assembly of the whole tribe before we declare war. Once we have done that, we will be ready to act.'

No one could deny that this suggestion was level headed, and there was general assent from the clan. Young Minshaaf agreed to take the message to the marabouts and to raise the clans. When everyone had nodded agreement and there were no more dissenting voices, old Belhaan called for more tea, and began to pass the tobacco around. 'It will take a long time to gather the clans and form a large enough raiding party to enter Delim territory,' he commented, blowing out smoke. 'God alone knows, but I have a feeling the raiders will be back before then.'

4

A WEEK LATER AND A HUNDRED miles away to the west, a man with a V-shaped scar on his cheek watched the Delim couch their camels in the crumbling courtyard of the Ribat.

Both men and camels were covered in dust and looked exhausted. Yet still they were a spectacular sight, he had to admit, in their uniform blue robes and black head-cloths, with their antique one-shot rifles slung across their backs. The Delim had been the ideal people for the job, he told himself. Having once been the masters of the desert here, they had lost their ascendancy to the more powerful Reguibat, and they resented it. Their resentment had made them bitter and vindictive, a savage and merciless fighting machine ready to kill almost anything that moved. These were qualities Von Neumann could use.

Von Neumann was standing at the door of the Ribat or Islamic Monastery, which lay on the banks of the Wadi Seluan at Smara in the Spanish Sahara. It had been built by a Muslim saint called Ma al-Ainin back in the 1890s, but had long been disused. Von

Neumann had chosen it as a base from which to launch his search for the boy. It was only a couple of days now since he had set up his wireless and antenna on the roof, and none too soon. Only this morning he had received a message from Steppenwolf that Sterling would very soon be on his way. Von Neumann's orders were clear. He must find the *Rose of Cimarron* and the boy if he were alive. If not, he must find out what happened to him and to Craven's map.

Sterling was only useful in that he might be able to identify the boy for them – after that he was expendable. 'Wolfgang' had been assigned to ensure that the Englishman didn't get lost or killed by bandits on the way. Von Neumann didn't know who Wolfgang was, but he didn't need to know. All that really mattered was *Sonnenblume*. Very soon, after eight years of waiting, *Sonnenblume* would be avenged.

Viktor Von Neumann accepted now that the dreams of a *reconquista* they had nurtured in 1945 were further from fruition than ever. *Sonnenblume* was the only ambition he still had.

The son of a salesman for Mercedes-Benz, he had not had a deprived childhood compared with many, though few in Germany had been well off in the 1930s. But his mother had been fickle and flirtatious, entertaining boyfriends when his father was away, which was frequently. His father had lived for the job – he'd been almost a stranger to young Viktor, who'd grown up without any true figure of authority in his life. Tall, blond and blue-eyed, he'd been the ideal 'Aryan' type, and when a friend already serving in the SS had suggested he should apply, he'd done so, swearing his oath of allegiance to the Führer. It had been the best move he'd ever made. In the SS he'd found the family he'd always craved, a cure for depression and alienation; something decent and solid in which he could finally believe. Despite Hitler's death, despite losing the war, he had never quite given that up.

The code of honour he'd learned in the SS, and the rigid hierarchy with its relationships, obligations and privileges, had suited him. In 1941 he had volunteered for the Fifth Airborne Division under General Student, and had taken part in the drop on Crete – the first major airborne operation ever mounted. He'd been proud to be part of history, but it had been a terrible fight, which the Germans had only won by the skin of their teeth.

Von Neumann's reputation for efficiency had got him noticed, and in 1943 Otto Skorzeny had recruited him as adjutant for his operation to snatch the Italian dictator, Benito Mussolini, from Gran Sasso in the Italian Alps. The operation had worked like a dream, and the only casualties had been sustained when one of the gliders carrying the assault party had crash-landed. Von Neumann had been on that glider and had narrowly escaped death; a piece of twisted fuselage had pierced his right cheek, leaving the distinctive V-shaped scar. Koerper, the sergeant whom Sterling had bashed with a phone-box door back in London, had saved his life by pulling him clear an instant before the glider had plummeted down the mountainside.

In '45, when they all knew it was going to pot, Skorzeny had asked Von Neumann to become quartermaster for 'Werewolf', a secret organization dedicated to reviving the Third Reich in exile. Von Neumann's courage had been more of the 'fight to the last ditch' kind, but ever since Gran Sasso he had idealized Skorzeny as a father figure, and could not refuse him. Under the leadership of Skorzeny and Gehlen – intelligence chief on the Eastern Front – Werewolf had made plans to smuggle thousands of key Nazi personnel and billions of Deutschmarks-worth of treasure and cash out of the country.

As 'Q', Von Neumann had been in charge of operations to move resources out of Germany. *Sonnenblume* had been one such operation. It had been under Von Neumann's personal leadership,

101

and he had been the sole survivor. When Skorzeny had picked him up afterwards, piloting the light plane, Von Neumann had felt so inadequate he'd actually wished he'd died with the rest. He'd vowed then, that Reich or no Reich, he'd one day set *Sonnenblume* right.

Von Neumann had never seen Skorzeny since that day. The commando chief had been arrested by the Americans in 1945, and put in a de-Nazification camp. Von Neumann had skipped to Brazil. When he'd heard that Otto had simply walked out two years later, though, he hadn't been surprised. Soon after, Von Neumann had received a telegram asking him to reopen investigations into *Sonnenblume*. The message had contained certain references to the Gran Sasso, and other operations known only to himself and Skorzeny, which had convinced him that his correspondent was none other than his old wartime chief. The telegram had been signed Steppenwolf, a code name that Skorzeny had used occasionally during the war.

Von Neumann had been thrilled to hear from his master, and had begun work at once, painstakingly collecting such personnel from the old Waffen SS and Brandenberg Divisions as he could. He had worked with the Brandenbergers in North Africa after Crete, and still had many contacts among them. They were particularly useful for civilian ops, because most were expatriate Germans who could pass as Americans, Australians, British or South Africans. The work had been slow and circumspect – always a jump ahead of the British MI5 and American OSS agents who'd been on their trails, but Steppenwolf had passed him messages by various agents, had left him phone numbers and drop locations. To Von Neumann's disappointment, though, they had never met.

It had been Steppenwolf's idea to pass themselves off as British plain-clothes policemen while in London, and it had appealed to Von Neumann and his men at first. It had been the perfect disguise, opening doors and silencing objections with an effectiveness that had astonished them. The British public seemed to have a faith and trust in their 'Bobbies' that Von Neumann thought naïve and ill founded. His men had all been Brandenbergers who spoke English more or less fluently. They had practised talking loudly in Cockney, calling each other by assumed ranks – 'inspector', 'sergeant' and 'constable' – and had had some laughs learning rhyming slang – *Mickey Mouse*, house; *whistle and flute*, suit; *apples and pears*, stairs. It had taken Munz and Koerper quite a while to understand that it was only the non-rhyming part of the phrase you actually used. Wohrmann, the signaller, who was mustard at codes and ciphers, had picked it up immediately, though. Steppenwolf had even supplied them with forged warrant-cards, which had proved extremely useful. But in the end it hadn't delivered. Someone had got to Corrigan before them, and Sterling had escaped with the map.

The same night, when his men were sound asleep in the hotel at King's Cross, Von Neumann had walked a couple of blocks until he found a telephone kiosk. He dialled Steppenwolf's emergency number with a black-gloved hand; almost at once, a woman's voice said, 'Yes?'

'This is Freidrich,' Von Neumann said. 'I have to report that the mission failed. Someone got to the American before us. We found the Englishman there, and I am certain he found the map. He got away. That is all.'

The voice on the other end was ice-cold and the accent so neutral that he couldn't tell if the woman was English or German.

'Steppenwolf is not pleased,' the woman had said. 'You should have contacted this number before, Freidrich. The situation has changed. Another cell took care of the American, and he talked.

103

He did not have all the information we wanted, but enough. The map is no longer a priority.'

'But how can Steppenwolf be sure?' Von Neumann cut in. 'The Englishman has—'

'The map is no longer a priority,' the woman repeated.

'And the Englishman?'

'Don't worry about him. Wolfgang has been assigned to him.'

'Then what are my orders?'

'Steppenwolf says you are to visit the drop tonight for redeployment instructions. You are going after the boy.'

It was while serving in North Africa that Von Neumann had learned Arabic – it had saved his life during the *Sonnenblume* fiasco. He had a certain disdainful admiration for the nomads, acknowledging that, despite their racial inferiority, they lived by a code of honour not dissimilar from that of the SS.

Now, Von Neumann watched the nomads' leader, Amir ould Hamel, as he walked towards him across the rubble-strewn court. The Arab's unhurried dignity betrayed nothing, and Von Neumann was suddenly filled with anticipation. He had supplied the Delim with all the details Steppenwolf had obtained from Corrigan. Had they found the *Rose of Cimarron*? Had they discovered any news of the boy?

Amir halted before Von Neumann, a small, tightly built man, as all the nomads were, with brooding eyes under saturnine eyebrows, a disdainful hook of a nose and slivers of moustache and beard. He looked as poised and graceful as a ballet-dancer, Von Neumann thought. They shook hands and exchanged the courteous desert greetings, then Von Neumann invited the chief inside the partly ruined hall, where he'd had a carpet and cushions laid out. He snapped his fingers for tea, which was quickly brought by his servant, a furtive Senegalese.

104

Von Neumann watched as Amir swallowed three glasses of tea, one after the other, and finally set the glass back on the brass tray. The chief waved the servant away imperiously, and leaned towards Von Neumann, ready to talk. 'We found it,' he said. 'The big bird – it was there, on the Ghaydat al-Jahoucha, just where you said it would be. But by God we were taking a risk venturing into Reguibat land.'

Von Neumann watched the nomad hungrily. 'Did you inspect the aircraft?' he demanded. 'Did you find anything?'

Amir surveyed Von Neumann haughtily, his satanic eyebrows creased with displeasure. 'No,' he said, 'we didn't stay long. That place is evil, it is peopled by jinn, and even the local clans don't go near it. Then, on the way back, fortune smiled on us. We found a Znaga camp, unprotected, and we demanded information. The serf was stubborn, so we did a job on his wife and children. In the end he squealed. He told us that there is such a boy as you mentioned, who came down in the iron bird on Ghaydat al-Jahoucha. The Znaga said he is alive and living with the Reguibat. He swore he didn't know which family or clan the boy lived among, but he knew his name – Taha Minan Nijum, Fell-From-The-Stars.'

Von Neumann could scarcely conceal his delight. The Delim had done better than he'd dreamed possible. If the boy was alive, he could be found. If he could be found then the answers that Von Neumann had sought for so long – the answers to the *Sonnenblume* riddle – could soon be within his grasp.

'That is what we discovered,' Amir was saying. 'And as we risked our lives for you, you will now keep your part of the bargain: five bales of blue cloth for every man and ten for myself.'

Von Neumann smiled. The blue cotton cloth, imported from France, had provided the key to buying the Delim's services. To the nomads it was a currency. They even liked the blue stain the dye left on their skin, which they said gave them extra protection against the sun. It was a small price to pay compared with the riches of *Sonnenblume*.

'You'll get your blue cloth,' he said. 'But you must go back.'

The sheikh looked at him sharply. 'You pay us now,' he said sourly. 'We did not agree to go back a second time. It was only because we were moving fast that we managed to return without a fight. After the war between the tribes the councils of the Delim and the Reguibat agreed that neither would enter the other's territory without permission. We have violated that agreement and that is an act of war. When the Reguibat gather they are many – as many as the crows in the sky. Our party cannot fight an entire tribe.'

The German's eyes were gleaming, and the sheikh did not miss it. 'You have a plan?' he asked.

'You could fight a whole tribe if you had modern rifles,' he said. 'You could fight almost anyone.'

For the first time, Amir dropped his languid pose. 'You mean Mother-Of-Ten-Shots rifles?' he asked. 'The ones that carry a store of bullets and you pull a handle back to fire one after the other?'

Von Neumann held up a hand. He rummaged under the cushions behind him for a moment, and brought out a long object wrapped in waxed paper. He unwrapped it carefully and removed a heavy wooden-stocked rifle, still covered in its factory grease. He held it up with both hands, then passed it to the sheikh.

'Look that this,' he smiled. 'It is a Mother-Of-Eight-Shots, an *Amerikani* rifle. The one they call Garand. This one will fire many bullets without even pulling a handle. It is the best rifle in the world.'

Amir was sitting up straight, cradling the weapon as if it was a baby, his eyes ablaze. Von Neumann saw that he was virtually drooling as he examined the weapon.

'By God,' Amir said. 'With such weapons as these we could defeat the entire Reguibat tribe. We could even regain our territory from them and drive them into exile. Better still, we could slaughter the men and take their women and children. A rightful revenge for the years of humiliation they have inflicted on us.' He glanced at Von Neumann avidly. 'How many of these do you have?' he demanded.

'Enough,' Von Neumann said. 'But don't get any ideas. They're safely stored and you don't get them unless you agree to the deal.'

'My word is my bond. What do you want us to do?'

'This time I want you to find that boy, Taha Minan Nijum. I don't care how you do it, but you must find him and bring him back to me – *alive*.'

'But the Reguibat . . .' Amir protested. 'We can't just ride up to them and say, "Where is Taha Minan Nijum and what clan does he belong to?"'

'Go back to the iron bird. Start from there. Send patrols out to all the nearest encampments. If anyone resists, kill them. Do what you did with the Znaga – take prisoners, force them to talk. You will soon find what you are looking for. I also want you to keep a look out to the northwest, on the plain you call the Zrouft. If you find any travellers coming from that direction, stop them. If you find any *afrang* among them, you must bring them here to me.'

A frown creased Amir's brow. 'It will be difficult to do all that quickly,' he said. 'The Ghayda is hard to get into from the south – on one side there is a quicksand and on the other high dunes. We have no one who knows the way through the quicksand, so we must go through the dunes, but it is dangerous. Last time we lost three camels. And what of the Reguibat? Once they hear we have re-entered their territory they will gather a pursuit party.'

'You won't have to worry about them,' Von Neumann said. 'First, because you will have the new rifles, and second, because I shall be organizing a small diversion in their rear. Simple military tactics. Believe me, they won't want to worry about one boy and a handful of nomads.'

'How many bullets do we get?' Amir demanded.

'Thirty-two each – four full magazines.'

'Thirty-two! But that is nothing!'

Von Neumann grinned. 'It's plenty,' he said. 'That way you won't go blasting off rounds for fun. Make every shot count. You do the job properly and you'll get more ammunition than you ever dreamed of, and many more rifles. Enough for the entire Delim. And you will be in charge of the ammunition, which will make you the most powerful man in the tribe. Once you have the guns you can do what you like. Wipe the Reguibat off the face of the earth for all I care.'

5

FOR SIX DAYS STERLING AND CHURCHILL had seen no one else but their companions, nothing but the terrible black plain of the Zrouft going on and on until its emptiness scoured their minds. At times Sterling felt they were no longer on the planet earth at all, but had passed through the eye of uncertainty into a parallel universe where they were the only moving things. Nothing else lived here. After the first day they had passed no tracks, no animal droppings, no sign of human life, and thereafter not a single tree nor blade of grass. There were no hares, no snakes, no desert rats, no lizards, no skinks, no scorpions – not even flies. It was a sterile universe, as strange and un-lived in as Mars. It was an effort to remember that beyond all this there were teeming cities: the world had been whittled down to their tiny group of survivors, and Sterling experienced weird paradoxes of scale. When he turned his gaze to the distant horizon, it seemed that their small caravan was as insignificant as an amoeba oozing across an ocean: when he turned inward to the group, though, every action and every word seemed of epic significance – as if you were close up to a giant cinema screen.

Every day was hell in its own way. Every day a furnace wind blew in their faces, beginning lightly as they set off after sunrise, and growing in strength towards noon. By mid-morning it was almost unbearable, and soon Sterling's lips were cracked and broken, his face reduced to a mass of itching sores – he began to wish fervently he had worn an Arab head-cloth to keep out the biting sand. By now they had to ration their water to a few cups a day each, and the hot wind began to leach their water-skins dry. They ate only in the evenings – Arab bread cooked in the sand under the embers of a fire, so dry that Sterling had to force it down.

Churchill never complained, but he became morose and short-tempered. Often he cursed his stupidity in taking on the assignment at all. During the long, painful, silent hours of the day, his mind would constantly replay the scene of his first meeting with Sterling.

When he'd walked into Sterling's spacious terraced house in Kew, he'd immediately classified him as a 'boffin type'. Sterling was slightly built, and had been sloppily dressed in an old pepper-and-salt jacket, khaki shirt and squinted tie. Churchill thought he was probably in his forties, with a foxy face, keen eyes and greying, curly, uncombed hair. 'George Bridger Sterling,' the boffin had said, extending his hand. 'Thank you for coming.'

Actually, Churchill had been surprised at Sterling's appearance. He had imagined a broad-beamed and ponderous burgher of the old school. By contrast, Sterling seemed positively eccentric, a man whose almost palpable energy – or perhaps it was inherent nervousness – kept his body ceaselessly on the boil. He had looked defensive. His clear blue eyes had appraised Churchill

110

carefully, then he'd gestured to a wooden upright chair by the fire. 'Chilly, isn't it?' he'd said, in the same slightly nasal voice Churchill had noticed on the phone. 'Whisky?'

'I could murder one,' Churchill nodded, and sat down, stiffly upright, in a wooden chair. Sterling returned from a side-cabinet with whisky in two tumblers and handed one to Churchill. 'Afraid it's neat,' he commented. 'I've run out of soda.'

'You can't get it for love nor money,' Churchill said, shaking his head wryly, taking the whisky. 'Heavens – these days! The things up with which we have to put!'

While he sampled the whisky, Sterling contemplated him uneasily. There was a matching straight-backed chair on the opposite side of the fireplace, but he didn't sit. He played with the whisky glass, his eyes flickering nervously, and Churchill realized that he was anything but at ease.

'So,' Churchill began. 'Tell me about your son.'

Sterling paused. 'Billy was fourteen,' he said. 'Still a child, really. I blame myself for letting him go off to Morocco at that age, but my wife, Margaret, was suffering from depression, and couldn't look after him. During termtime it was all right. Billy was away at boarding school. But it was the summer holidays and he had time on his hands. As for myself – well, it was just after the war, you know. I wasn't exactly in a fit state to entertain him, and of course I had the business. . .we were just setting it up then.'

'Dakin and Sterling's?'

'Yes. Vernon Dakin – the man who recommended you – was an officer in the Royal Tank Regiment during the war. Quite a broad thinker for an officer, if you know what I mean. With my record he could have been excused if he . . . Anyway, he's a good businessman. I'm a chemist, so we were complementary elements, you could say. I look after the technical side of the business and he does the management . . .'

111

'So how come you sent Billy off to Morocco?'

'His grandfather, Arnold Hobart, was out there at the time. He was some sort of attaché to the British Embassy. Since Margaret and I couldn't look after Billy, Margaret asked her father to have him for a few weeks, and he agreed. At the time it seemed the perfect solution. I took him out there on the new air-service to Casablanca from Paris. Billy loved aeroplanes. Did you ever come across Arnold Hobart when you were in Casablanca?'

Churchill reflected for a moment. 'Broad-chested fellow?' he said. 'Half-Colonel? Head like the Sphinx?'

'Sounds like him.'

'Remember him well. I was a military cop originally, but in forty-five Field Security was transferred to the Intelligence Corps, where it should have been from the beginning. Same job, different badge. Hobart was Intelligence Corps, so our paths crossed from time to time, that's all.'

'Anyway,' Sterling went on grimly, 'Arnold had a friend called Craven – Major Keith Craven, a former Long Range Desert Group pilot in the war. One of the few army men to win the DFC. Did you know him?'

'*Ravin'* Craven? Heard the name, certainly.'

'Arnold had been in the LRDG before the Int. and he and Craven had been pals. In nineteen forty-six, Craven had got his demob and was working as a pilot for Atlantic Air Transport, a civilian company in Casa. He was flying a Douglas Dakota, an ex-USAF kite called *Rose of Cimarron*. One day he offered to take Billy on a flight. Billy leapt at the idea, probably, and knowing Craven was a very sound man, Arnold agreed. It was only meant to be a quick there and back – Casablanca to the Foreign Legion post at Zagora– a round daytrip. Some brilliant views of the High Atlas. Only thing was, the *Rose of Cimarron*

112

never arrived. She went down in the mountains somewhere – at least that's what we thought – and no trace of her was ever found: no pilot, no crew, no Billy – nothing. Until now.'

For a moment Sterling's eyes moistened. Churchill polished off his whisky and, in the absence of a table, laid the glass on the floor.

'I presume a search and rescue mission went out?' he commented.

'Not just one. Several. Arnold and I did hardly anything else for almost a year but search for Billy. After Arnold moved back to Britain, I went out there on a regular basis every summer for five years. We scoured the route between Casablanca and Zagora with a fine-tooth comb. Nobody knew a thing.'

'What about the company? Weren't they interested in a lost aircraft – I mean, they're not cheap?'

'They just wrote it off for the insurance. They were so disorganized that they didn't even know who'd been on the aircraft with Craven. Their paperwork was an unbelievable mess and, of course, there was no radar or anything out there: it was like the Dark Ages as far as technology was concerned. In the end the French authorities concluded that Billy and Craven and the rest of the crew were missing presumed dead.'

'So what happened? You said "until now", and you mentioned new evidence on the phone.'

Sterling had paused. 'I'd better tell you the whole story,' he'd said.

He had related the details of his meeting with Corrigan, and how, only hours earlier, he had found the man's mutilated corpse in a garret in Rotherhithe. Churchill had listened with an attention that became increasingly rapt as Sterling described his escape from the police.

When he'd finished there was a pregnant silence. Sterling

113

stared at Churchill, who squirmed in his seat, and cleared his throat.

'Well, Mr Sterling,' he said finally. 'It's certainly a tale and a half. But to be honest I hadn't reckoned on this business of the police. I mean, I was a military cop myself, you know. I don't normally touch anything illegal. Wouldn't you be better just to hand the map over to them and come clean, as your father-in-law said?'

'After running from the scene of Corrigan's death and assaulting a police officer? I've got a record. They'd throw the book at me.'

Churchill considered it carefully. 'Maybe,' he said uneasily. 'But we're talking about some real nasty stuff. I mean, that wasn't an amateur job, not unless you imagined the piano-wire round the neck. You have to be trained to use that stuff – some commandos used it in the war. The Brandenbergers – Hitler's special service troops – used it, but the British did too. Maybe the mafia, like Arnold said, and you wouldn't want to get mixed up with that lot, believe me.'

'The question is, do you believe *me*?'

Churchill wriggled his big body awkwardly. 'As I say, I normally do aircrew,' he said. 'It's plain sailing. Most of the ops are on record. Even if we find *Rose of Cimarron*, so what? Your boy's not going to be there, is he?'

'Maybe not, but as Corrigan said, you have to have a fixed point to start with.'

'But I mean, sorry to say it, but even if Corrigan *was* telling the truth, it was a long time ago. Even if your boy wasn't killed by the Arabs – look, I have to speak frankly – he might have died of disease, or in an accident. There are no hospitals or doctors out there. You might not even be able to find his body – it could have been picked clean by vultures or hyenas by now.'

Sterling had regarded him with disappointment. 'Look,' he'd said, 'my business partner said you were a good man. If you don't want the job, say so now. I'm not poor, Mr Churchill. I'll pay you well – anything you want.'

'That's tempting,' Churchill had said, apparently wrestling with himself. 'Still, I . . .' He'd straightened his dicky-bow, thinking that he had done as much bargaining as he needed to. 'All right,' he'd said. 'To hell with the police. After all, assuming you've told me the truth, you've done nothing wrong really. You've got a deal, but we'd better get weaving right away before any unwelcome visitors start knocking at the door.'

As the days passed, the terrible aridity of the Zrouft began to take its toll. Gone were the cosy night-time conversations that had marked the first leg of the journey. Instead, while Sterling curled up in his sleeping bag as soon as they had eaten, Churchill would wander off into the darkness, carrying his kitbag, returning perhaps an hour later. Sterling noticed that the camel-men found his absences curious, even comical. They never went far from the camp to relieve themselves, and for privacy merely turned their backs to the group, covering themselves with their long shirts. Sterling wondered if Churchill was suffering from the Mahdi's Revenge, and was too proud to mention it.

They slept fitfully. Sterling was often woken from his first doze by Churchill's return, and then frequently by the big man's polyglot rambling in his sleep. It was mostly gobbledygook, but he once thought he'd caught the word Steppenwolf. He was intrigued. The only *Steppenwolf* he knew was the 1927 novel by Hermann Hesse, but, though Churchill spoke German, he didn't seem the type for such esoteric tastes. When he asked his companion about it in the morning, the big man croaked gruffly that he'd never even heard of Hermann Hesse, only Rudolf Hess. Sterling guessed he had misheard.

* * *

115

On the seventh day the water ran out. Sterling had been thirsty before, but never like this. This was pain – agony in the kidneys, constriction in the throat, tongue like sun-dried leather, the eyes burning, feeling as if they were sinking into the skull. Hamdu taught them to tie lengths of cloth tightly round their stomachs, which seemed to ease the pain for a while, but they were too weak to walk or talk, unable to do anything but lean groaning over their saddle-horns. Churchill's bulkiness worked against him here, and Sterling often shot him worried glances. At times he seemed almost catatonic – his lips crusted with white mucus, his face a mask of purple and grey. Frequently, Sterling felt himself succumbing to the seductive tranquillity that beckoned beyond his eyelids, but he dared not yield to it. There was no guide but himself and his compass. He had plotted the next well, Ain Effet, on his survey map, and without the compass they would never make it – just one moment's inattention, a fraction of a degree off, and they might all be dead. In the borderlands of dream and reality, it was Billy who kept him going. Billy was not dead. He existed in a state of uncertainty, neither dead nor alive.

Finally that afternoon, just as Sterling felt that his eyes were failing, he made out a wall of dunes on the skyline, ghostly and insubstantial as clouds at first, but as the sun dipped and the wind fell, he realized that they were really there. His heart leapt. The well of Ain Effet was at the base of those dunes. As they approached, Sterling realized how high the dunes were – perhaps 700 feet from the *sebkha* to the crests – and he wondered how they would get the camels over them. His thoughts were interrupted, though, by a cry from Hamdu, riding next to him. 'See!' he cried. 'Ain Effet! The well is over there!'

Sterling strained his already weary eyes, but could make out only an overhanging rock cliff poking out of the dunes, with a long skirt of sand beneath it. 'I don't see any well,' he said.

'It is under the overhanging rock,' Hamdu said. 'Sheikh Mafoudh described it. To get to the water you have to climb down between the rock and the sand.'

Within half an hour they were couching their animals by the overhang, where for the first time in a week they saw animal tracks and droppings, a sure sign that men had been here in the past. 'But long ago,' Jafar croaked. 'No one has been here this year.'

For a moment Churchill sank exhausted into the sand, drawing a white-crusted tongue over chapped lips. He fixed Sterling with eyes so clogged and irritated with dust that they were almost closed. 'We did it,' he said breathlessly, as if unable to credit it. 'But by heaven, I wouldn't want to do it again.'

Hamdu dismounted painfully and staggered over to the over-hang. He looked gaunt and haggard; the buoyant bulk and springy step that Sterling had first noticed about him had gone. His face was greyish now, the tribal tattoos standing out strangely, his eyes red-rimmed and sunken into the skull. 'Come, look!' he said groggily. 'It is as Mafoudh said.'

Sterling and Churchill raised themselves with the ponderousness of submerged divers. A drop of sweat ran down Sterling's face and he caught it greedily with his mucus-crusted tongue. Hamdu pointed out a narrow crevasse between the rock and the sand, falling almost sheer into darkness. 'It will not be easy,' he said. 'We will have to climb down there on ropes, fill our skins, and drag them up again.'

Churchill groaned. Jafar came to inspect the crevasse, slinging his precious Martini-Henri over his shoulder, brushing grit off his face with his head-cloth. His long hair was so full of dust that it no longer looked black, and the sand had crept into his eyebrows, nostrils and ears. He shook his head balefully at the depth of the crevasse, and tried to lick a bloated tongue. 'We have to go down on ropes,' he agreed. 'It's the only way.'

117

'But how?' Churchill said. 'That looks about thirty feet or more. We don't have a rope long enough.'

Jafar sniffed and blew dust from one nostril, covering the other with his thumb. 'If we take all the camels' head-ropes,' he said, 'and all the packing-ropes and harnesses, we may have enough.'

Hamdu and Faris nodded, and soon Sterling and Churchill were helping to hobble the exhausted camels, unthreading and un-knotting all the ropes, while Jafar joined them length-to-length, and Hamdu laid out the empty water-skins. It was painfully slow work; every movement seemed clumsy and uncoordinated. Often, Sterling sank down on his haunches and drifted off into a waking dream, only to be shaken awake roughly by Churchill. At last the rope was assembled. 'All right,' Churchill panted. 'Who's going down?'

The two ex-slaves were big-framed and heavy, which ruled them out. Churchill was even bigger. Sterling weighed himself up against Jafar and found the other was doing the same. 'It's me!' they both said together.

'No,' Sterling insisted. 'I am certainly the lightest.'

'No,' Jafar croaked, almost comically, through bloated white lips. 'It is I.'

Churchill knitted his heavy brows. 'God help us!' he grated. 'We're dying of thirst here. What the hell does it matter? Sterling is the lightest, Jafar. Let him go.'

The ex-herdsman stepped back reluctantly. 'If it is God's will,' he said.

Churchill cursed under his breath, and began tying the rope round Sterling. Hamdu handed him one of the water-skins, and Faris gave him a leather satchel containing a torch and a metal bowl. 'You might find the water covered in sand,' the black man said. 'You will have to dig it out with the bowl, then use it to fill the skin.'

Sterling nodded, and walked over to the cavity under the

overhang. The rock wall there had been carved with what looked like runic letters, and small matchstick figures of animals, including unmistakable giraffes and elephants. 'The nomads call it the work of the Bafours,' Jafar said. 'The Old People. Myself, I don't believe there were ever such animals here.'

'Let's get on with it,' Churchill snapped.

Sterling looked down into the dark shaft, while Churchill braced the rope around his own shoulder. 'I'm going to be anchor,' he croaked. 'At least I can manage that.'

'*Gusenkian Travelling Circus*,' Sterling grinned. 'Just like old times for you.'

Churchill grimaced. 'Tug once on the rope when you want to send the skin up,' he said.

Sterling began to slither down through the narrow chimney, which was only just wide enough to take a human being and a water vessel. After the first few yards it became dark, and Sterling felt like Alice falling into Wonderland. He scrabbled down through a series of sand-ledges, smelling the dampness. The proximity of water, far from easing the torture in his stomach, made it more acute.

At last he was crouching on a sandy floor. He took out the torch, switched it on and stuck it in the sandy wall. He was in a chamber only just wide enough to stretch out in. He crouched down and felt the sand – it was wonderfully damp to his touch, and he was almost tempted to take a mouthful and suck it.

Clumsily, he began to scrape away the sand, until he had a small hole in which clear water quickly gathered. He filled the bowl with water and brought it to his lips ready to swallow it, but something stopped him. It was nomad custom, he knew, never to take advantage of one's companions by drinking before they could. A silly rule, maybe, but he guessed the others would be offended. He steeled himself and poured the water into the

119

skin. The hole filled up quickly, and he repeated the action again and again, his head spinning dizzily. It seemed forever before the skin was full. He tied it securely, knotted the rope to the drawstring and tugged. The skin shifted, then began its slow ascent up through the chasm.

'Pull me up next!' Sterling shouted, his grating voice sounding like the rasp of metal on stone. Minutes later the rope descended. Sterling grabbed it, looped it round his waist and tugged. At last, he thought, he would be able to drink. There was a lurch as his body was dragged upwards, and he used his feeble limbs for extra purchase on the ledges. He had just reached the light end of the ravine, and could hear his companions' voices growling above him, when without warning the rope went limp. For a second Sterling scrabbled at the sandy ledges on both sides with his hands, but the loose sand gave. With a scream, he fell tumbling back down the shaft, bumping against the ledges, until his body hit the wet sand at the bottom with a resounding thump. A shower of sand fell after him.

For a moment or two he was dazed and scarcely conscious. Then it occurred to him that the whole shaft might cave in on top of him, and his heart began to beat a tattoo. 'Jesus Christ!' he bawled frantically. 'Pull me up! Pull me up!'

There was a sudden jerk on the rope, and Sterling felt his body being drawn up again. This time, he did not rely only on the rope, but made sure he had good purchase on the ledges as he rose. It was agonizingly difficult, and by the time he reached the top of the crevasse, his ears were buzzing and his vision swimming in and out of focus. He was only aware of arms dragging him and a bowl of water thrust to his lips. He gulped and drank greedily, letting the precious liquid splash down his jacket. He could feel the water moving through him, pulsing into his blood, giving him new life. When he was able to focus again, he saw Churchill sitting in a heap in the sand, and Hamdu standing over him. In the ex-slave's hand was Churchill's own pistol. 'What the hell is going on?' Sterling said.

'The captain tried to kill you,' Hamdu spat. 'He let go of the rope. Thank God you are still alive.'

Churchill knitted his brows and stared at Sterling appealingly. 'I fainted, George,' he said. 'It was too much strain. It was just like being at the bottom of that human pyramid back in the circus again. I actually thought I was there for a moment. I couldn't help it, I just blacked out.'

Sterling rose unsteadily. He realized no one else had yet drunk. 'Give him some water,' he said. 'Everybody, drink.'

Faris and Jafar began to argue about who should drink first, each insisting the other should take priority. Sterling lost his patience. 'What the hell does it matter?' he said. 'Drink both of you, for God's sake!'

Hamdu let Churchill drink, but he continued to point the pistol at him, even when he took the bowl himself. He swallowed the liquid quickly. 'Thanks be to God,' he said.

'Now,' Sterling said. 'What's this about the captain?'

'It's true,' Faris said. 'He let go of the rope on purpose. He wanted to kill you. He is no friend of yours.'

Churchill screwed up his face. 'George,' he said, his voice smoother now that he had drunk. 'I just had a blackout. Why on earth would I want to kill you? You employed me to come with you – if you don't make it I don't even get paid.'

'He just let go of the rope,' Hamdu insisted. 'I saw him.'

'That's impossible,' Sterling said. 'You were mistaken.'

'No,' Hamdu insisted. 'This man is no good, by God. Even Sheikh Mafoudh didn't trust him – that's why he turned back. And where does he go, walking off every night after eating, huh? He stays too long for just doing his business!'

Churchill groaned. 'This is paranoia induced by thirst and hunger and fatigue,' he said. 'I've seen it happen before. Mafoudh turned back because he was chicken-shit scared of the Zrouft, whatever he might have said to you, Hamdu. If he didn't trust me he could have turned the whole thing down at Tamerdanit, or even before. All right, so I like privacy when I answer the call of nature, and all right so I've been a bit queasy. So what? As for the well, I had a blackout, that's all. Now let's be sensible.'

He was right and Sterling knew it. 'I think it was just an accident,' he said. 'Give him back his pistol, Hamdu.'

The next morning, feeling stronger than they had done for a week, Churchill and Sterling climbed the dunes behind the well. It was hard work, traversing the slopes, using a camel-stick to probe for soft sand. At the crest they threw themselves down panting. For a moment, Sterling closed his eyes, then opened them suddenly. The dune slope fell away beneath them to reveal a vast open plain, but one very different in texture from the dreadful Zrouft. To the north, the dunes grew thicker and more impenetrable, and on two other sides the plain was hemmed in by sharp pinnacles and serried ridges the colour of glazed red earthenware. The valley itself was criss-crossed with patches of low crescent dunes and punctuated with dry washes and little copses of thorn and tamarisk trees. Almost in the centre of the plain, something glittered silver in the early sun. 'Hey!' Sterling said, prodding Churchill.

The big man looked up. He brought out a worn pair of army-issue binoculars and scanned the plain below. 'If that's not the *Rose of Cimarron*, I'm a Dutchman,' he growled. Sterling heaved up into a kneeling position beside Churchill, suddenly reluctant to take a look. It had been too long, he thought. Seven weary years since he'd last seen his son, and the last seven days had been the worst of all. Churchill thrust the binoculars into Sterling's hands. 'Look for yourself,' he said.

Sterling weighed the glasses, hesitating. He had come a long way for this, and now he was afraid of what he might find. He took a deep breath and peered through the lenses. The silver speck evolved into a length of polished fuselage and the unmistakable crosshatch of a tailplane. The rest of the aircraft was hidden under what appeared to be a mound of blown sand. He lingered on the sight for a moment, then handed the binoculars back to Churchill.

'Come on,' he said.

6

JUST AFTER SUNSET THE FOUR ULAD al-Mizna spotted
the flicker of a wood fire and at once halted. Taha, Fahal,
and the brothers Quddam and Auwra slipped from their mounts
silently and crouched in the darkness, knowing that they had
caught up with the enemy at last. It was now five days since the
two Znaga scouts had ridden into their camp on camels half dead
with fatigue, to announce that they had picked up fresh tracks
heading north towards the Ghaydat al-Jahoucha. The Znaga had
no doubt that they belonged to Delim raiders, and they were
many – even more than last time.

Belhaan had called an immediate meeting of the clan council
to consider the situation. Minshaaf had not yet returned from his
journey to consult the marabouts and raise the tribe, and already
the raiders were back, just as the old man had predicted. The
clan agreed that they could not sit by and do nothing – the Delim
had already done the unpardonable – yet they themselves were
only eleven men in all, and the scouts estimated the Delim party

to be at least twenty-five. After a long debate it had been agreed that Fahal would lead a tracking party, with Taha and the brothers Quddam al-Ghazal, *Outruns-a-Gazelle* and Auwra al-Kilaab, *Hunter-with-Dogs,* two of the best trackers and rifle-shots of the tribe. They would follow the Delim until a larger party arrived.

The night was dark, with a sliver of moon. From below, the Reguibat couched their camels carefully. They had chosen the clan's best raiding-animals: male geldings that could be relied upon not to make a noise – or almost relied upon. Camels were not entirely predictable. They were still essentially wild animals and could be trained only to a point. Some tribes tied their camels' mouths with cloth during raids, but this practice often caused more trouble than it was worth.

The four youths poised tensely in the darkness. Taha felt the sand under the soles of his bare feet, still warm from the day's sun. They were in an almost imperceptible depression where a little rain, perhaps two years back, had raised clumps of esparto grass, amid stunted saltbush and Sodom's apples. The poor vegetation gave them a little cover. Taha could smell the wood smoke now, just as he could smell the Delim camels. Turning his head and cocking his ear, he could even pick up the raiders' harsh voices on the night air. The enemy were not more than a rifle shot away, and, confident in their numbers, seemed to be taking few precautions.

Fahal gestured to the others. They formed a close group so that they could confer without their voices carrying. 'We could take those camels,' he said. 'All of them. We could creep up and take them before the enemy know what's happening and disappear into the night.'

Auwra, the youngest of the four, was a spindly youth with a long, narrow face so smooth and hairless that the others sometimes made fun of him over it. Despite his age he had already made a name for himself by training his dogs to run down hares – a feat almost unknown among the nomads, who generally left dog-lore to the hunter-gatherer Nemadi. Auwra made a giggling sound, which he stifled at once. 'They'd have a long walk back to Delim country,' he whispered.

Quddam, his elder brother, was similarly built but taller, with long, slim legs that made him the fastest runner in the clan, outclassing even Fahal in sheer speed, though not in staying power. He was more soberly inclined than Auwra. 'Belhaan did not tell us to steal camels,' he whispered. 'God knows, the Delim are twenty-five and we are four.'

'Yes,' Fahal hissed, 'but we are Ulad al-Mizna . . . and anyway, the night is on our side.'

Fahal looked instinctively at his brother. Taha considered it for a moment, then said, 'We should take only the camels that have wandered furthest from the camp. We will sneak up and un-hobble them, then drive them off silently. Let us leave the rest. Twenty-five camels are too many for us, anyway.'

'I should have liked to see them walk home!' Auwra chuckled.

'By God,' Quddam said. 'This is folly. They are too many.'

'Think of the songs the clan will make up about us if we succeed,' Fahal whispered. 'They will speak of us in hushed voices.'

'I'm thinking of Latif,' Taha said. 'Of his wife and children, and the camels these devils stole from the Znaga – *our* camels.'

'He's right,' Auwra told his brother. 'It is our duty to avenge Latif.'

Quddam shook his head, realizing he was outvoted and that he ran the risk of being called 'cautious'. 'All right then,' he said.

The Delim had made camp in a shallow dry wash the Arabs called an 'elbow', full of tamarisk and acacia, and the camels

126

had spread along it, browsing the shrubs. The four Reguibat crawled and monkey-ran silently, making cunning use of the shadows, until they were among the bushes on the western side. As they caught their breath among the trees, Fahal made a stabbing gesture with his finger. Not ten steps away, a large, fat-humped she-camel was feeding on a bush. Fahal pointed at himself, and began to crawl stealthily towards the she-camel. He reached her and crouched between her front legs, trying to undo the knot in her foreleg hobble. The others watched tensely, all attention on Fahal now. He pulled the hobble free, and at that moment the she-camel let out a deafening roar, hawing like a dissatisfied donkey. She skipped forward, kicking her back legs, knocking Fahal aside. He rolled in the dust, grabbed for his rifle and turned to run. Suddenly there were guttural shouts and shadows streaming through the dry wash. Shots rang out, a salvo of fire more intense than anything Taha had ever heard. Tree branches crashed and rattled, bullets whined off stones, Fahal grunted and fell. Footsteps padded in the sand, harsh voices approached.

Taha fixed his sights on one of the flickering shadows and fired. His old rifle kicked and slapped orange flame, and the shadow vanished. The others kept coming, but more cautiously now. Taha saw Quddam taking aim and shouted, 'Don't shoot. Save it!' He dashed forward, grabbed his brother, lifted him onto his shoulder by an arm and leg and ran. More crisp shots exploded behind them like rocks cracking in the heat, Taha couldn't tell how many. Rounds yawed and fizzed past him. He was vaguely aware of Quddam and Auwra running beside him, and the panting of his own breath as he struggled with Fahal's weight. In a moment they were back at their camels, and Taha tried to tie Fahal to one of them with rope. 'I'm all right!' Fahal gasped groggily. 'I can ride!'

His brother's face was ashen, Taha noticed, but he let him go, and kicked his camel till it rose. Then he un-hobbled the others while the two brothers stood guard. 'They're coming!' Auwra bawled. There was an almighty boom as he fired, a spear of orange and a scream from the other side. Taha glanced at the lean youth as he slipped the ramrod from under the muzzle of his weapon, stuck it down the barrel and started poking the shell-case out. Just then Quddam fired another ear-splitting shot. 'Got one, by God!' he yelled.

Fahal was in the saddle but sagging over the horn. Taha tied his head-rope to his own saddle, and leapt onto his animal's back. 'Come on!' he yelled.

The brothers jumped up and onto their camels in a few bounds. Taha was already racing away, with Fahal bouncing behind him. Flashes and the crack and thump of bullets pursued them into the darkness.

They did not stop until Fahal's screams were too much to bear and they were sure no raiders were pursuing them. They couched the camels in a copse of thorn trees, amid nests of giant boulders that would give them some protection if the enemy came, and Taha helped Fahal out of the saddle and laid him gently on a sheepskin.

He had been hit in the arm, and the bone was shattered. It wasn't a mortal wound, but he had lost a lot of blood – his *dara'a* was soaked in it. He apologized for screaming. At first, he said, he hadn't been able to feel it at all, but after a while the pain had set in, and the camel's jolting had caused the fractured bones to chafe, which had been agonizing. Unless the arm was set properly and treated soon, he might lose the use of it. 'And all for a stupid she-camel,' he choked. 'Never trust a female!'

In the wan moonlight, Taha examined the smashed arm as

well as he could, and saw that there were two wounds – an entry and an exit. 'May God protect us!' he exclaimed. 'The bullet passed right through.'

'They were using Mothers-of-Ten-Shots,' Quddam said.

'No,' Taha said, 'the fire was too rapid. I have never heard fire as fast as that.'

'We didn't stand a chance,' Auwra said. 'So much for "hushed voices". We'll never hear the end of it.'

'I hit one of them,' Quddam said eagerly.

'I think I did too,' said Auwra.

'You think they will come after us?' Taha asked.

'Not now, not till morning at least,' Fahal groaned. 'They're in hostile territory – and besides, they drove us off.'

Taha searched for his brother's pouch of evil-smelling ointment and began smearing it carefully on the crippled arm. Then he took out his knife and cut some lengths of green wood from a bush, stripping them of their bark-fibre, which he used to strap on the splint while his brother grunted and gritted his teeth.

'Where did you learn to do that?' Auwra asked.

'My father taught me,' Taha said. 'Belhaan.'

When the splint was fixed, the youths sat down and drank water from a skin – Fahal first. 'You have to take Fahal back to camp,' Taha told the brothers. 'He needs proper treatment from our father.'

'What about you?' Quddam demanded.

'I'm staying,' Taha said. 'Belhaan told us to stay with the enemy and one of us has to do it.'

'You must come back, Brother,' Fahal choked. 'Return with us. Father will be angry with you.'

Taha felt an unexpected strength flowing through him. He had been on his own in the desert many times. He had brought back the bezoar stones; he had killed the Twisted One: all his training in the desert had prepared him for this.

'It needs two to get you back to the camp,' he said. 'Father may be angry, but he will also understand that I am a man, and a man must follow his own path. Besides, I am not alone. God will be my companion.'

For five days Taha followed the trail, sleeping close by his camel at night, living on the water in his goatskin and on bread baked in the sand under the embers of the fire. Twice he tracked hares to their burrows and bopped them on the head with his club; once he dug a fennec out of its lair. He saw dorcas gazelle in the distance and even Hubara bustard, whose meat was tender and delicious; but he had only five rounds for his rifle and didn't want to waste any of them.

Being alone did not bother Taha. The long silences did not overwhelm him; indeed he relished the opportunity to become absorbed into the elemental tranquillity of the landscape. It was not empty – it resonated with the spirits of times past, the millions of souls who had crossed over it and through it from the dim reaches of the Time Before Time. Neither was it alien. The landscape had a familiar logic to it: regs – flat and stony desert plains – of wind-graded sediment with saltwort bush that not only provided fodder for goats and camels, but also stored dew in tiny reservoirs; pillow dunes or *sbar* with tamarisks in wind-scooped hollows, and white-spined acacias; grassy savannas that were home to the gazelle, the addax, the oryx and the wild boar. And almost every bit of it had been a camp, a hearth, a home at some time in the past – a place where ancestors had been born, lived rich lives, and died, their bodies giving substance to the land, giving way to new blooms. It did not matter to Taha that he was an adopted son of the land – he belonged to it, it was part of him. Life was like a wave, he thought, now ebbing back far into the distance, now flowing strong and powerful, but never fading out completely. Every day he came across sights that gave him a sense of connection with the eternal community of time: a primitive burial mound of a pattern unknown to the People of the Clouds, ancient runes on a rock, once a rare ibex scampering up a steep slope in the distance, and once a flight of cranes, so many that the sky was black with them, and the whole desert seemed filled with the swish of their wings.

On the morning of the fifth day, though, it was the circling of vultures in the near distance that drew his attention, and as he rode nearer he saw that they were of two kinds – the large black vulture and the smaller yellow-headed race, sweeping, dipping and banking in continuous play. As he topped a swell in the desert surface, an ugly sight met his eyes. There, in the dish-shaped depression beneath him, a family of six *lemha* had been butchered, their dark winter coats ripped and slashed by the carrion eaters to expose the ruby-coloured flesh beneath. He slipped from his camel to get a closer look, and a squad of vultures flapped away, gobbling and cackling in protest. The antelopes were lying in pools of blood and guts – a large bull, three cows and a couple of calves, all with spiral horns, white faces and tufts of dark hair on the forehead.

The carcasses had not been carved up for meat, merely left to rot, but each had been peppered with bullets – in the neck, head, and even the rump, as if they had been used for target practice. The sight sickened Taha. The nomads shot the *lemha,* or addax, occasionally for meat, or in dire need to drink the water from its stomach. But since nomad weapons had only one shot, the antelope had a more-than-even chance of escape and the hunter needed great skill. This purposeless killing was a crime akin to murder.

As he turned away from the sight in disgust, he noticed that the tracks of the Delim intruders had paused here. Men had

131

couched their camels and dismounted to inspect the carcasses. There could be little doubt that this was the work of the Delim and their powerful new rifles. Taha groped for some explanation as to why a desert people should have desecrated these animals, but could not explain it.

He led his nervous camel away, clearing the lip of the depression, and couched it to remount. He had slung his rifle from the saddle and was about to cock his leg over when the animal snorted and jerked up prematurely: Taha had to skip backwards to avoid being sent sprawling. Just then there was the crack of a rifle shot, and Taha felt the shockwave of a bullet as it zapped past him, burning air. He let go of the camel's head-rope and fell flat. The animal raced off, carrying his rifle with it. Taha crawled up behind some sedge and drew his dagger. Below him half a dozen men had sprung out of the earth itself – dwarf-like men in shapeless, dust-coloured cloths, with rags of the same shade over their heads, like hoods. Taha realized the men had been there all the time, lying flat with their coverings over them, blending in perfectly with the sage bushes and stones. His eyes, keen as they were, had not picked them out. They were not Delim. The men were fair-skinned but quite distinct in appearance from the nomads, with hairy hands, thick-bearded faces and large, splayed feet. They were pointing well-oiled rifles his way, and they looked angry.

Taha knew they were Nemadi, the almost-legendary hunting people who ranged immense distances on foot across the desert, with their dogs and donkeys. They were the best shots and trackers in the Sahara, capable of following spoor for days without food or water. They had no camels and did not live in tents as the nomads did, neither did they keep goats or sheep. They were said to be a very ancient folk, the direct descendants of the Bafour. It was said that the Nemadi were skilled herbalists and medicine men, whose knowledge of the properties of desert plants and animals was unequalled even by the marabouts. Taha had once heard a story of how a Nemadi hunter had sucked the venom from the foot of an Arab woman who had been bitten by a puff adder, a treatment unknown to the nomads. The woman had survived.

Taha also knew the little men had been trying to kill him and that he'd been saved only by the nervousness of his camel, and the protection of the spirits. He did not know why the hunters wanted him dead, but, small as they were, he knew he wasn't capable of killing all six with his dagger.

He slipped it back into its sheath. When the Nemadi were within fifty paces of him, he stood up suddenly holding his hands high. 'I am Taha ould Belhaan of the Ulad al-Mizna,' he cried.

The little men halted, but did not fire. One of them stepped forward, a squat but immensely powerful-looking man, who moved with dignity and grace despite his dwarfish appearance. 'I am Bes,' he said in a high-pitched voice. 'And my name means no more to you than yours to me. I see only one of the camel-folk, the "hook-noses"; the same folk who slaughtered the *lemha* for cruelty alone. You deserve to die for what your people have done here.'

He spoke Hassaniyya with an odd inflection, using archaic words and expressions, and with a curiously grave tone that Taha found slightly comical. But there was nothing comical about the six rifle-muzzles pointing at him, and from what he'd heard of the Nemadi they weren't likely to miss. It was said a Nemadi hunter could hit a running gazelle at three hundred paces. Taha knew he was trapped. His missing finger-joint began to throb suddenly.

'I had nothing to do with this carnage,' he said. 'It was done by my enemies the Ulad Delim. I have been tracking them for ten days, almost since they entered our territory. Five days ago

133

they shot and wounded my brother – I continued after them alone.'

Another man, leaner and younger-looking than Bes, stepped forward, whipping off his hood to reveal a broad, pug nose that looked as if it had been squashed, and a bald pate. 'Ulad this, Ulad that,' he said. 'You are all of one folk – hook-noses, with your big camels and your goats that go gobbling up the ranges. What squabbles you are having between you are no concern of ours. Hook-noses are hook-noses, sir. As for the land being your land, the hunting-folk were living here long, long before your hook-nose grandfathers came. Before there *were* camels here. When the land was still green and rivers running. This is not your land, sir, it is the land of the Great God.'

Taha nodded, realizing that he would have to choose his words carefully. His fate hung in the balance.

'God knows, you are right,' he said. 'Only these men have killed more than the *lemha*. They have killed defenceless people under our protection – women and children, too. They have powerful weapons – look at the damage they have done to the *lemha*. Could I have wreaked such havoc with my poor old one-shot gun? They have guns that fire many bullets without needing to be reloaded, guns made by the Christians. If they are allowed to escape, they may wipe out all the *lemha* in the desert, and God knows they are already few.'

Taha stopped for breath. Bes halted one pace in front of him, and Taha saw that his eyes were green, not blue-grey or brown like those of the nomads. The little hunter peered into Taha's face. 'Words,' he said. 'You camel-folk are skilled at weaving them, but we hunting-folk see the deeper language, the language of the earth.'

Taha did not flinch, knowing that death faced him now. 'I speak truth,' he said simply.

Bes hesitated. 'It is true,' he said, 'that the *lemha* were killed

134

with weapons we have never seen before. We have heard of Christian weapons, and of the Christians – the people of the iron chariots. They have no respect for the animals. Only two summers back some Christians in iron chariots shot eighty *lemha* in one hunt and took only their horns! Eighty! Enough to feed every man here and his family for a year. By the Great God, such obscenity cannot go unpunished.'

'Kill him and be done talking,' the bald man said. 'He seeks to trap you with words. He is a hook-nose. He is one of them.'

Bes looked at him, then at Taha, examining his face curiously. 'No, Hawwash,' he said. 'This one is strange. He is a hook-nose. He speaks their language, but there is something . . . aah!'

Bes's eye had fallen on the severed leopard's paw that hung around Taha's neck – the paw of the Twisted One, mummified and withered now, and so light that Taha scarcely noticed it. The small man's eyes suddenly opened wide as if he had had a sudden epiphany.

'*Qalb al-Kuhl*,' he gasped. 'The Black-Hearted One. By the Great God!' His eyes fell on Taha's left hand and the missing finger-joint. 'You are he!' he said with awe in his voice. 'He who killed the demon leopard. They said his name was Fell-From-The-Stars and that part of his small finger on the left hand was missing. You are surely he!'

Taha nodded. 'Thank God, who guided my hand.'

Bes lowered his rifle and smiled, showing perfect white teeth. 'My cousin was killed by that beast,' he said. 'You have avenged his death. I am now in your debt, sir.'

'God was with me,' Taha said again, scanning the other faces, seeing hesitation. Bes was evidently their leader. Only the bald Hawwash seemed unconvinced.

'He is a hook-nose,' he piped again. 'I say we should kill him anyway.'

Bes glanced at him. 'He avenged Rass,' he said. 'It would be a disgrace. The blessing of the Great God is upon him.'

He let his weapon drop and offered Taha a hand like a huge knot of old rope. Taha shook. 'Come, get your animal back,' Bes said, pointing to where Taha's camel stood browsing in salt-wort, a hundred paces away. 'Let us leave this place of ill omen. You shall eat our poor fare with us, sir, and afterwards you shall tell us of the Black-Hearted One and how you killed her.'

The Nemadi had made camp in some saltwort north of the depression where the addax had been slaughtered. To Taha's eyes it was a poor place, where a trio of bony donkeys were hobbled and animal skins had been thrown over the bushes to make low shelters, invisible until you were on them. A pack of wild-looking hunting dogs pelted towards them as they arrived, yapping and barking, only to be driven off by some fierce curses from Bes. The Nemadi had left two children to look after the animals, boys not much older than Taha's own sons, who stared at him with wide eyes as he couched his camel. As soon as they had arrived they began to prepare the meat of a gazelle they had shot the previous day, cooking it on a pile of red-hot stones.

As the meat was roasting, Bes pressed Taha to describe how he had killed the Twisted One, and the hunters murmured with understanding and admiration, plying him with questions and making him tell the tale over and over again.

'Truly,' Bes commented, 'there is no more fearsome animal than the leopard. The lion is stronger but neither so fast nor so brave.'

When the meat was done, Bes divided it carefully into nine equal portions with a razor-sharp knife. He presented the first portion to Taha, then, as he called out the names of each of his men in turn, they came forward to take their share. They ate silently, using their knives and stones as plates. Taha found it succulent and delicious after the fennec-meat the previous night. When all was eaten and the bones and scraps thrown to the dogs, Taha offered to make tea for the company, which was politely refused. 'We drink neither tea nor milk, sir,' said Hawwash smugly. 'On the hunt we drink water but once, before sunrise, and then not again till sunset.'

'But how do you get your water?' Taha asked. 'Many of the wells are too deep to draw water without camels.'

Hawwash gave a superior smile. 'We rarely use the nomads' wells,' he said. 'We know many small watering places that the hook-noses do not know, sir. We know the hidden paths and secret places both in the south and the north. Their secrets have been passed down from father to son, sir, across the ages of time.'

Bes noticed the bezoar stones around Taha's neck, and asked him about them. Taha recounted how he had tracked and killed a white antelope up by the Jebel Sarhro as an initiation test. In turn, he asked about the Nemadi's wanderings in the desert, and the animals they hunted.

Bes explained that they had left their womenfolk and other kinsmen in the Tekna, far to the south, to look for *lemha*, which had almost disappeared there. Once upon a time ostrich had been their preferred quarry – ostrich meat was rich and full of grease that could be stored in skins, and they could trade the ostrich feathers for guns and cartridges. 'But the ostrich is hard to kill,' Bes explained. 'She will take a bullet at fifty paces and not even falter in her step, unless you hit her vitals – and she can outrun a galloping horse.' He shook his head sadly. 'But the ostrich is almost hunted out,' he added. 'First by the hook-no— I mean the camel-folk, and then by the Christians in their iron chariots. We made a pact with the Ostrich Spirit that we would hunt them no more, but go after the *lemha* instead.'

Bes described how they had tracked the family of addax for six days with their dogs, intending to kill only the bull. The hunters never killed female animals or young if they could help it, he said. The trail had led them directly to the carnage Taha had seen, and they had decided to lay in wait there for two days to see if the killers would come back.

'What would you have done if they had returned?' Taha enquired.

'Why, we should have slaughtered one of them for every animal they slaughtered,' Bes said.

'And yet you kill the *lemha*,' Taha observed. 'We too.'

Bes smiled but his eyes were grave. 'There is a connection between the Great God, the hunter and the prey,' he said. 'When we merge in half-death trance, the Great God gives us the prey – the addax, the oryx, the antelope, the ibex, the ostrich – but the animal itself is willing. For while we eat its flesh, the essence of the animal lives on eternally, forever renewing itself, just as the stars appear each night though they vanish during the day. The ones who slaughtered those animals did not eat their flesh – they killed them without purpose, interrupting the flow of spirit.'

Taha scratched his head, not fully understanding, but Bes seemed reluctant to go on. There was a pregnant silence until finally a hunter named Pyet, who was almost as broad as he was high, spoke up. 'Bes is *inhaden yenun*,' he said. 'One who talks with the spirits. It is difficult for him to explain such things in the language of words. That is what he meant when he talked about "earth language". Some things cannot be perfectly explained.'

Taha nodded, remembering his own initiation vision, induced by *afyun*, in which he had felt himself unite with the soul of the white antelope. 'I understand,' he said. 'My father, Belhaan, is also *inhaden yenun*.'

138

Bes croaked as if clearing his throat. 'The world is One,' he said. 'Have you not observed it yourself? It exists in perfect harmony. No part of it can be taken away without another part being affected. Before the hunt, we become one with our prey. The spirit flows like a river between the hunter and the hunted: they fit together like lovers. Our prey is sacred. To kill it in the manner of the Delim is an insult to the Great God. An abomination.'

'Bes,' Taha said. 'Will you come with me and punish the desecrators of the *lemha*. Like this, you will propitiate the Great God.'

Bes considered it for a moment. 'Take not the name of the Great God in vain,' he said coldly. 'We have no wish to become embroiled in the feuds of the camel-people. What goes on betwixt you is not our concern.'

'But what of these new guns?' Taha asked. 'They are surely a threat to the flow of spirit?'

Bes was cutting a toothpick from a branch of white-spined acacia. His eyes, lapped in folds of wrinkles pickled by the sun, were distant. He sighed. 'The time of the hunters has almost passed,' he said. 'It is as the Great God wills. Whether we avenge the spirit of the addax or not, these weapons will prevail.'

He placed the toothpick in his mouth and gazed at the horizon. 'The way of life of our people is written upon the rocks of the desert,' he said distantly. 'Have you not seen them? Pictures made by the *inhaden yenun* from the dimmest depths of time. Where there are now regs there were once forests. Where there are now dunes there were once rivers; where there are now sand-seas there were lakes filled with fish, with crocodiles and hippopotami – creatures we know only from stories our grandmothers tell us.'

'I have seen these pictures,' Taha said.

'In those days the hunters used only spears and bows and arrows. They had no metal – spearheads, arrowheads and knives they made of stones shaped with great skill. Some of our people still have this skill, but few now. The great veldts our fore-fathers, the Bafour, knew, have slowly become unstitched like a jerkin, split at the seams. The forests have gone, so that only few of the old *tadout* trees can be seen, and there are no saplings. Instead there is saltwort, white-spined acacia, tamarisk, Sodom's apple. The lakes and rivers have dried up and been replaced by sands. The days of the great beasts have passed, just as the day of stones has passed, just as the use of our old rifles will pass. Just as everything will pass. It is the way of the Great God.'

Taha nodded again. 'Then you will not help me?'

Bes smiled enigmatically, then closed his eyes and opened them. 'We shall ask the Great God,' he said.

7

THOUGH HAMDU FOUND THE PATH THROUGH the dunes on the edge of the Zrouft, it was still late afternoon before Sterling's caravan reached the *Rose of Cimarron*. Even closer up, little more of the aircraft's shape was revealed. By chance she had landed in a great field of fish-scale dunes and the restless sands had covered her almost completely. No wonder, Sterling thought, she had never been located from the air. The dune-field was punctuated by islands of wind-mangled acacia and tamarisk, and in the distance, perhaps half a mile away, there was a school of yardangs – rocks with slender stems and bloated heads like petrified fungi.

About fifty yards from the aircraft, Hamdu halted his camel and made the sign against the evil eye. 'This place is cursed,' he said. 'I go no nearer.'

'Nor I,' Faris agreed.

'Oh Lord,' Churchill said. 'You survived a sandstorm and a week in the Zrouft and an aeroplane gives you the heebie-jeebies?'

141

'I go no nearer,' Hamdu scowled.

'All right,' Churchill sighed. 'We'll go on foot.'

While the others unloaded the camels, Sterling and Churchill walked towards the aircraft, but within twenty yards, Churchill paused to take in the sight. 'Damn,' he said. 'Knew I should have brought a camera. This would have looked marvellous on my wall. See, she made a crash-landing – the undercarriage folded, but she's intact apart from that. Blow me, if you could rebuild the landing gear you could probably even fly her out.'

Sterling was only half listening. He was staring at the bulk of the aircraft under the layers of sand, his head full of images of Billy. His son, here, alone, in this stultifyingly empty wilderness. He shivered and felt tears in his eyes. He brushed them away, and approached the sand-covered aircraft.

Churchill went to inspect the props and the twin 1200 HP Pratt & Whitney engines in the nascelles on the wings, while Sterling, beginning at the opposite end from the tailplane, began to clear away the sand with his bare hands. It was not difficult work, and soon Churchill joined him. The sand was warm on the surface from the day's sun, but cold underneath. Clear of the sand, the fuselage looked as if it had been recently burnished and, just below the cockpit, he found the legend *Rose of Cimarron* in black letters, only just legible after years of abrasion by the moving sand. When he had uncovered the side door, Churchill called Sterling over. 'Are you sure you want to do this?' he asked.

Sterling looked at him, knowing that it was the moment of truth, knowing that Corrigan's tale might have been a lie, and that all this effort might have been for nothing, or that his son's corpse might lie on the other side of that door.

'Dammit, Eric,' he said. 'I have to know.'

He wrenched on the door and it opened easily.

Then both Sterling and Churchill screamed.

Swinging out of the door was the most ghoulish figure Sterling had ever seen. It was neither a corpse nor a skeleton, but a frame of bones with the skin dried on them like a tight suit, a skull whose jaw was opened in a monstrous grin, whose rotten hair still stood like tufts on its pate, whose vacant eye-sockets glared at them balefully, whose knuckle bones broke through parchment skin on its fingers to jab and poke at them.

Sterling leapt backwards as the ghoul seemed to take a step towards them, then it tripped and tumbled forward, crashing awkwardly in the sand, no more than a lifeless bag of bones.

'Jesus Christ!' Sterling said.

Churchill knelt down to examine the corpse. 'It's completely mummified,' he said. 'See – skin and ligaments, but no organs at all and no smell.'

The corpse wore some kind of orange suit, in strips and tatters, and Churchill began to feel for the pockets. 'There's something in here,' he said but, before he could find it, Sterling pointed to a nametag on the orange funeral-wrap where the left breast pocket might have been. *Maj. K.L. Craven*, it read.

Almost simultaneously, Churchill pulled a wallet out of the remains of the map pocket. He examined the contents carefully. There was no map, but there was a pilot's licence and other documents in the name of Keith Craven.

'God Almighty,' Churchill half whispered. 'What do you know? It's Ravin' Craven, the blue-eyed war hero, the army air ace; so cool that butter wouldn't melt in his mouth. This is how he ended up. Jesus Christ! Doesn't look so cool now. So are the mighty fallen: hoist by their own petards.'

Sterling stared at him in surprise. 'What do you mean by that?' he demanded. 'I thought you said you only knew Craven by name.'

143

Churchill looked suddenly embarrassed, as if he'd been caught out. 'Name and *reputation*, I should have said.'

Sterling had returned his attention to the mummy. 'Thank God it's not Billy,' he said.

Churchill looked doubtful. 'It certainly doesn't look like it,' he said. 'But someone *could* have changed clothes. Can we be a hundred per cent sure?'

'This can't be Billy,' Sterling said. 'Because Billy was missing the joint of the little finger on his left hand. He got it caught in a wire fence when he was eight and it was ripped off.'

Churchill glanced at the left hand of the mummified corpse. The joint was intact.

'He always reckoned it affected his batting in cricket,' Sterling said almost to himself. 'But the truth was he just found cricket deadly boring.'

They clambered inside, Sterling first, followed by Churchill. It was dim in the cabin, but not dark – the portholes let in enough light to see. The first thing that struck Sterling was how well preserved the aircraft was. It was almost as if it had come down only days, not years before. The passenger seat-slings along the sides were still intact, and the three static-lines originally attached to parachutes were still firmly clipped to the horizontal bar over-head. The floor was covered in packets of cigarettes, chewing gum, chocolate bars and tools. There were several US army-style water-canteens, and an overturned jerry can with the British MOD arrow on it – all of them empty.

'Look!' Churchill said excitedly, and Sterling glanced up to see him pointing to a long narrow tank that seemed to run almost the whole length of the cabin. The big man tapped it with his fingers and the metal made a hollow, ringing sound. 'Spare tank,' Churchill said. 'Hobart was right. They fitted an extra tank to extend the range, so they weren't going to Zagora at all.'

Sterling stood next to Churchill and laid his hand on the cool metal. 'You mean Corrigan was lying,' he said.

'At least about that. He wanted to cover up Craven's intentions, that's for sure.'

There were more surprises in the cockpit. The control panels were intact, and an old leather flying helmet was tied to the pilot's seat. There was a little pile of goodies on the floor – a carton of compo rations, a length of cord, a hatchet, a wrench, a flashlight – looking as if someone had only this moment collected them. Sterling picked up a half-finished packet of hardtack biscuits, which at once dissolved into powder. Clipped in a bracket next to the seat was a thermos flask. Churchill pulled it out and unscrewed the cap. 'Good God!' he exclaimed. 'Look at that – there's still coffee in there.'

It was a relief, though, to find no other corpses. Whatever had happened to Billy, at least Corrigan's tale had held up in that respect. On the way back out through the cabin, Churchill's face suddenly assumed a puzzled expression. He glanced around. 'Doesn't it strike you that something's missing?' he asked.

Sterling stared at the empty space beyond the seat-slings. 'What?' he asked.

'The cargo,' Churchill said, grinning. 'Corrigan said they were carrying supplies . . .'

'No,' Sterling corrected him. 'That was what Arnold told me. Corrigan didn't mention the cargo. Arnold said they were carrying food supplies for the French army in Zagora. Craven's company had the contract.'

'Did you see the manifest?'

'Yes . . . well, no, actually, but it was confirmed by a French army clerk we spoke to.'

'Then where is it?'

'Somebody looted it, obviously.'

Churchill raised an eyebrow. 'Maybe,' he said. 'But where's the evidence? Everything else is here, even the cigarettes and chewing gum, but no cargo. No bits of broken boxes or wrappings inside or out and ; . .' His eyes lit up and he pounced on a dark mass of webbing coiled at the back of the cabin. 'Look at this,' he said excitedly. 'Baggage nets. Any cargo has to be lashed down with these things, but they haven't even been unfastened. Are you telling me that the looters took the stuff and then neatly coiled and fastened up the nets afterwards? It doesn't make sense.'

Sterling considered it, flicking through the probabilities with scientific intensity.

'They could have jettisoned it,' he said, 'when they knew the crate was going down.'

There was an expression of triumph on Churchill's face. 'George,' he said. 'Corrigan never mentioned jettisoning cargo, did he? You said he never mentioned cargo, and that's because they weren't carrying any. They never intended to go to Zagora at all – if they had they wouldn't have needed the extra fuel. This tank must hold what – three or four hundred gallons. A Dakota C forty-seven like this has a three thousand five hundred kilo payload, but not with that extra tank on board. They couldn't have carried anywhere near the full payload. It just wouldn't have been economical.'

Sterling looked confused. 'Why would the French military clerk lie?'

'Maybe they were going to pick up cargo rather than deliver it. Maybe it was something they didn't want to advertise. Maybe the clerk had been slipped something to keep his mouth shut.'

'You mean Craven was into something illegal?'

Churchill frowned and crosshatches appeared on the high forehead. 'That company he worked for had some very dubious

146

connections. I told you that when I was in Casablanca it was part of my job to investigate links between the mafia and the Forces. Didn't Corrigan say he wanted to come out here with you? Pretty crazy move unless he was after something they left out here.'

'That's what I thought initially, but if he was after something it had to be on the aircraft, because that's all that's shown on the map. There's nothing here, and if you're right there never was. What you're saying doesn't add up anyway, because no one in their right mind would have taken a boy with them on a flight involving something devious. I mean, nobody forced Craven to take Billy, and if Billy had seen anything odd he'd certainly have told Arnold. It would have been a pretty stupid move.'

Churchill blinked, apparently convinced. 'You're right,' he said. 'He'd have had to be an idiot, and with the DFC and bar he can't have been that, can he? I mean, he was mister blue-eyed boy, wasn't he? He was mister butter-wouldn't-melt-in-my mouth, who sported the old-school tie and used to shit roses.'

There was a bitterness in Churchill's tone that Sterling hadn't heard before, and he looked at his companion enquiringly.

'Hey, it's getting late,' Churchill said, recovering. 'We ought to give Major Ravin' Craven, DFC and bar, a decent Christian burial, don't you think?'

'All right,' Sterling said.

Outside the dusk was gathering. The last golden rim of the sun lay on the dunes, with streamers of colour laid at angles across the darkening sky. The utter silence of the desert engulfed them, stranger and more pregnant than ever.

As they looked around for a suitable place to bury the corpse, the silence was shattered by a gunshot from the direction of the camp, followed by a raucous shout.

Churchill and Sterling stiffened and stared at each other for a split second.

'Just one of the boys shooting a hare,' Churchill said calmly. 'Nothing untoward.'

Before he had finished the sentence, more shots crackled out of the night, so fast and furious that they sounded almost as if they came from a machine gun. Churchill knitted his brows and drew his Smith & Wesson. 'Those were semi-automatics,' he whispered. 'Our boys don't have those.'

After that last salvo there had been no more shots, and the night silence had descended again by the time they reached the camp. They came in slowly, cautiously, Churchill in the lead, taking in the glowing embers of the fire, the saddles and water-skins hanging from them, untouched.

Sterling saw Jafar first. The ex-Znaga was face upwards, his long hair, wet with something slick, fanning out around his head like a garment, his eyes bulging, his chest a morass of blood, still grasping his ancient Martini-Henri rifle in his right hand, as if he had refused to be reduced to his former vassal status even in death.

Faris was dead, too. His body was face-down in the dust, and a shot had sliced off the back of his head as cleanly as a blade. Even in the moonlight, Sterling could see bits of brain and fragments of bone, like eggshell, among the blood.

Hamdu was still alive. He had been shot in the face – a bullet had passed through one side of the jaw and taken the other half off on exit. Sterling knelt beside him and saw that he was beyond communication, his fingers twitching spasmodically as if grasping for an unseen support, his eyes opaque, his breath coming in ragged spurts.

'Jesus wept!' Churchill whispered. He turned away, making gagging noises, and just then a camel groaned somewhere. The detective stopped gagging and pulled himself up. He moved towards the sound with his revolver extended before him in both hands. There was a rustle behind them. 'Eric!' Sterling hissed.

Churchill had half turned to see what it was, when a dark ghost, hooded and in flowing robes, suddenly appeared from behind a thorn bush in front of them, shrieking like a banshee. Sterling's blood ran cold. In the same moment he saw Churchill move like lightning, dropping and firing two shots, as calmly as if he had been snap-shooting on the ranges. Sterling saw the muzzle-flashes, saw the dark figure go down. An instant later all hell was let loose.

Robed men appeared from all directions, screaming, shooting, brandishing long curved daggers. There seemed to be scores of them. Churchill yelled something that sounded like '*Bastards*!' and fired once more. Then he was obscured from Sterling's view by four or five ghosts with clubs and knives, who flung them-selves on him with the hunger of starving jackals. His pistol fell. For an instant the big man struggled loose, his fists flailing, sending men staggering back. Then they were on him again, even more than before. Sterling was dimly aware of arms grabbing his, and then a battering ram connected with his skull, and a host of comets scored channels across his pupils, like diamonds cutting glass.

Churchill was kneeling with his arms lashed behind his back when Sterling regained consciousness. They had been dragged to another clearing, away from the bodies of Hamdu and his companions. Hamdu had to be dead by now, Churchill thought. A fire had been kindled and a group of shadows in flowing robes and head-cloths was squatting round it. Churchill could see others moving in the middle distance around a tightly packed troop of kneeling camels. The men by the fire were talking in loud, grating voices. There were at least twenty of them.

Sterling groaned as he came round, his lips moving silently. His face was a mask of blood running from an open wound on his head. Churchill winced at the sight, and hoped fervently that the wound wasn't as bad as it looked. Kneeling was painful; as he tried to shift position, the leather bindings cut painfully into his flesh.

One of the figures by the fire seemed to notice the movement, rose and came towards him. The man was small and moved with the lightness and grace of an acrobat. Closer up, his eyes looked dark and hooded in the firelight, his aquiline nose emphasizing an expression of arrogant disdain. He was barefooted and wore a cartridge belt around his waist, with a hooked dagger in a sheath in the centre. His hands were calloused, broad and strong, and in one of them he held a slender camel-stick. He stood before Churchill and let loose a stream of Arabic that the big man couldn't catch. He repeated the words slowly and with sneering emphasis, and Churchill suddenly understood. The Arab was cursing him for killing one of his companions. The Arab spat on the ground in disgust. He kicked the big man's leg with his bare foot, repeating the sentences, and suddenly whacked Churchill's ankle with his stick. Churchill winced but did not cry out.

Sterling also hadn't grasped the Arabic, and he stared at Churchill, horrified, struggling to get loose. 'What does he want?' he gasped. 'Who the hell *are* these people?'

'Bandits,' Churchill croaked. 'They want to know what's inside the aircraft.'

'Why the hell don't they just look for themselves?' Sterling groaned.

'They're scared stiff of it. Think it's guarded by evil spirits.'

Sterling snorted. This was evidently the wrong thing to do, because the small man shouted to his companions, who quickly gathered round him. Their faces under the enveloping dark head-cloths were stony. The leader snapped a crisp order, and two or three men ripped away the legs of his trousers up to the crutch. 'What the hell are they going to do?' Sterling stammered.

The leader whacked him with his camel-stick across the calf and he screamed.

The man looked impatient now. He repeated his earlier questions to Churchill, and the big man shook his head. The leader made a sign to one of his men, who pulled a red-hot brand from the fire and brought it over to Sterling, holding it up a yard or so away from his eyes.

'I'm sorry, George,' Churchill said. 'Unless you or I tell them what they want to know, they're going to start with your feet and end up with your balls.'

'Why me?' Sterling yelled.

The leader repeated the same question and Churchill shook his head again. The Arab made a sign to the man with the red-hot brand, who leaned forward, grinning. Sterling watched the glowing end of the wood with horror-filled eyes. His mouth had already begun to form a scream of anticipation when there was a dull thud like a boxing glove striking a punchbag. The man with the firebrand lost his grin, and his lips groped soundlessly for a question to which there was no answer. Time changed direction with staggering abruptness. The man with the firebrand seemed to be falling forever, and it was only after aeons that Sterling realized there was something anomalous sticking out of his back – the handle of a dagger. The chief and his cronies seemed literally petrified, their eyes starting in disbelief. Sterling kicked instinctively to prevent the body rolling on him, and at that moment the fire erupted in a supernova of light.

The explosion lasted a fraction of a second, but was enough to momentarily blind everyone around the hearth. Almost

151

simultaneously, gunshots rang out of the night. Sterling's eyes opened in time to see an Arab fall into the fire. His head-cloth caught light immediately, and he leapt up, screaming and dancing, wearing a halo of flame. Men were rushing in every direction, jabbering, and beyond them the camels bellowed, lurching up and breaking their hobbles.

A robed figure, indistinguishable from the rest except for a white band round his black turban, appeared out of the shadows, walking unhurriedly towards Sterling and Churchill. Four feet away, he stooped, snatched the dagger out of the dead man's back, and used it to slice through their bindings. One of the bandits crashed into him, and Sterling saw the dagger that had cut his bonds plunging in and out of his assailant's belly faster than the eye could follow.

The lower part of their rescuer's face was veiled, but Sterling saw bright eyes shining like opals in the moonlight. '*Ajri! Ajri!*' the man yelled. 'Run! Run!' He pointed towards a clump of dark tamarisks in the distance. Another bandit closed in on him, and Sterling recognized the 'chief', his hawkish features contorted with hatred as he slashed at the white-banded man with his dagger. '*I am Amir ould Hamel of the Ulad Delim,*' he thundered.

There was a clash of steel as the man with the white band parried the thrust.

'*I am Taha Minan Nijum of the Ulad al-Mizna!*' he roared back.

The chief seemed startled. He took a step backwards, and in that moment the one named Taha grabbed Sterling's arm and ran. Sterling just had time to see Churchill fell an Arab with a smashing blow from the butt of the man's own rifle. There were more resounding thumps as the big man laid about him with the whirling rifle-stock, but already Sterling was leaping after Taha.

A volley of shots kicked up the sand around Sterling's feet

152

and burned past his ears, but he kept on running, faster than he'd run from the police in London, faster than he'd ever run in his life. From the darkness among the trees came muzzle-flashes and then the blast of answering shots. The grotesquely distorted tamarisks loomed up out of the moonlight, growing on an island in the centre of a deep hollow from which the sand had been scooped by the prevailing wind. Taha disappeared into the depression, and a moment later Sterling threw himself down beside him. His head felt top-heavy and tight, as though he was wearing a helmet.

His head wound was bleeding again. Sterling wiped blood out of his eyes, and only then did he realize there was someone else inside the hollow. A yard away was a dwarflike man with a black beard and large hairy hands, who was shoving a flat-nosed round into the breech of his rifle, his heavy jowls set in grim determination.

Taha skittered down to the base of the hollow and crawled back up the slope carrying two rifles. He thrust one at Sterling, but Sterling shook his head. Taha made a sound of derision, and monkey-ran up to join the dwarf. There was the clunk of a weapon cocking, then a *krrraaak*, and a flatter snort of fire from the dwarf's gun. Sterling felt as though his eardrums had been ruptured. He smelled cordite and the odour of the men nearby – gunpowder and animal grease.

He pulled himself up beside them and peered over the edge. Eric Churchill was limping towards them, with a dozen Ulad Delim close on his heels, like a bear pursued by wolves. He was carrying his kitbag on his back and it was slowing him down. 'Drop the kitbag!' Sterling bawled.

Shots whined above Sterling's head, slapping into the trunk of the tamarisk behind him. He ducked, and when he looked again a Delim with a smooth-shaved skull was springing across the sage-clumps after Churchill, a dagger in one hand, a rifle in the other. He was within only five paces of the big man when there was a *krrraack* and a flash from the dwarf's rifle. The running Delim dropped without a sound. A moment later Churchill crawled over the edge of the hollow like a tortoise, still dragging his kitbag with him.

The dwarf fired again, grunting with satisfaction. Taha pointed to Sterling. 'You come with me,' he snapped in Arabic. 'The hunter will take your friend.'

He began to slide down towards the tamarisk trunk at the bottom of the hollow. Sterling hesitated and shot Churchill a nervous glance. 'Go on!' Churchill wheezed. 'I'll be all right.'

Sterling followed Taha, slithering down towards the mass of wormlike tamarisk roots at the bottom of the hollow, and creeping up the other side. Shots whizzed and cracked in the high branches. Under the bank of the hollow a camel was couched, and by the time Sterling got there Taha had whipped off the hobble and was holding the animal still by its head-rope. '*Arkab! Arkab!*' he told Sterling urgently, pointing to the space behind the saddle. 'Ride! Ride!'

The moment Sterling had slung his leg over, the animal began to rise, shunting forwards and backwards and forwards again. Before it was on its feet, Taha had hoisted himself into the saddle.

He headed the camel up the gentler slope on the other side of the hollow, shielded from enemy view by the branches of the tamarisk. Seconds later they were on the open plain, trotting southwestward into the night.

After the first rush to get away, Taha slowed his camel to a walk. He slipped off its back, taking the head-rope and leading it forward. Taha never spoke to Sterling or gave directions, and Sterling gripped the saddle-horns dumbly. As the shooting faded,

154

the night grew deathly silent, with no sound but the crunch of the camel's feet in the gravel and the slap of water in Taha's skins. Sterling's head ached savagely. He was tortured with thirst, but he did not ask Taha to stop.

For long periods he stared vacantly at the stars above him. The night was so clear that the Milky Way was visible, a nebula of stardust like a path twisting through the heavens. Nausea and faintness came in waves. His head swam, his vision fuzzed and the blood pulsed like a drumbeat in his ears.

There were voices inside his head: Billy's voice saying, '*Come on, dad, you can make it.*' Billy, aged eight, holding up the bloody, severed joint of his little finger, making a whimpering sound, but bravely holding back the tears. Billy, thirteen years old, confronting him angrily after a term of baiting from the other pupils at Scowcroft, and more than one fist-fight to defend the family honour. '*Why dad? Why don't you just fight like all the rest?*' The gut-wrenching feeling that his own son was ashamed of him. '*I know you're not really a coward, dad. Why don't you just show them?*' The terrible inability to explain. He gasped out loud. His head, until now top-heavy, felt suddenly light, as though it was floating. He heard, as if from afar, his own voice again, murmuring, '*We shall not flag or fail. We shall go on to the end . . . whatever the cost may be. We shall fight on the beaches, we shall fight on the landing grounds, we shall fight in the fields and in the streets, we shall fight in the hills; we shall never surrender.*'

He smiled fondly. Then slowly, with a momentum that felt wholly inevitable, he surrendered, crumpling, toppling out of the saddle.

When Sterling came to it was half light, and he was lying on soft sand. The camel was couched in the shelter of some high

155

rocks, munching grain from a nosebag. The water-skin slung from its saddle looked inviting; his mouth was as dry as parchment. He got up unsteadily, feeling his head, and staggered towards the camel. It was then that he saw Taha.

A black head-cloth and blue *dara'a* lay airing out over a couple of thorn bushes nearby, and Taha, naked but for a short loin-cloth, was crouching over a flickering fire with his back to him. Sterling saw a lean youth's body with a taut back, and arm muscles like rope, long legs, a tangle of dark hair that fell to his shoulders. It was the body of a gymnast, flesh burned down to hard fibre by years of activity and little food and water.

The youth fished a kettle off the fire with a twig and turned suddenly to face Sterling. The shock was so swift and powerful that Sterling felt as if he had been punched. The breath hissed out of his lungs, and he teetered to his knees. The youth stopped in his tracks and their eyes locked for an infinite second.

The face raced at Sterling out of the landscape, a face within a face: older, more mature, but one he had seen grow and change from infancy to near adulthood. The face of a little boy he had brought up, the features of the woman he had loved. A face imprinted on him for all time, a face he could have picked out of a million. His eyes fell to the youth's left hand, and he saw that the joint of the little finger was missing.

'*Billy?*' he whispered. '*Billy, is it really you?*'

8

THE WORDS CHIMED IN TAHA'S HEAD, familiar yet somehow crippled, as if heard distorted on a wireless. He studied the *afrangi*'s face closely for the first time, and knew it was the face that had haunted his dreams, the face he had deliberately rejected on waking as a visitation from the spirit world.

'Billy?' the man said again.

The name was a key unlocking an ancient rusted door. The dam Taha had built inside him burst, a torrent of images came gushing out with such force that he began to shake. The lid of the box he had kept closed for so many years was blasted off.

'Dad?' he said, his voice trembling. *'Dad?'*

They threw their arms around each other, and Sterling felt tears streaming down his face. Taha fought to control his wildly conflicting emotions – fear, anger, joy, disbelief. Two distinct personalities grappled for supremacy within him: one a man of the desert; the other a child with memories of a different place and time. It was like looking out at the world through two

157

windows at once, each viewing the same thing with a different perspective.

He remembered the man's face, yet it was also different from the way he remembered it – unnaturally pink, and of a curious shape and colour. The man's behaviour and the way he held himself seemed uncouth and primitive compared with the Blue Men. The man's clothes too, were familiar, yet they looked outlandish – even ridiculous. The battered, broad-brimmed hat gave him the look of an imbecile. And Taha recalled suddenly how the previous night the man had refused the rifle – the one he'd stolen from the Delim. He'd refused to fight, even in defence of his friend. The memory embarrassed Taha – courage was one of the five qualities that together comprised 'humanness'. To be without courage was a disgrace.

And yet, this odd-looking stranger was *dad*, there could be no doubt of that. A million images of his previous life were blinking in his mind like mirages on the open Zrouft. Taha felt dazed, reduced to silence by the unfathomable mystery that had brought this man here. He felt reverent, just as he had on the day he had shot the white antelope and retrieved the bezoar stones. The Divine had brought Sterling here, to the same spot as Taha, and placed his life in Taha's own hands. There was purpose in it, Taha knew. First the Delim had come looking for him; now this. The seeds of these events had lain in his falling out of the sky seven summers ago, a lifetime ago. The purpose had lain dormant all that time, just as the seeds of the desert grasses lay dormant in the sand for years, awaiting a downpour of rain. Now was the time of its fruition. The purpose was still opaque, but would become clear very soon. It was a simple matter of patience, and if there was one thing the Blue Men had taught him it was patience.

The *afrangi* was holding him, tears running down his cheeks. His face, thin and sallow, still stained with blood, showed a

158

shifting storm of emotions. '*Billy!*' he repeated like a half-death chant. '*Oh Billy!! You're alive!*'

Taha held Sterling back gently with both hands. '*Dad,*' he said. 'No *Ingilizee . . . Ana nasit . . .* I have forgotten. No Billy . . . *Ismi* Taha Minan Nijum. I am Fell-From-The-Stars.'

Sterling pressed Taha to him possessively, caressed his hair. 'It doesn't matter,' he said. 'Nothing matters. All that matters is that you are here.'

Taha was distracted by the faint sound of camel pads on the sand. He made an urgent sign to Sterling and fetched his weapon, crouching among the rocks with the rifle at his shoulder. A moment later the camel swung into the wadi, casting a vast, spiderlike shadow in the light of the new sun. The other *afrangi* – the big one – was riding it, while Bes the Hunter led it, rather disdainfully, by the head-rope.

'*Yak la bas?*' the dwarf said to Taha. 'No evil?'

He jerked the rope and the camel sat down heavily, squalling. Churchill slid off the animal's back and looked at Sterling, unsure what to do next. 'All right, George?' he said.

Bes handed Taha the head-rope and went and sat by the fire. 'The Great God be praised!' he said, rubbing his hands. He held them up, splaying the big, stubby fingers, his face thoughtful. He clenched the fingers into fists. 'You knifed two,' he said, and two fingers popped up. 'I shot four.' Six fingers were showing now. 'By the Great God!' he said, counting them. 'That is six! Six Delim for six *lemha*. The Spirit of the *lemha* is avenged!'

'I killed three,' Taha said. 'I killed a sentry and took his weapon.'

Another finger popped up. 'Seven!'

Taha nodded towards Churchill. 'And the big *afrangi* here, he killed one too!'

'By heaven!' Bes growled. 'That is eight!'

Taha nodded and led the camel over to where his own was munching grain. He couched it there and examined it critically, observing the Delim brand-mark on its flank – an inverted arrow with a dot. 'A fine beast,' he said.

The creases on the dwarf's thickly bearded face elongated, and he bared gleaming white teeth. 'It was easy enough to get,' he said. 'They were running about bleating like frightened goats. I could have bagged half a dozen, but *achh*, they are horrible stinky beasts, their meat is like old boar-skin, and their milk tastes like piss. By the Great God, I don't know why you hook-noses prize them so. Give me a good hunting-dog any day – now *there*'s a beautiful animal.'

'I thank you for your help,' Taha said.

'*Achh!*' the little man swept the thanks aside with his hirsute hand. 'The thanks is to the Great God, who guided us. We are only the instruments of his will.'

'The praise be to God.'

'The Great God is eternal. Man's life is short, but He endures forever.'

'*Amen.*'

After he had fitted a nosebag of grain over the camel's muzzle, Taha shook hands with Churchill. 'You saved us,' the big man said in Arabic. 'We are in your debt – both of you. But how did you make the fire explode like that?'

Taha tossed his long hair back and watched Churchill carefully. Living in the desert, one learned to read faces, and while Sterling's face was entirely open, the big *afrangi*'s features told him that he had something to hide. He was certainly brave and strong, yet there was something in him that was difficult to fathom. Taha decided to let it ride for now, knowing that there was purpose in this too.

'Flash powder,' he said. 'My father makes it.'

'Who were those people?'

'Ulad Delim, our enemies. I have been following their tracks for more than a week. We heard them when they attacked your camp and killed the people with you. We came close, too late to save them, but I heard the Delim talking. They were expecting you. The Delim are good shots and they have new rifles. They could have killed you easily, yet they did not. Why?'

'God knows,' Churchill said.

Sterling stared at him enquiringly, but Churchill shook his head. 'You look on your last legs, George,' he said. 'That cut in the head needs treating. What's up?'

'It's Billy,' Sterling said, pointing at Taha.

Churchill's face went slack with amazement. He took a step backwards, staring automatically at Taha's left hand. 'He's got the right sign,' he stammered. 'But this chap's a wild man. I saw him kill two people myself. You sure you're not jumping the gun, George? I mean, Billy wasn't the only boy in the world with a missing joint on that finger.'

Sterling shook his head. 'No,' he said. 'It's him. I know my own son.'

Churchill was visibly shaken. He stared hard at Taha. '*Hatha sahih?*' he asked. 'Is it true that you're Billy Sterling?'

Taha surveyed him solemnly. '*Kaan yom min al-ayam walad ismu Billy,*' he replied. 'There was once a boy called Billy. He came from the world outside, he floated down out of the night. But the boy is dead now. I am not him. I am Fell-From-The-Stars of the Ulad al-Mizna.'

'*Jesus!*' Churchill gasped. 'It *is* him.' He pointed at Sterling and said in Arabic, 'The man you just saved is your father!'

The little hunter had been watching from the fire, trying to follow what was going on. 'What does he mean?' he demanded. 'How can an *afrangi* be your father? You are Taha son of Belhaan.'

161

'The *afrangi* is not my father,' Taha said. 'At least . . . I have two fathers.'

The dwarf snorted. 'Are you the first man in all creation to have two fathers, then?' he said. 'By the Great God, why did I get mixed up with Christians and hook-noses? Their ways are the ways of madmen.'

'Billy . . . ?' Sterling began.

'Who is Billy?' Taha asked evenly, in Arabic. '*Billy ma mowjuud.* Billy is not here. Billy vanished the day after the iron bird came down. He waited for you but you didn't come. Grandfather didn't come. Only Belhaan came. Billy died that day and Taha was born. *Hassa' kaayin Taha utauf.* Now there is only Taha.'

'But Billy,' Sterling said, also speaking Arabic now, 'I tried. Grandfather and I, we searched every inch of the route. We just didn't know where the plane came down . . .'

'Perhaps,' Taha said grimly. 'But it was God's will that Belhaan found me. Billy is gone.'

Sterling shook his head in confusion. Of all the possible outcomes of his search, this was one he hadn't envisaged.

Churchill saw the expression on Sterling's face and made a pacifying gesture with his broad hands. 'All right,' he said, in Arabic. 'Now maybe we should calm down a bit. We've all been through a lot. Let's have a glass of tea and think about this. By God, we should be drinking a toast to the reunion!'

'We must move on,' Taha told them. 'Now the Delim know you are here they will come after you. They have good trackers and they will be angry that so many died or were injured.'

Sterling looked at Churchill with new concern. 'Move on?' Churchill said. 'But your father and I came to take you *back*.'

Taha stared at him. '*Back*?' he repeated. 'Back where?'

'Back to *Balad al Ingliz*,' Churchill said. 'To England, where you belong.'

'*England*?' Taha said wonderingly. He shook his head. 'No,' he said. 'I don't belong there. *This* is where I belong.'

'But Billy . . . !' Sterling gasped. 'You can't mean that. You can't have forgotten. You *are* Billy. You are Billy Sterling, my son.' He grabbed Taha's left hand gently and held up the mutilated little finger. 'I remember the day you got this,' he said. 'You jumped over a fence and got your hand stuck. The fence was sharp steel and it took the top of your finger off. You came running to me with the end of your finger and wanted me to stick it on. That was *you* – not Taha. You, Billy! Don't you remember? You have to come home with me.'

Taha removed his hand from Sterling's grip and his eyes turned cold. 'We must move on now,' he said.

They walked, leading the camels, with the little hunter guiding them. Sterling tramped behind his son dejectedly, not trusting himself to speak. Taha seemed unconcerned, as if the fact of his father's arrival after seven years was meaningless or simply hadn't sunk in yet. Or maybe he was also thinking about it deeply, but wouldn't let it show.

Sterling was shattered, but wise enough to glimpse a reason for Taha's behaviour. It was the syndrome that had been reported from the recent war in Korea, he told himself, in which prisoners-of-war had begun to identify with their captors. The boy had been abandoned in the wilderness, and had been obliged to identify with the desert people in order to survive. He couldn't believe that Billy would choose to live among this filth and hardship and squalor if he had a true choice. Sterling's head was brimming with questions, but he knew it was too early. Billy was still getting used to the idea that his situation had changed. It would take time.

Taha's world seemed very much an exterior one, Sterling noted. His son constantly pointed out features of the landscape that neither Sterling nor Churchill would have picked out without a guide: the track of a ground squirrel, the burrow of a ratel or honey badger, the tail prints of a *mushlud*, or monitor-lizard. He showed them the dark spikes and granite ridges or *guelbs* that emerged like great jagged whalebacks from the hammada, reciting their names and the myths surrounding them, and indicated how the sun created lakes, ravines and hills in the emptiness – the mirages that the nomads called Satan's Mirrors.

Sterling, listening silently, was astonished at Taha's knowledge. Glancing at his son from time to time, he got images of Billy as a child, interspersed with images of a stranger. This was a man who had just killed three people with a dagger, who had calmly cast explosive powder into a fire, walked through a horde of enemies and rescued him and Churchill, without even knowing who they were, and probably saved their lives. This was a man who had tracked these bandits alone for a week, who handled camels as if born to it, who had just guided him for a night through trackless desert, who seemed to fit the landscape like a hand fits a glove. Billy had always been stoic and resourceful, yet this was not Billy. Billy had been a boy. This was a man, confident, mature; capable of killing calmly and efficiently. A man Sterling didn't know.

After an hour, Bes halted and pointed out a single tree far away on the skyline. Between themselves and the tree was a flat, brown plain, utterly featureless in all directions. 'That tree is a day's journey from here,' he said.

Sterling gasped. 'It can't be,' he said. 'You're talking about more than twenty miles.'

'By the Great God, I tell the truth,' Bes growled.

He thrust his knobbly hand out in the direction of the tree, fist clenched. 'The plain between here and the tree looks like any other,' he said. 'But it is treacherous. It is the Umm al-Khof, the quicksand, the Mother of Fear.'

164

'Whole herds of camels have disappeared into it,' Taha added.

'Aye,' said Bes darkly. 'And more than camels, too.' He lowered his fist a few degrees. 'See that black dot a little further down from the tree?'

Sterling strained his eyes, and Churchill pulled out his old field glasses. Sterling could see the black object, but it could have been anything from a tin can to a house. There was nothing around it to judge its size at all. Even Churchill's binoculars wouldn't reveal further information. 'What is it?' Churchill asked.

'I won't tell you,' Bes said. 'You must observe. We shall be at that spot by noon, but from now on you must be very careful.'

'But the surface looks all the same,' Sterling said. 'How can you be sure we won't blunder into the quicksand?'

The little man squeezed his bulbous nose, then pointed out a plant growing nearby, with dark green stalks a few inches high. 'Askaf,' he said. 'The askaf shows the way – it grows only where the sand is solid. Where there is no askaf, I look for the tracks of the burrowing skink. It will only burrow into hard sand. There is only one plant that grows in the sands – the jurdu – a grey spiky tree with no leaves. If you see a jurdu, steer clear of it.'

As they toiled on in the mounting heat, their eyes returned to the black dot with increasing frequency. Apart from the ghostly silver lights that blinked at them out of the quicksand, and the single tree on the skyline, there was simply nowhere else to look.

The conversation dropped, and finally gave way to silence, but for the flap of the camels' soft pads on the sand. The sky was a polished sheen of luminescent blue, blurred at the edges by the tremors of heat-haze. Nothing else moved.

After a while, Churchill halted, and Sterling saw that he was peering ahead through his field glasses again. 'By God,' he said excitedly in Arabic. 'That black thing's a motor vehicle. How the hell did it get in here?'

165

Bes said nothing, but led them on. The black object was still much further away than it seemed. They tramped on doggedly for another hour, and were almost up to it before their naked eyes could make sense of its shape and size. 'You were right, Eric,' Sterling said. 'It *is* a vehicle. Looks like a Jeep.'

Taha wanted to stop here to rest the camels, but Bes seemed troubled. 'This is a place of ill omen,' he said.

After a long discussion, though, Taha persuaded him to make camp a little further on. While Taha and the hunter unloaded and fed the animals, Sterling and Churchill trudged back to look at the Jeep. 'Careful!' Bes shouted after them. 'One false step and you'll be in. Then only the Great God can save you!'

The Jeep was painted in military colours, and was still more or less intact, although the tyres had perished, and the entire front section was nose down in the soft sand. Churchill examined the back, touching mounts that had obviously once held machine guns. He retracted his hand quickly. 'Struth!' he gasped. 'You could spit a chicken on that!'

'It's a military vehicle,' Sterling said. 'Maybe Spanish Foreign Legion?'

'Could be anybody,' Churchill said. 'Tens of thousands of these were turned out in the war –but not many had weapons-mounts like these. Yank Rangers used them, the British SAS and the Long Range Desert Group. Leclerc's Free French too.'

'Whoever it belonged to, why try to drive through a quick-sand?' Sterling asked. 'I mean, it would have been suicide.'

'Unless they had a guide.'

'Yes, but then why ditch it? These things are four-wheel drive, and they could easily have winched it out.'

There were spiky, leafless trees growing beyond the vehicle, and Sterling began to walk around the Jeep in their direction.

'Stop!' a voice bellowed. 'Don't take another step!'

Sterling froze and turned to see Bes behind them. The little man had approached in absolute silence and his face was contorted with anger.

'Did I not tell you?' he demanded. 'Jurdul trees grow in the quicksand. Those are jurduls. Step back in your own tracks!'

Sterling let out a gasp and began to retrace his own footsteps until he was back with Bes and Churchill.

'It's impossible to tell,' he said.

'We call the jurdul the Siren of the Quicksand,' Bes said. 'Many's the stranger who has been given a false sense of safety by its presence.'

'Thanks,' Sterling said.

'The thanks is to the Great God.'

Churchill turned his attention back to the Jeep. 'You know who left it here?' he asked.

'Come, sit in the shade,' Bes said. 'It is hot at midday and the heat makes you sick without your knowing it. Come, and I will tell you the story.'

Taha and Bes had rigged up a shelter with blankets tied across lengths of wood stuck in the sand. As they crawled into the few square feet of shade, Taha offered them water in an esparto bowl. Both drank avidly. Taha squatted on the edge of the shade and made a fire with bits of wood he had collected that morning. Bes settled in front of them, cross-legged.

'So,' Churchill asked. '*Shin-hi al-gissa*. What's the story?'

Bes took a deep breath. 'It was some time ago,' he said. 'Maybe . . .' He held up the splayed fingers of both hairy hands and folded the thumbs. 'Eight summers back.'

Churchill did a quick calculation. '1945,' he said.

The hunter nodded without comprehension. 'I did not see it, I only heard from a hunter called Barra who was here tracking oryx alone. He was following the path through the Umm al-Khof

167

one day, when he heard a sound like thunder. He hid himself at once and only just in time, because soon a big caravan of these chariots passed him, the like of which no one had ever seen.'

He held up all the thick fingers again, folded them, then extended five. 'Fifteen,' he said. 'Some of them were big, big chariots, and others were small like this one. There were men with them – all Christians – one in each chariot. In the first chariot there was a hook-nose. The hunter took him to be the guide. There are a few hook-noses who know the path through the Umm al-Khof. Well, as I say, they were going very slowly, and Barra was able to follow them. They did not see him. When they got here, all the chariots stopped and the men got out. Then they did a very strange thing. They pushed the big chariots one by one into the quicksand.'

'What?' Churchill gasped. 'Why?'

'Only the Great God knows. I was not there and I cannot tell you I saw it, but this is what Barra told me. They pushed all the big chariots into the sand until they were completely covered, and only six small chariots like this one remained. Then the strangest thing of all happened. Two of the Christians got up on the back of one of the small chariots, which had some weapons mounted on it, like big heavy rifles with drums on top. It looked as if they were going to make a speech, because the other men gathered around. Then suddenly the two men on the vehicle started firing the guns. *Kraaak-kraak-kraak*! Like that! The other men weren't expecting it and most of them were killed at once – the hook-nose guide was amongst them. One of the victims managed to get a pistol out and he shot one of the two on the Jeep in the leg. A moment later, he too was killed. Barra said it was the most evil thing he had ever witnessed. Indeed – excluding your presences, sirs – the Christians are a cruel people, cruel beyond all imagining.'

'Jesus wept!' Churchill exclaimed. Then he said in Arabic, 'But who were these Christians – Spanish? Who?'

168

'They were *afrang* and *afrang* are all the same.'

'So what happened after that?' Sterling asked.

'When all were dead except for the two, the injured one wrapped his leg in cotton, and then they threw all the dead bodies into the quicksand. They removed weapons and tins from four of the chariots and pushed them in too – this one here was the last one, and for some reason they couldn't get it in. Perhaps their strength failed them, and it was stuck, so they just left it. They cleared up everything on the sand – not a trace remained. Even the bloodstains were covered. Then they got in the last remaining chariot and went back on their tracks. Barra followed them for a while until they got onto the stony desert, the serir, then they headed north towards the Maghreb – Morocco, too fast for him to follow. He never saw them again.'

Churchill and Sterling were staring at him. 'But are you certain of this?' Churchill asked.

'I did not see it with my own eyes,' Bes said. 'But Barra had no reason to lie. Indeed, among my people lying is a great sin. Did I not say the ways of the Christians are strange beyond fathoming?'

Churchill shifted position, easing his body further into the limited shade. He looked at the little man inquisitively. 'Did he notice how these men were dressed?' he asked.

Bes scratched his onion of a nose and blinked. 'He said they were wearing clothes the colour of sand,' he said. 'All the same clothes, with head-dresses similar to the ones the hook-noses wear, but not black. All the same sand colour.'

Churchill nodded. 'Khaki drill,' he said to Sterling in English. 'They must have been military, at least.'

Sterling said in Arabic, 'Couldn't your friend have found out where these er . . . chariots came from? I mean, he could have followed the original tracks back to the source. After all, there must have been more to the story.'

'Aha,' Bes smiled. 'He certainly would have done, but there had been a terrible *irifi* blowing for a week before that day, so all trace of where they had come from had vanished.'

The water in the kettle had boiled, and Taha was setting glasses out on his small brass tray. He poured out a glass, tasted it, then poured it back. Then he carefully doled out three glasses, offering one first to Bes, who refused. 'We Nemadi drink no tea,' he said.

'I had forgotten,' Taha said, offering the glasses to Churchill and Sterling, who took them gratefully.

Taha took the last glass and slurped the tea experimentally. 'I have heard this story before,' he said. 'But there *is* a little more to add.'

Churchill balanced the tea glass in his large palm and looked out at the heat-devils steaming in the distance, then back at Taha. 'Oh?' he said. 'What?'

'A caravan of iron chariots was seen by nomads of the Tekna some days earlier,' he said. 'Crossing the border from the Maghreb – Morocco. The Tekna are a people who live in that region. They told my father . . .'

Sterling swallowed hard at the word 'father' and fought back a comment, but Taha seemed not to have noticed any discrepancy.

'They told my father that these chariots were being driven by Christians – two in each lorry. There were no small chariots with them.'

Churchill scratched his head, puzzled, but evidently deeply interested. 'So we've got a convoy of ten trucks coming down from Morocco, manned by twenty men,' he growled. 'And some days later we've got the same trucks – probably – being pushed into the quicksand, but by now there are only fifteen men and another six vehicles, this time Jeeps. We've gained six vehicles and lost five men.'

Sterling put his tea glass back on the brass tray, and Taha

refilled it. He lifted it pensively to his lips, but did not drink. 'More, surely,' he said. 'The maths doesn't add up. Unless they found the Jeeps abandoned in the desert, there'd have been at least one driver for each Jeep. That means a minimum of ten had vanished by the time they got here, but probably more still because the Jeeps would have had gunners as well as drivers. The probability is at least fifteen.'

'Whatever the case,' Churchill said, 'only two survived.'

'No,' Taha said. 'There was another.'

He filled a second glass for Churchill, who lifted it, his eyes squinting in the sun.

'That is what the Tekna said,' Taha went on. 'At about the same time as the hunter saw the Christians here, another Christian was found in a well, far away in the Reg al-Harra.'

'In a well?' Churchill said. 'I don't believe it!'

'As God is my witness. It was a very deep well. The Christian had been fleeing enemies and had jumped in the well. He hid there for two days and then he was pulled out by the Tekna. God had preserved him. At first they believed he was a *jinni*, and they wanted to kill him, but he spoke some of the language of the desert folk, and he persuaded them to let him live. He stayed with them a while, and they were wondering what to do with him when an iron bird arrived and picked him up.'

Churchill's eyes were narrowed now. 'Did these people say anything about this Christian?' he asked. 'Where was he from? What did he look like?'

'They said that he was a tall man, very, very tall, and that his hair was yellow, like the sand of Wadi ad-Dheheb.'

'Blond?' Churchill murmured. 'Hardly Spanish.'

'Why not?' Sterling said. 'Blond Spaniards are not that uncommon.'

'And there was another thing,' Taha added. 'He had a scar –

171

here, like this.' He pointed to the centre of his tanned right cheek, then drew the shape of a 'V' in the sand.

Sterling swallowed hard and caught Churchill's eye. 'But that sounds like—'

'We must go,' Taha said suddenly, glancing at the sun.

The afternoon was another gruelling march through an unearthly stillness, where the only movement was the play of heat along the margins of their vision. While Bes chose the way, Taha brought up the rear, constantly checking to see if there were raiders behind them.

'Don't fear,' the little hunter told him. 'The Delim do not know how to get through the Umm al-Khof. If they try they will all be lost.'

'God is all-knowing,' Taha said. 'But it is not impossible that one of them knows the way. A nomad only needs to see the path once – I shall never forget it now.'

They were heading directly towards the tree on the horizon, but to Sterling its size kept fluctuating: now larger, now smaller. Sterling was fascinated by the illusion, just as he had been by those on the Zrouft, and he occupied himself in trying on and rejecting successive theories to explain it. He told himself that in fact there was no objective tree, only the way the tree appeared to the observer, and that depended on his speed.

No matter how he tried to occupy his mind, though, his thoughts returned constantly to Billy. In a sense the problem was precisely the same as that of the fluctuating tree: Billy kept on appearing in Taha's expressions and actions, then receding into the distance to be replaced by the stranger Sterling did not know. Like the tree, there was no objective Billy, only his son's reflection on himself and the other people around him.

At last the tree was no more than a stone's throw away, and

172

the sun was a billiard ball rolling along the sleeve of the day. The heat-devils along the horizon had been replaced by a pink glow, outlining purple shadows, and above the sky had lost its polish, its blue radiance now fading to onyx and jade.

The last sparklers of the sun were strobing the sky by the time they reached the tree. Up close it was an unimpressive white-spined acacia of moderate size, its branches hacked about for firewood. Churchill and Sterling were exhausted and flung themselves down in the sand. Beyond the slight rise on which the acacia stood, the landscape changed abruptly. Gone was the featureless plain, and in its place were brakes of acacia and tamarisk, low skirts of dunes, cragged ridges and a network of wadis.

Bes couched the camel he'd been leading. 'Thanks be to the Great God,' he growled. 'We have crossed the Umm al-Khof. It is behind us now.'

'The praise be to God,' Taha intoned.

He hobbled the camels while Bes picked up deadfall, took a handful of straw from one of the saddlebags and struck a light with his dagger blade against a flint. Soon the fire was smoking.

'My work is done,' he said. 'I will spend the night with you here, but I shall be gone with tomorrow's sun.'

'It is as God wills,' Taha commented. He caught Sterling's eye. 'I can find my way back to the camp of my people from here.'

Sterling was about to say something, when Churchill laid a big hand on his knee.

Taha set up the tea things once more, and Churchill took a tin of antibiotic powder from his kitbag and applied it to Sterling's head-wound with gauze. 'I'm glad you have something worthwhile in that bag,' Sterling said. 'It almost cost you your life.'

'I doubt it,' Churchill beamed. 'Like young Bi . . . I mean Taha, said. They weren't shooting at us, not really. I guessed that at the time. They had Garand rifles, did you see that? M-ones – brand new, state-of-the-art semi-autos. Even if they weren't good shots they could have brought us down by sustained fire.'

'Why the hell didn't they? . . . Ouch! Careful with that stuff!'

'Sorry, old boy. I don't know. Your guess is as good as mine.'

It was dark but the moon was out, and the desert glowed pale in the moonlight. Flames licked up between the three stones of the hearth, on which Taha had set the kettle. As Churchill took his place by the fire, he tripped and stumbled, putting out a size eleven foot to steady himself and upsetting the kettle. Water spilled, the flames sizzled and died.

'Stupid of me!' Churchill growled. 'Sorry! I'm so clumsy. Let me refill the kettle. No, no, I insist. It was my fault.'

He picked the hot kettle up gingerly, dropped it, cursed, and picked it up again, then carried it over to where the water-skins were hanging from the saddles in the shadows. The camels were munching grain contentedly nearby, their heads oddly truncated by their nosebags.

A moment later Churchill returned with the full kettle and Taha set it on the fire.

There was silence for a moment, but for the rhythmic grind of camels' jaws.

Churchill cleared his throat. 'Taha,' he began. 'I need to ask you some things about the iron bird, you know, *Rose of Cimarron,* and the day you came here . . .'

Bes glared at him. 'If you are starting this crazy talk again, I'm going,' he said snippily. 'There's a gazelle track over there that I'm going to look at – maybe I can bag one for breakfast.' He rose and faded quickly into the shadows.

'Tea!' Taha called after him. Then he stopped himself. 'Oh, I forgot . . .'

'How can he follow a track in the dark?' Churchill asked.

174

Taha shrugged. 'There is moonlight. The Nemadi have eyes like eagles and ears like fennecs.'

He made no attempt to follow up Churchill's earlier statement, and Churchill didn't repeat it. When the water was boiling he made tea, offering glasses to Churchill and Sterling. Churchill waved his plump hand. 'No,' he said. 'You drink. I have an appointment with nature.'

He rose heavily, picked up his kitbag, and tramped off into the moonlight.

Taha's eyes followed him. 'What does he need in that bag?' he asked in Arabic.

Sterling heard suspicion in his voice. '*Wallahi mani khaabar.* I don't know,' he said. 'He always takes it when he answers the call of nature.'

Taha's eyes switched back to Sterling reluctantly. Sterling sipped tea.

'You have known him a long time?' Taha asked.

'No,' Sterling said. 'He's a detective who finds lost people. I employed him to help me find you.' He hesitated. 'It's just wonderful to find you alive, but I hadn't really expected that you would be so . . .'

'You thought somehow I was still a child? Still the Billy you knew?'

Sterling put his glass back on the tray. Taha made to fill it, but Sterling put his hand over the top. Taha looked at him in surprise. 'You must,' he said. 'You must drink three.'

Sterling took his hand away. 'So much to learn,' he said.

Taha filled his glass, then poured one for himself. He sipped it. 'I'm sorry,' he said. 'I am glad you are here, and I know God has ordained it for a reason. But it's difficult. You must give me time . . .'

'I know. I'm sorry too.'

'I wanted to ask,' Taha said, putting his empty glass down. 'I was wondering . . .'

'Yes?'

'Where is mother?'

Sterling smiled awkwardly. 'Well . . .' he began, but he was cut short by a hoarse shout from out of the darkness.

'Bes!' Taha cried, lunging for his rifle. He grabbed it and rushed into the night, Sterling after him. After only a few minutes they almost ran into the giant form of Eric Churchill, towering over the diminutive Bes, and saw that Bes was holding him at gunpoint. The big Englishman, at least twice Bes's height and weight, was looking around him shiftily, embarrassed and angry, his hands up in the air. The little hunter was growling at him. 'He's up to no good,' he said. 'I don't trust this one.'

He pointed a broad finger at the ground, and Sterling gasped. On the desert floor was a wireless transmitter. Sterling recognized it from his wartime days as a 'biscuit set', a lightweight wireless small enough to fit into a Huntley & Palmer's biscuit tin. In fact, there was a battered biscuit tin next to the set, together with a morse key attached to it on a wire, and an unspooled antenna laid out on the surface. Sterling knelt down and examined the equipment.

'What the hell is this, Eric?' he demanded. 'I'm damn sure you weren't listening to the BBC.'

Churchill beamed, but not convincingly this time. 'I can explain, George,' he said in English. 'Just call this little sod off.'

Sterling stood up awkwardly. 'I think you'd better explain *before* I call him off,' he said in Arabic.

Taha nodded. 'I never trusted you,' he said to Churchill. 'Hand over the pistol you're carrying.'

Sterling looked at him in surprise. 'He lost the pistol in the fight with the Delim,' he said.

176

'No,' Taha said. 'He picked it up when we were running away, and he has been wearing it secretly under his coat. Perhaps he thought I wouldn't notice.'

Churchill made an exasperated sigh and slipped the pistol from its holster, handing it to Sterling. 'Watch you don't shoot yourself in the foot,' he said.

Sterling ignored the sneer. 'You've been lying,' he said. 'Hamdu and the boys were right. That's where you disappeared to every night when we were in the Zrouft. It wasn't a queasy tummy – you were sending a message to someone on *this*. What is this about, Eric? Who are you talking to? Why?'

'All right, George, ' Churchill said. 'Maybe I haven't told you the *entire* truth. But call the dwarf off and I'll explain.'

'Walk back to camp,' Sterling said in Arabic, so that the others could understand.

Bes nodded. 'Walk slowly,' he snapped. 'Don't try anything, because I am a very good shot.'

Sterling picked up the biscuit transmitter and packed it into its tin. He stuffed it back into the kitbag, and they made a solemn procession towards the fire.

It was a different Churchill, a shade haughtier and more arrogant, a shade less jolly, that Sterling saw in the light of the fire.

'So much for your fine speeches,' he said, still speaking Arabic. 'You've been working behind my back ever since we started.'

'Treachery is the most disgraceful of all sins,' Taha said.

'*Gif*!' Churchill said. 'Now hold your horses, boy. I have shaved the truth a bit fine, maybe, but believe me I have always had your dad's interests at heart.'

'What do you mean?' Sterling demanded. 'How can you have when you kept this wireless a secret? Who have you been talking to, Eric?'

177

The big man shrugged. Taha noted that he did not seem too concerned about his predicament, as if he knew something they didn't. It worried him. So did the unaccustomed feeling of acute drowsiness that was seeping through him.

'Spill,' Sterling said.

'All right,' Churchill drawled. 'Remember the night we met at Kew? The same day you found Corrigan dead?'

'Of course I do.'

'All right. Well, after I got home, I phoned Vernon Dakin, the man who gave you my name. It was just insurance, George. I wanted to be certain you were on the up and up – the thing about the police worried me silly. Dakin vouched for you all right, but he asked me if there was any way I could keep in touch when we were out here. Well, I'd trained as a TG op in the war, and I happened to have this biscuit set that was still in working order. I suggested the idea to Dakin and he jumped at it. Had a pal who was a wireless ham, he said, and he knew a bit about wireless, too, having been in the Tanks, so we set up frequencies.'

'That's shit, Eric. A biscuit set doesn't have the range to transmit to Britain from here.'

'No, but we arranged a series of relays through Layoune, Casablanca, Tangiers and Lisbon.'

'Why the hell would Vernon go to all that trouble to keep in touch?'

'I don't know. He sounded worried – said he couldn't afford to lose you.'

'Why didn't you tell me?'

'Dakin said not to, that's all. Said you wouldn't take kindly to being treated like a schoolboy.'

Taha slumped suddenly and recovered himself. His eyelids were flickering. 'What is it?' Bes demanded.

'Just sleepy,' Taha slurred.

'It has been a tiring day,' Churchill said. 'Do you need to know any more, George?'

'I damn well do,' Sterling said. 'I don't believe a word of it.' He was amazed to hear the words come out sluggishly, as if he were drunk.

Bes was staring at him. A small grin played around Churchill's mouth. 'You look tired, George,' he said.

Sterling suddenly felt *very* tired. His limbs had gone limp and his head was swimming, just as it had done during the previous night. 'This is a farrago of lies,' he said, but found the words came out in a slur. His eyes were closing of their own accord and he fought to keep them open. The moon suddenly seemed blinding. He closed his eyes for what seemed like a second, then pushed his eyelids up physically and saw that Taha had fallen asleep on the ground next to the fire, and that Churchill had somehow taken the little hunter's rifle off him and was covering him with it. Bes looked flushed, and Sterling knew he'd missed some exchange, but could not imagine how.

'Whatever you believe, George,' Churchill said, 'it doesn't matter now. You see, I laced the tea water with a Mickey Finn when I refilled the kettle. Billy is out for the count, and you will be too any minute. I think I can take care of our little non-tea-drinker here. I've already sent my message, anyway, and there's an aircraft on its way from Layoune to pick us up right now. It will be here by first light, but you won't see it because the stuff I gave you lasts twenty-four hours, and by then we'll be back in Layoune.'

'You bastard,' Sterling slurred.

'Oh I really don't think so, George,' Churchill said in English, but only Bes the hunter was awake to hear it, and he didn't understand.

9

T HE FIRST THING STERLING HEARD WAS the sound of the
sea, and he wondered how the sea could be here in the desert.
When he opened his eyes, he was not in the desert, but in a
bedroom with sunlight streaming through an open window. The
smell and the sound of the sea came from beyond it, and he had
the impulse to get up and look out. But the bed he lay in was too
comfortable. The sheets were crisp and fresh. He was no longer
wearing his dust-caked clothes, but a clean white nightshirt. His
body had been scrubbed and his face shaved, and a proper dressing
put on his head-wound. The room was large, almost luxurious,
with Persian rugs and baroque armchairs. Eric Churchill was sitting
in one of the armchairs reading a newspaper, wearing half-moon
glasses that Sterling hadn't seen before. A bone-china tea set stood
on the table beside him. He was dressed in a white shirt and cream-
coloured slacks, his tentlike brows knitted in concentration. For a
moment, Sterling had the uncanny feeling that Sir Winston
Churchill was sitting in the room with him.

180

Sterling pushed himself up on an elbow, and found that he had a splitting headache. Churchill looked round, saw him, and put the paper down. His trusty kitbag was at his feet, Sterling saw, and he wondered if his Smith & Wesson was inside it.

'Where's Billy?' Sterling groaned

Churchill shifted an upright chair to the bottom of Sterling's double bed and sat down. 'George,' he said earnestly. 'I'm glad you're back in the land of the living. I got a bit worried that I'd overdone it with the Mickey Finn. I'm hardly an expert at this kind of stuff. How do you feel?'

Sterling scowled. 'Who did this,' he demanded, pointing to the dressing on his head. 'I mean, how did I get like this – clean and shaved?'

'I did it,' Churchill said. 'With some help from the staff. It's all right, George, I had six younger brothers and sisters, I'm used to looking after people. I explained to the people here that you'd had an accident out in the Blue and I'd had to give you a sedative. They were really helpful when they heard the story about you and Billy.'

'You lying swine, Eric . . .'

Churchill made the familiar pacifying gesture with his hands. 'It's not what you think, George,' he said. 'I'm still on your side, always have been. You're in the Hotel Majestique in Layoune, and you are signed in as a private citizen. I squared it all with the immigration people, and told them the story about how we'd found Billy – leaving out certain details, of course. Said we'd blundered across the border. You can leave when you want. Billy's asleep in the next room with a bellboy watching him, and I'll be checking on him any minute.'

'Why did you do it?' Sterling said.

'The Mickey Finn? Had to, George. I played it by ear for a bit, till I realized there was no way on earth young Billy was going to come with us – surely you realized that? It was either dope him or jump him and clobber him and, you have to admit, he's a pretty tough customer. Then we'd have had to tie him up and drag him here, and I didn't think you'd take kindly to that. Was I right?'

'Of course you were right, but I'd never have agreed to either option. Is that why you doped me too?'

'I did consider telling you I'd got the stuff with me, but I reckoned you'd put the kibosh on it, yes, and then we'd be in a quandary, so I kept quiet and just took it into my own hands. It would have been difficult to add the drug to the tea without doping you too, and I thought, anyway, it'd probably be easier without your objections.'

'It was a barbiturate, wasn't it? Barbital or phenobarbital – they're the only ones that knock you out for twenty-four hours.'

'Phenobarbital. Only, as I said, I wasn't too sure about the dose.'

'You were playing with fire, you bloody fool. You could have given us an overdose – killed us both. What about the little fellow? He didn't drink any tea. Did you shoot him or what?'

Churchill snickered. '*George*,' he said, 'what do you think I am? I just tied him up, made sure he'd have to do a short walk before he got to his weapon, and left him free with two camels and plenty of food and water when the aircraft came in.'

'You're a bastard, Eric.'

Churchill's face crumpled. 'I was hoping you'd see it my way, George. I'm a professional, and I don't jump in with my eyes shut. All right, I kept the wireless quiet. But it got us here, so it did its job. When we were in Casablanca I made arrangements with a charter air company here in Layoune to pick us up on my signal. They arrived at first light yesterday morning in a Fokker Friendship. While you and the boy were out cold, I got busy laying out a do-it-yourself landing strip. I thought I'd done pretty well, actually.'

Sterling sneered. '*Pretty well*? Eric, if it was so easy to get an aircraft to pick us up, why the hell did we risk our lives crossing the damned Zrouft by camel? And what about Hamdu and the others? You are damned well responsible for what happened to them!'

Churchill removed his glasses and looked at Sterling with compassion, as if talking to a half-wit. 'We'd never have found Billy if we'd gone in by air, you know that, not even if we'd spotted *Rose of Cimarron* which, given the way it was covered in sand, we probably wouldn't have done. As it was, we ran across him by pure and unadulterated kismet, George. The deaths of Hamdu and the other boys were kismet, too. There was nothing I could have done to prevent it.'

'*Christ*,' Sterling said.

'Of course, when we started I didn't know any more than you did that Billy was alive, but I did consider what he might be like if he was, after seven years in the Blue. You see, I know what it's like – the pressure to adapt to a new culture. Billy may have spent fourteen years in our world, but then he had a traumatic shock – dropped suddenly into a totally different world from on high just at the time when he was in transit from boyhood to manhood. It must have been like going through adolescence on the moon. He's had an experience so powerful that we can't even begin to imagine it. It's as if he was living in another dimension. You've seen the way he refuses even to try to speak English although he obviously understands it? He's no longer Billy, George. He's someone else. Living with the nomads for seven years has penetrated his soul – he'll never be the same again. Sorry to say it, George, but, despite your scientific training, I don't think you anticipated that.'

'Maybe, but you still had no right to dope us.'

'Without it the mission would have been a failure.'

183

'The mission? Jesus Christ, Eric. Billy was just getting used to the idea that he had a father after seven years. He had a right to decide what he wanted, and so do I. You can't just go around slipping people barbiturates and carting them off without even consulting them.'

Churchill looked peeved, as if he'd expected gratitude. 'It got the job done,' he said. 'And that's what counts.'

Sterling shook his head despairingly. 'If you really think that's all that counts, you're a bigger fool than I thought.

Churchill looked away, apparently stung. 'Have it your own way,' he growled sullenly. 'I expected a little resistance, but I thought you'd see the light when I presented it as a *fait accompli*. If I hadn't done it, we'd all of us be out there in the Blue. We'd have been lucky to get out alive.'

'Lucky to be . . .' Sterling stopped suddenly, and threw the bedclothes back. He stood up, facing Churchill. Apart from the headache, he felt surprisingly sound. He squared up to the big man menacingly. Churchill was taken aback. Sterling seemed suddenly dominating and powerful, just as he had that day in the desert when he had gone back for Hamdu.

'You damn hypocrite, Eric,' he spat. 'Billy . . . Taha . . . said those bandits had been looking for us. How did they know we were coming, eh? It can only have been that bloody wireless of yours. You were reporting our movements all the way, and whoever you were reporting to sent a reception committee. Who was it, Eric?'

Churchill scratched his nose with a long finger. He glanced up at Sterling, and for a split second Sterling saw something wary and dangerous in the face. He recalled vividly how Hamdu had been convinced that Churchill had tried to kill him at Ain Effet, and how Billy had said he didn't trust the man. Then it was gone, and the pugnacious but benevolent bulldog face was back.

'As far as I know, I was transmitting messages to Vernon Dakin,' he said, 'who was worried sick that his brilliant partner was going to leave his bleached bones in the desert. You may know better, but I don't believe he's bosom pals with any Arab bandits. Look, I've risked my life more than once on this trip, George. I did the job you asked me to do, even if I didn't do it the way you wanted, but actually right now I don't give a damn. There's a ship leaving for Spain in a few days. I'm going to be on it. Why don't you just take Billy home before he gets hurt any more?'

Churchill's indignation didn't convince Sterling. The man was an actor and poseur from start to finish, with his Churchillian speeches and his 'minor branch of the family' routine. He'd started off as a circus performer and he hadn't changed, Sterling thought. It was just one act after another.

'I wasn't born yesterday, Eric,' Sterling said. 'It's more than just Billy. First Corrigan wants to come out here with me, then he's murdered, possibly by the mafia, possibly in revenge for having cheated them years ago when he was in Casablanca. *Rose of Cimarron* wasn't flying stores for the French military and she wasn't going to Zagora. You say she might have been going to pick something up rather than deliver it – something Craven had dumped in the desert previously. You admit you knew Craven a little better than the "I've heard the name" you told me originally. And by great coincidence, you yourself happen to have been in Casablanca in nineteen forty-five. Meanwhile, we almost get our throats cut by bandits who apparently knew we were on our way, and to cap it all you are sending reports out secretly by wireless. Eric, I may not be a military type nor Sherlock bloody Holmes, but I'm not a moron. There's something more to this than Billy, and there has been from the start. What is it?'

The big man shrugged his round shoulders massively. 'Blowed

185

if I know, George,' he said. 'You're the scientist. You compute the probabilities.'

'All right,' Sterling said. 'This is connected in some way with those vehicles that were driven into the quicksands in forty-five. And the blond chap Taha said they pulled out of the well. You didn't seem to want to talk about it, but the man had a scar like the one I saw on the so-called "police inspector" at Corrigan's flat.'

Churchill did a raspberry. 'Pooh,' he chuckled. 'Scars are legion, George. It was only hearsay, anyway, and it might not even be accurate.'

'It's too much of a coincidence.'

'You were tired, George. In the desert things seem different. You forget there's a big world beyond the sand. Everything starts getting connected with everything else.'

'You know more than you've let on, I'm sure about that.'

Churchill paused. 'All right,' he said. 'I do know a bit more – not much, mind. I told you that when I was in Casablanca in forty-five I was investigating links between the mafia and the Allied military. Well, I *heard* things about Craven and the shower he worked for, Atlantic Air Transport. They were as bent as they come, and I'd swear Craven was in it up to the hilt. I could never prove it, but my guess was that they were siphoning off contraband – maybe guns or drugs – from the mafia and storing them out in the Blue. I got so far in my investigations, then I was warned off by my brigadier. When I objected, I was handed my bowler hat. That made me very peeved– you see I was a substantive captain, and could have gone higher. I was good at my job. I knew I'd never have got in among the old boys' club if it hadn't been for the war, but I was in and I wanted to stay in afterwards. Could have been a brig by now. But they gave me the boot and I've never forgiven them. When you offered me the chance to come out here again, I admit I was wary at first. But then I saw that I might get a chance to get my own back – at least morally.'

'On whom?'

'I don't know. Only, put it like this: there was somebody quite well up in the British military establishment who didn't want anyone breathing down Craven's neck. He was the blue-eyed boy, the celebrated war hero. It was probably a crazy idea, but I thought I could kill two birds with one stone. Only I'm none the wiser, really. At least you have Billy back, and I reckon you ought to get him out of here as quickly as you can . . . What's that, for God's sake . . . ?'

The furious battering on the door made them both start, and a moment later the door crashed open and a dark-haired man stormed into the room. He was followed by another in a bellhop uniform, who was vainly trying to restrain him. For a moment Sterling didn't recognize the man. His hair had been cut coarsely, and he was dressed in clothes that, though new, were far too big, and flapped scarecrow-like on his arms and legs. The man was barefooted and his hands and feet were gnarled and calloused by years of contact with the earth. He looked forlorn and ridiculous in the clothes, his eyes rolling so wildly that for a moment Sterling took him for an escaped lunatic. Then his face fell, as he realized it was Taha.

The bellhop was a robust black man and he had his arms around Taha's waist now. The youth wrenched his hands back, twisting the fingers until the man howled in agony. 'Take your wet slave hands off me!' he screamed in Arabic. 'How dare you touch me, son of a dog? I am of the People of the Clouds!'

The bellhop staggered back, moaning, bent double and clutching his fingers. 'This man is mad!' he shouted, eyes bulging. 'Mad!' He stepped back into the corridor outside, and

Taha slammed the door after him. He turned to face Churchill, hate written all over him, and tugged at his shorn hair. 'Pig and the son of a pig!' he spat. 'Who gave you the right to cut my hair? The hair is the mark of a man. It may not be cut.'

He advanced on Churchill and, despite the fact that the big Englishman had a foot on him and was probably twice his weight, Churchill stepped back, eyeing his kitbag.

'*Laysh inta shilta ar-ruh haqqi*?' Taha demanded. 'Why did you take my spirit? Where are my weapons? No warrior must be without his weapons, not even for a moment. Where are they?'

'I left them with the little fellow,' Churchill stammered. 'Out in the desert. You won't need them here, Billy. This is Layoune.'

'Fool,' Taha said, advancing. 'You think the Ulad al-Mizna have no enemies in Layoune? I should have left you to the Ulad Delim. I have told you that there is no Billy. Billy *was*. Taha *is*.'

Churchill bent suddenly and whipped his pistol out of his kitbag with remarkable speed, but Taha moved with the quickness of a cobra, grabbing the muzzle of the weapon and sending Churchill crashing back over the low table. It gave under his weight and the china tea service leapt into the air, hitting him in his face. The teapot and cup smashed and Churchill howled as the hot tea spilled over him. When he sat up he found himself looking down the barrel of his own weapon. He lifted his hands in a gesture of surrender and grinned sheepishly.

Sterling couldn't help himself. He rocked with laughter. 'It's what you deserve, Eric,' he said.

'You're probably right,' Churchill said, heaving himself up. 'Anyway, it's not loaded.'

Sterling shook his head at Taha. 'Please,' he said, 'put it down. I'm sorry for what has happened. It was not my plan, but maybe it's for the best. This man meant well.'

He put out his hand for the weapon. Taha blinked at him and let it drop, but did not give it back. He fumbled with the unfamiliar locking-catch and finally got it open. There were no rounds in the chamber. He gave Churchill a glance of derision and offered it back to him, handle first. 'To draw a weapon on a warrior of the Reguibat is to invite death,' he growled. 'I advise you never to try it again unless you wish to kill me.'

Churchill took the revolver, made an apologetic sound in his throat, and flapped a hand. His tanned face was bright red where the tea had scalded it. 'All right,' he said. 'I suppose that's fair.'

Sterling turned to Taha. 'Look,' he said, 'I didn't know what Eric here was going to do – he "took my spirit" too. But I am your father: you know that. I came to look for you, for me, for your grandfather who blames himself for what happened, and for your mother, who is dead now. I know it's terribly difficult for you, but please give it a try, for her sake. She loved you.'

Hearing the past tense, Taha looked shocked for a moment, and Sterling suddenly remembered he'd never got round to telling him that Margaret was dead. 'How did she die?' he asked.

Sterling sighed. He conjured Margaret up in his mind, trying to will back the warmth of her, the feel of her body. 'She was beautiful,' he said, finding the Arabic words difficult. 'But she was, well . . . she used to get depressed sometimes, and I couldn't talk to her. It was as if she'd gone into a different world and no longer knew us. Then, when I went to prison, it got worse, and of course as soon as they let me out I was sent off to France as an ambulance driver. She found it hard to cope on her own. Later, when you didn't come back, it was too much for her. She always kept your room exactly as it was, as if you were expected back any time, and kept on writing letters to you in Morocco, once a week. Arnold and I spent months – years – searching for you, but never found any trace. After a while Margaret just gave up. One day I came home to find her dead. She had taken her own life.'

'God have mercy on her,' Taha said. He opened his mouth as if to ask another question, then stopped and glanced about him like a trapped animal. He looked like a beggar in these ill-fitting clothes, Sterling thought, with his chopped-about hair and calloused feet and hands. In the desert he had looked like a king, had moved with the grace and confidence of an antelope, had seemed equal to any situation. Surrounded by these four walls he looked pathetic and out of place, ill at ease, diminished and disempowered.

Sterling glanced at Churchill. 'Would you mind leaving us for a moment?' he asked. Churchill nodded, picked up his kitbag and went out.

Taha watched him go. 'I don't trust that man,' he said.

He sat down, cross-legged on the floor, and for a moment he was Billy as a small boy again. Sterling sat in the armchair. 'He's only doing what I asked him to do,' he said in Arabic. 'Even the wireless – it was just extra insurance, and it paid off, because he was able to use it to call the aircraft that brought us here.'

'I still don't trust him.'

'All right, you don't have to. But do you trust me?'

'I don't know. I think so.'

'That's good, Taha. Now, I want you to do one thing for me, for the sake of your mother. I want you to stay with me here in the town for a week, and see if you can get used to it . . . to the things you learned as a child. If, after that, you still want to go back to the desert, then we'll have to reconsider. But promise me you'll give it a try, that you won't run away for seven days.'

Taha gave him a long, deep look. 'All right,' he said. 'I give my word. But if anyone tries to touch me. . . If that Eric tries to pull a weapon on me again, then the deal is off.'

* * *

190

When Wohrmann woke him, Von Neumann sat up shuddering. For a moment he had been back *there*, in that deep well with water up to his chest, looking up at a circle of hazy greyness, feeling dust drifting down and touching his face like ghostly fingers. The two days he'd been stuck down there had been the most terrifying of his life: he'd been constantly aware that if he fell asleep even for a few moments he would drown. He was in a hundred-foot hole in the middle of one of the most desolate places on earth, and there was no guarantee that anyone would come by and find him before he succumbed. He'd doubted that he could last a third night. It had been the stuff of nightmares – he could not believe afterwards that he'd kept his head, though he'd never been quite the same since.

Just jumping into the well in the first place had taken nerves of steel – he wouldn't have been able to do it at all without his airborne training. A hundred-foot plunge into the darkness of a shaft could easily have been fatal, but to stay in the open with all that shooting going on would have been worse, and his calculation had been correct, because he had turned out to be the *Sonnenblume* mission's sole survivor. He remembered hearing the voices on the second day, over the roar of the storm, infinitely far away, perhaps in his imagination only, then realizing that there were darker shadows at the lip of the well above him. How he had implored, begged, pleaded with them to pull him out! The Arabs had been terrified – they believed wells were inhabited by evil spirits and for a long time he'd thought they were actually going to go away and leave him.

But in the end the desert people were a practical folk, and they'd put a rope down and hauled him up using a camel. Sitting there at the wellhead, he'd felt the wind lashing him through his wet clothes, adding a new, even more surreal dimension to the scene. The father and son who'd saved him had looked like Old

191

Testament figures, their head-cloths and ragged robes flying in the wind. They had pointed their rifles at him and debated shooting him – he'd been saved only because of the Maria Teresa silver dollars he kept for emergencies, and because he spoke Arabic. The sandstorm had hidden from his view any relics of the battle with the British commandos. And when the storm had subsided after a week, and Skorzeny had picked him up in the light aircraft, all trace of the convoy had disappeared off the face of the earth. The *Sonnenblume* mission that had started off so confidently from Vichy-French Morocco had simply vanished into thin air. None of the drivers or guards was ever seen again.

He shivered again, and Worhmann stepped back, startled by the look on his face. Von Neumann saw that the wireless operator was wearing a long Arab shirt, and had a signals form in his hand. Sunlight was coming through the window of the room in a single thick shaft, suspended by dust. His nose wrinkled, remembering the smell of the storm, the accursed *irifi* that had allowed the British commandos to escape. 'What is it?' Von Neumann snapped.

'Sir,' Worhmann said, 'a signal from London. Steppenwolf is on his way. His ETA is one week.' He thrust the form at Von Neumann, who took it and read the signaller's crabbed decryption.

At last, he thought proudly. He and Otto Skorzeny would meet again, and the humiliating memory of his failure would be redeemed.

'There is another thing, sir,' the chunky Swabian added. 'An Arab runner arrived at first light. Amir and his party encountered the boy Taha Minan Nijum, but he escaped.' Wohrmann paused, expecting a cascade of vitriol that never came.

'How?' Von Neumann asked quietly.

'They don't know exactly, but apparently two Europeans were with him.'

Von Neumann smirked. 'Then he's safe. Anything else?'

'Yes,' Worhmann said. 'Amir's party found out which clan the boy's been living with and where they are located. They are proceeding there to put pressure on them, but are worried about reprisals from other Reguibat clans.'

Von Neumann stepped out of his sleeping bag, yawned and ran a hand through his blond stubble. 'Send the runner back to Amir,' he said. 'Tell him no killing. We want the boy's people as hostages. And tell him not to worry about reprisals. The Reguibat will not come to help the boy's folk: a five-hundred-strong raiding party of the Delim is already attacking them in the rear.

For Taha it was more difficult to keep his promise than Sterling could ever have imagined. Taha had grown to manhood in the wide panoramas of the desert – even his people's tents were open to the elements – and to confine himself voluntarily to living within walls was a torture. Although George's arrival had opened up the floodgates of his memory, his life in England was still dim and unreal, like a tale of the Time Before Time. Although he found he could understand English, the wrong words came out when he tried to speak it. He had to admit to himself that he no longer *wanted* to speak it – the tongue of his childhood had become foreign to him.

The bed he had woken up in felt strange and cloyingly soft, and he quickly moved his sheets to the hard floor. Sterling came to show him the use of the flush-toilet, but to Taha who had learned to squat when relieving himself, and to use stones to clean himself afterwards, it now seemed an abomination. He could not believe that good water was wasted in such a fashion. The first morning, Taha had found a way out into the garden behind the hotel, where ladies and men were sitting sedately at

193

tables under umbrellas. He squatted down in the flowerbeds to relieve himself, feeling the awkwardness and immodesty of his new clothes. He had hardly started when the ladies began to scream and point, and several waiters in dark uniforms and red sashes at their waists came sweating up to him, apparently horrified. He held them off with a stick pulled out of the hedge until Sterling arrived.

That evening he went to dinner in his ill-fitting European clothes, barefoot because no shoes would fit him after going unshod for seven years. The dining room was large and carpeted, with enormous chandeliers and bay windows overlooking the sea, its round tables with white tablecloths and accessories, set with silver cutlery and crystal glassware. Taha gazed around him in bewilderment at the tables, touched the cutlery and glasses wonderingly. So much was wasted here, he thought. These city people had so many things – objects, possessions – that they were weighed down by them. The men wore white colonial dinner jackets and bow ties, the ladies low-cut dresses: clothes that seemed tight and as uncomfortable as his own. Their faces were cold masks of arrogance that Taha sensed covered doubt and insecurity. Their bodies were water-fat and fleshy and they moved with a ponderous clumsiness. They sweated and covered themselves in sickening perfume that did not disguise their disgusting smell. They talked a great deal in loud voices, but they seemed miserably unhappy.

Though everything here was easy, he thought – water came through a tube in his room at the movement of a hand, blinding light at the touch of a button. Outside in the street he had seen the iron chariots he remembered from boyhood, but now they seemed different – ugly, noisy, smelly contraptions. Here there was food in plenty – more than anyone could eat – and no apparent threat from enemy tribes; at least, none of the men

194

carried weapons. Yet far from being contented, the people seemed grey and lifeless. Taha saw almost at once why this was – they were trapped in buildings like prisons, cut off by their machines and possessions from the spirits of the earth.

As they moved through the great dining room, Sterling and Churchill nodded and shook hands with people. Many had heard the strange story of the Englishman whose son had been lost in the desert and found after seven years. They seemed interested and shook hands with him, but Taha read amusement in their faces. Some of the ladies were the ones who had screamed at him in the garden earlier. The dark-clad waiters who strutted among the tables glanced at him with obvious derision, deliberately staring at his bare feet and unkempt hair. This made Taha seethe. Many of them, he could tell from their features, belonged to inferior tribes or were *haratin* – freed slaves whose families worked the palm groves for their warrior-masters. Outside this place, they would have paid for such expressions with their lives.

Sitting on a chair at a table was agony for Taha. His muscles had grown accustomed to sitting on the ground, and he was used to eating from a communal dish with his hand. He remembered knives, forks and spoons from his childhood, but they seemed clumsy and unnecessary. It was said in the desert that only the *Ajam* – the despised Tuareg nomads from the east – ate with utensils from their own dishes. This was not the Arab way. On that first night he sat, shifting uncomfortably on his chair, while the waiters served food from silver dishes, standing at his shoulder in a way he found threatening. He looked at the food on his plate – a mess of white flesh – and wrinkled his nose. 'What is this?' he demanded. '*Shin-hu hatha?*'

'It's very good,' Sterling said, 'try it.'

Taha took a handful of the white flesh and put it in his mouth. Then he spat it out on his plate. 'It is *fish!*' he said.

195

'It's freshly caught today,' Churchill said.

Taha stood up. 'The People of the Clouds do not eat creatures from the sea,' he shouted. 'It is forbidden!'

There was silence in the dining room as people turned enquiring faces towards him. Someone snickered. Taha threw down the useless white cloth Sterling had told him to cover his clothes with. He tore off the tight white jacket and slapped it down on the floor. Then he turned on his bare heel and marched out.

Sterling found him later, sitting on the roof under a dense carpet of stars. It was a hot night, and Taha had removed all his clothes but his trousers. Sterling sat down beside him quietly. 'What's the attraction up here?' he asked softly.

Taha pointed east with a closed fist. 'Can't you smell it?' he asked, still speaking Arabic. 'It is the wind off the desert, the free wind unfettered by walls. It blows on and on from as far away as the land of the Nile, and nothing stands in its way. It tells me that my people will be leaving their spring camp soon and moving closer to the water-sources in the inner desert.'

He looked at Sterling. 'Have you ever seen the People of the Clouds on the move? They are called the People of the Clouds because they move vast distances in search of grazing, following the rain-clouds. They move further than any other tribe. Everything they own is carried on the backs of their camels – women and children ride in litters, the warriors of the tribe ride ahead as scouts seeking out the pastures and watching for raiders. By God, it is a fine sight!' He sighed. 'Better than a thousand iron chariots.'

George took a deep breath. 'Taha,' he began. 'I came here to take you home, to the country you grew up in. Whatever you may think, you *do* belong there. I can understand that when you

196

were lost in the desert you thought you'd been abandoned, and you had no choice but to become one of the . . . Blue Men. You had to survive. But you aren't really one of them – you're English. Their lives are hard. I saw that even in the short time I was in the desert. In England we live a peaceful life. It's a place where you don't have to worry about the basics all the time – where to find food and water and shelter. You don't have to be looking over your shoulder constantly in case there are raiders about. You don't have to carry weapons. There, every child can read and write, everyone can go to hospital when they're sick.'

'You make it sound like heaven. But I remember when men came to take you away because you wouldn't fight. They locked you in a room. The other boys at school made fun of me because of it. It is just as dishonourable to be a coward there as it is among us, except that in our world no one can force you to do anything. You are free to make your own choices.'

Sterling swallowed. This was proving more difficult than he'd anticipated, especially speaking a foreign language.

'Look,' he said, lapsing into English. 'There are many problems there, I don't say there aren't – it's not heaven, but it *is* civilization. In nomad society everyone has to do exactly what their parents did. There is no innovation, no invention, no improvement – nothing new, not even a new song. It's a society living in the past. In England there is progress: things move forward and get better. Cures are found for terrible diseases; every day we find new and better ways of doing things; we can travel all over the world. You don't have to stay in your own little bit of the earth – you can see new and wonderful things, find out just how varied and fascinating the world really is. You think you are free, Taha, but really you are bound by a set of rigid codes of conduct much harsher than anything we have back home. You are hemmed in by superstitions – spirits, ghosts and nonsensical

197

beliefs about the earth and the stars. In fact, you are not free at all. You can never develop your own potential; never really fulfil yourself in such a life. You can't be anything but a herder of animals, a shepherd. You are bound to live just as men have lived for generations in the desert, a life that is nasty, brutish and short.'

He paused for breath, squinting at Taha's passive face in exasperation. 'Don't you have any happy memories of England, Billy? Don't you remember how we used to go and stay in that cottage at Woolcott, near the sea? You used to love it there. We used to play football on the lawn – you, me and mummy. We used to go swimming in the sea, even though it was so cold.'

Taha smiled. 'I remember,' he said. 'We used to dig holes in the sand. You used to say we were digging to Australia. When the sea was rough we used to watch them putting out the lifeboat. I remember the men in their funny yellow coats and hats.'

'That's it!' George said, encouraged now. 'When it rained we used to go to the cinema and watch Charlie Chaplin. How you laughed! And do you remember when we went to see *Snow White and the Seven Dwarfs*? You were so frightened when the queen turned into a witch that you hid under the seat and wouldn't come out until mummy offered you a box of popcorn!'

Taha chuckled. The cinema. It was something he hadn't thought about in years. He suddenly remembered the taste of popcorn and ice cream. He remembered riding a bicycle, playing pirates, going to the circus, rides at funfairs, hide and seek. The magic of those days came back to him so suddenly and powerfully that he gasped.

'Come back with me, Billy,' George implored him. 'You're all I have now that mum's gone. I need you.'

Taha looked at Sterling more closely and placed his hand on his father's arm. 'I know you are a good man, Father,' he said. Sterling realized suddenly that it was the first time Taha had called him that. 'I know you love me. I know you feel you are doing the right thing in bringing me here. But it is too late. I feel no desire to go back. I long only for the desert. It is the one thing that does not change.'

The following days were the greatest trial of Taha's life, but for Sterling's sake he forced himself to wear the clownish clothes, to endure the agony of shoes, to sit on chairs, to eat his food with a knife and fork. He never got used to the toilet, but grew cunning and used the garden at night when no one was there to see him. He never mentioned Belhaan or his wife and children to Sterling, but his thoughts were always with them. He was growing increasingly anxious. What was happening in the Seguiet al-Hamra? What had the Delim raiders done after he and the *afrang* had escaped? Several times the big one, Eric, had tried to talk to him about the iron bird, Corrigan, Craven, and the *Sonnenblume* map, but when he did so the light of avid interest shone in his eyes, and Taha became wary and pretended to know nothing.

During the morning, Sterling would sometimes accompany him outside, and they would walk through the streets. Taha was disgusted by what he saw, by the putrid smell of the place. Some of the people he encountered were from tribes he recognized, revealed by the way they wore their head-cloths and *dara'as*, yet these people had given up the desert life for the town, and appeared only half alive. The crowded conditions, the squalor of the town, appalled him after the cleanness of the open ergs and regs. None of the people he met, not even the Blue Men, seemed friendly or hospitable – most looked at him as though he was invisible. The worst thing of all, though, was that there were no tracks here. Out in the sands one could read the comings and goings of people like a book. Here, all was confusion. He remembered Belhaan saying that the city was 'the place where tracks ran out.'

On the evening of the sixth day, there was a reception in the hotel, to which Sterling and Churchill were invited. Sterling insisted that Taha went with them. Apart from the Spanish Colonial officials, there were high-ranking local Arabs present in clean blue robes and head-cloths. Taha longed to be able to dress like them. The reception was held in the dining room, but the tables had been pushed back so that the guests could wander about. Sterling seemed cheerful, but Taha felt more out of place than usual. At least ordinary mealtimes had a certain ritual quality that he had managed to adapt to, but this was quite another thing and Taha did not know how to comport himself. There was discordant music and people danced to it in a strangely rigid manner that was particularly ugly. Several people seemed drunk. Women giggled stupidly. Churchill tried to press a glass of wine on him, but he found the taste revolting and thrust it away.

Sterling introduced him to a Spanish official, whose name Taha had no interest in catching. He was fat, as most of them were, with a red face and grinning, pugnacious features that made Taha want to hit him. He had had too much wine and leered at the youth. 'So,' he said in Arabic, 'you are the boy who has been running round with the savages out there in the Seguiet al-Hamra, eh?'

'My people are not savages,' Taha said.

The man giggled stupidly. 'Oh, *my people* is it? Well, let me tell you, my boy, those primitives won't be running about there with their camels much longer. No, the mineral rights and mining rights have all been handed out. There's phosphate out there, a lot of it. In a few months the mining companies will be starting their operations. We can't afford to have a lot of idiots with guns taking pot shots at them. It's all been decided. The nomads will be rounded up and settled – it will be better for them – with schools, hospitals and police to see that they observe the law. It's high time it happened – you'd think we were living in the dark ages. Oh yes, things are going to change.'

'But the land belongs to God,' Taha said, stunned, thinking the man was making fun of him.

The Spaniard winked and glugged red wine. 'Not any more,' he said. 'Soon *your people* will all be living in towns like this one.'

Taha staggered backwards as if he had been struck. Seeing the expression on his face, the Spaniard began to laugh. Taha felt instinctively for his dagger, remembered it wasn't there, then turned and ran out of the room, out of the hotel and into the street.

He paused only to kick off his shoes and socks, rip off his jacket and tie and fling them into the dust. Then he ran blindly along the road that skirted the sea, not knowing where he was going, only that he had to get away from the vile atmosphere of the hotel with its hypocrisy, its elaborate and meaningless rituals, its lousy, stinking toilets.

He ran in the direction of the Arab quarter, the shantytown he had skirted once with Sterling, thinking that he might find someone from his tribe – someone who could understand his talk, a friendly face. He ran through the empty marketplace and a moment later he was in the labyrinth of the shanties. The European Quarter had been deserted, but the streets here were at least full of people – a confused mixture of slaves, Znaga and Arabs, men and women. Some of the women were unveiled and called to him, the men stared, taking him for a white man, and some pointed and jeered. '*Nasrani!* – Christian!' Children threw stones and ran away shrieking. Taha looked around him desperately for some sort of refuge, but there was none. Crowds hemmed him in on all sides, eyeing him curiously. Taha's head whirled, confused by the utter profusion of hostile faces. His senses began to swim, his ears throbbing, his heart pounding. 'Why don't you listen?' he bawled at them. 'I am Taha Minan Nijum!'

Suddenly a man stepped out of the crowd, his dark eyes fixed on Taha's. He was wearing a robe so dark it was almost purple, and an elaborate head-cloth that half shrouded his face. His eyes were deep and hooded and he had a long nose, turned sharply down at the end like a fishing-hook. He was holding a dagger in his hand.

'Taha Minan Nijum,' he repeated, 'the son of Belhaan. So, God brings you into my hands to destroy you before you destroy me!'

The crowd, thinking this was part of the game, cheered. Taha's blood ran cold. He recognized the man. It was Agayl ould Selim, who had killed Belhaan's small son, Asil, during a raid.

Taha came to his senses quickly. He was unarmed and Agayl was only a couple of paces away from him. He remembered how he and Fahal had tracked him to his cave in Jebel Zemmour, just missing him on two occasions. They had discovered from some itinerant smiths that Agayl had fled to Layoune to evade the retribution that would inevitably fall on his head, even should it be forty years in coming. By killing Taha, Agayl would be ridding himself of a sworn blood enemy.

Agayl slashed with the dagger, catching Taha on the arm. Taha gasped as the blade stung him, but moved at the same time. Agayl tried to retreat but he was too slow – he had been too long in the city, Taha thought. He grabbed the hand that held the dagger, snapped it back until Agayl squealed out, and wrenched the dagger out of it.

The crowd had begun to widen the circle around them, no longer cheering. Taha skipped a step nearer, feeling all the pent-up frustrations and hatred of the past week driving him forward as he plunged the dagger into Agayl's guts. The Delim belched blood and staggered, doubling up. Taha brought the knife out and plunged it into the yielding flesh again and again and again shrieking, 'Die you filth! You murdered my brother! Die in agony, you pig!'

He was still stabbing long after Agayl was dead, his clothes saturated with the man's blood. He let the ravaged corpse fall to the ground, looked at the silent, staring faces of the crowd and at the knife in his hand. He let it fall onto the hard, salt-caked mud. He did not hear the shouts of 'Police! Police!', nor see the crowd scatter. He did not see the four big Spanish colonial policemen closing in on him until his arms were forced behind his back, and iron shackles snapped painfully upon his wrists.

Jose Fernandez, the police commandant, was dark and handsome, his hair slicked with oil, his white uniform immaculate. He wore black, highly polished knee-length cavalry boots. He had one eye on the gilt-framed mirror as he politely offered Sterling a cigar from a rosewood box. The room was small and functional, decorated only with the mirror and a collection of framed photos of Fernandez at leisure, horse-riding and fishing.

Sterling declined the cigar. Fernandez took one with a flourish and sat down in his chair behind the bare desk. He scratched his dark moustache with it but did not light it. 'I'm sorry, Mr Sterling,' he said in adequate English. 'But the charge against this person – whom you say is your son – is very serious. He murdered a man in cold blood in the street, in front of witnesses.'

Sterling gulped. He had been stunned by the news of Taha's arrest and his crime. The youth had seemed to be readapting slowly to civilized ways again, and now he was to be snatched away from him once more, and this time to face what was for Sterling the unimaginable cruelty of capital punishment.

'He could be shot,' Fernandez said abruptly, then he seemed to regret the outburst. 'Of course,' he added, 'it depends on the Municipal Court.'

'But he's my son,' Sterling said. 'He's a British citizen.'

Fernandez frowned and put the cigar down on the desk. 'Forgive me,' he said. 'You *say* he is a British citizen, but where's the proof? What I see is a savage, a wild nomad from one of the desert tribes. He's a shade lighter of skin, but then the tribes do not all have the same features, some are lighter, some darker. You admit this person has no passport. You show me a paper purporting to be his birth certificate, but the man himself speaks no English and insists that he is Taha Minan Nijum of the Reguibat. You and your companion entered Spanish territory without visas, and are here only with the indulgence of the Immigration Authorities. You insist he is your long-lost son, and it is a touching story, but how do I know you haven't simply – how shall I put it? – *taken a fancy* to him? The English have a penchant for young Arab boys, no?'

'That's preposterous,' Sterling said, fighting to control his temper.

The commandant picked up his cigar and stuck it rakishly in his mouth. 'Perhaps,' he said. 'But even if you could prove he is your son, and British, this does not make him innocent. Spanish law is impartial.'

He beamed, struck a match and lit his cigar, then stood up with a scraping of chair-legs and a cloud of blue smoke.

Sterling stood too. 'Can I at least talk to him?' he asked.

Fernandez glanced at the mirror. 'Of course,' he said. 'But you must obtain official permission from the authorities. It will take time.'

* * *

204

At first, Taha had tried to smash his way out of the stinking cell, but the big *afrang* policemen had soon stopped that by clapping him in shackles again, and then knocking him down repeatedly with their fists. They hit him in the stomach, careful not to leave marks.

The policemen had gone, but the cell remained the same, hot as an oven in the day, with only one tiny window up in the corner of the room, too high to see through. The hotel room had been bad enough, but the cell was torment to one used to the freedom of the desert. Taha had heard the stories of desert men who'd been locked up by the Christians, pining to death. Only his vague memories of another life prevented him from going insane. His childhood had been like this, he remembered, stuck in a small room in that place, that school, shut up in the dark when he had committed some petty breach of school rules. To Taha, all his life before the Blue Men had found him seemed now to have been a dark prison cell like this one. And now he was back, even though all he had done was what honour demanded of him. To avenge the death of Asil's murderer had been a sacred duty, which would have been celebrated by his tribe. Instead, he was locked and shackled in this filthy place.

The jailer was a slave called Shamsu whose belly protruded from the filthy white uniform that had lost many of its brass buttons. He was surly, ashamed of his lowly origins and determined to prove his newly acquired authority by shouting and laying about with his club. At first Taha had tried to reason with him to remove the shackles, but the jailer had just grunted, and beaten smartly on the cell door with his stick. 'You will be shot like a dog,' he'd said, grinning through ravaged teeth. 'Where are your People of the Clouds now?'

On the morning of the third day, though, Shamsu disappeared and was replaced by a tall, spare man, as dark skinned and raggedly dressed as the other, but with a reserved graciousness that told Taha he belonged to the *haratin*.

As soon as they were alone, the *hartani* let himself into Taha's cell. 'I know you,' he whispered. 'At least, I have heard of you. Your father is Belhaan bin Hamed. My name is Abboud and my family tends the palms of the Ulad al-Mizna in the Seguiet al-Hamra. We are sworn to be loyal to your people, just as you are our sworn protectors. By God the Great, I am sorry to see a warrior reduced to this. Your crime was no crime according to desert law, but the Christians think differently. I cannot set you free – then I should be shot by the Christians – and I have only a short time with you.'

'Unlock my shackles,' Taha said.

'I cannot, as God is my witness. I am here only because I bribed Shamsu.'

'God will requite you a thousandfold,' Taha said. 'Unlock me. Let me out.'

Abboud glanced over his shoulder furtively. 'I cannot,' he said. 'And now you must listen, for I have terrible news for you. Your brother Fahal is here, hiding in the brush outside the town.'

'Fahal is here!' Taha exclaimed. 'But how did he find me?'

'Listen,' Abboud said urgently. 'Your brother has a message for you. A week ago raiders of the Ulad Delim struck at the camp of your people. It was a surprise attack by night.'

'By night! That is against all— '

'Quiet!' Abboud hissed. 'I have only a short time. The fat one will return. Your camp was attacked by night and your clan were taken by surprise. One of the men was killed. All the women and children and the other men were taken prisoner by the Delim, and the camels and goats stolen. Your brother, Fahal, was the only one who escaped, because he was out with the herd at the time. He was alone and didn't know what to do. Then he met with a Nemadi, who told him you'd been taken to Layoune with some *afrang* in an iron bird. He rode straight here on his camel and made enquiries about you. He discovered that you were in jail for killing Agayl and . . .'

There were footsteps in the corridor outside and Abboud rose quickly. 'I must go,' he said. 'Your brother is hidden in the Wadi of Lizards to the north of the town . . .'

Taha held out his shackled hands to the *hartani*. 'Unlock me!' he said desperately. But Abboud was already letting himself out of the cell. 'God's peace be upon you!' he said.

A moment later Shamsu's double-chinned face was pressed through the barred part of the door. 'Good news?' he tittered.

Something in Taha exploded then. He leapt up, roaring with anger, and smashed at the door with his manacled hands. The smile was wiped off the slave's face and he backed away. Taha hurled himself at the door, roaring like a beast, clashing the irons against it again and again and again, until his wrists and arms ran with blood.

When Sterling was shown in, Taha was sitting ashen-faced, staring at the wall. He was exhausted, his manacled hands hanging limply, streaked with blood. He turned to look at Sterling as he entered, his eyes blank and lifeless.

'Why?' Sterling asked.

Taha looked away. 'You brought me here against my will,' he said, his voice distant, strained to near breaking point. 'You asked me to try your way of life, and I did so and it is not a way of life. It is death in life – just one prison after another. I spent much of my life before the desert in such a prison as this – at least that is how it seems to me now. I was lost in the desert and you did not come for me. Belhaan found me and became my father, and his family became my family. Now I am here and your people have locked me up again for an act that was entirely honourable, while my wife and sons, and my father and cousins lie in the hands of Delim raiders. Better that I died in their defence than rotting here.'

Sterling gasped. He tried to speak but words would not form. He felt himself flush, and suddenly tears were streaming down his face. 'My God,' he whispered, 'what the hell have I done? I just didn't know . . . I didn't know you had a wife and children. It . . . never even occurred to me. You never told me . . .'

He took a deep breath, and wiped tears off his face with a hand. 'I didn't know,' he said again. 'I told myself you couldn't *really* want to stay with those people. I thought you were a kind of prisoner. I never guessed . . . I've been stupid. Selfish. Even when you were small and I could have spent more time with you, I just sent you off to that awful school. Then you vanished and it was too late. You see, I wanted to make up for the way things were before, but I've been lying to myself. You can never go back, and you don't get a second chance. Children grow up and become strangers . . . you have to love them for what they are.'

He put his arms round Taha.

'Father,' the youth whispered. 'Get me out.'

It was dark when Churchill pulled up in the yard of the hotel in the newly acquired Jeep. The quays reeked of algae and rotten fish, but there was a dry breeze rasping out of the desert that seemed to sterilize the place.

Sterling was waiting for Churchill when he arrived. The big man made his bulldog face. 'What do you think?' he bubbled. 'Cost a packet, but it's your money after all, and I'm going to enjoy driving back through Morocco with you and Taha. For me it'll be just like old times.'

He jumped out, and pointed to the rows of jerry cans strapped in the back. 'Enough petrol there to get us to Casablanca,' he said. 'It's got everything: four spares, water, an awning for the sun. It's ex-military – it's even got weapons-brackets on the bar in the back. I managed to get some compo rations off the army as you suggested and . . .' He picked up an elongated leather case and held it up. 'Maybe you won't approve. This is my own addition – a hunting rifle. Taha would like to eat fresh meat. Got plenty of ammunition, too.'

He caught sight of Sterling's grim face and stopped suddenly. 'When does he get out of jail?' he enquired.

'When we get him out,' Sterling said.

'What?'

Sterling glanced around him. 'Get in the Jeep, Eric,' he said. Churchill clambered back in and Sterling got in on the other side. 'Drive,' Sterling said.

Churchill had the 'officially nonplussed' look on his face that Sterling knew well and no longer trusted. 'Where to?' Churchill said. 'What's all this about? I thought they were going to let Taha out with a slap on the wrists and we were all going to drive home together. Have a bit of a safari.'

'That's what I wanted you to think,' Sterling said. 'But I don't believe you really swallowed it, Eric. Anyway, you've been devious with me, and now it's my turn. We aren't going to drive back through Morocco. We're taking Taha back to the desert. His people have been kidnapped by raiders, and we're going to help him rescue them. After we've broken him out of jail, that is.'

Churchill's face dropped theatrically. 'You're off your rocker!' he said.

'No I'm not,' Sterling said. 'This is the first sane thing I've done for years. I had the chance to make Billy happy when he was a kid, but I fluffed it every step of the way. I'm not going to do that again. Not even if it means breaking laws. Not even if it means getting myself killed.'

Churchill stopped the Jeep on the quayside, where the lamp-light from the buildings threw long blocks of light on the rippling sea. He turned to Sterling, and suddenly his manner changed. The wary, calculating Churchill that Sterling had glimpsed the day after their arrival was looking at him in the dim light, out of the same face.

'That's fighting talk, George,' he said. 'Sure you can take the consequences?'

'I'm determined to get Taha's people back. He has a wife and children, Eric. My grandsons.'

'Jesus. He never breathed a word about that.'

'I know. Now, the question is, are you with me? Or do I have to do it on my own?'

Churchill laughed, and this time it was a genuine laugh, not one of his hail-fellow-well-met ingratiating chuckles. 'If we break Taha out of jail,' he said, 'what's to stop the Spanish air force sending an aircraft out after us?'

'Nothing,' Sterling said, 'except that this afternoon I had a word with the chief mechanic at the airfield and made a very substantial contribution to his family's welfare. He predicted that all local planes would be grounded for three days.'

Churchill's surprised look was patently authentic this time. 'Good God!' he exclaimed. 'You've certainly got it all worked out.'

'I had a good teacher,' Sterling said. 'So. Are you in or out?'

Churchill took a deep breath. 'All right, George,' he said. 'I may as well see it through to the end.'

The local lock-up stood on the quayside, a primitive building of white adobe, without even a fence or a guard. Sterling supposed that they didn't have many jailbreaks here, or many prisoners, for that matter. The place was a good hundred yards from the next house, so Churchill simply drove up and parked the Jeep outside.

'Now what is our strategy going to be?' he asked Sterling.

Sterling scratched his head. 'I reckon we'll just go up and knock on the door.'

Shamsu was surprised and annoyed when the Englishman appeared at the door asking to see Taha. Who did he think he was? He, Shamsu, was in charge here. 'Where is your permission?' he demanded insolently, holding the door open a crack. 'Visitors are not allowed at night.'

Suddenly the door was pushed open violently with a force that sent Shamsu tottering. When he looked up, there was a man he hadn't seen before, a bear-like *afrangi* with a ferocious face, pointing a pistol at him. 'This is our permission,' the *afrangi* croaked. 'Unlock the cell of the prisoner Taha. Unlock his shackles, or you will be meeting your maker sooner than you counted on.'

The bear-like man looked serious and quite capable of carrying out the threat. Shamsu began to tremble. 'B-but I don't have the keys of his shackles,' he stammered.

'No?' the man said. He eased his big frame into the office and the smaller one shut the door. 'Then I don't need you, do I?'

He clicked the safety catch with a giant thumb. Shamsu's eyes started out of his head. 'No!' he whimpered. 'I have the keys! Don't shoot!'

He led the big man to the cell and unlocked it. Taha recognized Churchill and stood up, backing away warily, holding up his shackled hands as his only weapon. 'What do you want?' he demanded.

'Don't worry, son,' Churchill said. 'I'm on your side. I always have been.'

211

He made Shamsu unlock the shackles. Taha's wrists were bloody and the skin chafed through. 'Now,' Churchill said to the fat man, '*you* put them on.'

Shamsu began to whimper and plead, but Churchill poked him with the revolver. 'Put them on,' he said. 'Or I'll put a bullet right through that fat gut of yours.'

Shamsu clapped the irons on his own fat wrists, crying like a baby. Churchill locked them, then drew a long piece of cotton material out of the pocket of his smock and tied it firmly round the jailer's face. 'That ought to shut you up,' he commented. He nodded at Taha who was standing back, rubbing his arms. 'Come on,' he said, 'your dad's out there. Let's go.'

Sterling was tempted to hug Taha again when he appeared, but restrained himself. Churchill closed the cell door, locked it, and pocketed the keys. 'They'll have a hard time finding these where I'm going to drop them,' he grinned.

Outside, the night was cool and quiet, pervaded by the soothing rhythm of the sea. There were pinpoints of light from the other buildings along the quay, but there was no one about. Churchill jumped into the Jeep and Sterling pressed Taha into the passenger seat, taking up his position with the petrol and water in the back. Churchill gunned the engine. 'I'm sorry,' Sterling told Taha. 'This time it's the iron chariot or nothing.'

Churchill changed to second and the engine burst into life, burning rubber along the metalled road, heading north. 'I hope you know your way back to your camp,' he said.

'No,' Taha said. 'But my brother does. He's hiding in the Wadi of Lizards, just north of the town.'

10

TAHA AND FAHAL WERE SO DELIGHTED to see each other that they remained locked in each other's arms for several minutes. Taha broke the embrace only to examine his brother's injured arm, which was still strapped up but on the mend, thanks to Taha's splint and Belhaan's ministrations. 'I can just about hold my camel's head-rope,' Fahal explained. 'But I can't fire a rifle.'

He showed Taha the heavy pistol that their father had given him, and Taha made a grunt of approval when he saw it was a Colt .45 revolver. 'If you hit someone with that, they don't get up,' he commented.

It took him a long time, though, to persuade Fahal to leave his camel and join them in the Jeep, and the delay made Churchill nervous. He knew the police probably wouldn't find Shamsu till morning, but he wanted to put in some miles between them and Layoune across the open desert to be on the safe side. 'What's his problem?' he growled at the brothers out of the open door. 'Let's get a move on.'

'Fahal's afraid,' Taha said. 'He's never been in an iron chariot before.'

'Get him in, for God's sake!'

Reluctantly, Fahal loosed his camel from its hobble and drove it off with a smack on the rump. He hated parting with the animal: he had reared it himself and it was like a child to him. He hoped it would reach his camp eventually – camels' homing instincts were very strong, but these days you never knew if someone would steal it or butcher it for meat, despite the Reguibat brand.

Churchill moved Taha into the back and put Fahal in the passenger seat, since he was to be their guide. He drove off fast, but soon Fahal made him stop. 'The chariot moves too fast,' he said. 'We are past the marks I am looking for before I know it. I am used to the pace of a camel.'

Churchill scratched his thick jowls. 'What about the stars?' he asked.

'I know them,' Fahal said. 'But you must drive slowly.'

Though they did not get as far as Churchill had hoped, they had made a good hundred miles across the gravel plains by the time they stopped in an area of grass-covered sandbanks, acacias and tangled tamarisks. No aircraft had come after them yet, but Churchill parked under the flat-topped spread of a white-spined acacia just in case. The first thing he did on cutting the engine was to hurl the lock-up keys as far into the desert as he could. 'I hope they've got spares!' he said.

Churchill and Sterling shifted jerry cans of water and cartons of provisions from the back of the Jeep, while the brothers lit a fire quickly and efficiently. The big man gave the nomads a bag of flour and some dried meat, and opened tins of beans and sausages, slopping the contents into a mess-tin. 'You keep your Arab bread,' he told them wryly. 'I had enough of it in the Zrouft to last me forever.'

Taha and Fahal moved away and made a second fire in a sandy patch. Taha mixed flour and water in a bowl and began to knead the dough rhythmically, while Fahal made tea. As they worked, sitting shoulder to shoulder, relaxing, happy to be in each other's company, Fahal described how he had been herding his camels a day's journey from Lehauf, and had returned one morning to find that the camp had gone. 'Vanished,' he said. 'Tents, water-skins, everything. Then I heard whimpering, and I found Auwra lying by his two hunting dogs – what was left of them. You remember how he loved those animals? Their heads had been cut clean off by the Delim. Auwra was barely alive.'

The Delim had fallen on the camp by night, a thing unheard-of in nomad tradition. They were many – more than before – perhaps forty or fifty, and all with the new rifles. The clan had been taken by surprise. Old Saqr Tayaar had grabbed a club and knocked five or six of them down before they felled him. Auwra himself had set his dogs on the raiders. They hadn't expected this, and at first the dogs had scared them, but then they had taken courage from their numbers and killed them. Auwra had resisted, and they had shot him through the chest. The strangest thing of all, though, was that instead of just stealing the camels and goats, they had disarmed the men and forced everyone to strike camp. Taking prisoner an entire clan was something new.

'Our father believed the Delim had sold themselves to the devil,' Fahal said. 'But by God, it's a human devil. Whoever gave the Delim those rifles is behind this.'

Taha paused in his kneading and considered it. 'Between us, with God's help, we killed or wounded eight Delim on the Ghayda,' he said. 'Then there are the two or three we shot the time you were hit. That's a lot for a raiding party to lose. It would have been perfectly understandable if the Delim had wanted to take revenge. But capturing a whole clan like this is

215

very strange. You're right, Brother, it's as if they were being instructed by someone else – someone ignorant of our ways.'

Fahal yanked the kettle off the fire with his good hand. 'Auwra said they asked after your family,' he said. 'That is, Father, Rauda and your boys.'

Taha leapt to his feet. 'God's curse on the Delim!' he bawled. 'I swear I shan't rest until I have killed them all!'

Churchill and Sterling, surprised by the outburst, were staring at him in alarm. Fahal banged on his leg. 'Calm down, Brother,' he said gently. 'I found Rauda's tracks among the rest, and those of the boys, and Father's. They showed no sign of having been harmed.'

Taha squatted down again, picked up the bowl and the dough and began kneading furiously.

After a few more minutes he took out a clean cotton cloth and tipped the dough out on it, then began to shape it into a flat, oval loaf. With his good hand, Fahal added twigs to the fire to make it hotter for baking.

He rocked back into a cross-legged position, and told Taha how he had left his milch camels with some Znaga. 'I was returning to Lehauf to pick up the tracks of our people again,' he said, 'when I met a hunter of the Nemadi who had your camel with him, and a stolen Delim camel. His name was Bes. He sat with me for a while, and told me about the *lemha*, about what had happened on the Ghayda, about the two *afrang*, and about how the big one had taken your spirit, and tied him up. He was furious about that. He said that an iron bird had come to take you away, but that he heard the big Christian mention Layoune. He was sure you'd been taken there. The news gave me hope, though, because I knew that I couldn't do much alone, especially with my arm as it is. I decided to go to Layoune and find you. After all, doesn't the old proverb say: "two can do together what is impossible for one"?'

216

Taha nodded, breaking the burning twigs down to embers with a heavy stick.

'So Auwra died peacefully?' he asked.

'He'd lost too much blood,' Fahal said. 'He became quiet, and by sunset he was dead.'

'God have mercy upon him. We shall take his price.'

'By God, we will. But will these Christians help?'

'I think so. The shorter one – he is my father. I mean my *afrangi* father, the one I had before I became one of us.'

'God works in strange ways.'

'Amen. He is a good man, but he does not understand anything. The other man, the big one, is a friend of his. My father does not carry arms, but the big man is a fighter whom my father hired to help him. I do not trust him, but I think he will help us for his own reasons, or for money.'

'Bes said he knocked you out with some kind of medicine.'

'That is so. I cannot understand him. He is a shape-shifter who wears different masks.'

Fahal sucked in breath. 'That is the worst kind of man,' he said.

The wood had burned to glowing embers now. Taha raked them aside with a stick and scooped a shallow hole in the sand. He placed the raw dough carefully in the hole, then drew a thin layer of sand over it, followed by the hot embers.

While the bread was baking, Fahal brought Taha his spare *dara'a* and head-cloth. Taha put them on gratefully, and threw his European clothes into the fire. Churchill had already offered to treat his chafed and bloody wrists with antiseptic powder, but Taha preferred the fish-oil ointment his brother kept.

As Taha swept back the burned-out embers and flipped the hot, hard-baked loaf out of the sand, Churchill and Sterling joined them, eating beans and sausages out of mess-tins. Taha borrowed

217

Fahal's dagger and scraped the excess sand and soot from the loaf. Sterling had always marvelled at the accident of chemistry that somehow prevented the sand and dust from mixing with the wet dough. Finally, Taha slapped the loaf with his hand, set it back on the clean cloth, and began to carve it up with the dagger. The delicious smell of freshly baked bread touched their nostrils. Taha offered pieces to Churchill and Sterling, who declined. Then he and his brother began to eat ravenously, a quarter of a loaf in one hand and a glass of tea in the other. 'By God!' Taha commented through a mouthful. 'This is good. The first proper food I've had for more than a week!'

After they had finished, Churchill hefted a long canvas bag over to their fire and opened it. Taha's jaw fell slack with amazement as the big *afrangi* took out two brand-new Garand M1 rifles, a Bren gun, and a bunch of Mills grenades. He handed an M1 to each of them. 'Presents,' he growled. 'I thought since we're taking on that Delim mob, we may as well even the odds a bit.'

The brothers took the weapons and examined them with reverence.

'These are really for us?' Fahal asked.

'All yours,' Churchill said, setting his chiselled chin. 'Of course they're from George here, really. He paid for them, only he didn't know about it.'

Sterling was looking on in bemusement. 'When did you get these, Eric?' he demanded.

Churchill shrugged. 'Someone was selling them on the black market in Layoune yesterday and I couldn't pass up the chance. Got plenty of ammo too.'

Sterling cocked his head to one side. 'But yesterday we didn't know anything about this,' he said suspiciously.

Churchill smiled to himself and ran his big hands over the

Bren in the moonlight, fiddling with sights and settings. 'I thought they might come in handy,' he said. 'I never really thought you'd take Taha to England. I had a feeling we'd end up taking him back to the desert.'

Sterling shook his head. 'You never cease to amaze me, Eric,' he said.

'No?' Churchill said seriously. 'Thing is, George, I'm always one jump ahead of you. Learned that in the spy-catching business.'

He lifted the Bren as if it was a toy, snapping its bipod down. 'Best light machine gun ever made,' he said. 'Fires five hundred and twenty rounds a minute, effective range six hundred yards.' He cocked and released the mechanism, clicked on a curved magazine, stood the weapon on its bipod and surveyed it proudly, as if it were a baby he'd just set on its feet. 'That's for me,' he said. 'Used to be a marksman with it.'

Fahal was still staring at his new weapon. 'By God!' he said. 'That's the best present anyone ever gave me. I just wish I had two sound hands so that I could fire it.'

'All in good time,' Churchill said.

Taha had thrown away an M1 he'd taken from the Delim guard on the Ghaydat al-Jahoucha for lack of ammunition, but he remembered how good it had felt to fire, and the feeling of power when the new cartridge was thrust into the chamber without any effort on the firer's part. His eyes lit up as he realized the rifle was really his, and he began to tinker with it, opening and closing the breech.

'But why did you get two Garands?' Sterling asked. 'You didn't even know Fahal would be joining us?'

Churchill blinked at him 'The second one was originally for you, of course, but you can take the Remington hunting rifle instead. That'll be better for you. It's a sniper job – five shots, bolt action, small calibre.'

Sterling grinned sheepishly. 'You're joking,' he said. 'Anyway, I wouldn't even know which end to point at the enemy.'

The big man shrugged and rubbed grease off his hands. 'Never too late to learn,' he said. 'Maybe you'll change your mind.'

'I've managed without up to now.'

Churchill winked and nodded towards Taha. 'He's got a wife and sons, you said? Mass war's one thing, but when it comes to your own kids it's another. In the end, a man has to look after his own.'

Churchill sat down opposite Taha, and poked up the fire with a stick. 'I know you don't trust me,' he said. 'And you have good reason. I knocked you out with that medicine, but only so we wouldn't have to fight each other. I did it with the best of intentions, you have to believe that.'

Taha glanced at him sceptically. 'All right,' Churchill said. 'I understand how you feel.' He looked around, scanning the faces of both Sterling and Fahal. 'Unless I am very much mistaken, we are all going to come across some very strange things in the next few days. All I want you to remember is this: whatever happens, whatever I say or do, I'm really on your side.'

Taha watched firelight flickering across the big face. For a moment he remained motionless with the new rifle clasped across his knees.

'Now,' Churchill went on, 'I think it's time you told us all you know about Craven and Corrigan.'

Taha cocked the unloaded Garand with a furious action, and squeezed the trigger so that the working parts crashed forwards.

Churchill winced. 'You don't want to do that too often,' he said. 'Wrecks the springs. Let it go forward under pressure. Hold the cocking handle and squeeze.'

Taha studied him carefully, wondering if the weapon was a simple bribe – paid for by someone else's money. Churchill was showing a different face now, but was it his real face, or just another mask? He thought about it for a while, watching the flicker of the flames in the hearth.

'Among my people,' he said, 'possessions are nothing. Honour is everything. If a man does not keep his word, he is nothing. Would you agree?'

Churchill brought out the stump of his cigar and stuck it in his mouth unlit. 'A man must be loyal to his beliefs and commitments, yes,' he said, nodding.

'Very well,' Taha said. 'I want you to swear now in front of the others, by everything you hold dear, that you will help me to free my people, even at the risk of your own life.'

Churchill was suddenly still. He removed the cigar stump from his mouth and scratched his ear with it. 'I'm not much on God and religion,' he said, 'but I believe in my country. I am its adopted son as you are of yours, but I'm ready to die for it if I have to. I swear now, in the name of the British Empire – what's left of it – that I will help you to free your family, whatever the cost may be.'

For a moment Sterling thought he was going to tilt into the 'fight on the beaches' speech, but he didn't.

'God is your witness,' Taha said. 'And if you break your word you can never hold up your head again. Even if everyone here is dead, your name will be cursed throughout this country, wherever one tribesman remains alive.'

Churchill nodded gravely. 'Yes,' he said.

Taha heaved a long sigh. 'All right,' he said. 'Keith Craven was a liar and a traitor. The word in our language is *bowqaa*. I met him at the place of iron birds in Casablanca one day and he asked me if I'd like to go on a trip to Zagora. I said I'd have to ask grandfather, but he told me he'd already spoken to him, and that it was all right. It was a lie. The iron bird did not fly to

221

Zagora, but into the desert. Then something went wrong with the navigation instruments. I don't know what it was, but the iron bird began to lose height, and Craven panicked. He jumped out, leaving me behind with Corrigan. It was Corrigan who saved me by pushing me out – I was afraid, and he punched me to stop me screaming. I fell over and my watch was ripped off.

'It was night when I landed, but when it got light I found Craven's body hanging from a rock. He was dead. I picked up his map-case, thinking it might help me, and fled. I spent the next day and night hiding in the iron bird. That night, Corrigan arrived at the aircraft, but he made no attempt to find me. Instead he found Craven's body, cut it down and buried it in a shallow dune. In the morning I came out and found the body was gone. I ran back to the iron bird, frightened, but Belhaan had arrived. He took pity on me, knowing I would not survive in the desert alone, and he carried me home with him. That is how I became one of the Blue Men.'

Sterling felt tears in his eyes and fought them back, overwhelmed by his admiration for Taha's fortitude, and by his sorrow for the missing years of Taha's youth that could never be retrieved.

'I don't get it,' Churchill said, chewing on his cigar. 'Your father told me Corrigan's story. He reckoned he arrived next morning and found you'd already been kidnapped.'

'That's another lie, by God,' Taha said. 'At first light I found Corrigan's barefoot tracks in the sand near the iron bird. I didn't know they were his at the time, of course, but he must have come in the night, because I was woken by a noise while it was still dark. He must have known I was there, at least by the time it got light – he would have seen my tracks. But he didn't call my name or try to find me.'

'But how do you know all this?'

'Later, Belhaan, my father, told me he'd seen the strange tracks and was certain they belonged to an *afrangi*. Since Craven was dead it had to have been Corrigan. My father returned to the wreck many days later, found Craven's body where it had been hastily buried, and hung it from the door of the iron bird, to scare off any snoopers.'

'Damn near gave me a heart attack,' Churchill muttered.

Sterling looked mystified. 'But why the hell didn't Corrigan help you?' he said. 'I mean, he'd already saved your life. Why dump you in the desert?'

Taha remained quiet for a moment. Then he said, 'My father is one of the best trackers alive. He found evidence that Corrigan had searched Craven's body for something. It could only have been one thing – the map I took from near his body. When Corrigan pushed me out he didn't know that Craven would be killed, or that I would end up with the thing he wanted.'

Churchill leaned closer now, but his eyes were pools of shadow and Taha could not make out their expression.

'What was this map?' Churchill asked.

'It showed the whereabouts of something that had been hidden in the desert. That's what Craven wanted. That's why he came. I didn't know that at the time, but I do now.'

Churchill stuck the cigar behind his ear and leaned forward excitedly. 'What was it? What was hidden in the desert?'

Taha watched him, his face darkened by the shadow of his new head-cloth. 'Something evil,' he said.

'But you still have the map? Or you know where it is?'

Taha didn't answer. There was silence but for the low crackle of the fire. Somewhere a desert cicada started up.

Churchill sighed, realizing there was no point in insisting. He leaned back on his big haunches, pulled the stump of his cigar from behind his ear and lit it with a glowing twig from the fire.

Fahal glared at him. 'You don't want to do that too often,' he said. 'Never take a burning twig from the fire. You must find an unlit one and light it, or you will attract the evil eye.'

'Point taken,' Churchill chortled, puffing at the stump to get it going. 'But I think the evil eye's on my case already.'

He blew out a long stream of smoke with satisfaction. 'Well,' he said. 'My nose was right about Mister Ravin' Craven. DFC and bar, my pimply arse!'

He smoked contentedly, but there was still something Sterling wanted to ask. 'All right,' he said. 'If Craven was trying to find whatever it was that was hidden in the desert, why on earth would he take *you*?'

Taha sighed. 'God alone is all-knowing,' he said.

It took three days to reach the cliffs of Lehauf. They arrived there on the afternoon of the third day to find that only the jetsam of Belhaan's former camp remained: stones set out in oblongs which had marked the placement of tents, dried and broken water-skins, fragments of ruined ropes and hobbles, shards of pottery. Auwra's grave, freshly dug, lay under the rock-shelters of the cliff, but apart from that and the ancient runes and rock draw-ings, the place that had been Taha's home had reverted to wilder-ness once more.

Sterling, Churchill and the two brothers climbed out of the Jeep and began to inspect the camp-rubble silently, the sun casting their long shadows across hard-baked ground. Fahal and Taha found the swath of tracks made by people and animals as they left the camp, heading towards the south. As they crouched down to examine them, Taha said, 'Where are the other clans? Why have they not come to help?'

Fahal shook his head. 'That is the worst news,' he said. 'On my way to Layoune I met with some Znaga who told me that a big raiding party of Delim, made up of hundreds of tribesmen, has entered our territory from the south. They have attacked many camps. Every Reguibat that can be spared has ridden to fight them. Our clan has been forgotten in the excitement.'

Taha shook his head, as if refusing to believe it. 'This is war,' he said. 'War between the tribes.'

Fahal nodded. 'But there is someone else behind this. The Christians, without doubt.'

Taha considered telling Fahal what the Spanish official had said in Layoune, but decided against it. 'Listen, Brother,' he said in a low voice, keeping Churchill and Sterling in sight. 'Tell the *afrang* that they must go on a little way with you, while I pay my last respects to Auwra. As soon as you have moved on, I will dig up the *Sonnenblume* map.'

'You think that's what all this is about?'

'Did you not see how avidly the big one asked about it? Belhaan always said this would happen one day, but I didn't believe it. I could not imagine that the *afrang* would go to such lengths for gold. Now I have been back into their world, I remember. They dream of riches and possessions. They do not perceive that their lives are as a breath of wind blowing across the plains.'

'God protect us from the stoned Devil!'

'Give me your satchel.'

After the Jeep had moved off, Taha located the place where his tent had stood, found the fireplace, and dug into the ground beneath with a flat stone. The tin box was still there, and the map was still inside. He placed the box in the leather satchel Fahal had lent him, and sprinted to catch up with the others.

He found Churchill swearing in frustration under his breath with Fahal a hundred paces ahead. 'Can't we go any faster?' the big man demanded.

Taha gave him a dismissive glance. 'How can my brother track sitting in this machine?' he asked.

They continued in fits and starts, and after a couple of hours topped a rise, looking across a long brown valley – ochre gravel beds, sifts of sands, razor-back ridges, thickets of dry acacia, sedge fields, the occasional lone withered tamarisk, and on the horizon a plug-shaped hill like a giant termitarium.

Fahal and Taha, who had both been walking ahead, waited for the Jeep to approach just below the skyline. 'There they are,' Fahal said to Churchill. 'They will have spotted us already. The Delim have eyes like hawks.'

Churchill stepped out of the Jeep and took his binoculars up to the head of the ridge for a better look. Sterling and the brothers followed and crouched down next to him. Churchill scanned the distant plain in confusion. 'Where are they?' he demanded. 'I can't see them.'

Fahal pointed the clenched fist of his good hand. 'See the stump on the horizon?' he asked. 'That is Guelb Richat. See, there is a trace of smoke in the air above it? That is where our people are being held. The tracks also lead that way.'

'But how come you're so sure?' Churchill asked. 'I mean, that smoke could be from anyone?'

'No,' Fahal said. 'The Ulad al-Mizna never make fires in the Guelb. To us it is a *haram*, a place sacred to the old spirits from the Time Before Time. No animal may be killed or tree felled here, no blood spilled, or fire lit. It has to be Delim.'

Churchill focused his field glasses. 'I can see loose camels moving about under the stump,' he said. 'Look like ants from here.'

'Grazing,' Taha said. 'They are probably our camels, too.'

Churchill rolled away from the skyline and sat up. The others joined him.

'Well,' he said. 'That's our target. But we'll never get anywhere near them without being seen, at least not in daylight. It's got to be a night attack.'

'It is against our traditions to attack at night, or even by surprise,' Taha said.

'It won't make any difference anyway,' Fahal said. 'They already know we're here from the dust. And they'll hear the noise of this machine long before we get there.'

'Listen,' Churchill said. 'You want to get your folks back, right? Then let's forget tradition for once. The odds are stacked heavily against us, whichever way you look at it. I'd feel far better with a squadron of Shermans and couple of Lancasters to back us up. We'll take a compass bearing on the hill, and we'll approach after last light.'

'We should go on foot,' Taha said.

Churchill scratched his unshaven jowls. 'No,' he said. 'We'd lose any advantage we have. I mean you said they were . . . how many? Forty or more? There are only four of us: one's a noncombatant and the other – all due respect – the other's only firing on one cylinder. Without the Jeep we'll be stuffed. It gives us mobility and fire power. Is there a way into that place wide enough for the Jeep to get through?'

'Yes, there is a canyon.'

'Good. And how will the Delim fight?'

Taha slapped the stock of his weapon moodily. 'It is our way to fight in the open,' he said. 'Standing up, face to face with the enemy.'

'That's stupid,' Churchill said.

Taha looked at him sharply. 'It is not stupid,' he said. 'It is how brave men fight. It is not how many you kill that is important but your name, your honour – whether or not you show courage.'

227

Churchill stifled a snort. 'I didn't notice the Delim standing up and fighting like men when they jumped us before,' he said. 'They sneaked up on our camel-boys and shot 'em point-blank, then tried to pull the same trick on us. And didn't you do the same thing when you put the flash-powder in the fire?'

'Don't insult me!' Taha retorted angrily. 'When I threw that knife, and the powder into the fire, I was standing in full view of the enemy, with a white band round my head to distinguish myself. I walked up to free you, I did not run.'

'Sorry,' Churchill said. 'I didn't mean anything – only those fellows . . .'

Taha scowled. 'They were honourable tribesmen once, but it is true they have become dishonourable of late. That means they are nothing – a man without honour is not a man. We cannot guarantee they will fight like men, especially as we come at night.'

'We'll go in slowly with the lights off,' Churchill said. 'And if they're waiting for us we'll draw fire. As soon as we see the flashes we'll dazzle them with our full headlights and race in shooting. I'll set the Bren up on the bracket in the back – I wonder how five hundred and twenty rounds a minute will suit them? Can you drive, George?'

'I should say so,' Sterling said. 'Ex-Auxiliary Ambulance driver first class.'

'Christ, yes, I'd forgotten. Good. That frees me to handle the gun.'

'But isn't this going to be suicide?'

'Your father-in-law's lot, the LRDG, got away with it dozens of times in the war,' Churchill said. 'Used to drive into Eyetie airfields right into the centre of machine-gun nests. Amazing how people keep their heads down when faced with a fast vehicle spitting fire. And remember, we're not fighting Eyeties or Jerries.

These fellows aren't used to mechanized war. They'll have no idea what our intentions or capabilities are. We'll put them to flight, capture the camels and free the hostages.'

'I hope you know what you're talking about. They got those M1s from somewhere and they seemed to know how to use them last time.'

'If I recall it was Taha, Dwarf and Churchill eight, Delim three, in the first round.'

'Yes, but maybe they'll be shooting *at* us this time.'

'Let's eat,' Taha said. 'Then we shall be ready for the fight.'

One of Amir's men had spotted the dust cloud first, and now Von Neumann lay on a ledge of the crater, scanning the horizon with his field glasses. It was the enemy, all right, and they were equipped with a single Jeep, just as he'd been told. They had stopped just below the distant skyline.

'They'll move at last light,' he told Wohrmann, who was lying next to him. 'I estimate they will be here within two hours.'

When he'd noted their position, Von Neumann put the field glasses away and slid down the scree into the canyon. The signaller followed. Further along, on the sandy bed of the crater, the forty-five Delim were encamped with their camels, saddles and equipment laid out neatly, every six or seven men crouching around a cooking fire. A vapour of blue smoke filled the gorge.

On the far side of the crater, under the rock overhangs, Belhaan and his clan sat stoically eyeing their captors with curiosity rather than fear. The clan had been disarmed and their livestock stolen and now they were prisoners. Such conduct was unknown in the annals of desert raiding. For Belhaan's people it was the worst disaster in memory, and yet in the long run it would be far worse for the Delim. When the news of their transgressions became known, no other tribe would trade or co-operate with them and their very name would be reviled forever. They would be shunned as outcasts, spat upon even by the smiths.

Belhaan had seen the four *afrang* who had been waiting for them here in their two iron chariots, and now he knew where the Delim had acquired their new rifles. He had guessed the Delim had sold themselves to the devil, and now he had seen the devil. He also knew what it was these particular devils sought. The thing he had feared ever since Taha had come, ever since they had found the *afrang* graves, had finally come to pass. It was like a terrible *irifi*, threatening to uproot his people and draw them into its very eye. And yet Belhaan didn't reproach himself for having adopted Taha. The boy had been a real son to him, had become a man to be proud of. The rest was the work of God, who moved in opaque and mysterious ways. For now, their captors were giving them food and water, which meant they were needed alive. For the future, he would trust in God and wait and see.

Five hundred yards away, at the Delim camp, Von Neumann and Wohrmann seated themselves cross-legged at the hearth next to Reuth, Van Neumann's second signaller, and Franz, his driver, both of them ex-Waffen SS. Seated across the fire from them, Amir doled out glasses of tea.

'It is almost time,' Von Neumann said to Amir. 'After we have eaten, your men must get into position.'

Amir made a gesture of impatience. 'The enemy are so few,' he said. 'Why do we need to hide from them?'

Von Neumann smiled indulgently. 'They were few on the Ghaydat al-Jahoucha,' he said. 'But still they managed to escape.'

Amir glared at him, then lit a dry twig and blew on it. He put a filled brass pipe in his mouth and lit it with the spill. 'You told me not to kill them,' he snapped. 'If not for that, I would not have lost so many men, by God. This time we shall kill them all.'

'No,' Von Neumann growled more harshly than he had meant to. 'No. There will be no killing. Our intention is only to capture, not to kill. Besides, one of these men is working for us.'

Amir regarded him quizzically. 'How will we know him?' he demanded.

'He will identify himself as Wolfgang,' Von Neumann said. 'You should know him – he is one of those you captured on the Ghayda. One of those who escaped.'

Amir scowled.

'These Arabs you have captured are our hostages,' Von Neumann went on. 'Once the boy has shown us what we are looking for, and we are sure it is all there, then you can dispose of his people as you wish.'

Amir rubbed his chin. 'The name of our people is already accursed for what we have done,' he said. 'But no matter. It is too late now. All that matters is to repossess our rightful lands from the Ulad al-Mizna. As for these worthless Reguibat, the men are forfeit in revenge for those of us their people killed. The women are our prizes. I shall personally take Taha Minan Nijum's wife. She is a beautiful one. I shall enjoy taming her.'

He puffed out smoke, and at his shoulder Wohrmann coughed.

Von Neumann glanced at him. The signaller's pink face looked out of place framed by the dark head-cloth. 'Is the wireless fully operational?' Von Neumann asked.

'I will check it now, sir,' Wohrmann said, gulping down his tea. 'But there shouldn't be a problem. Steppenwolf is due to cross the Moroccan border tomorrow with the transport column.'

Von Neumann clenched his fist. 'Just one more day,' he said. 'And it will be within our grasp.'

Taha had been deafened to the night-sounds by the roar of the engine, and blinded by the headlights, the speed and the dust.

His liking for iron chariots had not improved. For the past half-hour they had been driving by moonlight only, and therefore much more slowly. Taha knew it would make no difference whatsoever to the Delim – they would be watching.

As Churchill cut the Jeep's engine a hundred paces from the canyon that led to the interior of the Guelb, Taha squatted among the sedges and tamarisk thickets trying to reorient himself, letting the night come into focus. It was clear, with a three-quarter moon and the familiar constellations twinkling above. The stars gave the sky a soft silken blueness, against which the outlines of the Guelb were starkly visible. Taha waited silently, letting his senses reach out to the night, feeling the tremors of small desert creatures, hearing the flap of an owl's wings. He was suddenly suffused by the same feeling he'd had the night he'd shot the Twisted One – the knowledge that there was something dangerous hidden beyond his vision, waiting to attack. It was as if the whole landscape was waiting. The missing part of his little finger pained him.

He picked his way casually back to the Jeep, his bare feet dislodging no pebble, making no sound. The vehicle smelt evil, a hostile, chemical smell that was out of place in the desert. 'I don't like it,' he told Churchill in a whisper. 'They must know we are here, yet I sense no movement at all.'

The big man shrugged, but his face, wan in the starlight, betrayed nervousness.

'Don't worry,' he said. 'I know they'll have an ambush set up somewhere in the canyon. They'd be stupid not to. The point is to go through them like a dose of salts.'

Churchill sprang out of the driving seat and went round to the back. Sterling got down and Churchill slapped him on the shoulder. 'You're at the wheel now, George,' he said. 'The whole thing depends on you.'

Sterling grinned in the darkness. 'So,' he said. 'No pressure at all!'

Sterling climbed into the driver's seat, adjusted it, tested the gearstick, felt for the controls with his toes and twiddled with the light switch. It was a familiar drill, remembered from scores of dark, fearful nights like this one, but with the boom of guns, the rattle of small arms, the thunder of bombs, the sirens of diving Stukas, instead of this silence.

Churchill took the Bren out of the canvas bag, clipped it onto the weapons-bracket behind the seats and cocked the mechanism with a jolt. The clack of metal on metal startled everyone.

'Christ!' Sterling said. 'If they didn't know we were here before, they do now!'

Churchill frowned and checked the Smith & Wesson in his belt holster. Fahal took up a position behind him with his Colt .45 at the ready in his good hand. Taha swung into the passenger seat next to Sterling, riding shotgun. Sterling smiled at him. *This can't be real*, he thought. *I am driving into battle with my son Billy armed to the teeth beside me, to rescue his wife and children, whom I have never seen.*

Taha cocked his rifle and the snap brought Sterling out of his thoughts.

'All right,' Churchill said from behind. 'Take her forward, George, right into the canyon. When I give the green light, put the lights full on and stick your foot right down on the accelerator. Nobody shoot till you see my tracer, all right?'

There were grunts.

'*And darkling they went,*' Churchill growled. '*Under the lonely night.*'

'Winston?' Sterling asked, reaching for the starter.

'Not quite,' Churchill said. 'Virgil.'

Sterling gunned the engine. It stalled and he started it again, then began to inch the vehicle across the flat gravel towards the canyon opening, guided left and right by the keen-eyed Taha. There was no sound but the low purr of the engine and the crunch of the tyres on gravel. The gates of the canyon loomed darkly over them, and suddenly they were within it, enclosed on two sides.

To Sterling it was like entering a great railway tunnel. If they were ambushed there would be no chance of turning round. He hoped Churchill's predictions about the way the Delim would behave were well founded.

Time seemed to run on endlessly as the Jeep crept forward at no more than ten miles an hour. Sterling felt every muscle in his body tense, and his breath came in stabs. He did not need Taha's experience to tell him something was wrong. He slowed the Jeep, his senses screaming, wondering when Churchill was going to give the order to put on the lights. At that moment there was a dull *plop* sound that was anything but threatening, and a second later a brilliant corona of light filled the canyon, scarlet and crimson rills spreading in concentric rings like the tail of a painted peacock.

'Flare!' Sterling hissed, crossing his eyes with his forearm, but too late. Taha, momentarily blinded, jumped up in his seat and opened his eyes to see a host of dark figures scuttling like demons across his vision. He raised his rifle to shoot, but found it snatched suddenly out of his arms from behind. Sterling blinked. The red flare was fading, but the Jeep was already surrounded by dozens of bobbing men in dark head-cloths, pointing their rifles at him, grabbing at him like demented beggars. He put his hands up, just as there was an ear-splitting crack from Fahal's Colt .45 behind him, and a yell of 'Wolfgang! Wolfgang!' from Churchill.

Taha lashed out at the grabbing hands with his fists, and turned

234

to get his weapon back, only to find Churchill holding it in one immense hand, wrestling Fahal's revolver from him with the other. Taha reached for the dagger that wasn't there, then hit out at Churchill's leg. The big man bellowed and kicked him, and quickly the Delim grabbed him from behind.

Two Delim swarmed up on the back of the Jeep to help Churchill subdue Fahal, and Taha heard his brother scream as one of them twisted his injured arm. Churchill made a tut-tutting sound and jumped down, pushing his way through the jabbering, truculent tribesmen, until he was face to face with Taha and Sterling. He sloped the M1 over his shoulder, and for a moment starlight played on a gallery of white teeth, bared in triumph. 'All right, boys,' he said. 'We're here.'

By the time they had been marched into the Guelb, the moon had risen fully and the night was light enough to read by. The Delim had tied their arms behind their backs, and Churchill strode before them nonchalantly, rifle slung over his shoulder, like a big-game hunter leading porters carrying his trophies. Von Neumann and Amir were sitting at the hearth and rose to greet him. 'So,' Von Neumann said, shaking hands. 'You're Wolfgang?'

'I am he,' Churchill said. 'And you are Freidrich.'

Suddenly Amir froze and grabbed the hilt of his dagger. 'You!' he hissed. 'You killed Barahim!'

With astonishing speed Churchill whipped the M1 off his shoulder, brought it to bear on the Arab and cocked it with a sharp metallic clack. A Garand weighed almost nine pounds, but in Churchill's hands it looked like a toy.

'Be careful, Sheikh,' he growled. 'This thing fires eight bullets auto-loading, as you well know. You will be dead long before you get that blade out. And by the way, I haven't forgotten that whack on the leg you gave me. I still have the scar.'

235

Amir stood poised like an acrobat, his body ready to spring, his hand still on the dagger, his hard eyes fixed on Churchill's face. 'Don't be too sure,' he said slowly. 'I have been throwing knives since I was a baby.'

The big man settled his features into a mask of contriteness. 'Look,' he said sincerely. 'I'm sorry about Barahim, but he gave me no option. He shouldn't have jumped me like that.'

Amir was unconvinced by the rhetoric. 'You must pay,' he said. 'A life for a life.'

Von Neumann put up a pale hand. 'Come now, Amir,' he said. 'Mistakes are made in the heat of battle, and you will recall I told you explicitly to capture the *afrang* alive.'

'He must pay.'

Von Neumann sighed. 'Very well,' he said. 'You have my word that you will be paid blood money in full – for all of the men you lost. But please do not touch Wolfgang, he is one of us.'

Amir spat on the ground, but he stepped back and dropped his hand from his dagger. For a moment his eyes remained fixed on Churchill, glowering, then they swung towards Taha. 'This one, too,' he said. 'He took at least three lives.'

Taha drew himself up and returned the hawkish stare haughtily. 'You dishonour the name of your tribe,' he said. 'Dog and son of a dog, chief pig of all pigs, whoreson of the great whore. You slaughtered children, you butchered unarmed Znaga, you—'

Amir grabbed Taha's hair, but Von Neumann pulled him back by the arm. As he did so the Arab struggled, and the German's head-cloth was knocked askew.

Suddenly Sterling's eyes fixed with horror on the V-shaped scar on Von Neumann's cheek. 'It's you!' he gasped. 'You were at Corrigan's flat.'

236

Von Neumann pulled off his head-cloth completely, revealing the stubble of blond hair. 'Indeed, Mr Sterling,' he said. He made a sign to the Delim, who forced the prisoners down to their knees by the fire. A large ring of armed Delim tribesmen sat down behind them. Taha stared at the flames, breathing deeply, trying to master himself, knowing that his wife and children and his father depended on him still, and that he was ready to give his life in their defence.

Amir made tea sullenly, handing the first glass to Churchill as a sort of peace offering. The big man took it and sipped. Sterling glared at him. 'You lying piece of shit,' he spat. 'You and your patriotic crap and your bloody Churchill speeches. You've been in on this from the start. You knew they weren't policemen. You've lied and cheated every step of the way.'

Churchill put the tea glass back on the tray and waved his big hand, as if accepting a tribute. 'As I have already told you, old boy, I have been a jump ahead of you all the way. Now, I have no doubt you're a brilliant chemist, George, but you're incredibly gullible – what Winston would have called "a sheep in sheep's clothing".'

'Why did you try to persuade me to take Taha home?'

Churchill squeezed the small glass as if he wanted to crush it. 'I had to reinstate my credibility after the Mickey Finn business. Had to try to persuade you that I was working in your best interest, but there was no way Taha would have left this country.'

'You gave your word,' Fahal spat.

Churchill sneered at him, and passed the glass back to Amir. 'Only a fool believes in someone's word,' he said. 'What do I care about your schoolboy "code of honour", or whether my name is cursed or not cursed? I couldn't give a monkey's. You think yourself so clever. Look at you, mister one-armed bandit: too scared even to ride in a motor car!'

Sterling stared at the German, the Arab and the Englishman, and decided that it was Churchill he despised most.

'You're a damn traitor,' he said. 'A disgrace to your country.'

Churchill hooted with laughter. 'Now that *is* funny,' he said. 'Coming from a yellow-belly like you. You know what Winston said: "Anyone can rat, but it takes a certain amount of ingenuity to re-rat."'

'It wasn't Dakin you were talking to on the wireless, was it?'

Churchill took another glass of tea and paused, studying it. 'No, it was Steppenwolf,' he said. 'The one who killed Corrigan; the one who's been controlling all this from the start. I nearly gave myself away when I was rambling in my sleep, didn't I? That's why you came up with the question about Hermann Hesse?'

'Who is Steppenwolf?'

'You will find out soon enough,' Von Neumann cut in. 'He will be here tomorrow, all being well, with the transport column.'

Sterling's eyes widened. 'Transport column? For what?'

Von Neumann and Churchill exchanged a glance, and Von Neumann nodded towards Taha. 'Ask the prodigal son,' he said. 'He's the one who caused all the trouble. If he hadn't interfered, none of this need have happened.'

Sterling looked at Taha, who was still staring into the flames. He lifted his head and his eyes suddenly caught the firelight, gleaming eerily.

Amir shivered and made a sign against the evil eye. 'The Twisted One!' he muttered. 'The spirit of the leopard is within him!'

Von Neumann seemed unperturbed by Amir's outburst. 'Your people are here in the crater,' he said. 'And they will remain unharmed as long as you give me the map now.'

Taha looked into his eyes and raised his chin.

Von Neumann chuckled. 'You don't seem to understand, boy,'

he said. 'What I am saying is that, if you don't help me, this minute, I shall order Amir to have his men slit the throats of your sons, rape your wife, and then kill her. I shall not desist until all your family is dead.'

'And if I give you the map?'

'Then they will be spared. As soon as we have got what we came for, you will be free.'

'Free for the Delim to shoot us like crows with the guns you gave them?'

Von Neumann made a gesture of hand washing. 'That is not really my concern,' he said. 'But you will at least have a sporting chance.' He studied Taha carefully. 'Eight years ago,' he said, 'I had a similar sporting chance not far from here. I was obliged to jump into a well a hundred feet deep.' He shuddered involuntarily and took a glass of tea from Amir. 'I admit that I wouldn't want to repeat it but, as you see, I survived, against all the odds. Now, when you give me the map, my ordeal will all have been worth it. Where is it?'

Taha glanced around at the stony eyes of the Delim guards, who were silently enjoying his humiliation. Churchill was watching him keenly. Sterling and Fahal were staring at the ground.

'Very well,' Taha said. 'You don't have far to look. The map is in my bag.'

Von Neumann seemed delighted. He nodded to Amir, who made a sign to two tribesmen seated behind Taha. They ripped off his leather satchel and brought it to the German. He rubbed his hands, his eyes shining in the moonlight, and was about to open it when he stopped. 'Wait!' he said. 'This might be a trick.' He glanced at Churchill. 'You open it,' he said.

Churchill grunted, took the bag and delved into it, coming up with a rusted metal box. 'Key?' he asked.

'In there,' Taha said.

Churchill rummaged once more and came up with a key that looked tiny in his large fingers. He opened the box with exaggerated care, and took out the folded piece of cardboard inside. He was about to unfold it when Von Neumann stopped him. 'No!' he said. 'I have waited a long time for this. Let me!'

Von Neumann switched on a torch and studied the map in silence while the tribesmen around them fidgeted and mumbled amongst themselves.

'Most interesting,' he said at last. 'I trust we can work out the location without too much difficulty. Tell me, boy, have you been there?'

Taha raised his head. 'My father and I found the graves marked on the map,' he said. 'Nineteen graves. *Afrang* soldiers, all shot.'

'Ah yes,' Von Neumann said. 'Those were my less fortunate colleagues.'

'Christ!' Sterling swore softly. 'What the hell is this all about?'

Von Neumann looked at him. '*Sonnenblume*,' he said. 'It was an operation to conceal a very large amount of treasure belonging to the Third Reich here in the Spanish Sahara in nineteen forty-five, when things looked bad for us. The treasure, mostly gold bullion, had been collected from various sources . . .'

'You mean from the Jews you murdered at Buchenwald and the other gas chambers,' Sterling said bitterly.

Von Neumann smiled at him indulgently. 'The treasure was trans-shipped to Spain under the aegis of the "Werewolf" organization. It was intended as part of a salvage operation that would one day enable the Reich to counterattack the Allies. Spain was neutral, but it wasn't safe because there were Allied agents everywhere, so we decided to shift it to West Africa, from where it could be flown to Brazil. This was operation *Sonnenblume*.

The treasure was shipped across the Moroccan border in ten trucks, but on the third day it was seen by a British spotter aircraft. The aircraft shouldn't have been flying in the area, which was officially neutral, but it was, and it put a squadron of British commandos on our tails. Of course they too were violating Spanish neutrality, but once they were after us there was no escape. They attacked at night under the cover of a sandstorm.

'The crews were willing to surrender, but when they went forward with white flags, the commandos simply shot them down. I couldn't understand this at the time, but I didn't wait to find out why. We had camped near a deep well, and I saw it was my only hope. I jumped in. When I was finally pulled out by Arabs, two-and-a-half days later, the sandstorm was still blowing and there was no sign of the convoy or the British. Even the bodies had gone. I stayed with the Arabs until the storm blew out, then I was picked up by my chief in a light plane. We scoured the whole area, but the convoy had vanished without trace. Of course, it slowly dawned on us what had happened. The British commandos had hidden the treasure in the desert in order to come back for it later, and somehow disposed of the trucks. They had decided to keep the treasure for themselves.'

Sterling's face was pale and drawn in the moonlight. 'And this map?' he stammered. 'Craven's map. This shows where the treasure is hidden?'

'Of course.'

'But I don't understand. What did Craven have to do with it?'

Von Neumann gave a snort of derision. 'Surely you must have realized,' he said. 'Major Craven was one of the leaders of the British commandos, and the only one to survive. We found out later he had massacred his own men in order that no one else would know the secret . . .'

241

'But wait a minute,' Sterling said. 'I heard that story, and there were *two* survivors.'

'Originally yes, but one was badly wounded in the skirmish and didn't make it back. So Craven ended the war with a secret worth millions of dollars. He was determined to come back to find it – that was undoubtedly the reason he got the job with the civilian company in Casablanca in the first place. We knew nothing about him or his crash in *Rose of Cimarron*, though, until Steppenwolf put us on to Corrigan. We tracked him for a long time, and finally caught up with him in London in February – as you well know, because you were there at the time. But another cell had been sent to deal with him and they got there before us. They didn't find his map, so they tortured the information out of him. Corrigan knew nothing about *Sonnenblume*, but Craven had let him in on the fact that they were going to retrieve something valuable from the desert, and he wanted a piece of it for himself. After *Rose* crashed, he went back to her to find Craven's map, but discovered that Taha here had taken it. That is why I say, if your son had simply left it with Craven's body, all this could have been avoided.'

Sterling stared at him, and now there was cold fury in his eyes – the look that Churchill himself had seen several times and learned to respect. 'All right,' he spat. 'I don't give a tinker's cuss for you or your shitty, pathetic "Werewolf", or your ludicrous quest for bits of gold you and your schizophrenic cretins extracted from the teeth of poor defenceless Jews. You can stuff the whole lot up your backsides – you and your British commandos, too. There's not one of you here – including you Eric, *especially* you – who's good enough to wipe my son's arse. A child dumped in the desert, fourteen years old, and he survived and became more of a man than you damned Werewolves could dream of in your wildest fantasies. Now I want someone to

242

explain what it had to do with him, and *why the hell was he on that aeroplane?'*

Von Neumann's eyes had fired up a little, but he wasn't going to get riled because of the insults of a man whose hands were tied, and who would be dead soon anyway.

'For that, my dear fellow,' he said languidly, 'you would have to ask Major Ravin' Craven. And he has been dead for seven years.'

11

THE TRIBES CALLED IT KIDJAT AN-NUHUR, the Plateau of Rivers, though no water ran there, or had done in living memory. From far off it appeared like the rotten carcass of some unimaginably huge titan from the beginning of time, its skin scorched and withered by the desert's fire, flaked and cracked into a billion facets. As Churchill halted the Jeep outside the gorge into the massif, Taha made the sign against the evil eye. The Kidja was the haunt of the most fearsome of all demons, lurking in its maze of sheer-sided channels, strange chamberlike bays and rock overhangs. In places, the walls were almost obliterated by the paintings and etchings of the Bafour, but here, as nowhere else he knew, the images were huge – creatures with men's bodies and the heads of vultures and lizards, or with heads like opaque globes, or with stalk-necks and no heads at all. The very thought of them made Taha shiver.

The Jeep Churchill was driving carried Taha, Sterling and Von Neumann. Fahal had been left in the crater. Franz drove the

244

wireless vehicle behind them, with Reuth the signaller, and the two cars were outridden by an escort of thirty armed Delim, led by Amir and mounted on magnificent camels. The prisoners were no longer tied. That morning, at first light, Von Neumann had taken Taha far enough across the floor of the Guelb crater to identify Rauda, his sons, and Belhaan, who were made to stand up and wave, but were too far away to communicate. Taha had viewed them with cold fury welling up inside him, but had said nothing. This was not the time for threats.

'Now this is how it works,' Von Neumann had told him. 'My friend Wohrmann will remain here with one wireless, and Reuth will man the other in my wireless vehicle. I shall be in contact with him every half an hour. If for any reason I fail to contact him, Wohrmann and the Delim will start killing your people. If that is fully understood, I will remove your bindings.'

It had taken most of the morning to reach the Kidja, because they had been obliged to move at the pace of the camels. All the way, Von Neumann had checked their position as accurately as possible on the one-to-one-million scale Spanish map he carried, similar to the one Sterling had brought with him for crossing the Zrouft. The map had been compiled mostly from aerial surveys and was not very accurate. On the way, they had halted at Hassi al-Abyad, a deep well in the middle of a concave plain. Von Neumann had jumped out and inspected it excitedly, leaning over the parapet and letting a pebble fall into the shaft. 'This is it,' he announced grimly. 'My prison. I spent almost three days in the bottom of this.' He shuddered.

Churchill ambled up to him, a smouldering cigar hanging from his mouth. 'So this is where it happened?' he said. 'The attack?'

Von Neumann's eyes narrowed as he tried to recall landmarks on the almost featureless plain, dotted with bare acacias, nests of egg-shaped boulders, rock outcrops like the ground-down molars of giant sheep. 'It was here,' he growled. 'The British commandos came by night under the cover of the sandstorm. We never even heard their engines.'

There was silence for a moment as Von Neumann remembered the screams of his men, the merciless thud of the British Brownings and Lewises audible even over the roar of the wind. He remembered jumping into the cab of one of the trucks, switching the headlights on, seeing that Jeep roaring out of the storm, spitting bullets. He remembered the face of the man behind the wheel, capless, a huge head like some kind of hero out of Wagner, long hair streaming wildly in the wind. A face he would never forget.

Churchill puffed the cigar and scanned the horizon. The sky was that familiar aniline blue, untainted by a single whiff of cloud. The air above the edge of the plain wobbled slightly with the heat-haze. 'Well,' Von Neumann said, 'so much for nostalgia. Let's move.'

The Kidja had not been visible from the well, but within an hour it had leapt suddenly at them out of the heat-haze. Taha had told Churchill to halt when they first sighted it, and stood up in the back of the Jeep. 'There,' he told Von Neumann. 'That is the place shown on Craven's map. Your people are buried just before the gorge.'

Now, Taha showed Von Neumann the German graves, each marked by a cairn. Von Neumann had a couple of shovels brought from his Jeep and told Sterling to dig. Churchill helped him. The sand beneath the cairn was soft and in only a few moments the shovels uncovered mummified human bones, tightly wrapped in parcels of skin and shreds of sand-coloured cloth. Churchill's powerful thrusts loosened a gaping skull with tufts of hair attached. The big man turned pale. The skull's teeth were intact and one molar on each side had been replaced by a gold filling. There was a neat bullet hole drilled in the forehead, and the back of the cranium was missing where it had been blasted out by the round's exit.

'Looks like a forty-five-calibre dum-dum,' Churchill said, swallowing hard to dissipate the nausea. 'Tommy-gun job. *Coup de grâce.*'

'Yes,' Von Neumann said, rubbing his scar. 'They left no wounded.' He turned to Taha. 'You exhumed all the corpses?' he demanded.

'No,' Taha said, 'only three. We counted the cairns and there were nineteen.'

Von Neumann took out Craven's map, which snapped slightly in the breeze. 'All right,' he said, 'we have seen enough. Fill in the grave.' He turned towards the grotesquely weathered façade of the plateau. 'Now,' he said, orienting the map. 'Craven's first clue is *Grave one, five hundred and seventy yards, three hundred and forty degrees north by northwest, Rum Flask.* That's almost a kilometre into the plateau.' He stood as near to the grave as possible and checked the prismatic compass hanging from a lanyard round his neck, adjusting the screw, aligning the phosphorescent marks, then setting a bearing of 340 degrees which directed him through the gorge. He kept the compass in his hand and called to Amir, who was standing by his camel. The Arab chief strolled up nonchalantly, his Garand slung over his shoulder, his hooded eyes flicking from Churchill to Taha and back again. 'We shall leave the camels here,' Von Neumann told him. 'Half your men will remain to guard them and the other half will come with us.'

Amir made the sign for protection against the evil eye. 'God protect us from the stoned Devil!' he exclaimed. 'That place is full of jinn.'

'Very well,' Von Neumann said. 'But this will affect the number of rifles you are given.'

Amir gulped, turned briskly and began shouting orders to his men.

Von Neumann smiled and pointed to Taha. 'You will walk in front with me,' he said. 'Mr Wolfgang, you will drive, and Mr Sterling will sit next to you. The wireless vehicle will follow, and the Delim will form an escort.' He beamed at everyone, the excitement showing in his eyes. 'Very well,' he said. 'Let's go.'

Not even Von Neumann had been expecting the tortuous labyrinth of channels and galleries that lay beyond the entrance-gorge, and he looked around at the weathered and eroded facades in something like panic. The Delim muttered superstitiously, staring wild-eyed and holding up their first and second fingers against the evil spirits that evidently abounded here. Sterling's attention was captured by the rock itself, its incredible burls, warts and nubbles suggesting an army of demons frozen in the act of bursting out of it. It was sandstone, weathered by ancient rivers and by sand and wind, but the substance of the rock had once been the bed of an ocean that had lain here in the Cretaceous era – 300 million years ago. Contemplating such an expanse of geological time made Sterling gasp, and for a moment forget the deadly earnestness of the quest they were engaged in. He was brought out of his musing by a curse from Von Neumann. 'This is a lie!' the German snarled. 'It is impossible to walk five hundred and seventy yards on this bearing. These channels are curved.'

'Maybe he didn't mean literally in a straight line,' Sterling said. 'Maybe just as near as dammit.'

Von Neumann grunted and followed the natural curve of the rock, keeping as near as possible to the bearing. After a few moments, the narrow corridor – only just wide enough to admit

248

the Jeeps – opened out into a massive sandy-floored boulevard, with the sandstone pinnacles towering as high as skyscrapers about them.

'This is it!' Von Neumann said.

They proceeded much faster now, Von Neumann whispering out the number of paces to himself, until the canyon closed in tightly again. At the base of the rock, exactly where the bottle-neck began, Taha's keen eyes spotted a small cairn with shards of pottery interspersed with the rocks. He sprang forward and Von Neumann started, pulling a Luger from beneath his Arab shirt. 'Stop right there!' he bawled.

Taha froze, holding up a fragment of brown glazed pot with a tiny neck containing a dried cork.

Von Neumann put the Luger away and took the shard. 'The rum flask,' he said. Then he looked sharply at Taha. 'You've been in here before?' he snapped. 'You found the treasure?'

Taha returned the gaze poker-faced. 'The treasure is still where Craven left it,' he said.

Suspicion slowly faded from Von Neumann's eyes as he examined the pottery. Churchill jumped down from the Jeep and joined him, picking up more brown shards. 'See!' he said, pointing to some letters stamped on one of them. 'SRD. Only the Long Range Desert boys got issued with rum in jars like this. They used to say SRD meant "Service Rum Diluted", but it probably meant something else.'

Sterling got out of the Jeep and peered at the pottery. 'Long Range Desert Group?' he said. 'Are you saying it was the LRDG who did this?'

'Who else?' Churchill said. 'Craven was an LRDG officer, even if he did fly aircraft for them.'

'But I can't believe . . .'

'What?' Churchill sneered. 'Did you think our boys were all

249

like Santa Claus? The blue-eyed boys with their ever-so-nice accents who always did the right thing? Think again, George. The Nazis weren't the only ones capable of atrocities.'

Sterling glared at Churchill angrily. 'I think I saw enough of the war to understand that,' he said. 'But Craven was a war hero.'

An expression of deep hatred wrinkled Churchill's face for a second, then it was gone.

Von Neumann let go of the shard he was holding and it struck a stone, shattering into smaller pieces. Glancing again at the instructions on the map, he took a new bearing on his compass. 'Come on!' he said. 'We are looking for "Wilkinson's Arrow" now.'

The way led them down a side-wadi that grew increasingly narrower. In places large knobs of sandstone had detached themselves from the walls and lay strewn across the sandy floor. Finally the vehicles were forced to stop. Only twenty yards further on, Von Neumann spotted a slim-bladed knife with a knurled handle stuck in a log of dried wood. He tugged it out and examined it curiously. 'Wilkinson's arrow?' he said. 'What does it mean?'

Churchill grinned. 'That's a commando knife,' he said. 'Wilkinson Sword made them – they churned out about a quarter of a million between nineteen forty-one and nineteen forty-five, but only the first five hundred had the famous cross-swords logo. Actually they were rubbish: a knife's no good if you can't cut with it, and they were made for stabbing. Someone among the great and good thought we were still fighting the Wars of the Roses.'

Von Neumann examined the weapon with approval. 'Still,' he said, 'it has something.'

He stuck it in his belt, then looked at his watch and walked back to the wireless truck. He leaned over the seat and told Reuth to tap out a message to Wohrmann back at the Guelb. He added the secret call sign that only he and Wohrmann knew, so that the wireless op would be certain it was him.

Von Neumann called Amir, who was skulking moodily behind the vehicle with his men, and told him that the Jeeps would remain behind. 'Tell your men to carry shovels,' he said.

He rejoined the others rubbing his hands. 'The last leg,' he said. 'We're almost there.'

The third and final bearing led them up a narrow defile between narrow walls that were painted with intricate and beautiful images of wild animals – elephants, ibex, antelopes, ostrich and giraffe, careening and leaping, with the unmistakable figures of humans and dogs pursuing them. Von Neumann had no time for the rock-paintings, though. He was almost panting with anticipation now. 'They must have carried the gold over this last stretch,' he told Churchill as they walked.

'How the hell did they manage it?' the big man asked.

'The bullion was in ingots weighing about a kilo each,' Von Neumann said. 'There were twenty ingots to a package, padded and roped up in hessian sacks, so that one man could easily carry one package. There were over five hundred packages – ten thousand kilos . . .' Churchill whistled.

Von Neumann stopped suddenly. The narrow path curved down into a steep-sided inlet about ten yards across with a sandy floor and no apparent way out. 'This has to be it!' he gasped. 'At last!'

There was a dead thorn tree on one side of the gorge, and Churchill spotted something out of place there. It was another knife, stuck in the trunk. This time the knife had a sabre-like hand-shield, which doubled as a knuckle-duster. Chuckling, Churchill brought it over to Von Neumann. 'This is another kind of commando knife,' he said. 'Issued to Middle East commandos. It's called a Fanny.' He grinned and poked a thick finger through the hand-guard. 'I don't know why.'

Von Neumann didn't get the joke, and wasn't interested. He was already calling forward two of the Delim with shovels to start digging at the base of the thorn tree.

The rest of the tribesmen gathered round. Despite himself, Sterling was fascinated.

There was silence now except for the scrape of the shovels in the sand. The men dug without enthusiasm, and after a moment both Churchill and Von Neumann grabbed shovels and joined in. The sand piled up quickly. Five minutes passed, then ten. Von Neumann paused for breath. His face became paler and he glanced at his watch, then he threw himself into the work even more feverishly. After another five minutes the hole in the sand was a yard deep, but there was still no sign of the packages. Von Neumann halted and ordered the other Delim to start digging. 'It has to be here somewhere!' he shouted. 'This place is only ten yards across. There were five hundred packages!' The tribesmen grunted and complained, but Amir urged them on and they began digging furiously.

Suddenly one of the men let out an exclamation. Von Neumann sucked in his breath and rushed over to him. The tribesman was laughing, holding up a torn piece of hessian with a broken rope dangling from it. The German snatched it out of his hand. The other Delim had downed tools and now they were laughing uproariously, letting go of the tension that had built up since they'd entered the Kidja.

Von Neumann wasn't laughing, though. His face was deathly white. He pulled out his Luger from beneath his *dara'a* and pointed it at Taha. His hand shook slightly. 'You lying little swine!' he said slowly. 'It was here! It was here! It was here and you and your stinking Arabs moved it! I ought to put a bullet through your head right now.'

The laughing stopped. Shovels crashed into the sand as the Delim unslung their rifles. Sterling stood petrified, tensing himself to make a spring, determined to protect Taha whatever happened.

For an instant Von Neumann pointed the pistol at Taha's head. Then he let out a long breath. 'No,' he said. 'Why kill you? It takes ten minutes to get back to the wireless truck, and it is now twelve minutes exactly till my rendezvous time with Wohrmann. That means you have exactly two minutes to tell me where the treasure is. If I am even one minute late for the RV, Wohrmann will start killing your family.'

He let the Luger fall but kept his watch-hand raised. Taha eyed him defiantly. Sterling's senses raced. He itched to do something – anything, but Von Neumann had anticipated them. Any attack on him would result in Taha's people dying.

He bit his lips.

'Thirty seconds!' Von Neumann snapped.

Even Churchill had turned pale now, Sterling noticed. He stared at the big man bitterly. For a second their eyes met, then Churchill looked away.

'One minute!' Von Neumann announced.

Taha glanced at Sterling then at Churchill, then back to Von Neumann.

'One minute thirty seconds!' Von Neumann said. 'If we do not return to the wireless truck in thirty seconds, your family are dead. Now, for the last time. Where did you move the treasure?'

Taha's chin dropped to his chest. 'We didn't move it anywhere,' he said. 'Craven did.'

* * *

Back at the entrance to the Kidja, the rest of the Delim were sprawled out in the shade of rocks near their couched camels. They sat up expectantly as the vehicles rolled slowly out of the gorge. It was mid-afternoon and the heat was beginning to drop. A caravan of puffball clouds broke the monotonous perfection of the desert sky.

Von Neumann retired into the shade of a giant upturned boulder and sucked water from a military style canteen. Churchill, lounging under the Jeep's awning, passed his water-bottle to Taha and Sterling, who drank circumspectly.

Von Neumann called them over, and spread Craven's map out in the oval patch of shade. 'All right,' he said to Taha, 'where is it?'

Taha pointed a grizzled index finger to the elaborately drawn north–south arrow on the map, standing east of the shaded area of the Kidja. 'Nobody noticed,' he said. 'Not even me, not until much later.'

Sterling, Churchill and Von Neumann stared at the device. Suddenly Churchill gasped. 'It's upside down!' he said. 'North is where south should be!'

'Right,' Sterling said, seeing it at once.

Von Neumann glanced at the compass. 'Then it's not meant to be a north–south indicator at all.'

'No, and there's something else,' Taha said. 'Look at the centre, where the north–south and west–east lines cross.'

Sterling looked, and could just make out the shape of what might have been a tree, thick and upright. 'X marks the spot!' he gasped. 'And there's the faint outline of a tree or something at the place where the lines meet!'

'A tree!' Churchill gasped. 'A tamarisk!'

Von Neumann watched Taha suspiciously. 'There are a million trees like that out here.'

254

'Look again,' Taha said. 'The tree drawn in the cross is large and straight. There are no straight tamarisks in the desert. All are twisted. That tree is a tadout, an ancient cedar, and it is very rare. It is a tree left over from the Time Before Time, when the desert was green and streams gushed through the Plateau of Rivers. There are no more than a dozen in the whole of the Sahara. There is one due east of the Kidjat an-Nuhur.'

He stood up and pointed with two fists due east. Sterling could just make out what looked like a column on the horizon. Distorted by the heat-haze, it might equally have been a tree or pinnacle of rock.

'That is where your treasure is buried,' Taha said.

'If this is a trick . . .' Von Neumann growled.

Taha shook his head. 'The treasure was in the Kidja originally,' he said, 'but Craven moved it. I knew that because we dug for it in the same place years ago and found just torn sacks.'

Von Neumann looked startled. 'Why would Craven want to go to so much trouble,' he said, 'when he was the only one who knew where it was?'

Churchill gave an amused grunt. 'That's obvious isn't it?' he said. 'Because he *wasn't* the only one who knew where it was.'

They spent the night at the entrance to the Kidja and at first light Von Neumann was woken by a wireless message from Wohrmann in the Guelb, reporting that Steppenwolf was in the area with a column of five heavy trucks. Von Neumann was excited when he read Reuth's decrypt. At last he would be meeting his wartime hero Otto Skorzeny again, and just at the moment of his final triumph. Von Neumann didn't care much about the gold, nor did he really believe any more in the renaissance of the Reich. The only real ambition left to him had been to vindicate himself from

255

the stigma of *Sonnenblume*, and reinstate his reputation in the eyes of Skorzeny.

He passed Wohrmann the details of the new site and ordered him to relay them to Steppenwolf, saying that they would be at the tadout within two hours. The morning was still and crisply cold. Amir and his Delim were already crouching round fires making tea. They had been up since before dawn, moving the camels to graze in the saltwort a few hundred paces away. Von Neumann squatted next to Amir, accepted a glass of tea, and explained the day's plan. Then he woke Churchill and his own driver, Franz, and had them warm the Jeeps' engines.

It actually took less than an hour to reach the tadout, and close up the site looked very different. The tree itself might have been 500 years old – a fluted, columnlike trunk thick enough for ten men to stand around it shoulder to shoulder, and short stumps of boughs. There was no sign of leaves, but the tree was evidently alive – it stood in a saucer-shaped dip that had once held water, with sandstone outcrops weathered into shapes as fluent as sculptures. To Sterling, the tadout looked like an ancient shrine, a totem pole from a lost age.

Almost as soon as they had halted, Von Neumann had everyone digging, apart from Taha, his wireless operator, Reuth, and a few Delim guards. He stood watching by the ancient tree with Taha next to him. 'Now,' he told the youth, 'if this turns out to be another waste of time, I assure you—'

He was interrupted by a yell from one of the men, and turned to see two of the Delim manhandling a bundle from the sand. It was roughly cylindrical – a thick hessian sack that had been padded inside and tightly bound with rope. The Arabs dumped the package at Von Neumann's feet.

Von Neumann's eyes were shining now. He felt for the commando knife he had brought from the Kidja the previous day and squatted down. The knife was blunt and Von Neumann was wheezing with anticipation by the time he'd cut through the rope. He threw the commando knife aside with disgust, and asked Amir for his dagger. It was razor-sharp, and he sliced through the hessian and the cotton rags underneath in a couple of slashes. Yellow metal gleamed in the sun. With trembling hands, Von Neumann pulled out a gold ingot. It was oblong, not much more than a thumb and forefinger span in length, with a large swastika stamped on top. Churchill and Sterling gasped. Taha, Amir, and the gathered tribesmen made the sign against the evil eye.

Von Neumann pulled another ingot out, then another, shredding the sackcloth with Amir's knife. He stood up, his eyes brilliant, clutching two of the bars in his hands, holding them up like trophies. 'At last!' he croaked. 'At last!'

He knelt and started wrapping the ingots up in the sack. 'Dig!' he shouted. 'Dig! Let's get it all!'

The men worked with more enthusiasm now, and within minutes another bundle was unearthed, then another and another. Quickly the packs of gold were built up into neat stacks of twenty. Sterling, sweating with his shovel, was astonished how fast the stacks went up, and how small the area required to conceal 10,000 kilos of gold.

Sterling had just paused from the work to take a swig of water that Churchill offered him, when one of the Delim guards bawled out a warning. Churchill jumped out of the trench to join Von Neumann, who was already scanning the horizon with field glasses in the direction the tribesman was pointing. Sterling and Taha both stepped out of the diggings to watch. By now five vehicles were clearly visible – tiny darkling beetles, appearing motionless in the haze shimmering on the edge of the landscape. 'Finally,' Von Neumann said, 'Steppenwolf.'

Sterling watched the vehicles with dread, knowing that the

final act was fast approaching. Von Neumann glared at him. 'Get digging!' he ordered.

Sterling threw his shovel down. 'Dig it yourself,' he said.

Von Neumann ignored him and began counting the sacks of gold, pausing every few moments to monitor the approach of the convoy. It seemed forever before the lorries arrived, but they seemed to burst into life suddenly, racing out of the landscape. Everyone stopped to watch.

They were Mercedes-Benz four-tonners painted desert pink. The roar of their engines came only distantly, with the scent of diesel exhaust fumes. They had dark tinted windscreens, so that the faces of their drivers were not visible, and they travelled in Indian file. The Mercs grated forwards until the first was within no more than a hundred yards of the tadout, then they fanned out in line abreast as if on manoeuvres. Once they were in line, the engines cut abruptly. There were a few seconds of silence, then a hatch on the cab of the left-hand truck opened with a dull thud, and a man with a beard and unkempt hair popped up, grinning. He did not speak or wave, but set up what was evidently a machine gun on a bracket in front of the hatch.

A moment later the door of the same truck opened and a figure dropped out, paused, then began to walk towards them.

Von Neumann watched him come with anticipation. The man was dressed in Afrika Korps fatigue trousers, desert boots, and a British Special Forces smock with the hood up, shadowing his features. He carried a Thompson sub-machine-gun at waist height, supported by a sling across one shoulder. Von Neumann was surprised that Skorzeny should carry a Thompson. Otto had always said they were too heavy, and insisted that the Schmeisser was the best sub-machine-gun ever made. Then Von Neumann noticed that, though the man was powerfully built, he was relatively short. Otto was as tall as himself. And, unlike Skorzeny, this man walked

258

with a pronounced limp. The heat of excitement began to chill in Von Neumann's blood. He put his hand on the Luger under his *dara'a*, but the figure had halted before them now, only ten paces away, and the muzzle of the Tommy gun was pointing in his direction. The man pulled the hood down with one hand, revealing a massive leonine head, features chiselled from rock, swept-back hair, cold blue eyes, and a Kitchener moustache.

Arnold Hobart stood before them.

It was Von Neumann who seemed the most shocked. For a second his mouth worked like a mechanical toy, but no words emerged. His head reeled and spun, the image of that night eight years ago crashing into it like a comet: the noise and smell of the sandstorm, the roar of the Jeeps, the clatter of the Brownings, the brilliant flash of verey lights, red and green, and the sudden knowledge that the enemy had found them; switching on the headlights of the nearest truck in panic, seeing the Jeep flying out of the storm like a vulture, and the face of this man behind the wheel, illuminated for an eternal moment, before the machine gun shot his lights out and forced him to jump out and run. The commando's face – wild, predatory, exultant – was etched on his memory forever, and it was that face, in front of him now, where Otto Skorzeny's face should be.

'You . . .' he stuttered. '*But how* . . . ?'

Hobart turned the ice-blue eyes slowly in his direction. 'Craven got clever,' he said. 'We buried the gold in the Kidja together, but he came back and moved it.'

Von Neumann shook his head, as if denying that he was really seeing what he was seeing. 'But you're dead,' he protested. 'Craven was the only one left alive.'

Hobart guffawed. 'No,' he said. 'Not unless I'm a ghost and didn't know it. I survived, as you see. The story of Craven being the only survivor was given out by Steppenwolf, when he took charge of the *Sonnenblume* salvage operation. Since I'm Steppenwolf, it wasn't so difficult to convince people – especially you, Freidrich.'

Von Neumann put his hands over his ears, as if trying to block out the voice. '*Skorzeny* . . .' he moaned.

Hobart chuckled again. 'Poor Otto,' he said. 'He wasn't quite the same man when he walked out of the de-Nazification camp in forty-seven. Oh, he wasn't broken or anything, but he had certainly got himself de-Nazified. He'd already realized the truth: that there would be no renaissance from exile, no revival of the Third Reich. It was finished. The dream was over. All that remained was to feather one's own nest. He was happy for me to play the part of Steppenwolf, and he'll receive his whack of the gold in due course.'

This was too much for Von Neumann. With a Neanderthal cry in his throat, he leapt at Hobart, drawing his Luger in one hand and the British commando knife in the other.

The machine gunner on the lorry cocked the weapon but, before he could fire, Hobart's Tommy gun blazed out, *thump-thumpa-thump*. The Delim scattered at the sound of the weapon, but didn't fire. Sterling and Churchill threw themselves flat. Von Neumann was hit in the throat and keeled into the sand, coughing and spitting blood. He tried to rise up on his hands and knees, and Hobart shot him again, the heavy rounds flaying flesh from his ribs like a whiplash. Von Neumann coughed once and lay still, blood soaking into the sand.

Franz and Reuth sat motionless in their Jeep. Neither of them was armed. Churchill cocked his Garand and pointed it at them and they raised their hands. 'I wouldn't try anything if I were you,' Churchill beamed at them. 'I would just see which way the wind blows.'

260

Suddenly, Taha let out a howl like an injured wolf and rushed towards Hobart, who swivelled and turned the Tommy gun on him. 'Stop it, Billy!' he snapped, in Arabic. 'I don't want to shoot you. Your people are all right. Wohrmann's dead. My own boys are there.'

Taha skidded to a halt as the words sunk into his consciousness. He blinked at Hobart incredulously. 'Grandfather!' he whispered.

Hobart smiled but made no move towards him. 'You're a good boy, Billy,' he said in Arabic. 'You're a tough one and no mistake. Not like your father . . .' He glowered at Sterling, who was picking himself up and gaping at Von Neumann's shattered corpse. 'You never knew how much I despised you, George,' he said, switching to English. 'I had to put up with you and your crap all those years because of Margaret – she was always loopy, but I had a soft spot for her. And I admit you were a pretty bright chap in your own way, and I thought you might make a bit of dosh and help me out in my old age. I don't need it now, do I?'

Sterling was already as white as a sheet. He began to shake his head as Von Neumann had done, as if trying to deny what he was hearing.

Hobart snorted. 'Pathetic,' he said. He nodded to Churchill. 'Good man, Eric,' he said. 'You played a blinder with the wireless reports. I couldn't have done it without you.'

Sterling let out a cry and sank to his knees. Taha stood very still, knowing that all the tracks of all the years were suddenly joining into one – that the spirits had guided their footsteps here for a purpose. He had recognized his grandfather almost at once, and suddenly the whole thing came into bright focus in his mind. His grandfather was a murderer and a thief. His grandfather had killed his own men and thrown their bodies into the Umm al-Khof. His grandfather had unleashed the Delim into Reguibat territory and given them the new rifles. His grandfather and Craven had been in it together – and all for this yellow stuff buried in the sand. Bits of metal that he and Belhaan had known about for years, and which weren't worth the life of one nomad child. Taha had understood enough of what Hobart had said to know that his clan were no longer under immediate threat, and they were his first priority. He would do nothing until they were completely safe.

Hobart and Amir were shaking hands cordially now, and the Delim had relaxed. They didn't seem perturbed by Von Neumann's death. Hobart was speaking to them in Arabic, explaining that Von Neumann was a traitor, assuring them that the original bargain would be kept. Hobart would have the gold; the Delim would be supplied with weapons and ammunition and would take over the Reguibat land that they believed was rightly theirs.

There was a slamming of doors and Taha saw that a dozen men had jumped out of the trucks, and were smoking and making tea on little oil-stoves in their shade. The men were all Christians and most were armed. Taha saw that the machine gunner on the last lorry remained at his post.

Hobart was rubbing his boxer's hands. 'Come on then,' he said. 'Let's get the rest of the stuff out and loaded in the lorries. I want to be off by this afternoon at the latest.'

The Delim resumed work, their shovels crunching in the sand. More bundles of gold came up. Hobart brought his janissary-faced pipe from his smock pocket and stuck it in his mouth. He walked up to where Sterling knelt, his arms crossed over his chest, rocking back and forth.

'Sorry, old man,' he said, 'but I've waited my whole life for this.'

'Arnold?' Sterling was repeating, as if he still couldn't believe the man standing there was his father-in-law. '*You* killed Corrigan?'

Hobart removed the pipe, brought a pouch of tobacco from another pocket and began to fill it. 'You supplied his address,' he scoffed. 'The man was out of his tree, of course, or he'd never have trusted you with it. I'd been trying to find him for years. Someone spotted him hiding out in Fez in nineteen forty-six and told me. Von Neumann had been on his trail ever since he became operational again in nineteen forty-seven, when Skorzeny gave me his name. Von Neumann revered Skorzeny and wanted to put his blunder right – he thought Otto was Steppenwolf.'

Sterling turned lifeless eyes to Hobart. 'But why did you try to persuade me to go to the police?' he asked dully.

Hobart shrugged. 'Just covering myself. I knew you wouldn't. Not with that stretch in the Scrubs on your record. Knew you wouldn't touch them with a bargepole. But even if you had it could have been worked out.'

'And that stuff about the mafia . . . ?'

A big smile creased Hobart's massive face. 'I thought that was rather good,' he said. 'There was no such person as Frank Quayle, and I never made any phone calls to old colleagues that night – as if I'd really have compromised myself! The story about Corrigan half-inching fifty grand from the mafia was just made up to explain why he might have been murdered. You fell for it lock, stock, and beer-barrel.'

'All these years,' Sterling whispered. 'I thought . . . you were an honourable man.'

'*So are they all, all honourable men*,' Hobart said, striking a match and lighting the pipe. 'I found out early that honour means having a big bank account,' he went on bitterly, letting smoke trickle out through his teeth. 'That's all it means. All I wanted, George, was to have the money to live up to the

263

family name, to live like a member of the gentry was meant to, not to be a damned civil servant. You understand that, don't you? *Sonnenblume* was my big chance. You see, in forty-five I was attached to the Int. Corps and sent to Casablanca on Operation Esperance – that was the Allied op to stop Nazi funds getting out of Europe. I was lucky. I got wind of a big treasure convoy and I kept it to myself – myself and Craven, that was. We'd known each other well in the LRDG in the Western Desert. In fact, I wrote the citations for his DFC and bar – they were spurious, actually. Craven was mouthy, but in the end he was chicken-livered. Anyway, we thought, why should the bloody Allies have the Nazi gold when we'd risked our necks for five years? I'd lost my son on Crete and my wife in the blitz. We decided to keep it for ourselves, you see. I sent Craven out in one of those little Wacos he liked to fly, and he spotted the convoy. He landed the kite at Zagora, and I picked him up. We led the LRDG patrol in together. I think you know the rest.'

Sterling shook his head again, as if he had something in it he wanted to get rid of. 'You . . . murdered your own men,' he murmured, hearing his own voice coming from far off.

Hobart made a helpless gesture. 'Had no choice,' he said. 'There's no honour among thieves, George. Can't keep ten thousand kilos of gold a secret among fifteen men for long. Somebody was bound to squeal. You know how it goes: "*Fifteen men on a dead man's chest – Yo ho ho and a bottle of rum – Drink and the devil had done for the rest.*" Only it wasn't the bloody SRD rum that did for them, it was me and Keith.'

He blew a smoke cloud, his eyes distant, as if musing on his dead comrades. Sterling gagged at the sheer callousness of Hobart's words. 'All right,' he said slowly. 'But I have to know. . .why Billy? What did he have to do with it? Why did

264

you have to wreck his life and mine too? You caused your own daughter's suicide.'

Hobart took the pipe out of his mouth, and his expression turned black. He glared at Sterling with a look of repulsion. 'Lip, George,' he snapped. 'Margaret had had it the day she teamed up with a limp-wrist like you.'

He looked at the piles of bagged gold, and his expression relaxed slightly. 'Can't change it now,' he sighed. 'It was you and Margaret who wanted Billy to come to Morocco. Like a bloody fool I accepted – never could deny Margaret anything, not even marrying you. Should have known Craven would take advantage.'

Sterling watched Churchill sidling nearer to them. The big man stuffed a half-smoked cigar into his mouth and sat down in the sand, listening. 'Got a match, Arnold?' he asked.

Hobart passed him a box of Swan Vestas. 'You know what we used to say?' he commented.

'Yes,' Churchill sniggered. 'Your face and my backside.'

They both chortled like schoolkids.

'How did Craven take advantage of Billy?' Sterling insisted, looking at them as if they were both mad.

'Craven was scared,' Hobart said, the grin fading from his lips. He took the matches back from Churchill. 'As I said, he was always chicken-livered under the bluster. He'd seen the way I'd dealt with the patrol, and he thought I might whack him out too. While I was in hospital in Algiers with my leg – it had turned gangrenous and I almost lost it – he came back out here with two vehicles and a crew of five prisoners of war, and moved the gold from the Kidja. God knows what he'd promised those poor buggers, but he certainly lost them on the way back. I don't suppose they'll ever be found. Anyway, by the time I got back to Casa, Craven was the only one who knew where the treasure was.

'I didn't see him for a while, but in forty-six, when I was a half-colonel working for the Int. attached to the British Embassy in Morocco, Craven turned up as a civilian working for Atlantic Air Transport. He came to see me and explained he'd moved the stuff in case I got any funny ideas. He was going out to get it, he said, but he needed my swing to square things. He said I'd get my share – half – as long as I didn't try anything nasty. He noticed Billy and asked who he was. I should have paid more attention. See, Billy used to hang around the aerodrome a lot – he liked aircraft, as all kids of that age do. One day, out of the blue, I received a phone call from Craven saying he was going to get the gold, or the first lot of it, and he was taking Billy with him as "insurance". His plan was to leave Billy with some nomads in the desert while he ferried back the gold – it would have taken four trips, he reckoned. There were ten thousand kilos and the crate could take about two thousand five hundred a trip with the extra tank fitted. If I tried anything untoward, he said, Billy would get it. That was the idea, but of course, it never came off. *Rose of Cimarron* went down, Craven snuffed it, and Billy walked off with the map. The gold was lost to the outside world, and I had to pretend to you that I had given Billy the go ahead, that it had all been on the up and up, and that *Rose* had been flying to Zagora. I got heartily sick of searching that bloody road, knowing the kite had never been anywhere near there!'

He puffed on his pipe and Churchill blew smoke from his cigar silently. The Delim were working less enthusiastically now, tiring, but the work was almost done. Hobart began to count the packages. When he was satisfied they were all there, he called one of his drivers to bring the first lorry over. Churchill noticed that the machine-gun sentry on the left-hand lorry had changed – Hobart's men didn't look like soldiers, but they knew their jobs all right.

266

The first four-tonner roared up in a cloud of dust, and the driver – a dark-skinned Spaniard with shoulder-length black hair – jumped out and opened the tailgate. There, under the canvas awning, were strapped a score of boxes. Hobart pointed at one with his pipe, and the driver clambered up into the back and unstrapped it. Hobart yanked it half out by its rope handle, and Amir sprang to help. The driver jumped down, produced a jemmy and levered the top off, his long hair swinging as he worked. Inside were a dozen Garand rifles packed in greased paper. 'All yours,' Hobart told Amir. 'A thousand rifles, straight out of the factory.'

Amir picked one up and shucked the paper. His eagle eyes gleamed. 'With these,' he said, 'we shall obliterate the Ulad al-Mizna from the face of the land.'

He stared at Hobart. 'Where are the bullets?' he said.

'Fifty thousand rounds, and more to come whenever you like.'

Amir grunted.

'Let's get to work,' Hobart said.

It took more than two hours to unload the rifles and ammunition and load the packs of gold. The lorry crews worked in a methodical and disciplined way, bringing only one truck forward at a time, always maintaining a sentry on the machine gun and another on foot with a Tommy gun or a rifle. The pile of crates grew taller; those of the gold diminished. Churchill lounged in the shade of one of the sandstone dolmens, smoking a cigar and watching. Sterling and Billy sat together in silence.

When the last truck was loaded and the tailgate slammed shut, the driver moved it to where the others were drawn up, already gunning their engines. Hobart called Amir and whispered something to him, pointing to the two Germans, who were sitting in the shade of the wireless truck. Amir barked an order, and a dozen tribesmen ran forward. The two men lurched up, terrified,

267

but in a moment they were engulfed in a tide of blue-robed figures. Sterling jumped to his feet. 'No!' he screeched, but no one was listening.

He saw daggers flash, heard animal grunts and squeals of terror. When the Delim withdrew, two more mangled, bloody corpses lay in the sand. Amir pointed to Sterling now, and the tribesmen moved towards him ominously. He saw savage eyes shaded by head-cloths, blood-smeared daggers in dark hands. Taha stood up and moved in front of him as gracefully as a leopard. He had a sharp stone in each hand.

'*I am Taha Minan Nijum of the Ulad al-Mizna,*' Taha yelled. '*I slew the Twisted One, and by God, the first man to touch my father shall die.*'

There was power and authority in his voice, and the Delim halted, reluctant to move forward. Amir cursed and lifted his rifle.

'Stop!' Hobart shouted. 'Don't shoot. I need that boy!'

He limped up to Taha, who watched him coming warily, the stones gripped tightly in his hands. 'Grandfather,' he said quietly in Arabic. 'I mean it.'

Hobart laughed. 'You're a real chip off the old block,' he said. 'But in your case it skipped a generation. I don't know why you bother. What did this yellow bastard ever do for you?'

Taha said nothing.

'All right,' Hobart said. 'I'll make you a bargain. In fact, I'll make you two bargains. Just to ensure that we get away clean, I shall be taking the route through the Umm al-Khof, the quicksand. Now, if what my friend Eric Churchill reported is correct, you're the only "Arab" who's been through it. Eric has too, of course, but, with all due respect, I wouldn't trust his tracking skills. You've lived here all these years so I'd trust yours. Now, you agree to guide me through the quicksand and I won't kill your dad here or your folks back in the crater.'

Taha's eyes opened wide in alarm.

Hobart laughed. 'Von Neumann's trick was quite astute,' he said. 'And I've taken the leaf out of an expert's book. I left a couple of men back there when we passed through, and I am in wireless contact with them. I shall be calling in every hour until we are clear, with a special codeword. If I don't call in, or the codeword is missing, my boys will tell the Delim with them to start shooting your adopted family.'

Taha glared at him. 'If I refuse?' he said.

Hobart frowned. 'Then your dad dies, you die, and all your people die, too.'

When Taha was seated in the first lorry, Hobart called Churchill and took him aside. 'You've done a good job, Eric,' he whispered. 'And you'll get your whack, I promise you. When we're over the horizon, though, bump George off, will you? We don't want any more accidents, you know.'

Churchill nodded grimly. 'What about the people back at the Guelb?'

'Wait till I'm through the Umm al-Khof,' Hobart said. 'Then you and the two chaps I left back there can deal with them. You can soon catch up with me in your Jeep, and my boys will have the wireless to keep in contact – just follow my tracks through the quicksand.'

Churchill grunted. 'And Billy?'

Hobart shrugged. 'He can either come home and be the heir to a fortune, or I can leave his body in the Umm al-Khof. It's entirely up to him.'

Hobart stuck the pipe back into his smock, hobbled back to the lorry and climbed up into the cab beside Taha. The driver hooted and the convoy began to pull out.

Churchill stood watching them for many minutes until they

merged into the dust-haze, then turned to look for Sterling who was examining the bodies of Franz and Reuth, probably wondering if he could do anything for them. The Delim were ignoring him now. They had brought their camels up, couched them, and were busily breaking open boxes of rifles and ammunition and loading them onto the beasts' backs. The men jabbered and bawled at one another and the camels jumped up, throwing their loads, while the tribesmen yanked them down, cursing. Two of the men were actually fighting. Despite the bloody murders he had just witnessed, Churchill grinned. It had been a long time, he guessed, since the Delim had seen such bounty.

He shouldered his M1 and marched towards Sterling, knowing he would have to move quickly now. Sterling saw him coming and stood up. He did not back away and there was no fear in his eyes.

'Did you see that?' he said distantly. 'Billy stood up for me. He said *"the first man who touches my father will die."* Ironic, isn't it, Eric, if you think all I ever wanted to do was to sell aspirins.' He sighed. 'Still, I suppose it's a good enough declaration of love, in its way.'

'George,' Churchill said urgently. 'See the Jeep over there? When I say "go", run like hell to it, get in and start driving. I'll be right behind you.'

There was a grave smile on Sterling's face. 'No more tricks, Eric,' he said. 'If you're going to kill me, you'll have to do it face to face.'

'You idiot! I told you the first day out of Layoune that whatever happened, whatever weird things you saw, I would always be on your side. I'm not working for Hobart and I never have been. Can you imagine a man like me ever ratting on my country? Now, if we don't move quickly those Arabs over there are going to get curious.'

270

On a sudden impulse, he pulled the Garand off his shoulder, slipped out his pistol and thrust both weapons into Sterling's hands. Sterling took them, wondering what it meant, and Churchill saw a sudden flame of hope flicker in his eyes.

'We have to save Billy,' he growled. 'But that means getting to his folks before Hobart's boys start shooting. Come on, George. I can't kill you without a weapon.'

Sterling took a deep breath, knowing that he was once again in the land of uncertainty. Churchill had lied to him: there was no doubt about that. It was quite possible that the big man had some other trick up his sleeve. But if he did nothing, he was going to lose Billy again. He had to make one final leap of faith.

'All right,' he said.

Churchill watched the Arabs for a moment, and saw that they were still preoccupied. 'One, two, three,' he whispered. '*Go!*'

The two of them sprinted towards the Jeep, covering the ground in seconds. Sterling leapt into the driver's seat and turned the ignition switch. The engine fired. He put the vehicle in gear, feeling the springs give under Churchill's weight when he jumped into the back. As he let the clutch out, jabbing down on the accelerator, he heard Churchill cocking the Bren mounted on the rear bracket. The tyres hummed and sawed across the gravel. There were shouts and raised voices behind them, and then cracks as a couple of bullets seared past his ears. Drum-fire rattled from the Bren in answer, and then Sterling slipped into second, and the Jeep's engine roared. In less than sixty seconds they were out of rifle shot, and racing back towards the Guelb.

12

IT WAS A GOOD TWENTY MINUTES before Sterling slowed, and Churchill dropped into the seat beside him, his face and shirt covered in dust. 'Brilliant driving, George,' the big man mumbled, reaching for a canteen of water. He uncorked it and offered it to Sterling. 'No Mickey Finns,' he grinned, 'I promise.'

Sterling made a face, took the water and swigged. It was warm and tasted earthy. He handed it back to Churchill, who was slapping dust off his clothes. 'It'll take them a long time to catch us, anyway,' Sterling said.

Churchill glugged water and corked the canteen. 'Don't underestimate camels,' he said. 'They're in their own country here.'

He took the Smith & Wesson from the seat where Sterling had laid it, blew dust off it and checked the chambers, then restored it to its holster. He picked up the M1 and clipped it in the bracket behind the seats. 'We're well set up,' he said. 'I halfinched all the spare petrol from the Jerry wireless truck while the Arabs weren't looking, and the water. We've got ammo, too.'

Sterling's eyes were fixed on the desert ahead. Evening was approaching, the sun about five inches above the horizon, the air cooler, but the landscape still palpably radiating the heat it had absorbed during the day. The wind-graded serir was easy driving, but the occasional patches of pebbly hammada were harder and had to be avoided, like the dune-fields and soft flat sand. Sandstone buttes reared out of the desert around them like the serrated fins of mythical sea-monsters, holding lakes of shadows among their scales, or chiselled by wind and grit into hammerheads, obelisks or giant chessmen. A slight breeze whipped up strings of dust around their bases.

After a while, Churchill stopped Sterling and got out of the Jeep with his prismatic compass in his hand. 'I've got a back-bearing on the Guelb,' he said. 'But the compass is no good in the Jeep – the engine's magnetic field throws it out.'

'We can use the stars,' Sterling said. 'Use Polaris in place of magnetic north.'

Churchill slapped his pockets for matches and came up with a packet. He lit his cigar. Sterling looked at him and shook his head. 'Last time you lit that thing,' he said. 'You had to ask Hobart for a match. I have to hand it to you, Eric, you're a bloody good actor.'

The big man got back in the Jeep and they started. 'I wanted to hear what was being said,' he told Sterling, puffing the cigar. 'And yes, you were right about that, George, I had good training in playing roles in "Gusenkian's Travelling Circus". You see we had to do everything: we were ticket-sellers, ringmasters, seat-ushers, programme-sellers, clowns, acrobats – you name it. Each part required a different face, a different mask.'

'And that stuff sneering at "codes of honour" – that was all garbage?'

Churchill took the cigar out of his mouth. 'George,' he said.

'I meant the oath I made to Taha, just as I meant the oath to King and country when I joined the Military Police. I've been a patriot all my life – refugee syndrome, remember? Things other people took for granted, like democracy and freedom of speech, fairness; all that really *meant* something to me, because I knew, at least my parents drummed it into me, what it was like to be without it. Now, I'm no saint, George – I've been economical with the truth at times, maybe, and I've always had a bit of a weakness for the ladies, but a traitor to Britain, no. God forbid.'

The Jeep throbbed across the vast plain, and Sterling wiped dust out of his eyes. 'No bloody windscreen,' he complained. 'Still, I suppose it wouldn't be much good in the desert.' He changed gear smoothly. 'I can't believe this,' he said, keeping his eyes ahead. 'Hobart always seemed so cut up about Billy – I always thought he was so . . . well, such a decent bloke.'

Churchill grunted. *'To what do you not drive human hearts, cursed craving for gold!'*

'That's not Winston, is it?'

'No. It's Virgil again. Winston's repertoire is actually a bit limited. Hobart's a monster, him and Craven both. Arnold couldn't live with the fact that his grandfather squandered the family money.'

'But I still don't understand . . .' Sterling trailed off.

Churchill rearranged his big body in the seat and took the cigar from his mouth, watching the horizon.

'All right,' he said. 'You deserve an explanation, George. I'm sorry about the web of deception, and I'm sorry about knocking you out – and Taha. I thought it was necessary at the time, and I've explained why. As for the rest . . . the fact is, yes I *have* lied to you about myself. I wasn't kicked out of Field Security in Casablanca in nineteen forty-five, but I did have to hang up my forage cap. After that I simply went covert, and became an

asset rather than an operational officer. I'm not claiming to be
– who's that fellow in Ian Fleming's new book? You know *Casino
Royale* – James Bond, Double-O-Seven, or something?'

Sterling's mouth fell open and he stared at Churchill for a
second. The Jeep bumped over a stone and Sterling had to wrestle
with the steering wheel. Churchill sucked in his breath. 'Christ!'
he gasped. 'Keep your eyes on the road or we'll end up in the
ditch, and that'll put the mockers on everything.'

'Sorry,' Sterling said.

Churchill was quiet for a moment. 'Look,' he said, 'if I'm
going to tell you the truth, you'll have to promise not to lose
your concentration.'

'All right.'

'Right. The fact is, George, I've been doing unofficial work
for MI5 for years – the Craven Patrol case was only one of the
things I've done. I was in Casa in nineteen forty-five, when
Craven came back having lost an entire LRDG patrol – thirteen
highly trained commandos – claiming it had been wiped out by
a Nazi column heading for West Africa. Well, anyone who
believed that would believe anything. That was more men in one
go than the LRDG lost in the entire North Africa campaign. But
we couldn't prove a damn thing. At first we didn't guess that
Hobart had been in on it – his story was that he'd been shot in
the leg by a Nazi agent while working undercover. I was on
Craven's arse, though – I knew from the start he wasn't what
he was cracked up to be. Then his name came up in connection
with five Italian POWs who went missing from a Moroccan
camp in nineteen forty-five. Again there was no proof.'

Sterling steered around a bowl-shaped depression, changing
down into second gear. 'And that stuff about the mafia connection,' he said. 'That was all eyewash?'

Churchill shrugged. 'I'm sorry about that,' he said. 'But I

didn't know how far I could trust you. That's been a bugbear from the start. When you told me Hobart's story about Corrigan and the mafia, I just elaborated on it a bit, to keep you off the scent.'

'And you weren't kicked out because you were getting close to Hobart and Craven?'

'No. There was just no need and no money for chaps like me when the war ended. I was a bit miffed about it, but since they kept me on as an asset, it wasn't so bad. I've done some good jobs for the Security Service over the years. I kept an eye on the Craven-Hobart business, of course, and I knew Craven had been lost in Morocco in nineteen forty-six. Then, out of the blue a few months back, someone handed me a report about Corrigan, a known associate of Craven's, who'd been spotted in London. The Office put me on alert: Corrigan, USAF deserter, is making enquiries about a certain George Bridger Sterling, who turns out to be Arnold Hobart's son-in-law. The dots start to join up. Sterling's son was on the kite with Craven when she went down. Sterling is the partner of a Major Vernon Dakin, ex-Royal Tank Corps, and a friend of a couple of my private clients. I get Dakin to feed you my name, just in case Corrigan manages to get in touch – and he does. Bingo! We're right on the money.'

Sterling chortled incredulously. 'But how did you manage to insinuate yourself into Hobart's confidence?'

Churchill sighed and picked a piece of tobacco off his lip. The sun was being sucked into the horizon now, losing its globe shape along the lower perimeter. Dust clouds fanned out like wings around it, their undersides turning to fire. Sterling changed down to negotiate a patch of loose sand.

'When I got home the night we met, I made two phone calls, neither of them to Dakin. The first was to the Office, to let them know I'd made contact with you. My boss thought about it, and

276

told me to get in touch with Hobart. It was a gamble, but it paid off. Your father-in-law didn't know I was an MI5 asset – thought I'd been out of it since forty-five, as officially I had. Actually, I knew him a little better than I let on. I'd run into him once or twice at reunions since Morocco, so we weren't strangers, and he knew I was in the private investigations business, anyway, so my cover story rang true. The conversation about the wireless actually did take place, but with Hobart, not Dakin. He leapt at the idea and told me I should address my reports to codename Steppenwolf. My codename would be Wolfgang. Sounded so *Boy's Own* that it was all I could do to stop myself laughing!'

Sterling slowed again and let the Jeep coast over a rocky hammada. 'But why did you try and persuade me to take Billy –Taha – home?' he asked. 'I mean, when Billy was the key to the whole case.'

Churchill threw the cigar-stub into the desert. 'You must understand, George, that I've been playing all this by ear. It started off as a case of suspected murder, that's all. We knew damn well something odd had happened to those LRDG boys, but we didn't know about *Sonnenblume,* Skorzeny or anything else. As it turned out, the disappearance of the Craven patrol was only the tip of the iceberg.'

The sun was a gold cartouche on the skyline and the dust clouds had turned to bats' wings. Sterling stopped the Jeep and a delicious silence absorbed them. 'We'd better eat,' he said, breaking the silence. Out there, nothing moved but a flight of crows flitting across the darkling sky.

In the Guelb, the Delim were carousing half naked round a bonfire and piles of hot stones, on which they were cooking haunches of camel meat. The meat had been sliced from one of Belhaan's prize racing-camels, which they had slaughtered at sunset. Its ravaged carcass sat a little way away in a swamp of giblets and gore. Someone was playing a tabla and some of the nomads were moving their bodies, swinging their long hair in time with the rhythm, apparently mesmerized. A few fired off shots from their new rifles into the night. Suddenly one of them dashed into the shadows where the Reguibat prisoners were gathered, and came back into the light dragging a girl by the arm. It was Rauda. Her head-veil had been torn off and her braided black hair fell to her waist. She clung to her flimsy *mehlafa* as the nomad tried to rip it away and expose her naked breasts. The audience clapped and cackled. Suddenly Rauda let the garment go, and the man took an unexpected step back. There was an audible '*Aaah!*' as the men stared at Rauda's body, naked but for her loincloth. In that instant, Rauda snatched the dagger from her assailant's belt, and held the point against her own breast, panting.

'Touch me, son of a pig!' she spat, her eyes flashing in the bonfire-light. 'And nobody else ever shall!'

The tabla stopped abruptly. The dancing men froze. The Delim who had seized her threw the *mehlafa* on the ground and stepped towards her, smiling truculently. Rauda raised the dagger higher. At that moment a frail voice said, 'Stop!'

As the Delim turned in surprise, an old man hobbled out of the shadows, barefooted, without head-cloth and wearing a torn and filthy *dara'a*.

The nomad who had threatened Rauda began to chuckle. 'Sorry, old man,' he said laughing. 'But you are no substitute for *her*.'

Uproarious laughter raced round the Delim. 'Give him a kiss!' someone shouted.

'Make him dance!'

The old man stood very still and the firelight played across his face. The laughing stopped. There was an unmistakable power and presence to the man, a stillness that was almost unnerving. 'I am Belhaan ould Hamed,' he said quietly. 'Sheikh of my clan. I am of the *inhaden yenun.*'

A murmur spread among the crowd. Some of the Delim made the sign against the evil eye.

'This is the Guelb Richat,' Belhaan continued. 'It is a *haram*, a sacred place, a refuge of the spirits of our ancestors – Ulad Delim and Ulad al-Mizna – for generations, back to the Time Before Time. It is forbidden to slaughter an animal here, even to light a fire. To molest a woman here is a disgrace. I speak not for myself but for you. The spirits will not forgive your impertinence.'

There was another moment of silence, and more murmurs among the Delim. Then a tribesman clad only in a loincloth stepped out of the crowd. His body glistened with sweat from the dancing, as he thrust the muzzle of his Garand towards Belhaan. 'You see this weapon, old man,' he growled. 'This is my new amulet against the spirits.'

He cocked the weapon. The sweat ran down his face and he blinked it out of his eyes. There was no sound but the crackle of the flames. The tribesman's finger tightened its pressure on the trigger, and Belhaan waited patiently for a shot that never came. Instead, there was a terrific explosion from across the floor of the crater, a brilliant gush of orange light and a shock wave that made the air tremble. The *afrangi* chariot, the one containing the two men who'd been left behind by the Lame One, had erupted into flame. The rifleman who'd been about to kill Belhaan dropped his weapon in astonishment. The rest of the Delim leapt up and yelled as if they had been stung by scorpions, firing off their rifles uselessly into the air, jabbering, making the sign against the evil eye.

279

Belhaan picked up the fallen rifle and shot the Delim at point-blank range. The round took the man as he ducked, passed through his ear and exploded from the other side of his head in twists of bone and flesh.

Almost simultaneously, the nomad who had dragged Rauda to the fire shrieked as his own dagger suddenly thumped into his chest. Rauda didn't wait to find out if he was dead. She strode quickly to her uncle, grabbed his arm, and dragged him back out of the firelight.

The iron chariot was burning over there across the valley. Powerful lights blazed up like giant eyes in the darkness, and the Delim howled. The lights were moving towards them fast, accompanied by the dragon roar and a thwack and whomp of shots that blistered the darkness, leaving green and orange trails. One nomad turned to face the great yellow eyes and a bullet smashed his forehead before he could get his rifle into his shoulder. Some of the Delim had simply flung their new weapons away and were now scrabbling up the valley's crooked stone walls. There was a last peppering of gunshots from the roaring monster and then it came to a rest by the burned-down fire. A bulky shadow moved on its back. Old Belhaan eased out of the darkness with his newly acquired rifle and fired one shot at it. The shadow fell. The old man was about to shoot again when his son, Fahal, knocked the rifle askew with his good hand. 'No!' he growled. 'Don't shoot! That is Taha's *afrangi* father in there!'

They laid Churchill on an esparto mat by the fire. He had lost some blood but was still conscious. The bullet had grazed his shoulder, slicing into the muscle before exiting, but mercifully it had not damaged the bone.

'Jesus Christ!' he grumbled as Sterling crouched over him,

dressing the wound. 'After all this, I have to get shot by one of the people I came to liberate!'

Sterling made the dressing as comfortable as possible and gave Churchill a shot of morphia from the medical kit. 'It should be all right,' he commented, 'but you won't be doing a lot of shooting, not for a while, anyway.'

'Rubbish,' Churchill declared. 'I'll use the other shoulder.'

Belhaan was sitting by the fire a few feet away, with Fahal and some of the other men of the clan. 'I'm sorry,' he said to Churchill. 'But my son told me you were a *bowqaa*, a traitor.'

Churchill blew air. 'Not his fault,' he said. 'Though I did tell him never to make that mistake. I suppose I was too convincing, that's all.'

Belhaan shook his head in confusion. 'This is not a way the Ulad al-Mizna understand,' he said. 'A man stands up and fights in the full view of his enemy, shouting his name so that all will know who he is.'

'Yeah,' Churchill groaned. 'Well, it's horses for courses, as they say, but probably yours is the way it ought to be, after all.'

Belhaan turned his eyes on Sterling with interest. 'So,' he said, 'you are Taha's *afrangi* father? I can see him in your face.'

Sterling felt a pang of resentment against this old man, who looked like a decrepit old savage, but who had won Billy's love and devotion, and who had shared with his son so many precious moments that should have belonged to him. 'I prefer just Father,' Sterling said.

Belhaan's eyes lit up. 'Ah,' he said. 'I understand. He is your son, but he is also mine. And then again, he is neither yours nor mine. Our children do not belong to us. They are not posses-sions, but are given into our keeping by God, lent to us for a short time. Taha fell from the stars and was given to me by God as a sacred trust. I have kept that sacred trust as well as I could,

281

but he is not mine. He is a man and belongs only to himself.'

Sterling was fighting back resentful words, when Rauda approached him leading two small boys by the hand, one about five and the other smaller. 'This is Dhaalib,' she told him, presenting the eldest boy, 'and this is Nofal.' The children were shy, but advanced towards Sterling warily with their small hands outstretched. 'I am Dhaalib ould Taha of the Ulad al-Mizna,' the eldest said proudly.

'And I am Nofal ould Taha,' the other squeaked.

Their likeness to Billy as a child was almost uncanny. The boys were a little darker, their hair perhaps a bit curlier, but they had the same expression, the same eyes, the same determined small mouths. Sterling gasped and hugged the children to him suddenly, one in each arm. Tears streamed down his cheeks. 'My grandchildren!' he repeated, incredulously. 'My grandsons!'

The resentment he'd felt towards Belhaan suddenly evaporated. The old man was right. Billy – Taha – had been given to them both for a while, but did not belong to either of them. Billy had dropped suddenly into this man's life, and whereas he might have mistreated him or abused him, even killed him, this man, this apparent savage, had saved his life, devoted himself to him, loved him as his own son. New tears fell down Sterling's cheeks. Ever since he'd entered the desert, he'd regarded the people who lived here as primitives. He'd been amazed and revolted that Billy had had to live amongst them. Now, though, face to face with his own grandsons, understanding hit him with the force of a hurricane. Billy was right. Life in the desert was hard and sometimes brutal, but, if civilization meant more than merely acquiring possessions, then it was here rather than in the city that true civilization lay. Sterling hugged the boys tighter, kissed them both and let them go. He turned to Belhaan.

'Thank you for looking after my son,' he said. 'I suppose there's enough love in the universe for us all.'

The old man pointed to the stars with a crabbed finger. 'The thanks is to God,' he said.

'This is all very touching,' Churchill croaked suddenly, sitting up and mouthing obscenities at the pain shooting through his shoulder. 'But Hobart's on his way across the Umm al-Khof right now with ten thousand kilos of bullion and Taha as a hostage.'

There was silence for a moment. The big man went on. 'Look, George,' he said. 'Frankly I'm just about *hors de combat*. I can't take bumping across the desert with this shoulder, and you're right, I can't shoot.'

'We will go after Taha on the camels,' Belhaan said. 'All of us will go!'

'No,' Churchill groaned. 'It won't work. First of all, by the time you get there on camels it'll be too late. Second, you'll have to leave women and children here, and unless I'm very much mistaken, Amir and his locusts will be here by first light, eager to help themselves to the womenfolk. So somebody's got to stay here to defend the place.'

Fahal banged his strapped arm against his knee. 'How can we fight so many?' he said.

Churchill curled a big hand around the dressing on his wound. 'There is a way,' he said. 'There's only one road into this place, right? We'll hold the pass with the Bren gun and all the Garands we've got. I've got Mills grenades and even plastic explosive in the Jeep, so we can make claymores. All right, so it's not fighting the honourable way, I know, but it will even the odds a bit. The women will have to fight alongside the men.'

Fahal brightened. 'It might work,' he said. 'But we will need you to show us how to do it.'

Churchill beamed as happily as he could. 'I'm not going anywhere,' he said. 'The question is, who's going for Taha?'

He looked around him with an expression of assumed blankness. 'We can spare two men.'

'I will go,' Belhaan said. 'I know a way through the Umm al-Khof – not the way you came through, but another one even the Nemadi don't know. It is quicker and will allow us to head off the iron chariots. But I cannot fight all those Christians alone. I need a warrior with me.'

Churchill nodded. 'The problem is,' he said, looking intently at Sterling, 'that there are no warriors here who can drive a Jeep.'

Sterling lifted his head suddenly and stared back at Churchill. He gazed at Belhaan, then at Rauda, then at his grandsons, and at the other Reguibat who were watching him expectantly. Any one of them, he guessed, would be willing to give his or her life for Taha, just as Taha had been willing to give his life for Sterling. Since childhood he had resisted taking up arms – he had even gone to prison over it, lost the respect of friends and colleagues. But that was different. What was it Churchill had told him? *'Mass war's one thing, but when it comes to your own kids it's another. In the end, a man has to look after his own.'*

Sterling picked Churchill's Garand from the sand next to him. He stood up, feeling a dam burst within him, years of repressed anger flushing away. There was no uncertainty now. He was sure that he was doing the right thing. He looked at Belhaan and cocked the rifle as if he'd been doing it all his life.

'Let's go for our son,' he said.

Hobart's convoy emerged from the quicksand at sunrise, when the desert night was splitting along the seams, spilling out starbursts of molten orange light. They had made good progress, despite following Taha at a crawl. At first, Hobart had been impatient with his grandson's pace, but the youth had explained that the route was a series of bottlenecks, wide in places, narrow in others, and could not be rushed. He could not navigate properly sitting high in the cab, and one wrong turn might mean losing a lorry. As they passed the Jeep half sunk in the sands, Hobart remembered how the surface had closed over the bodies of his dead comrades eight years earlier, and shuddered. After that he had argued no longer.

In one sense Hobart was glad that Taha was out of the cab: this way the youth couldn't know that he had lost contact with his men in the Guelb. *The best-laid plan . . .,* he thought. He wondered what had happened – whether the boys had simply got impatient and left, or whether the wireless was out of service. Whatever the case, if Taha realized Hobart had no communications, his hold over the youth would cease.

He wondered if Amir's men had arrived back at the Guelb to slaughter the men and take the women and children for themselves. He hoped they would enjoy it while they could. The original .30 ammunition Von Neumann had given the Delim had been good, but ninety-nine per cent of the rounds he'd brought with him on the lorries was dud. As soon as the original supply ran out, the Delim might as well use the rifles as clubs for all the good they'd be. That had been one reason he'd wanted to use the Umm al-Khof as an escape route. Unless the Delim had someone who knew the way through it – and Churchill had reported they hadn't – they would never be able to catch up with him now.

Churchill would have silenced Sterling hours ago, he reckoned. In fact, Churchill had proved a damn good operator all the way. Back in Casablanca in '45 he'd found him a bit overzealous: a mouthy type who'd got in by the back door because of his languages, and seemed more intent on doing his job than was

285

strictly necessary. Not really officer class. They'd heaved him out when the war was over; the chap had thought he'd got his foot in the door and resented it. He was a foreigner anyway – nobody with any breeding would have fallen for that 'minor branch of the family' routine. On this mission, though, Hobart had been more impressed. It was a pity he couldn't afford to share the gold with him. There was already Skorzeny to pay, and you couldn't mess around with Skorzeny. Churchill would just have to get lost on the way home.

Molly would be pleased about Sterling, Hobart thought. She'd been in on the *Sonnenblume* business since they'd met in Algiers in 1945 – she'd even acted as his contact agent and telephonist. She'd never been able to stand the sight of George Sterling, whom she referred to as 'the Wall-Flower'. Hobart agreed that his son-in-law was a lily-livered pansy: the fact that he'd won the GM in the Ambulance Corps was just a fluke. But, despite what Hobart had told him, he didn't even despise George, not really. He was simply indifferent to him. Since Hobart's own patriotism had been a mixture of bravado, chauvinism and lip service, privately he'd never been able to get too self-righteous about someone who just didn't want to play the game. To him, George was a nothing, a non-event. And now a dead non-event.

As for Billy/Taha, well Hobart had always wanted a son and heir, and Taha had grown into quite a tough customer, as Churchill had put it. But his grandson had unfortunately become a wog, and there was little hope of retrieval. Even if Taha wanted to leave his adopted folk, which he showed no sign of, Hobart knew that Molly would never accept a half-wild youth as a stepson. No, it was regrettable, but the very fact that Billy no longer spoke English, and was almost unrecognizable, made him all the more disposable. He was another one who wouldn't be making journey's end.

A hundred yards ahead, Taha had halted and was making a sign, opening both hands wide, his shadow elastic and surreal against the gold-tinted sands. Hobart took the sign to mean 'all clear', and heaved a long sigh of relief. He'd made it. He was home free.

He told the driver to slow down, and waved his hand out of the window to draw the lorries into line abreast.

Hobart yawned. This was as good a place as any to halt for a cup of tea and a bite, he thought. He wanted to press on fast from here for the rest of the day to make sure he put plenty of distance between himself and the Delim. Now he'd finally got the gold, he was going to make sure he hung on to it. This was also a good place to rid himself of Taha. He glanced down at his Tommy gun and wondered if he could do it. Margaret's face seemed to get in the way. But then Margaret was long dead, and Billy had been dead to him for seven years. This fellow in the ragged blue shirt was not Billy, he told himself, but a wog, a savage, and that's what he'd always remain. He'd even married and had sons now, for God's sake – he, Arnold Hobart, had wogs for great-grandsons! Imagine what Molly would say to that!

Hobart ordered the driver to stop, opened the door and dropped heavily into the sand. He adjusted his Tommy gun, and straightened up. As he did so, he saw to his great surprise that Taha was no longer alone – a gaunt figure in a *dara'a* and head-cloth seemed to have popped up out of the landscape, a second spider-leg shadow, dark against the rising sun. Taha seemed absorbed in conversation with the shadow, and from where Hobart stood the two figures looked like black chessmen facing each other, their features in perfect profile against the swelling light. The new figure didn't appear to be armed or menacing, but Hobart was suspicious and irritated at this unexpected development. He

287

cursed and limped towards his grandson angrily. 'Now who the hell is this?' he demanded.

There was a split-second's pause, and then Taha swung round on him, his face an oval of black against the sun. 'It's my dad,' he said. 'He's come to get me.'

At that moment the shadow threw back his head-cloth and *dara'a,* and Hobart realized with a shock that he was looking at George Sterling, down the barrel of the .30 calibre M1 rifle that was clutched firmly in his hands.

His first impulse was to laugh at the incongruous sight, his second to step back and release the safety on his Tommy gun. At that instant Sterling fired.

His first shot went wide, but before Hobart could let rip with the sub-machine-gun, Sterling pulled the trigger again. This time the bullet tore off Hobart's thumb, and he screamed in shock. He sank to his knees, blood pulsing out of the joint, spattering the cool sand. He watched incredulously as another slim figure popped up from the ground, from under a cloak the same colour as the desert surface, not a hundred paces away: a crabbed old beggar with a streak of white beard, holding a rifle in each hand. He held one of them out to Taha, who was already racing for it.

Hobart snatched at the trigger of his weapon with his left hand. The burst was wildly off-target, but self-preservation made Sterling drop, and in that moment Hobart turned and ran as fast as his stiff leg would allow.

He bellowed to his driver to open up with the Browning, still mounted on the cab. The driver was already through the hatch and was grabbing for the machine gun, when a shot from Belhaan took him through the chest. The driver's body snapped forward and drooped over the cab, his blood spilling, cleaning a path through the thick dust on the windscreen.

288

The other drivers were already panicking, reversing out of harm's way, gears grating, engines roaring. 'No!' Hobart bawled. 'Don't reverse!'

It was too late. There was a shuddering crash as one of the lorries backed into another, then a scream of gears as one big Mercedes began to tilt into the quicksand. The driver – the long-haired Spaniard – leapt out of the cab with a Tommy gun in his hand, but Taha, now armed with the rifle Belhaan had passed to him, put a round blast through the skull. For a moment the Spaniard's dark head was illuminated by a halo of pink mush, then his body buckled into the sand.

Hobart saw him fall, but still circled towards the lorries for the protection of numbers they promised. Sterling moved more quickly and cut him off. Hobart's game leg slowed him down, and he stopped, panting, blood still spurting from where his thumb should have been. His head reeled and he felt sick. He could not feel the pain in his thumb, but his leg was agony. He watched Sterling coming on; his small, tight figure had a determination about it that Hobart had never seen before, a sense of absolute purpose that was suddenly frightening.

Hobart's resolution deserted him, and he cast around for an escape route, the great head turning from side to side like a bayed lion. Fifty yards behind was a lone tree, leafless and spiky, and he hobbled towards it, his vision flitting in and out of focus, his mind spinning dizzily. He had gone only a few yards when Sterling shouted at him to stop.

Hobart swore obscenely, and staggered on another fifteen paces, until he had run out of steam. 'Stop!' Sterling bawled again.

Hobart's strength had failed him. He turned the leonine head slowly to find that Sterling was standing ten paces away, with the Garand held at waist-height.

'I should have killed you back there,' Hobart growled. 'At the tadout.'

'Yes,' Sterling agreed, raising the rifle to his shoulder.

Hobart clutched at his mangled hand, and tried to stop himself falling.

'All right, that was a lucky shot,' he groaned. 'But are you really going to shoot me dead? I doubt it.' He spat violently into the sand.

There was a rumble of shots, shouts, puffs of smoke, and the screech of brakes from the direction of the convoy. Hobart saw that two of the trucks had keeled over completely and were fast sinking into the quicksand. Those drivers and mercenaries who were not dead or wounded were being forced out of their cabs at gunpoint by Belhaan and Taha.

'Whichever way you look at it,' Sterling said, 'it's over.'

Hobart spat again. 'You and your idealistic bullshit,' he said. 'You could have been in on it with me. You can't change the world, George. Money equals power equals honour.'

'You're wrong,' Sterling said. 'Money doesn't buy honour, Arnold. There's a whole people out here whose society rests on honour without possessions. Taha is one of them.'

'Pah!' Hobart sneered. 'Savages!'

Sterling gave a hollow laugh. 'Perhaps you should look at yourself and ask who are the real savages,' he said. 'Us or them?'

'I haven't got time for your bleeding-heart garbage, George. I never have had. Now, if you're not going to shoot me, I suggest you let me go.'

Sterling lowered the rifle. 'I'm not going to shoot you, Arnold,' he said.

Hobart gave a triumphant leer. 'Didn't think so . . .'

'I don't need to. You see, you've blundered into the Umm al-Khof. Look at your feet.'

290

Hobart looked, and screamed. He had already sunk up to his heels without noticing. He whimpered and lurched forward, but the sudden movement took him even further into the sinking sand. He struggled, hurling the Tommy gun away in terror, and within a few seconds he was up to his knees. His head thrashed madly from side to side. 'George!' he bellowed. 'Help me!'

'I'm sorry, Arnold,' Sterling said. 'If I take a step further I'll be in it too. I tried to stop you back there. That spiky tree you were running towards is a jurdul.'

It was only then that Hobart remembered what he had once known – the quicksand started where the askaf stopped, and the only plant that grew inside it was the jurdul.

'George!' Hobart blubbered. 'George, please, there must be something—'

'There isn't,' Sterling said. 'Even if I went and got a rope, by the time I got back it would be too late.'

'*Pleaase, George*! For Margaret's sake!'

Hobart saw a chilling grimness in Sterling's face.

'I loved Margaret,' Sterling said quietly. 'Your greed took her away from me. You robbed her of her son, and me of seven precious years of his life. You broke the golden rule, Arnold – something I learned out here. In the end, a man has to look after his own.'

'*No*! *No*! It's not like that. Craven—'

'Sorry, Arnold,' Sterling whispered.

He turned, and as he walked slowly towards the lorries, the cries and imprecations grew fainter. By the time he got there, all trace of Hobart had gone.

Tifiski was over and the hot winds of summer were stirring along the margins of the red land. The caravan was making its way towards the pastures of the inner desert – the Jauf – where

291

Belhaan's people had summered since the Time Before Time. On the top of the escarpment, Sterling and Churchill halted the Jeep for a last glimpse of the People of the Clouds.

The camel-herd passed below them, a never-ending parade of animals, stalking on in trails of fine dust. Sterling had not realized how many camels Belhaan's clan owned. Behind the herd came the women and small children mounted on litters – tiny huts on camel-back. Woven hangings of many colours swayed beneath the animals' bellies, and their proud heads bristled with ostrich-feather plumes. After them came the strings of house-camels, laden like Christmas trees with tents and tent-poles, bloated water-bags, earthenware pots and wooden milking-vessels, iron-bound chests, faded leather saddlebags filled with everything the tribe owned. The goat flocks followed in the wake, five hundred paces behind, and scrambling to keep up. It was, Sterling had to admit, a magnificent sight.

Ten warriors formed a protective screen around the procession, trotting backwards and forwards along its flanks, their robes and head-cloths startlingly blue and black against the camels' pastel hues. Even from where he stood, Sterling could recognize the upright figure of Belhaan.

A week earlier, the old man had led the ritual purification ceremony to purge the Guelb of the transgressions that had occurred there, and the following day they had taken possession of the camels stolen from their Znaga by the Ulad Delim. Though Churchill had prepared the defence of the Guelb carefully, the expected attack had never come. In the south, the massed Reguibat clans had routed the Delim, and had then ridden fast under the guidance of young Minshaaf to deal with Amir's raiding party in the north.

They had intercepted the Delim on the plain outside the Guelb at first light, just as Sterling and Belhaan were halting Hobart's convoy. The Delim had been taken by surprise and, because their camels had been overburdened with rifles and ammunition, had been unable to escape. Amir and his men had stood their ground stalwartly for a few volleys, after which their rifles started to misfire, and they had begun throwing them away in disgust. The Reguibat had killed and wounded many, and lifted most of their camels, chasing the rest of the raiders to the borders of their own territory. Amir ould Hamel was not among the dead, and no one knew what had happened to him. It was clear, though, that he would never be trusted by any desert nomad again for as long as he lived.

Belhaan, Taha and Sterling had disarmed those of Hobart's mercenaries who'd remained alive, and sent them back to Morocco in an unloaded truck. As for the gold, Sterling had urged Taha to keep it. 'Remember what the Spanish official told you in Layoune?' he'd said. 'The land is being given to the mining companies. With the gold you could buy it back from them.'

The council had debated it long and hard, but in the end they had decided not to keep the treasure. It had come out of evil and could only bring evil, they said. And, as Belhaan had put it, 'If we offer the Christians gold for the land, we will be admitting that it belongs to them in the first place, when of course it belongs to no one but God.'

The following day they had thrown the gold, bundle by bundle, into the Umm al-Khof.

As Sterling watched now, one of the riders detached himself from the mobile patrol and halted below him. The Blue Man was completely enveloped in his *dara'a* and head-cloth, but Sterling knew from the way he held his body that it was Taha. Parting with his son and grandsons had been a great sadness for Sterling, but it was made all the more poignant by his knowledge

293

that time was running out for the Blue Men. For a million years man had made little mark upon this landscape, save a few rock pictures, but soon the corruption of the city would be reaching out into the sands. It was not only the last of the Sterlings, but an entire way of life that was passing away before his eyes.

The rider unslung his rifle, cocked it, and fired into the air. The gunshot cracked out, breaking the eggshell silence of the valley, evoking a salvo of echoes that pitched and sheered from rock to rock. With a lump in his throat, Sterling realized that it was a salute from one warrior to another.

As the echoes faded, the rider reined his mount round and caught up with the retreating caravan. Sterling stood and watched until the nomads merged with the landscape, far away, where the dark brown plain met the darkling sky.